BRIGANTIA

BY ADRIAN GOLDSWORTHY

The Vindolanda Series
Vindolanda
The Encircling Sea
Brigantia

Non-Fiction
Hadrian's Wall

BRIGANTIA

VINDOLANDA III

✠

ADRIAN
GOLDSWORTHY

HEAD
ᵒᶠ ZEUS

First published in the UK in 2019 by Head of Zeus Ltd
This paperback edition published in the UK in 2019 by Head of Zeus Ltd

9 7 5 3 1 2 4 6 8

A catalogue record for this book is available from
the British Library.

ISBN (PB): 9781784978211
ISBN (E): 9781788541886

Typeset by NewGen
Maps by Jeff Edwards

Printed and bound in Great Britain by
CPI Group (UK) Ltd, Croydon CR0 4YY

MIX
Paper from
responsible sources
FSC® C020471

Head of Zeus Ltd
First Floor East
5–8 Hardwick Street
London EC1R 4RG
WWW.HEADOFZEUS.COM

For Robert

Northern Britannia at the start of the Emperor Trajan's Reign

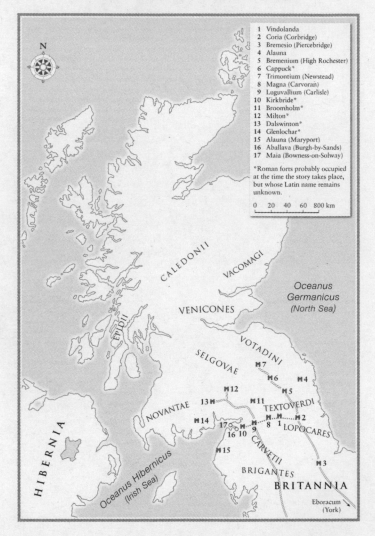

N

1 Vindolanda
2 Coria (Corbridge)
3 Bremesio (Piercebridge)
4 Alauna
5 Bremenium (High Rochester)
6 Cappuck*
7 Trimontium (Newstead)
8 Magna (Carvoran)
9 Luguvallium (Carlisle)
10 Kirkbride*
11 Broomholm*
12 Milton*
13 Dalswinton*
14 Glenlochar*
15 Alauna (Maryport)
16 Aballava (Burgh-by-Sands)
17 Maia (Bowness-on-Solway)

*Roman forts probably occupied
at the time the story takes place,
but whose Latin name remains
unknown.

0 20 40 60 800 km

CALEDONII

VACOMAGI

Oceanus
Germanicus
(North Sea)

VENICONES

EPIDII

VOTADINI

SELGOVAE

7

6

4

12

5

NOVANTAE

13

11

TEXTOVERDI

14

17   9

8   1   2

16 10

LOPOCARES

15

CARVETII

HIBERNIA

3

Oceanus Hibernicus
(Irish Sea)

BRIGANTES

BRITANNIA

Eboracum
(York)

Britannia AD 100

PLACE NAMES

Aballava: Burgh by Sands
Abus: River Humber
Alauna: Maryport in Cumbria
Arbeia: South Shields
Bremenium: High Rochester
Bremesio: Piercebridge
Bremetennacum: Ribchester
Brigantum: Aldborough
Camulodunum: Colchester
Cataractonium: Catterick
Coria: Corbridge
Corinium: Cirencester
Danum: Doncaster
Deva: Chester
Eboracum: York
Lindum: Lincoln
Londinium: London
Longovicium: Lanchester
Lugdunum: Lyon in France
Luguvallium: Carlisle
Magna: Carvoran
Maia: Bowness-on-Solway

Mediolanum: Whitchurch
Mona: Anglesey
Segontium: Caernarfon
Verbeia: Ilkley
Verulamium: St Albans
Viroconium: Wroxeter

PROLOGUE

T HE TWO MEN followed the path as it meandered up from the valley floor towards the lone farmstead. They were big men, one just slightly taller and the other broader at the shoulders. Each wore mail armour and helmet and had a sword on their left hip, and few among the Selgovae of these parts could boast such a fine panoply. The thicker set man also carried a torch held high in his right hand. There was no moon, but the heavens were an endless field of bright stars, and they did not need the torchlight to find their path. Instead it warned anyone who cared to watch that they were coming, two warriors well armed and grim.

'Are you sure this is a good idea?' the taller man said. His face was long, the skin drawn taut over the muscles, giving him the air of a leering horse. His companion ignored him and trudged on. Now and again the gentle breeze picked up and made the flame gutter and wave.

There was no sign that anyone in the farm had noticed them. It was much like the others dotted along the valley, indeed throughout much of Britannia, with a main house, its conical roof a little higher and broader than the round huts on either side. Below all was deep shadow, with the odd hint of movement as the livestock in the fenced enclosures shuffled and fed. Higher up the thatch was pale in the starlight. The Selgovae did not care to live too close to their neighbours. Men felt the need for room around them, so families lived apart and got on with the business of keeping their own flocks or herds and tending fields. Eburus, the old man who lived here, disliked company more than most, for the nearest homestead was nearly two miles away, and his own farm was perched on a narrow shelf halfway up the eastern side of the valley. Beyond the shallow ditch surrounding the three houses the slope steepened and then turned into high cliffs that were dark and brooding even on this bright night. No one could approach from that direction – or escape.

'I mean,' the taller man said, 'we could wait. Catch 'em tomorrow or the next day.' He spoke in Latin, the words clear and carefully chosen, albeit with the gruff accent of his people. Vindex was one of the Carvetii, a northern people who were close kin to the Brigantes, the biggest tribe anywhere in Britannia. For the last seven years he had led the scouts sent by his chieftain to serve alongside the Roman army.

Still his companion did not reply or stop. They were a good halfway up the slope, where the path reached a broad grey boulder and then made a loop around the mound behind it. There were two more big stones beyond the mound.

'Guess it could be a woman,' Vindex mused as they reached the pair of stones, round and evenly matched. 'Just lying there, waiting.' Someone must have thought the same, for the name of this place was the Vale of the Mother, or sometimes the Vale of the Queen, and perhaps a goddess had set her mark here as a blessing, for the barley in the fields around the farm was high and thick. 'Harvest soon,' he added. 'Although that lazy old sod Eburus will probably wait longer. Serve him right if a storm blows it flat.' He stopped and caressed one of the stones that might be breasts and smiled. He was fond of women, and had mourned two wives and not long ago taken a third. Before he left she had wondered whether she was with child. The thought was an exciting one, albeit salted by fear for her.

His companion continued to ignore him and trudged up the slope. He wore an iron helmet, with deep and wide neck guard, broad cheek pieces and a high transverse crest of feathers, which made him look taller. It was the way the Romans marked out their centurions, making it easier for friend and foe alike to see them in the chaos of battle. Flavius Ferox belonged to Legio II Augusta, but was on detached service as *regionarius*, the man tasked with keeping the peace and the rule of law in the area near the fort at Vindolanda. A few months ago the senior regionarius in the north had died an especially nasty death, and since then Ferox had acted in his stead. Even so they were a long way further north than any district formally organised by Rome or under his responsibility. No one but Ferox would have come this far in pursuit, especially with so few men. It was not the first time he had led Vindex off in this way and the scout doubted that it would be the last. In truth, given the odds they faced this night, he had to hope that it would not be the last time.

Vindex gave the stone one last pat and followed. Ferox was already a fair way ahead, climbing a little bank rather than following the path as it wound around it. He stood for a moment at the top, and a gust of wind hissed through the barley, rippling the feathered crest and making the torch flicker wildly. Ferox turned his back to the breeze and lowered the branch so that the flame recovered and did not go out. The wind slackened, and once he was sure that the torch was burning well, the centurion looked past the muttering scout down into the valley floor. The three points of light from torches like the one he carried were where they should be. Ferox grunted in approval.

'You're awake then,' Vindex said, staring up at him. 'Well, nearly.'

'Huh,' Ferox grunted again. The Carvetii talked a lot even compared to the rest of the Brigantes. Both made the Romans seem reserved.

Vindex came up to join him. 'How are they supposed to hold a torch and blow a horn at the same time?' he asked. 'Can you tell me that, centurion?'

The wind gusted again and Ferox turned and leaned over to protect the flame. He ignored the question because it was one of many he could not really answer. They had begun the chase three days ago. One of the scouts dropped out early on when his horse became badly lame. The day before last, their quarry met a lone rider who then rode off to the east while the others continued north and Ferox had sent another scout and one of his Roman troopers after whoever this was. The scout was not a true fighter, and the soldier a big Tungrian who would get lost inside a fort if left on his own, so the two would together make one capable man. The tracks suggested the fugitive was small, perhaps a youth, so hopefully the two should manage if they caught up, although anyone willing to meet the men they were chasing was bold at the very least. That was one more mystery in the bigger mystery, and Ferox was not sure why he wanted that lone rider caught save that he did not like loose ends. This whole business was odd, and something told him that it mattered and that nothing was quite what it seemed, so he had listened to his instincts and told them to bring the rider back, alive or dead, with everything he carried.

'That's if the buggers don't just go out before anyone has seen them.' Vindex spoke loudly over the wind, interrupting his thoughts, especially when the breeze dropped suddenly so that it sounded as if the scout was shouting. They both glanced up at the farm, but there was still no sign that anyone was paying attention.

'They'll hear.' Flavius Ferox spoke at last.

'They will, will they?' Vindex said once it was clear that nothing more was forthcoming. After all these years, he was used to his friend's ways. Not that that made them any less infuriating. 'Sure that little Greek can even blow a trumpet?'

'Philo talks all the time.' Ferox's tone implied that this well qualified his slave when it came to making noise. 'And he gave me the idea. Told me a story once about a hero of his people who crept at night with just three hundred warriors and surrounded the camp of a vast host of enemies. Each of them had a torch and a trumpet and they all blew at the same moment and waved the torches. Scared the enemy so much they panicked, killed each other by mistake and fled. A god clouded their minds.'

Vindex pulled up the wheel of Taranis that he wore around his neck and kissed the bronze. 'Have we got a god on our side tonight?' he asked.

'What do you think?'

'I'd settle for three hundred warriors.' Vindex sighed. 'If we wait, a patrol may catch up. The trail is clear. I could follow it with just one eye, half-open. You could follow it in your sleep.'

'And the girl?'

'If she isn't dead already, then why would they kill her now? They'd have to slaughter Eburus while they're at it. He may be a mean old sod, but he wouldn't have killing under his roof unless he's the one doing it.'

'Cistumucus would slaughter the world without blinking.' Ferox spoke bitterly. 'Rufus would do it with a big grin as long as he thought he could escape afterwards. One old man and his family wouldn't bother them or slow them down.' He paused, lifted the torch and gently waved it from left to right and then back again three times. Down in the valley the three points of light dipped in answer.

'And Rufus is there?'

'He's there.' Rufus was an army deserter who had left a trail of blood ever since he ran from his cohort eighteen months ago. Cistumucus was an outcast from one of the far northern tribes. Both were feared as truly bad men even in these hard lands, and it was clear that the rumours were true and they had banded together. 'They're both there along with a couple of warriors and the girl.' The tracks were plain, even with the ground hard after a month with unusually little rain.

'Now killing your host might not be something even those bastards will do lightly,' Ferox went on, 'but our horses are spent and apart from us we've only got the *tubicen* fit to fight, and I wouldn't count much on him. So we probably won't catch them tomorrow and if we do, the odds wouldn't be good in the open. If we wait for the others then they'll have too big a lead and they'll get away or kill the girl once they see us coming on behind.' He said no more and simply set off along the path.

'You ever met her?' Vindex asked once he had caught up.

'Met who?'

'This slave girl?'

'What's that got to do with it? You saw what they did.'

'Aye.' The woman was a slave, married to a slave, and both of them and their little boy were owned by an imperial freedman who had once been a slave, but Vindex had long since given up seeking reason in the ways of the Romans. The man was driving a cart full of goods belonging to his master when it was ambushed, and the solitary soldier who was presumably their escort could do no more than die with them. Pure chance had brought Ferox and Vindex to the spot half a day later. They had seen the corpses, wished they had not, and followed the trail for three days, riding hard. Ferox had sent a trooper back to Vindolanda asking for support, with little hope that it would arrive in time, and that began the depletion of the tiny band.

'They need killing,' Ferox said, his normally musical voice flat, which was always a sign that it was no use trying to persuade him otherwise.

'Aye, they do.' Vindex glanced at the other man. 'And there's plenty more out there like them.'

Ferox turned and smiled. 'You do not have to come with me.'

Vindex stopped and watched his friend stride on, his crest bobbing as he climbed the path. The iron helmet glinted red in the flames, as did his mail shirt. He did not look back.

Vindex sighed. 'That is true because it is not.' The words were no more than a whisper, for he knew that they did not matter. Brigantes were renowned for sticking with friends whatever the cost, and the Carvetii were known as faithful even compared to their kin. Ferox was his friend, whether the Roman liked it or not, and that meant Vindex would go with him now and always, as long as there was breath in his body. He raised the wheel of Taranis to his lips again, pressed it to them, and then slipped it down the top of his own mail cuirass. He patted the bronze dome of his old-fashioned army issue helmet to check that it was tied on securely and then gripped the handle of his long sword and gave a slight tug to make sure that it was loose in the scabbard. Then he shook his head. 'Bastard.' He said the word with great fondness, and followed Ferox.

The farm was close now, no more than a hundred paces away, and there was a brief jab of red firelight as someone pulled open the door of the main house and went in or out. Yet there was still no sign that anyone was paying them any attention. They were past the barley fields and into the open patch of ground in front of the farm. In spite of the long dry spell the path grew muddy from the passage of animals day after day. One of them, a pony with a broad white mark on its face, stared over the wattle fence of one of the animal pens alongside the huts. The ditch around the farm was shallow and from the smell filled with the waste of the family who lived inside. The Selgovae did not use their own dung on their fields, but tended to toss it aside and then forget about it. It added an extra layer to the odour of pigs, sheep, goats, ponies and rotting food.

There was a single causeway across the ditch, although that was rather a grand name for the earth they had simply not bothered to dig out. The ditch, like the fences around the animal pens, was there to stop the livestock from straying, and make it just a little harder for thieves to steal them without anyone noticing.

Ferox and Vindex stopped in front of the causeway. The centurion turned, and waved his torch for the second time. Down in the valley the three red lights dipped in answer. A bronze trumpet sounded a rising scale, then sounded it again.

'The lad's good,' Vindex muttered, knowing that this was Banno, the tubicen from Vindolanda. The last note faded and they waited for what seemed an age before there was a brief, high-pitched snort, then nothing, and then a thin, rasping note. 'Not so good.' That was Philo, a slave who waged merciless war against dirt in his master's quarters and with less success on his clothes. 'The music is not in him,' Vindex added sadly.

No one stirred in the farm, and even the white-faced pony turned away from them.

'Eburus!' Ferox shouted, so loud that Vindex flinched. For a man prone to brooding silence, the centurion had a voice of surprising power. 'Eburus! We are at your gates, my lord, and ask to speak with you!' The old man was neither a lord nor did he have any gates, but courtesies were important. Ferox spoke in the language of the tribes, and after more than a decade in the north, there was only a slight trace of the accent of his own people. Although a Roman and a centurion of Legio II Augusta, Ferox was born a prince of the Silures, a tribe who had fought Rome for twenty years and lost in the end. In his early teens he had been sent as hostage to the empire, educated like a good Roman, made a citizen and an officer. Vindex always felt that two different, even hostile, spirits battled for the soul of his friend.

They waited.

'Maybe they've killed each other,' Vindex said cheerfully.

Light spilled from the low doorway in the main hut. They could see a dark shape lurking there.

'Go away! You are not welcome.' It sounded like a boy's voice.

'Ah, the fabled warm hospitality of the Selgovae,' Vindex whispered, the words dripping with irony.

Ferox ignored him. 'Come forth, Eburus! We must speak.' He thought he heard some discussion.

'Who are you?' the boy called out.

'Ferox, the *centurio regionarius*. We must talk.'

'I have guests already and no room for more.' This voice was deeper and heavy with petulance. There was movement in the doorway, blocking most of the firelight, and then a spare figure unfolded to its full height. It swayed a little as it walked towards them. 'Be quick. My fire is warm and the night is cold.'

Eburus was more than fifty and looked a good deal older. He was taller by a head than Vindex, but thinner than seemed reasonable, his bare arms like sticks and his neck immensely long and wrinkled like a lizard's. The head of the household walked to the inner side of the causeway. 'Speak! And be quick!' He fumbled with his trousers and began to urinate into the ditch.

'You know me, Lord Eburus.' Ferox spoke over loud splashing that seemed to go on and on. He had met the man several times over the years, and once received the shelter of his roof and the warmth of his fire for the night. The house and its occupants were dirty and sullen, the hospitality sparing even by the thrifty standards of the Selgovae, except for the rich, deep flavoured beer that came in great bowls. Ferox was counting on the potency of that beer.

The old man seemed to consider before he replied, and all the while the flow of urine kept coming. The white-faced pony was back at the fence, watching and no doubt impressed.

'I know you,' Eburus conceded at last.

Ferox glimpsed movement in the doorway and raised his voice so that it would carry. 'I have come for your guests. For Cistumucus and the Roman once called Rufus and their companions. I shall slay them tonight or take them as prisoners to face just punishment. They are murderers.'

Eburus blinked several times, eyes peering from his wrinkled face as if he struggled to understand. At last the flow of liquid stopped. 'They are guests at my hearth.'

Ferox turned away and waved the torch. In answer the lights in the valley dipped once more. Banno repeated the short fanfare and this time Philo produced a louder, if wavering call.

'I have nine Batavian horsemen with me,' Ferox announced, facing back towards the old man. 'You know their fame as warriors. You also know the fame of Vindex of the Carvetii, who stands beside me. Six of his warriors wait in the valley below.' In truth there was only Banno, Philo and just one of Vindex's scouts. Philo barely knew enough to pick up a sword the right way, and the scout had injured his leg earlier in the day and could hardly walk. Some of the Selgovae were bound to have seen them. He had to hope that the ill-tempered old man had not spoken to his neighbours in the last few hours.

'They are my guests.' Eburus sounded more puzzled than anything else.

'And I must take them or kill them.'

'They are under my roof.' Eburus' temper was starting to fray and his words were slurring. 'Do you not know what that means?'

'He is a Roman,' Vindex said. 'They understand nothing except iron to kill and gold to hoard.'

'I make this offer to your guests.' Ferox shouted the words. 'Come out and fight the two of us. My men will not intervene. If they kill us, then I swear by the gods of Rome and by Sun and Moon that my men will let them go free and wait for two days before they chase. It is a fair offer.'

'The gods of Rome.' Eburus spat and then remembered to pull his trousers up properly and tighten his belt. He was unarmed and it was only now that Ferox noticed he was barefoot. 'What if they will not come out? They are guests and have my protection until the sun rises tomorrow.' The old man took a step onto the causeway. 'I shall not command them to leave. What if they will not come?'

Ferox admired the old man's pride and determination, and wondered whether Eburus knew or sensed that he was bluffing. 'They must come out!'

'Why?' the old man said.

Ferox thought he caught Vindex's muttered 'Why indeed?'

'Because if they do not come out and face us, then I shall put your farm to the torch and kill every man, boy and beast inside, and sell your women as slaves.'

Eburus spluttered with rage. 'You would not dare! You would not!'

'He is a Roman,' Vindex explained for a second time. 'They have no honour. Worse still, he is a Silure. Everyone knows the wolf people never let honour get in the way of vengeance.'

'The gods will curse you!' Eburus took another pace forward. Ferox simply shrugged. The old man was quivering, his hands twitching. 'My kin will hunt you down and kill you.'

'Plenty have tried,' Ferox told him. 'A few more will make no difference and it will not save you tonight. Ask your guests. Either all of you die in the flames or on our swords or they come out and face us. Then they will die or we will die, but you and your house will live.'

Eburus spat again, and Ferox felt some of it strike his face. He wiped it away with his free hand. 'Ask them.'

The old man walked off, murmuring a thorough and highly specific curse involving the Roman's blood, bones and guts. Finally, he crouched and went through the low door of the main house. Light spilled from the smaller hut on the left as someone watched them, but did nothing. Ferox transferred the torch to his left hand and gripped his sword, which as a centurion he wore on the left. It slid easily from the scabbard and he felt the familiar joy at its perfect balance. His grandfather had taken it from a Roman officer and given it to him when he was too small to lift it. The blade was an old one even then, for it was longer than the army issue *gladius*, of a pattern rarely seen since the days of the Divine Augustus. Holding this sword and knowing that he would soon have to use it brought a rare simplicity to life.

Vindex sighed and drew his own weapon, a longer and slimmer blade, and hefted the small square shield in his left hand. 'What if they don't come out?' he asked.

'We try to set the thatch on fire and then kill them one at a time as they come out.'

'Easy as that.'

13

'Not so easy. It will take a fair time and we'll get tired.'

A bulky shape emerged from the main house. As the man stood, light shone off his shaven head and glinted on the blade of the axe he carried. It was a woodsman's tool, not a warrior's weapon, but this was Cistumucus, and he liked to fight with the great axe, though he was happy to kill with anything, including his huge hands. He was not tall, but his chest was wide and looked dark, and, even though neither Ferox nor Vindex had ever seen the killer from the north, they knew that he was bare-chested, for his body was covered in thick hair. There were plenty of stories about the northerner and all were dark. Men called him the bear because he was so hairy and because of his appalling rages. They spoke of how he cut the head off anyone he killed, boiling the flesh away until only bone was left. It was told that he liked to take the skulls to the far west and cast them into the sea, and some said that this gave him power or that he had taken a vow and if he did this he could not die. Men said many things and some were true and some were not.

A taller man appeared, and then two more beside him. Each carried a long sword of the style beloved of the tribes, end heavy to give appalling force to a downward cut. One had a small shield like the one Vindex carried. Behind them came a warrior with a spear, and finally one who was bearded unlike the others and wearing a shirt of small bronze scales that took on a red tinge from the firelight. He paused and wrapped a cloak tightly around his left arm. In his right he held an army issue gladius, of the modern pattern with a shorter blade and point than Ferox's old sword.

'Didn't think they'd come,' Vindex said softly.

There was more movement in the doorway as two more men emerged.

'Bugger, they must have had friends,' the scout hissed.

'Must have met up with them here,' Ferox said.

'Still think this is a good idea?' Another man appeared, swatting away the assistance of a boy. Vindex sighed as he recognised the very tall, terribly lean figure. 'Silly old sod. Must be one of his boys.'

Ferox nodded. 'Only kill them if you have to.'

He was interrupted by a scream of rage as one of the warriors pelted towards them, little shield in front and long, blunt-tipped sword held high ready to sweep down. Some of the others came on steadily, but there was no time to watch them closely as the attacker was on the causeway. He was heading for Ferox, his high-crested helmet drawing attention as it always did.

Ferox and Vindex both took a pace back as the man stamped his left foot down and swept his sword at where the Roman had been. He recovered before the blade went too low, and that showed some skill, but then the centurion thrust the torch at him, the motion making the fire blaze dazzlingly bright. The warrior dodged, saw Vindex coming at him from the side and switched his shield in that direction just as Ferox jabbed with his gladius. The long, wickedly sharp point drove easily through tunic, skin and muscle, sliding into the ribcage from below. Gasping for breath, the warrior let his sword fall and staggered as the centurion twisted the blade and yanked it free. He sank to his knees, a trickle of blood coming from his lips, and tried to speak, but no sound came. Ferox kicked the dying man into the ditch.

'They should have rushed us then, while they had the chance,' he said, his tone almost disapproving of his enemies' mistake. He heard Eburus shouting something about a spear and shield, his tone as aggrieved as ever, and then his lad trotted over to the far hut. A deep voice protested, then spat a curse at the old man, and the other five came on, the bald axeman in the centre, two warriors on his left and the other on his right. The deserter hung back a couple of paces, sword held low in one of the standard guards approved by the divine Augustus in his regulations for the army. There was no hurry, or any sign that they had drunk too much of the old man's beer, which had surely prompted the other warrior's lone assault.

Ferox tossed the torch onto the causeway. It flickered, but continued to burn. Instead he drew his stubby *pugio* dagger in his left hand, thumb on the pommel and point downwards. Most legionaries either kept their daggers wrapped up and heavily oiled and polished, producing them only for inspection, or treated them casually for cutting their food. Fighting with one was a skill that took a lot of practice, but since he did not have a shield there was nothing he would rather have alongside his sword.

Cistumucus thrust out his matted chest and roared like a beast, brandishing the long axe above his head. The warrior closest to him held a heavy shafted spear. Ferox could see no sign of a sword, which meant that he was unlikely to risk throwing the spear unless he was sure of his mark. Thankfully none of the enemy had javelins, so perhaps some god was on their side after all.

The spearman was on the bald axeman's left, facing Ferox. Beside him the warrior jumped down into the ditch to threaten the centurion from the side. Rufus kept back, watching and waiting, ready to pounce. Before the deserter had gone over the rampart he had cut the throat of his decurion while the man was asleep. In battles and brawls he'd shown himself a vicious fighter, but he was not a man to take an unnecessary risk.

Cistumucus bellowed again and as he did stamped forward and swung the axe down so that it hummed through the air. Ferox dodged to the side, and only just had time to parry the thrusting spear point of the warrior in front of him, beating it aside with his gladius. He had to step back to keep his balance, and seeing the man in the ditch coming up the shallow bank he stepped back again. Vindex thrust his blade forward, aiming for Cistumucus' eyes, but the stocky man flicked the axe back up with staggering speed, blocked the attack, then was poised for another downward blow. The two men were a pace apart, eyeing each other warily, waiting for their chance.

On the axeman's right, the other warrior went into the ditch, moving warily, small shield up. Vindex's eyes flicked to watch him, then back to face Cistumucus just as the axe flashed down again. There was no time to raise his shield, so the scout slashed with his sword and swayed so that the blade of the axe glanced against his bronze helmet with a clang weirdly like a bell ringing. Vindex staggered, his helmet twisted round and chin bloodied where the cheek pieces had torn loose. His cut had lacked real force, but had gouged across the hairy belly of his foe. In the light it was hard to see whether he had drawn blood or whether the matted hair really was as thick as a bear's hide and the man could not be wounded.

Ferox jabbed with his dagger against the spearman, and gave a wild slash at the man coming up this side of the ditch. Both gave way for a moment, but the respite was brief and almost at once they came on again. The warrior in the ditch near Vindex saw the lean man staggering and bounded up the bank, then shrieked as his shoes slipped on piled excrement and he flipped backwards, arms flailing and legs in the air. It was so absurd that even the stunned Vindex snorted with laughter, his helmet falling off with the motion.

Cistumucus gave no sign that he noticed and raised the axe again, but the spearman's head flicked around to see what had happened. Ferox flung his dagger. The pugio was a heavy, clumsy weapon and he did not have a chance to ready it properly in his hand, but the range was short and all the years of practice made it fly true, the point burying itself into Cistumucus' great belly, making him grunt like an injured animal. Ferox whipped his empty left hand down and grasped the spear shaft just below the head, yanking it towards him. He swung to the right, putting all his weight behind his gladius so that the long triangular tip drove into the man's face so hard that it burst out through the back of his head.

The sword was trapped and Ferox let go of the grip just as the man in the ditch cut hard against his side. It was not a perfect blow, and a jab would have been more dangerous save that the warrior's sword had no point, but still it snapped one or two of the mail rings and felt like the blow of a hammer and he fell to his knees. He still had hold of the spear and he wrenched it free from the dead man's grip, then let himself fall because the axe was slashing at him. Cistumucus was screaming in high-pitched rage, and Ferox rolled aside an instant before the axe struck the hard ground and bounced up. The warrior in the ditch was crouching as he came up the slope. He dropped his sword and grabbed the centurion's leg. Ferox lashed out with the other foot, struck the man's face, and the heavy, hobnailed sole of his boot smashed his nose and drove him away.

'Bastard!' Vindex yelled as he went at Cistumucus, and the screaming man did not seem slowed or weakened by the knife sticking in his stomach for the axe was up and then sliced down. The scout blocked the blow with his shield, but such was the power that the blade shattered the board, which fell to pieces, the boss riven and Vindex's fist numb. Ferox managed to get his other hand around the thick shaft of the spear and he used all the strength he could muster to jab the point backwards, luck as much as aim driving it into the axeman's thigh. Cistumucus wavered and Vindex sliced down so that his long sword bit into the bald man's skull. Blood sprayed as he yanked the blade free and cut down again. The wounded northerner sank to his knees, flailing wildly with the axe so that Vindex had to leap back. Ferox pushed himself up, still clutching tightly to the spear, and ripped it free. Vindex came on again, slashing his sword down two-handed, and when the axe was raised to block the attack its haft was sliced in two. Ferox thrust the spear into Cistumucus' eye, this time rolling the point so that it came free easily. The two warriors in the ditch were both standing, staring up in disbelief at their dead leader.

A horn blew a ragged note from down in the valley, then the bronze trumpet showed how it was done. Rufus was nowhere in sight.

'The boys are coming,' Vindex said to the man who had fallen and was now covered with a reeking skin of manure and other filth. 'You giving up or do you want me to kill you now?' When there was no response he went down the bank, almost slipping.

The warrior knelt in submission. 'Spare me.'

On the other side the man with the broken nose made no effort to pick up his dropped sword. Ferox's side throbbed with pain and he wanted to know where the deserter had gone. He hefted the spear. The warrior stared at him blankly, neither defiant nor showing any sign of giving in. Ferox flung the spear, his chest screaming in agony with the motion. The iron spearhead had never been very sharp, and had blunted further in the fight, but the weight and sheer force of the throw punched through ribs into the man's heart. Ferox had turned away before the warrior fell. The centurion grasped his sword, placed a boot on the corpse's face and wrenched the blade free.

There was a shout of triumph from inside the farm as Eburus, wearing a battered old helmet, brandished his shield and spear in the air. The boy stood beside him, armed with a reaping hook. Then a scream came from one of the animal pens. Ferox ran into the yard, for it was the terrified cry of a woman.

Rufus rode through the open gate of the pen, mounted on the white-faced pony and driving the beast on with the flat of his sword, the other hand guiding the reins and holding down the struggling slave draped in front of his saddle.

'Coward!' Eburus yelled at his fleeing guest, while the boy sprinted at the rider, hook raised. Rufus turned the animal on a denarius, and the beast almost bounded at the young lad, who swung his blade wildly and missed. The deserter cut down once, the well-honed blade striking at an angle into the boy's neck so that the blood jetted high as he fell.

Ferox tried to get on Rufus' left as the horse reared, hoofs flailing. The woman shrieked and tried to wriggle free.

'Bitch!' Rufus hissed and punched down with his left fist. Eburus was on the other side, and the deserter managed to block a thrust from his spear. He kicked hard against the horse's sides. Ferox's sword was too low and he dropped it, instead grabbing with both hands for the woman's arms. The horse surged forward, stumbled, recovered and cantered for the causeway. As it stumbled, Ferox felt the woman's weight shift and she was falling onto him, and then there was red-hot pain in his thigh. His leg gave way, his hands slipped, he grabbed, felt something tear, then he hit the ground and the weight of the woman smashed into him.

Rufus galloped across the causeway. The kneeling warrior sprang at Vindex, knocking him against the bank. They wrestled, slipping in the filth of the ditch, and the scout pounded the man's head with the twin-pronged bronze pommel of his sword.

'Mongrel!' Eburus screamed. The woman rolled off Ferox, panting, her eyes wild with fear. He tried to push up, his leg screaming in protest. His trousers were slick with blood from the wound made by Eburus' spear. 'Why did you get in the way?' the old man yelled angrily.

Vindex had beaten the warrior to the ground. He kneeled, and drove the sword into the man with such force that it stuck in the earth. Trying to stand, he slipped twice before he managed to get up. One hand wiped dung from his face and he spat several times.

'Are you still sure this was a good idea?' he said.

I

FEROX CRAWLED THROUGH long grass. He could hear a woman singing a lilting song that was as old as the hills and told of a hero meeting a princess. 'I see a sweet country, I'll rest my weapon there.'

The grass was thick, almost like heather, so that he had to push down each blade, beating it into submission. He kept going, panting with the effort. The trees at the top of the slope seemed further away than ever. He wanted to get up and run, but knew that then they would see him and he would die. The grass had prickles and his fingers hurt as he pushed his way through.

The singing was getting fainter. He grabbed frantically at the grass and thistles in his way, flinging himself forward. The trees were there at last and he jumped up and ran into them. Branches like snakes writhed all around him, grasping his legs and arms. He could no longer hear the woman.

Ferox fought the trees, pushing on and on, and suddenly he burst through into the moonlight and saw the pool.

A scream rent the night air. She was standing by the far side of the water, hair bound up on top of her head with a ribbon, her slippers and robe on the ground. Her skin was white like ivory, her hair the purest gold and her shape the dazzling perfection of the divine.

Was this Artemis of the hunt, so that he would suffer the fate of Actaeon and be torn to pieces by her hounds? Part of him said that such a glimpse was worth the awful price. Another part recalled how much he disliked dogs.

'Oh!' The cry was one of annoyance without a trace of fear. The goddess leaned forward. One hand over her chest and the other between her legs, the posture covering little and somehow making her seem more naked, more desirable. This was not Artemis, or Diana or Luna of the Moon.

'Oh!' It was almost a gasp. She went down on one knee, both arms over her breasts, her bottom thrust out. This was Venus and not the untouchable Huntress. This Goddess offered love, even sometimes to mortals, her virginity renewed after each affair human or divine. He knew her face and dreamed of it so often.

She smiled and Ferox rushed forward into the water. It was black and thick like honey. After one step it was up to his waist. At the second it was around his neck. The goddess changed. She was clothed now in a long dress of many dazzling colours and seemed younger. As the black water reached his mouth she transformed into the Mother, spear in one hand and sheaf of wheat in the other. Then she changed again and was the hag, one eye pale and sightless, hair wild and skin showing the wrinkles of the centuries. Her laugh was a cackle of contempt.

The pool pulled him down into the blackness of the Otherworld.

Ferox felt someone shaking him and he woke with a start, blinking at the morning sunlight streaming through the window and gulping for breath. His body felt slick with sweat.

'Good, you are back with us.'

Vindex leaned over him. It was not much of an improvement over the hag, especially when he grinned.

'You are still alive then?' The scout was not the one speaking. This was a polished voice, whose simplest statement was beautifully pitched and composed from years of training.

Ferox sighed deeply. Vindex had moved away so that now all he saw was the beamed ceiling. Dimly he remembered arriving at Vindolanda, drenched and cold after three days of riding through near constant downpours.

'The *medicus* said that it should not do too much harm if we roused you,' the voice went on. 'That is if it did not kill you.'

Ferox stared at the ceiling. He did not want to talk, for he knew that voice all too well and usually it was the harbinger of some fresh ordeal. Why did the Romans have to jabber so much? Among the Silures every man was a warrior at heart, and a warrior knew the strength and the sheer joy that came from silence and stillness.

'Do you not wish to ask where you are or what day it is?' the voice went on. 'I do believe it is customary on these occasions.'

'I am in the *valetudinarium* at Vindolanda,' Ferox said, still staring at the ceiling and making no effort to rise. He was stiff and his leg ached. One of the rooms in the fort's hospital seemed the most likely place for him to be. 'And I presume that my Lord Crispinus has a task for me.'

Someone snorted with laughter, and Ferox gave in and sat up. Atilius Crispinus, the senior tribune of Legio II Augusta, was the son of a senator and would in due course join that council of elder statesmen. He was a small man, whose hair had already turned almost wholly white even though he was in his early twenties. Beside him sat a tall, very handsome man with reddish hair and a warm smile. Flavius Cerialis was the prefect commanding cohors VIIII Batavorum, the main garrison of Vindolanda.

Crispinus stared at Ferox, who stared back. At last the young aristocrat smiled. 'Surly and awkward as ever,' he said. 'Splendid. If you ever mellowed, I fear that you might turn into a far less capable officer, and that would never do. At least this way we can easily have you dismissed the service in disgrace if you go too far.'

'Easily,' Cerialis agreed. 'Even exiled. There must still be plenty of tiny rocks in the Mediterranean that do not yet have a prisoner lodged on them.'

'Dozens at least.'

Ferox waited. He noticed Philo hovering behind the two seated officers, standing beside Vindex and a man who was presumably the doctor or one of his staff.

'Well, since you lack the manners either to laugh at our wit or the decency to ask questions, then I suppose that I must shoulder the burden of this conversation,' Crispinus said with mock weariness. 'Such is the lot of the nobleman.'

'Yes, you are indeed at Vindolanda among the injured and sick. You have been here for six nights. When you arrived you were in a bad way, shivering from fever and your wound stinking and full of muck. I shall spare you the gruesome medical details, but there was talk of taking off the leg. This fellow...' he jerked his head towards Vindex '...threatened to fillet anyone who tried and had to be arrested. It was fortunate that the noble Cerialis and I returned from a hunting expedition at just the right time. We felt that it was better for you to take your chance and either die or live whole.'

'Thank you, my lord.' The gratitude was genuine for the thought of losing a limb terrified him. If he was not regionarius then there was little left for him in life.

The tribune spread his hands. 'You would be of little use as a cripple. So the good medicus was persuaded to try other means. He cleaned the wound and kept cleaning it and applied his potions and sacrifices. Mostly he doped you up with the juice of the poppy to stop you from thrashing about so much. At times they strapped you to the bed. You babbled for days.'

That was worrying, and not simply because it showed weakness.

'Like Marius in his illness you shouted out commands and war cries, striking at foes no one else could see.' Flavius Cerialis sounded amused, and as always pleased to parade his knowledge of Rome's history. The prefect was an equestrian, thus second only to a senator in matters of prestige. Yet he was always conscious that his father was the first in his line to become a Roman citizen, and although the family were part of the Batavian royal house that meant little outside the tribe.

'At times I am told that you were less fierce,' the tribune said, 'calling out softly for your mother.'

Ferox tried to read their faces. He liked Cerialis, admiring the man for his courage. The prefect was married to Sulpicia Lepidina, daughter of a distinguished if impoverished senator, by far her husband's social superior, and the union was a sign of the Batavian's immense ambition. Apart from her nobility and connections, she was witty, intelligent and beautiful. Venus or not, the face and form of the naked goddess in his dream were those of Sulpicia Lepidina, *clarissima femina*. She and Ferox had been lovers, and he was the father of her only child, young Marcus. It was a foolish, impossible love, and he could still not understand why she had taken such a risk. Deep down he knew that it made no sense, any more than a goddess choosing to lie with a mortal. Again his dream came into his mind and he knew that no mortal could resist, whatever the cost.

'I never knew my mother,' Ferox said after what felt like a very long pause. Crispinus always looked half-amused, as if he had seen the joke. Was there anything more behind the sparkle in his eyes? It was hard to be sure.

'Well, that is one of life's many sorrows,' the aristocrat said solemnly. The prefect was shifting restlessly on the folding stool. 'Yes, my dear Cerialis, I realise that time is pressing and you should go. We will join you very soon.'

The prefect stood, and smiled warmly down at Ferox. 'It is good to see you restored. My wife will be delighted when I send her the news.' There seemed no hint of irony or bitterness. A few years ago Ferox had saved Sulpicia Lepidina from an ambush, and only this summer had rescued her when she was abducted by a band of deserters and carried off to a distant island. 'She always says that whenever you are around her life turns into something out of a Greek novel!' He threw back his head and roared with laughter, for the moment looking far more the Batavian king than Roman officer. 'We both owe you so much.

'Well, I shall go, and make sure that everything is ready.'

'We will join you very soon,' Crispinus assured him. He snapped his fingers in the direction of Philo. 'Boy, bring boots and a cloak for the centurion.'

'Shall I shave him, my lord?'

'No time now.' The tribune grinned. 'He'll want a thorough clean afterwards, so no point wasting time now.'

Philo frowned. 'My lord?' The boy had firm opinions on matters of dress and cleanliness. 'It will not take long. And perhaps a clean tunic.'

Crispinus glanced at the slave for only a moment. Philo went pale and bowed. 'At once, my lord.'

'And fetch my hat!' Ferox called as the slave bustled out of the room. Philo hesitated for just a moment at the unwelcome request. 'Bet he won't be able to find it,' Ferox muttered, knowing just how much the boy disapproved of his battered old broad-brimmed hat

A nod from the tribune to Vindex and the medicus was enough sign for them to follow.

'You should have that boy beaten more often. Either that or free him, although perhaps the world is not ready for such passion for order.'

'My lord,' Ferox said flatly. In truth he had often considered both options.

'Still refusing to ask questions? We rouse you from deep slumber, prepare to drag you from your sick bed and you express not even the slightest curiosity as to why.'

Ferox pulled back the blanket and swung his legs out of bed, wincing when his thigh complained. He felt weak and filthy. Someone must have put him in a spare army tunic of the sort usually reserved for fatigues, and so off-white that it was nearly brown.

'At your command, my lord.'

Crispinus shook his head. 'You look terrible, but at least you remember your sacred oath to the emperor.' The tribune emphasised the last word, no doubt as a reminder that Ferox had also once taken an oath to the aristocrat's family. 'However, since you refuse to display the slightest curiosity, then I shall ask a few questions. You just happened to stumble across these corpses?'

Ferox nodded.

'I presume the dead soldier made it clear that they were more than just slaves?'

Ferox said nothing. He would have hunted the killers whoever the victims were.

'And, with hardly any men and little in the way of provisions, you gave chase?' Another nod. 'That seems bold. Why?'

'It is my job.'

'Did you know whose slaves they were?'

'Yes, Vegetus. And there was something not right. The warriors who had done this did not bother to search the cart thoroughly. I found a bag each of gold and silver coin, barely hidden under a pile of furs. The furs themselves were worth a year's pay.'

'Perhaps they were disturbed?'

Ferox shook his head. 'They knew what they wanted and took it, along with the girl. She should be able to tell us more once she has recovered. She barely said a word on the journey back.'

'Swathed in the cloak you so generously gave her.' The tribune must have spoken to Vindex or one of the others. 'Leaving you drenched to the skin and shivering from fever.

30

A generous deed, although such kindness was insufficient to persuade her to talk.'

'They murdered her child and her husband before her eyes. Then took turns with her. She will need some time.'

'No doubt.' The tribune's expression did not change. 'A ghastly business. So you chased them and killed them. All save this Rufus, who tried to take the girl rather than any other prize, and when you searched the corpses they had nothing of great value. Which suggests that the rider who split away took whatever it was they wanted with him. Did your men catch him?'

'In a way. The trooper was killed and the scout so badly wounded that he died an hour after he caught up with us.'

'It seems an ill-omened expedition.'

Ferox hesitated for a moment, and then decided that there was no harm in telling the tribune since he may already have heard from Vindex or one of the others. 'The rider they chased was a woman.'

Crispinus raised an eyebrow to register his surprise. Aristocrats loved to perform.

'The scout said that she came from nowhere, her blade moving faster than the eye could see. She killed the trooper almost at once, and he was a hard man. The scout said that she was alone.'

'When did this happen?'

'Six or seven nights ago.'

'So it was dark, and perhaps he did not see too clearly.'

If the tribune was unconvinced then that was up to him. Ferox knew the man had told the truth, for it made sense of the tracks he had seen.

'Well, whatever it was they wanted, we must assume that either this woman or whoever sent her has it now. In time we may learn from Vegetus what his slaves were transporting and understand why they went to such trouble.'

'The girl may know.'

Crispinus sighed theatrically. 'She hanged herself two nights ago. It seems that both your pursuit and your kindness was wasted.' He realised that Philo was at the door. 'Good, we can go. Put your boots on and come with me.' The boy shot in, a cloak draped over one arm and the boots held in the other.

'Go where, my lord?' Ferox asked as he lifted his feet in turn.

Crispinus smiled. 'You need to come with me to the latrine.'

II

THE SUN WAS warm on his face as they walked through the fort. Even so, Ferox was glad of the cloak, for it helped to hide the military tunic, which, ungirded by a belt, hung down almost to his ankles. He had to squint as they turned into the sun. Philo had failed to produce his hat. 'Being cleaned, my lord,' the boy had explained with unconvincing sincerity.

Summer was over and Vindolanda felt crowded now that so many detachments had returned to their base for the winter. A lot of faces turned to watch the elegant young tribune and the scruffy, bearded centurion limping along beside him. Crispinus ignored them all, and said little as they went down past the main buildings along the *via praetoria*. As they passed the prefect's house, Ferox glanced at the high, two-storey building with its rendered walls and tiled roof. He half hoped and half feared to glimpse Sulpicia Lepidina, until he remembered her husband saying that he would send word to her. Presumably she was away.

They turned at the end of the road and followed the track behind the rampart into the far corner, where the ground sloped down towards the steep valley behind the fort. Half a dozen Batavians stood guard outside the timber building standing beside the corner tower. The sentries on the tower were supposed to be watching the land outside against the improbable chance of any threat, but it was clear that they were keeping more of an eye on what was happening inside. A few fatigue parties had found an excuse to watch, and there was more than one face at the windows of the nearest barrack block.

The latrine block was set partly into the earth bank at the rear of the rampart. Ferox could see the tanks on its low roof and guessed that they must be nearly full of water after last week's deluge. A couple of times a day, someone would open a sluice, and the water would gather speed as it rushed down the channel before flushing out the latrine. Even so the place stank, just as every army latrine stank.

Cerialis was waiting for them by the door and wrinkled his nose in distaste. 'Sorry to lure you to this salubrious spot. Hard to think of a more awful place to die, isn't it?' He must have sensed Ferox's surprise. 'Oh, didn't you know?'

'Take a look,' Crispinus ordered. 'Take your time, and tell us what you think. The only witness is inside. Once you are done come to the *praetorium*. Then we can talk properly after you have had a chance to refresh yourself.'

Ferox opened the door, blinked as his eyes adjusted to the dim light of a pair of oil lamps and his nose was assaulted by the reek. Waiting inside was the medicus, and a soldier sitting glumly on one of the wooden seats in the row to his right. It was never very comfortable sitting there unless you were using it. Presumably this was the witness. His shield and spear were propped beside him, and he was wearing a dark cloak, so he must have been on guard. Someone had brought in two coils of rope.

'He's in there.' The medicus pointed to the row of seats along the opposite side of the block.

The row of seats was made up in sections, with three holes cut into a single frame of sanded and varnished wood, except at the corners where the board was angled to shape and each had only a single place. Each was hinged, so that it could be lifted and leaned back against the wall. There was space for fifteen men on either side of the long room, and in the centre two barrels of clean water, another overturned and empty, as well as a pile of fresh sponges, and a dirty trough where used sponges could be dipped before they were put into the buckets to be collected.

Ferox walked over to the middle of the left-hand row of seats. In the dim light it was hard to see much through the neat round holes in the wood. He leaned forward and almost gagged as the stench rose up to meet him. The darkness reminded him of the pool in his dream.

'This was how you found him?' He stood up and asked the question, as much to calm his stomach as anything else. He could not see anything definite through the seats, or smell anything apart from the overwhelming reek of filth, but it was clear there was a corpse down there.

'So he says,' the medicus answered when the soldier said nothing.

'Well, boy?' Ferox asked. The lad looked barely old enough to enlist. A lot of Batavians were like that, covered in freckles and so fair haired that they rarely needed to shave. 'What happened?'

The young soldier sprang to his feet and stiffened to rigid attention, staring at a point a foot or so above Ferox's head.

'Sir!' His voice cracked and the word came out as a squeak.

'No need to be formal. Sit down and take off your helmet.'

'Sir.' The straps on the cheek pieces were already untied, so the soldier slipped off his bronze helmet and put it down beside him. One hand brushed the moss that was glued to the top to look like fur, a peculiarity of the Batavians.

'What's your name, son?'

'Cocceius, sir.'

Ferox smiled. 'So, named after an emperor, just like me. Your father was in the cohort?'

'Yes, sir. In the century of Exomnius. He was discharged three years ago.' After twenty-five years of service auxiliaries like the boy's father were granted Roman citizenship for themselves, one wife and any children from the marriage.

'And when you were old enough you joined up?' A nod. 'Didn't fancy a legion?'

'Legionaries.' The lad brimmed over with all the contempt of his seventeen years. 'I've shit 'em!' He stopped, embarrassed and must have remembered that Ferox belonged to a legion. 'Sorry, sir, didn't mean no disrespect. Only ever wanted the Ninth, sir. It's the best cohort in the army.'

'I know, I've fought alongside you.' Flattery rarely did any harm. He patted the lad on the shoulder. 'Your folks still here?' Some soldiers could never quite let go and settled in the *vicus*, the civil settlement outside their old base.

'Nah, Mam and Dad took us home as soon as he was free. Got a nice patch of land and some prime cows.'

'But you grew up with the cohort?' Another nod. 'Good, then you're a veteran and I can talk to you man to man. When did you come down to the latrine?'

Even in the dim light Ferox saw the youth's eyes flick from side to side just once. 'Hard to say, sir,' he began.

'I do not care if you were on guard and nipped in here for a quick crap while no one was looking,' Ferox said. Sentries were not supposed to leave their post for any reason. 'It will be our secret, and I'll make sure there is no charge. Tell me the truth. You were on the fourth watch?'

'Yes, sir.' Cocceius licked his lips. 'Had to go, sir, had to, so I came down. Wouldn't have been gone long, I swear.'

'So what happened?'

'As I opened the door there was this scream from inside. Then this girl appeared. Must have been her screaming. She ran towards me. She was filthy, but her dress was all torn open, and they were out, her...' The young soldier struggled for the right word.

'"Tits" is the medical term,' the doctor said from the far side of the room.

Cocceius laughed nervously. 'They were out, bouncing everywhere. "They've killed him! They've killed him!' she yelled at me, and tried to push past. I dropped my shield and spear and tried to grab her.'

'I'll bet.' The medicus was obviously enjoying the story.

Ferox tried to ignore him. 'Go on. She got away?'

'Yes, sir. She was slippery. I tore her dress a bit more.' Cocceius frowned, and when the medicus guffawed the furrows on his brow grew even deeper, worried that he should not have done that. 'Didn't mean to, sir.'

'Then you're a fool,' the doctor muttered.

'Accidents happen,' Ferox said. 'So you grapple, but she slips past and runs?' Cocceius nodded fervently. 'You didn't follow.'

A shake of the head. 'I really needed to go,' the boy pleaded.

'Must have slipped over the wall,' the medicus cut in, serious at last. 'When the sun came up they found an old dress torn to shreds hanging from the parapet. It stank, so must have been our girl's.'

'And?' Ferox asked.

The doctor shrugged. 'A patrol took a look around. No problem finding volunteers to search for a naked woman, of course, but no sign.'

'Was she pretty?' Ferox turned back to the young soldier.

'Yes, sir.' Cocceius tried to grin like a man of experience and only managed to look more boyish.

'What did she look like?'

'She was big, sir, really big.' The boy winked.

'Was she tall?'

'I think so.'

'What colour hair?'

'Not sure, sir. Dark, maybe.'

'How did she smell?'

'Sir?'

'Never mind, only a thought. How old was she? Bit older than you?' A slight nod. 'Fine, so you let her run and then got to work yourself. Did you think about what she had said?'

'Only when I was done. Then I took a look around and thought I saw something down in the drain over there. Then I ran and gave the alarm.'

'As you should.' Ferox patted the lad again. 'Well done. Wait here in case I need to ask you some more questions.' He crossed to the other side to join the doctor. 'Give me a hand, will you?' They reached down and together lifted a section of the wooden seats. It was stiff at first, then gave suddenly and banged against the wall. The one next to it moved easily. 'You've already had a peek?'

'Yes.' They stared down, the medicus holding a lamp over the gaping hole. 'Not pretty, is it?' the doctor said. 'Nasty way to go, swallowing shit.'

The dead man lay face down, his head almost buried in the dark piles of excrement. His tunic was hitched up around his hips so that his bare buttocks looked very pale and plump. He was short, but fat with heavy arms and legs.

'Do we know who he is?'

The doctor sniffed. 'Reckon it's Narcissus from the procurator's staff. Or was.'

Another imperial freedman, just like Vegetus, and the coincidences continued to pile up suspiciously. Ferox took off his cloak and boots because there did not seem much choice. 'Get the ropes ready.' He prised up another of the stiff seats and clambered in, jumping down into the clinging and stinking contents, which came up to his calves. The stench became even worse. His first step took him deeper into the mire and he wondered whether his dream had been prophetic. Probably had a lot of business late in evening after men had eaten their *classicum*, the meal that came at the end of the day. This was one of four latrine blocks to serve the seven or eight hundred men and their families who were in the fort at the moment. Senior ranks had their own private facilities, but everyone else used these blocks, and the army diet of rough brown bread, vegetables and plenty of meat meant that they got a lot of use. Yet Narcissus was a guest of the prefect, so had no need to use this latrine unless he had a good reason, so why was he here?

Ferox went towards the body, steadying himself on the wall, when his foot slipped. Before noon a fatigue party – the men marked down as *ad stercus* on the duty roster – would come and make sure the drains were sluiced out thoroughly and give the place a clean. He would have expected the material to be harder by now, but it was like wet clay. That meant he was not the first down here. His foot brushed against something big and solid, and feeling about he discovered a belt with an open and empty pouch. The dead freedman's dishevelled tunic suggested that his body had been searched thoroughly. His best guess at the moment was that the woman had come down here. Most likely she had taken off her dress, then afterwards used the water from the overturned barrel to clean up a bit. Ferox examined the side of the drain pit. He could reach the top easily, and guessed a moderately sized woman could grab them, even if she needed to jump. With a hold on the lip of the wall, it should not be too hard to clamber up unaided. If you could get your elbows over it – and he could do that readily – then anyone fit could get out in a moment.

The medicus peered down, ropes in hand. 'Having fun?'

Might as well smile. '*Omnes ad stercus*,' he called up, using one of the army's oldest jokes. 'Let me have the first one.' He reached up for the rope. There was nothing more to learn, so they may as well get the corpse out and have a proper look. Ferox tied the end of the rope around the corpse's legs, and then took another and lifted him so that he could run it under his armpits. By the time he was done, his tunic, arms and legs were smeared thickly with filth. It was hard to imagine being clean again. He jumped for the lip of the wall, could not grip properly, so wiped his hands as best he could on his tunic. The second time he got a firm grip, hooked his elbow over the top and scrambled up. The medicus had not offered a hand and Ferox could not blame the man.

With the help of Cocceius, they hauled the dead body up and laid him on his back on the earth floor. Ferox went to one of the barrels, and gestured to the others to help because it was almost full and very heavy. They tipped water onto the freedman, pouring some, stopping, then letting another wave clean him.

'That will do,' the medicus said, and began to examine him.

'Well, the poor bugger did not choke to death,' he announced after only a cursory glance. 'That's a mercy.' He held up the front of the man's tunic, poking his fingers through a tear in the stained wool. 'Let's have some more water. No, better yet, soak a sponge.' Ferox did as instructed and then watched as the doctor half pulled, half dragged the tunic over the corpse's head. Taking the sponge he washed the chest clean around a small but deep wound just underneath the ribcage. 'Neat job.'

Ferox nodded, and was not surprised when after a thorough search the doctor declared that there were no other injuries. 'Would have killed him instantly.'

'A pugio?'

'Maybe. Any sharp knife really. Whoever it was stood very close and knew what they were doing.'

'A woman?'

The medicus snorted. 'You didn't know him, did you?' He took the sponge and cleaned lower down on the body.

'No women for this one. Not ever, I'd guess. They usually castrate them when they are young.' He seemed genuinely moved. 'Poor bastard. Hasn't had much luck in life, has he?'

'Have you ever met anyone on the procurator's staff who was poor?'

'Not much good if you can't enjoy yourself.' He sighed. 'Anything else to do now?'

'No, that is it for the moment. Have you got somewhere in the hospital where you can have him cleaned up and take another look?'

'Aye. I'll see to it. Doubt there's anything more to see, but will do my best.'

'I know,' Ferox said. 'Still, you know how it is when one of the emperor's servants is involved. Everything by the book. There was a work party waiting when I got here, so you will have plenty of help.' He went to the remaining barrel and washed his arms and as much as the rest of himself as he could. It was not much of an improvement and disturbing the filth only seemed to stir up the smell. 'Cocceius.'

'Sir.'

'Am I right in thinking that you didn't kill this man?'

'Sir?' The boy was genuinely puzzled. Like most auxiliaries these days, he did not carry a pugio. 'Thought not. In that case you are dismissed. Get cleaned up and report to wherever you should be now.'

'Sir!' He hesitated for a moment. 'Am I in trouble, sir?'

Ferox grinned. 'Shouldn't think so. You might want to practise catching slippery ladies though!'

'Yes, sir!'

After the soldier had gone Ferox had a thought. 'Tell the fatigue party to search for any knives or daggers in here,' he told the medicus. 'Doubt they will find anything, but no harm in trying.'

'Any theories?'

'Typical Greek!' Ferox chuckled.

'I'm from Leptis Magna.'

'Even worse, you Africans can actually think in a straight line! What do you reckon happened?'

'Someone murdered him.'

Ferox slapped his forehead. 'Eureka! Now I need a bath more than he ever did. I just hope the noble tribune has given the necessary orders.'

III

A BATH WAS ready in the simple but private room maintained by the prefect and his wife in their house. Before he was permitted inside, Ferox was taken to the courtyard of the praetorium and instructed to dunk himself thoroughly in a tall and wide barrel filled with water. His mind, always prone to wandering away, thought of the story of the Hound, one of the great heroes claimed by his tribe and just about everyone else. The stories were almost the same apart from some of the names and the identity of the enemy wherever you went and he had even heard ones very similar told in Gaul. After one battle, where the Hound had gone into his battle frenzy and butchered hundreds of enemies, he returned to the stronghold still lusting after slaughter. Terrified that he would kill all the men he found, even his kin, they sent out bare-breasted women to meet him. Modestly, the young hero turned aside – a part of the story that had never made much sense – and while he was distracted the men grabbed him, and plunged him into three barrels of water. The first burst asunder, the second boiled, and the third merely bubbled as the frenzy left him.

The only woman in the courtyard was an elderly slave, fully clad and smirking as the centurion stripped off his tunic and climbed into the water. Philo waited impatiently with a fresh cloak and a pair of the wooden slippers worn in a bath-house. The prefect's private bath did not have the heated floor, something impractical in a timber building, but when he reached the pool and shuddered as he lowered himself into the hot water, it was with an almost spiritual joy. Philo fussed, until Ferox sent him away, promising to let himself be shaved once he had finished. A hint that the boy was to make discreet enquiries among the other slaves and freedmen put a jauntiness in his step as he left. Philo dearly loved to be useful and thrived on gossip.

An hour later, clean shaven, dressed in his finest tunic, new breeches and best boots, Ferox was ushered in to a room Cerialis kept as an office. Only the prefect and tribune were there, which was surprising because normally the prefect's *cornicularius* would keep a record of the meeting. After a few questions about his wound and his welfare they let him report. They appeared to have known or guessed much of it already, and the fact that the freedman had been stabbed rather than smothered made little real difference. It was murder either way.

'Was it the woman?' Crispinus asked once he had finished.

'She may have killed him, but I very much doubt she could have heaved him down into the drain. He was well built, and a corpse is always awkward to handle. So either she had help or she got there after the real murderer had gone. The floor was too scuffed from soldiers' boots for there to be any clear prints.'

'Any idea when he was killed?'

'Sometime during the night.' Ferox doubted that the medicus would be able to make any better guess even after examining the corpse more carefully. 'The body was no longer stiff, so he probably had been there a few hours. Hard to say any more than that.'

'Indeed.'

Ferox could sense that both men were uncomfortable, even nervous, and some of that was surely because the dead man was no ordinary freed slave, but one of the emperor's household and a servant of the procurator. The procurator of Britannia was an equestrian, just like Cerialis and several score other officers, officials and wealthy people in the province. Lucius Neratius Marcellus was the *legatus Augusti pro praetore* of Britannia, the supreme representative of the emperor in the province, a former consul and a distinguished member of the Senate. Yet the procurator was also the emperor's man, charged with overseeing the finances in the area, from taxes to the revenue of imperial estates, and was in direct communication with the emperor. Friction between legates and procurators was not uncommon, especially under the more nervous emperors. Back in the days of Domitian, it was the procurator who had reported on the activities of Sallustius Lucullus, then legate in Britannia, accusing him of dangerous ambitions, and citing as evidence his naming a new pattern of *lancea* after himself. That episode ended in the legate's execution. Even his bodyguard, who carried the offending javelins, had been formed into a special unit as a punishment and sent to Moesia on the Danube. What was written in the procurator's confidential reports mattered a lot, even under the enlightened rule of Trajan.

'I take it that no trace was found of the woman?' Ferox asked.

'None,' Crispinus replied. 'The description was not exactly precise, and it does not sound as if you were able to coax any more from this soldier.'

'He is young, was tired and on his way to the latrine. Then a half-naked woman barges into him. What do you expect him to remember?'

Cerialis snorted with laughter. The prefect was in his late twenties and a vigorous man, who kept a number of attractive young slaves to attend to his needs, as well as making frequent visits to the special staff at the brothel on the edge of the vicus outside the fort.

'Do you think he is hiding anything, this soldier?' Crispinus ignored the commander of the Batavians and his gaze was hard.

'Cocceius has an excellent record.' The prefect spoke loudly, quick to defend one of his men. 'There is no reason to doubt him.'

Crispinus paid no attention and stared intently at Ferox.

'I believe he has told us all he knows, and he stumbled on all this by pure chance.'

'You are sure. Some women can get even good men to do what would otherwise be unthinkable.'

'I am sure.' Ferox glanced apologetically at the prefect. 'He's not the brightest. Certainly not to lie consistently over something like this.'

Cerialis chuckled. 'He's a good soldier. He doesn't need to be bright.'

Ferox bit back a suggestion that intelligence was equally not essential for senior officers. Instead he raised the matter that the others had oddly left out. 'Why was Narcissus here, my lord?'

The two officers exchanged a glance. 'If you are asking why he was in the north of the province,' Crispinus began, a hand smoothing his unnaturally white hair, 'then the answer is that he was assisting with the census in the Anavionestan districts, as well as helping Vegetus collect revenue from tenants on some of the emperor's estates, and also well as some matter of a legacy from the Brigantian royal family.'

The census had begun this summer, and in time would cover most of the Brigantes and their kin as well as those of the Selgovae and Demetae who were considered formal allies of Rome. As soon as he had heard the plan, Ferox had worried that it was needlessly provocative at a time when discontent was already bubbling away and the Roman garrison of the province was known to be weak. Plenty of rebellions throughout the empire had been sparked when census officials came around asking lots of questions that everyone knew were a prelude to fresh levies.

'I know you consider the census unwise,' Crispinus continued, making Ferox worry that he had betrayed his thoughts. He was tired, and everything was too much effort. 'However,' the tribune added, 'if you mean why he was at Vindolanda, he came to attend a dinner last night held in honour of our emperor's birthday.'

Ferox had lost all track of the date and was surprised to learn that yesterday must have been the sixth day after the Ides of September.

'I was the host, and issued the invitation.' Cerialis cut through his thoughts.

The tribune patted him on the arm. 'At my prompting, dear Cerialis, and it was a perfectly reasonable thing to do.

So it does mean that the prefect and I, along with his dear wife and their guests, were among the last people to see Narcissus before his untimely death.'

'When did you last see him, my lords?'

'The dinner finished sometime before the end of the second hour of the night,' Cerialis said. 'Several of the guests had an early start the next morning, so there was no taste for a late night. And most of the men had been hunting for the last few days and came back later than we had planned. We had ridden hard and while that gives one an appetite for food, none of us were in a mood for prolonged discourse. And then…' He trailed off. 'It was not the most successful of dinners.'

'Scarcely your fault, my dear friend. I invited him.' Crispinus stared at Ferox for a while. 'Your lack of curiosity can become tiresome. I had never met Narcissus before, but he carried a letter from my uncle, the noble Neratius Marcellus, and from other connections of mine. No doubt they had their reasons for writing,' he added sourly, 'but it was not because the fellow was a congenial companion. When he spoke it was often barbed.' The tribune glanced at the prefect.

'Perhaps you are aware, centurion, that my wife's brother has a somewhat…' He paused searching for the right word. 'Shall we say unfortunate past.'

'I am aware, my lord.' Ferox knew that Sulpicia Lepidina's older brother had been a young tribune much like Crispinus when he was caught up in Saturninus' plot against Domitian. That episode was a dark memory for Ferox, who had been tasked with investigating a number of senior officers accused of being involved. All had died, whether he had shown them innocent or not. Later, recalled by Nerva, the fool of a brother had been part of another conspiracy, this time by the provincial legate in Syria. That had meant a second disgrace. This, and the huge debts of her family, seemed the main reason why a senator's daughter had married a mere equestrian, and one of provincial stock. Petilius Cerialis was rich and known to have the favour of Trajan.

'Good,' Crispinus said, 'then we have no need to speak of such distasteful matters. Sadly, Narcissus displayed a vulgarity exceptional even for a freedman come into wealth, and thought it fitting to make jokes about this and other matters.

'My wife's brother is shortly to take up command of Legio VIIII Hispana,' Cerialis explained. 'That fellow hinted that he was on trial, with a last chance to prove his loyalty.'

That might or might not be true, Ferox thought, although it would seem a considerable risk unless the emperor was confident that the man would pass the test. Either way it was a surprising rehabilitation. Perhaps the brother had something of the ability and charm of his sister. From all he had heard, this seemed unlikely.

'Worse than the jokes were the silences,' Cerialis added and then went quiet. His normally cheerful face was grim.

'Narcissus listened too closely to be polite,' Crispinus explained. 'It gave the impression that we were all on trial.'

'Who else was there, my lords?'

The other guests were familiar. Aelius Brocchus commanded the cavalry *ala* at Coria, and he and his wife Claudia Severa were old friends, as was Rufinus, who led the cohort at Magna to the west. 'Oppius Niger is new to these parts,' the tribune went on, 'having just arrived to take charge of the cohort at Aballava. While you will remember Attius Secundus from when we stopped at Trimontium two years ago.' It took Ferox a moment to remember the tribune who had entertained them at that northern outpost. 'In contrast he is on his way home at the end of his tour.'

None of the guests appeared the type to stab a freedman and shove his body into a latrine, however vulgar the fellow was. On the other hand they might just order someone else to do the business.

'Do we know who was the last one to speak to Narcissus, my lords?'

'I believe it was that dubious character, the tribune Crispinus,' the young aristocrat said with an exaggerated raise of the eyebrow. 'He hurried after me as I went through the courtyard and begged leave to ask a favour.' Noting Ferox's questioning look, he went on. 'Nothing out of the ordinary. Did I happen to have an acquaintance who might introduce him to the king of the Coritani. I said that I would see what I could do.'

'And would you have done anything?'

'Impudent as ever. Well, centurion, I probably would have found someone. One does not have to like a fellow like that to realise that there is no harm in having him well disposed.'

'And perhaps great harm in having him ill disposed?' Ferox finished the thought.

Crispinus grimaced. 'Either you do not ask or are too direct for true courtesy. Better to say harm rather than great harm, but it is generally a sound policy to grant a favour if you can. Why run a risk even of that lesser harm unless it is necessary?'

'May I speak to the other guests?'

'Rufinus and Niger are still here,' Cerialis explained. 'Everyone else left before dawn. My wife and Claudia Severa are taking the children south for a few months, perhaps even for the winter if it seems likely to be a severe one. Brocchus and I may join them for a while, and for the moment he will take them part of the way and provide an escort of troopers for them. Secundus will ride with them to Coria, but planned to go ahead with his own servants from there.'

'That is unfortunate.'

'I doubt that you would learn much from them,' Crispinus replied archly. 'If your mystery woman was incapable of hefting a corpse about, then I trust that you are not hinting two noble ladies might have been capable of such a feat!'

'Of course not, sir. Perish the thought, sir!'

The tribune shook his head. 'Ah, the flat insolence of a soldier. How truly tiresome.' He let out a long breath. 'I dare say we can write and ask them if they know anything of importance.'

'Of course,' Cerialis said, bristling with dutiful eagerness. 'It is unlikely to be much, but you never know. I will write a letter before the day is out and send a swift trooper to carry it.'

'Does that satisfy you, centurion?' the tribune asked.

It did not, but there was no use saying so. 'Of course, my lord. Very generous of you, sir, to trouble the ladies.' Ferox hoped this face was an unreadable mask. 'What I do not yet fully understand is what you wish me to do.'

'I should have thought that would be obvious.' Crispinus spoke like a teacher addressing a slow pupil. 'Find out what you can about this affair. You will have to stay in the hospital for some days so you may as well earn your pay while you are there. Learn whatever you can. It may not be much, but you have a nose for the truth as good as those of friend Cerialis' hounds for a scent. Learn what you can and write us a report. As full a report as possible in the finest tradition of this scribbling army. Do it as fast as you can and then we can send it to the procurator and that should help shape his actions, and more importantly the story he chooses to tell to others.'

'Do you want the truth, or simply a truth fit for the procurator, my lord?'

Cerialis chuckled again. 'We shall make a philosopher of you yet, prince of the Silures.'

'More likely a legal advocate,' Crispinus muttered. 'I have asked you to do this because I want as much of *the* truth as you can find. My fear is that there will be little to learn, but that is neither here nor there. If this is somehow connected to the attack on Vegetus' people, then we should know. Do I detect surprise? Since you have failed to mention the possibility that our mystery woman was the same one who killed the two men you sent in pursuit, I felt that I ought to raise it. At this point it would at the very least be courteous to register surprise at my perceptive and suspicious mind.'

Ferox patted his brow with one hand. 'Wisdom of the gods, my lord. Too much for a mere mortal.'

'I truly hope not. Learn what you can. Perhaps this is to do with the census, perhaps not. You have spent the last weeks warning of trouble brewing among the tribes. On the other hand I have never met an imperial freedman who was poor, and I know this one was not. Money tends to complicate everything and that may well be behind this. I do not know, Flavius Ferox. All I do know is that I did not kill the wretched man, and I will lay you good odds that neither did any of the guests at dinner. So try to find out who did and why, and we may be able to smooth this whole business over. Will you do that for me?'

Ferox sprang to his feet. 'Sir!' The obedient shout was louder than he had meant it to be. Crispinus winced and Cerialis jumped in his seat. Then the prefect smiled.

'I shall check with the medicus, but I am sure that he would not object if you stayed in the praetorium rather than the hospital.'

'Thank you, my lord.'

'Now, if the noble tribune will excuse me, I shall enquire whether Rufinus and Niger are free to see you.'

Both of the prefects were indeed free, although they had little to say. Rufinus had met the freedman a couple of times, but the dinner was the first social encounter. 'Bit of a tick, but you have to be polite,' was his verdict.

Oppius Niger was from Antioch, almost as impeccably neat as Philo and with the same olive skin and eyes so dark that they were almost the black of his name. He had a slim face and an abrasive manner. 'Couldn't stand the little shit. Too oily. Reckon the shithouse was the best place for him.' He looked around twenty-three, just starting his first posting in the army after years of education and idle indulgence. Like of lot of equestrians at this stage in his career, he overdid the brusque fighting man act. 'No, never met him before. Never been comfortable around geldings, even to ride. They lack spirit.'

Little the wiser, Ferox decided to have a look around outside. Vindex appeared from nowhere, probably sent by a nervous Philo to persuade the centurion to make use of a wooden crutch or at least a staff. Ferox took only the stick and the scout said nothing, but carried the crutch with him. For a while they wandered around on the rampart either side of the latrine and he was shown where the torn dress was found. They left the fort and walked along to the same point beyond the ditch. The ground behind them sloped sharply down into a valley, and he soon found the trail. They followed it down, over the brook, crossing by a number of big logs laid there and then climbed the far hill up to the old abandoned hill fort.

'Wasn't hiding anything, was she?' Vindex commented as his friend struggled up the steep side of the hill, pushing his way through the heather. Broken fronds made the trail very clear. It was probably deliberate.

At the top there were prints from two horses and from the boots of a man. The woman had come here, met a companion, and most likely dressed herself before they rode away to the south.

'No point following on foot,' Vindex said. 'And the sun will be down by the time we could fetch horses.'

'Yes.' Ferox stared down at the fort and the vicus beyond it. It was easier to think up here away from the busy army base. Even so, he heard the clear call of a trumpet sounding the last watch of the day.

Vindex came to stand beside him. 'None of this makes much sense,' he said. 'So, are we already humped, or are we waiting for it?'

'Maybe both.'

'Same as usual then. Lovely.'

IV

FEROX WONDERED WHAT to write in his report. Five days had passed and the tribune was becoming impatient. There was some excuse because yesterday the garrison had paraded to witness the sacrifice of an ox in honour of the birthday of the divine Augustus and he had been required to attend the ceremonies and the dinner Cerialis gave for his own centurions and decurions. At least his leg was feeling better and he had tried to do a little more exercise each day. It was now an hour after noon and he had borrowed a practice sword and shield so that he could test himself at one of the posts on the training ground beyond the vicus. At this time of day it was usually quiet before training resumed later in the afternoon, and he had come here every day apart from the day of the parade. For the first few sessions he had contented himself with stretching, some short jogs, and throwing a javelin at one of the ox skulls mounted as targets at the far end of the field. Today he felt ready to use the overweight wicker shield and wooden gladius.

Vindex had wanted to come, saying that fencing with a real opponent rather than a lump of wood would be more useful, but Ferox needed to think and it was easier to do that on his own. The praetorium was too crowded to be peaceful, and even with the lady of the house, her children and attendants away, there remained a large household who seemed always to be busy. There never seemed to be any peace, even compared to the little outpost where Ferox spent most of his time when he was not riding abroad. He had been there for many years now and it was the closest he had to a home. Soon after arriving he had dubbed the place Syracuse, after the room in the palace where the emperor Augustus had gone whenever he did not want to be disturbed.

Eager for news from the wider world, Ferox had asked the scout to ride over to Syracuse and pick up any fresh reports or rumours. He would have preferred to do it himself, but the tribune was adamant that he was not to leave Vindolanda until the report was completed to his satisfaction. Ferox knew that he must sit down and do it. Hopefully the exercise would help clear his mind and perhaps let him glimpse some answers.

He began with the sword, cumbersome and poorly balanced compared to his own blade, and after some stretching made a series of mock attacks that stopped short of contacting the six-foot-high post set into the ground. There was no one else using the training area and that was good, but a straggle of children appeared and stared at him and this was less good. The oldest, a tall, raw-boned lad with hair so blond it was almost white, must have been nine or ten, the others younger. One, a little girl of four or five clutching the edge of the boy's tunic, had a squint, which made her steady stare slightly unnerving. All were no doubt children of the cohort, hanging around looking for something to do. Ferox found that he was a good deal more indulgent of all children ever since he had become a father. Even so, he could have done without their silent scrutiny. He could not help wondering whether they knew almost as much as he did about the murder.

For the simple truth was that in six days Ferox had learned almost nothing more. He wondered if everyone else was equally baffled and simply wanted to forget the dead man. The Batavians were a clannish bunch, and even though he had fought alongside them a good few times in the last years, he knew that he remained an outsider and wondered if they were telling him everything. Longinus, the trooper who had once been Julius Civilis, prefect and leader of the Batavian rebellion against Rome and afterwards vanished into the anonymous ranks of the army, might have told him. However, the one-eyed veteran had gone as part of the escort to Sulpicia Lepidina. Presumably he felt that no one would recognise him after almost thirty years, even if he went with the lady as far as Londinium and the big cities of the south. Oddly enough he had not been marked down for this duty, but two troopers had been taken ill with food poisoning early that morning and Longinus and another man assigned to take their places.

Ferox had had enough of mock blows and slammed the hardwood sword into the post strongly enough to leave a dent. He did not like coincidences, although in truth he had come across plenty of them over the years. A letter had come last night from Sulpicia Lepidina, expressing mild sorrow for the death of her guest while saying nothing of importance about him. Narcissus had not spent long this far north, even though he had been in and around Eboracum for over a year. In time Vindex might pick up some rumours about his business with the Brigantian royal family.

It was time to use the shield, and he was pleased to have found one shaped like the rectangular *scutum* used by legionaries rather than the flat oval type equipping the Batavians and Tungrians here at Vindolanda. He hefted it, testing the weight. In some ways it was easier having something balance the sword in his right hand.

At the far end a horseman walked his dark bay onto the training field. He was fully equipped, with polished scale armour, gleaming bronze helmet, uncovered shield and a long spear. He turned his head, nodding and raising the spear to acknowledge the centurion. Ferox waved his sword in reply, and was surprised to see that the cavalryman had a masked helmet, of the sort used in the cavalry games. He had heard that Cerialis was forming two teams so that he could put on one of these displays, even though they were normally the preserve of the better mounted cavalry alae, rather than mixed foot and horse units like the Batavians. Presumably one of the men was putting in some additional practice, getting used to riding with a mask, which reduced his vision to just a couple of slits. After the wave, he ignored the centurion and began walking his mount in a circle. The children, evidently bored by his ongoing duel with a lump of wood, decided that horse and rider offered better entertainment, and wandered over to watch him instead.

Ferox returned to his practice and his thoughts. Philo had learned far more than he had and the little Jewish lad from Alexandria had obviously enjoyed himself. He had charm when he wanted, and an innocence that seemed to appeal to women young or old. Slaves gossiped. Everyone knew that, although their owners often liked to pretend that they did not. Yet they rarely were so forthcoming to outsiders.

In the last few years Philo had become a favourite of quite a few members of Cerialis' household, even Privatus, the senior steward who recognised a kindred spirit in the boy's obsession with neatness and cleanliness. It had taken several days, and Ferox did not like to think how many favours or swapped stories, but soon the boy was getting some sense of Narcissus.

'They are collectors,' Philo told him, his face brimming with pride. 'He and his colleague Vegetus. You could call them friendly rivals.'

'Collectors?'

'Of antiques, my lord. Jewellery, silver and gold plate, helmets and weapons. They especially like anything associated with the kings and queens of the Britons. Some they keep, but most they hope to sell to wealthier collectors in Gaul and Italy. The profits are said to be substantial, although Narcissus' man Rivus says that they enjoyed most the thrill of the chase. When the cart owned by Vegetus was attacked, Rivus says that Vegetus' man joked with him that his master was behind it all!' He noticed Ferox's puzzlement. Philo shrugged, 'Apologies, my lord, I get ahead of myself. The cart carried a tall bronze helmet and a mail shirt said to have been worn by King Venutius of Brigantia when he led his warriors against the legions all those years ago. They had both heard the rumours that they had been given years ago to a chieftain of the Selgovae, and were eager to obtain them. Vegetus won, although not for long. Am I correct in assuming those items were not found with the cart?'

Ferox nodded, much to the boy's delight. 'What did Rivus think of his master?'

'He was not generous, but nor was he demanding. There is a saying that freedmen make either the very best or the very worst masters.'

'I have never heard it,' Ferox said.

'My lord, you have never been a slave.'

'No.' More than once he had wondered about giving the boy his freedom, before Philo's constant fussing made him dismiss the idea. Perhaps soon.

'Narcissus did not work Rivus too hard, and kept him even after he lost his arm in an accident.' That injury was the main reason why no one suspected the slave of the murder, since he could not have lifted the body. 'Mostly he was decent enough, although now and again he would lose his temper and beat him savagely. Rivus had been a slave of a high chief of the Brigantes and was given to Narcissus in part payment of debt. He wonders a little whether he was part of the collection. His master liked him to strip so that he could look at his tattoos.'

Ferox began to approach the post like a fighter, crouching behind the shield, left leg shuffling, followed by short step with right, sword ready to seek a gap. His thigh was sore, but he did not want to let it get stiff so he forced it to move. The rider was still doing circles, although he had changed rein to ride in the other direction. This appeared to be enough for him to retain his youthful audience.

That had been all Philo had to tell that first session, and had given Ferox plenty to ponder, until his mind was dragged into the present. After the boy had gone, one of Cerialis' slaves appeared. She was young, pretty like most of the women in his household, and he had seen her serving at table in the past.

'My master wishes your stay to be as pleasant as possible,' she had said, eyes staring down at his knees in the demure manner felt appropriate for servants. He guessed that she was a Gaul, pale skinned and with long brown hair plaited into a pigtail that reached halfway down her back. 'I am at your service.'

'That is kind of him,' was all that he could think to say.

With an easy gesture she slid her dress off her shoulders, letting the material fall to her waist. The belt unfastened almost as quickly and the whole garment rustled down. She was bare apart from a simple pair of sandals.

Ferox wondered whether this was some sort of test. Had he said something during his fevered dreams that hinted at his love for the prefect's wife or had Cerialis worked it out for himself? For all his open, enthusiastic manner, the commander of the Ninth Cohort was a shrewd enough man.

Philo disapproved, but the woman returned each night and attended to him efficiently enough, as she had no doubt entertained her master and a fair few of his other guests. Cerialis gave him a big wink the morning after her first visit.

Ferox hefted the practice sword and shield once again. It was better not to think, but simply to let his mind roam free. On the other side of the training field the rider clicked his tongue a couple of times as he changed direction again and urged his mount into a trot. The animal bounded, gave a small buck that prompted a scream from the little girl, and then gave in and obeyed. Ferox wondered whether he was still breaking in a fresh horse. The bay looked sleek, its hair recently trimmed and well brushed, two socks on its front legs and its face a blaze of white. When the man took the animal into a canter, still keeping to a tight circle, the group of children cheered.

Ferox did his best to ignore them. He was tired, weak from the illness and days lying idle, and his back was damp with sweat. Forcing himself to keep going for just a little longer, he stamped forward, punched the post with his wicker shield and followed with a thrust from the gladius at eye height, grunting with the effort.

Perhaps it was the nightly visits of the slave woman, but yesterday he had slipped a note to Flora, asking for an appointment. She had once been a slave, entertainer and prostitute, winning freedom and setting herself up in the same business, and was now owner of the most successful brothel in the north, catering for soldiers and, in more style and comfort, senior officers. Cerialis was a frequent visitor to the big house on the edge of the vicus, built partly in stone and with two storeys so that it stood out among all the other civilian buildings.

Earlier that morning, Ferox had gone at the stated time to see the mistress of the house. The place had a subdued, exhausted air after yesterday's festival, but the clerk and guards were as welcoming as ever. Flora had always been small, even though her voice and most of all her earthy laugh sounded as if they came from a great fat woman. Today Ferox thought she looked even smaller and a lot older. Now and again she coughed, a deep racking cough that shook her slight frame.

'Doesn't the sun ever get warm in this benighted place?' she had asked of no one in particular. Ferox was never quite sure why Flora had set up house at Vindolanda. There was an old bond with Longinus, but she had come here years before he arrived with cohors VIIII, so that did not explain it. Once, on a rare occasion when she had drunk so much that her tongue loosened, she had hinted at some trouble in Londinium years before.

'How's your boy?' Flora asked next. They were alone, sitting in her plain office as they had often done in the past. A slave had brought them wine, but the mistress herself poured it into crystal cups, adding plenty of water to the one she offered to Ferox. 'Glad to see you have stopped making a beast of yourself.' In the lonely years at Syracuse, rejected by the army, tortured by dark memories of interrogations and executions, and lost because the woman he had loved above all had vanished, Ferox had been prone to days of heavy drinking. Flora had stayed his friend throughout those hard years.

'I think Marcus is well,' he said after a moment. Ferox never knew how Flora had discovered that Sulpicia Lepidina's baby was his and not her husband's. She always seemed to know almost everything that happened in and around Vindolanda, and in the wider world.

'He is,' she stated firmly, pausing as she relished a long sip of her own wine. Even watered down, Ferox could tell that it was good. 'Poor mite was a bit crook last month, but he's better now. Good solid lad, although let's hope he takes more after his mother than his father.'

Ferox laughed. He had not seen Flora for months and had missed these quiet talks. They chatted for a while, for that was their custom, and then he asked a few questions about Narcissus.

'Don't know much.' Flora usually began that way, but this time there was some truth in it. She told him about the freedmen and their rivalry as collectors, adding only a little to what he already knew. Narcissus was not a visitor. 'And don't look as if I was stating the blindingly obvious. I've been in this trade more years than I care to remember and seen things even a nasty little sod like you wouldn't dream. Some eunuchs still like to be entertained.'

Vegetus was a regular visitor. 'The randy pig. Oh, doesn't do any harm, but the girls say he struts as if he's Herakles. Losing his wife made him worse, but he was bad enough before.' Two years ago, Vegetus' flirtatious wife had been abducted by warriors loyal to a savage priest who called himself the Stallion. They had meant to take Sulpicia Lepidina, but Ferox had saved her and still felt guilty because at the time he had given no thought to anyone else. He and Vindex had found the poor woman's corpse the next day.

'Did you get them all?' Flora asked.

The Stallion was long dead, along with a good few of his followers, but others were still out there, most of all Acco, a true druid who had aided the Stallion and then carved him up as a sacrifice once he failed. 'No, not yet,' Ferox said. 'One day I will.'

'The freedmen were up to something,' Flora said after they had sat in silence for some time. 'They may be the emperor's men, but that doesn't tie them to the same emperor we have at the moment.'

'Do you know something?'

Flora shook her head, which meant that it was a guess, but she had a nose for politics, which always made Ferox wonder all the more about her past. Once or twice she had admitted that she and Longinus had been through a lot together.

'Something is brewing. There's still folk out there who reckon Trajan is not the right man to be *princeps*. Others just out for the main chance. Three weeks ago a trader calling himself Domitius stopped for a few days. Old man – older even than me!' Flora laughed that deep, incongruous laugh of hers. 'A Gaul from his speech, but maybe not one who has been home in a long while. No ring, even though he threw money around as if he had no lack of it.' Equestrians were marked by a distinctive silver ring. 'I wondered whether he didn't want too much attention. Men of his type usually get a formal welcome from the prefect, however much he may pretend to despise people in trade.'

'Where did he stay?'

'Castus' place, so decent, but nothing special. Had a different girl each night and paid extra for the best rooms and the bath.' Flora's private bath was one of the great luxuries of her establishment. 'One of the twins saw him talking to that one-armed slave of Narcissus, and he stood drinks for a lot of soldiers in a couple of the bars. Never went to the fort, though, as far as I know. He was a man who was listening, and not here to buy and sell or I'm a virgin.'

Ferox smiled. 'You are always as fresh and fair as one.'

'Liar.' Flora was pleased, which only made her more gruff. 'Now go on with you. I have not had a chance to finish it all, but I will send a package to you later today. May be a help, where you are going.'

'Am I going somewhere?'

Flora smiled. 'Probably. At least if I'm any judge, but it's no job of mine to do the army's work for it and tell you where.'

That was one more mystery to add to so many others, although he had little doubt that she was right. He was still not much wiser about Narcissus, and whether or not his death was something to do with the attack on Vegetus' slaves. Like it or not, he would have to sit down and write the report, doing the best he could. Frustration led him into a furious assault on the post that left it leaning an inch or so to the side.

Ferox decided that he had had enough exercise, and laid the sword down on the ground with the shield over it so that he could do a few last stretches and exercises before quitting. Just then a woman shouted, yelling at the children to come. When they ignored her, she stamped out from behind a nearby house and called again. She was tall, her round face marking her out as a Batavian even though her hair was a dirty grey and no longer the gold or red it had once been. Life in a camp tended to age a woman. One more shout and the children started moving, shuffling their feet to show small defiance without actually disobeying.

The rider had changed rein again and was cantering a wider circle, the horse tossing its head. Ferox reached up and rubbed his neck with his hands, wondering whether tomorrow he ought to try and do everything wearing mail and helmet as well. He froze as the memory of the fight at Eburus' farm came flooding back. The sound of pounding hoofs was getting closer. He turned, saw the white face of the horse and knew it was the same one Rufus had taken that night.

Silent apart from the drumming of hoofs and clink of harness and equipment, the masked rider bore down on him like some statue come to eerie life. He was close, coming straight at him, and Ferox flung himself down to the right, hitting the ground hard and rolling. The rider pulled on the reins to follow, coming close so that Ferox was covered in dust thrown up by the horse's feet. Thrusting across his body to the wrong side, the spear did not have the reach to strike him.

The horseman yelled, an odd distorted sound through the small gap between the tinned lips on the face mask. He was already turning, and the horse reared as it fought against the brutal drag of the bit. Ferox pushed himself up, realising that his dive had taken him away from the shield and sword lying beside the post. Even practice weapons would be better than nothing. He tried to shout for help, but his throat was dry and he managed no more than a croak.

The expressionless mask stared at him and then the horse came at him, slowly this time, the rider taking care. Ferox waved his arms wildly and after a cough screamed a ululating cry, hoping to frighten the beast. It reared, hoofs thrashing near his face and making him jump back, but the rider was still in control and Ferox had to leap back again to avoid the glittering spear point coming for his face.

Another jab, and this time he leaned his body out of the way and tried to grab the shaft of the spear. It jerked back, and grazed his left hand as the edge slipped through his grip. The rider swung the spear, the wood hitting Ferox hard on the side of the head, so that he dropped to his knees. Reeling, he managed to throw himself under the horse and started to scrabble across the ground. One heavy foot landed an inch from his face, dust was in his eyes, and then the animal reared again, and the rider dropped his spear as he struggled for balance.

Ferox pushed up and half staggered, half ran towards the post. The spear was on the far side of the cavalryman and he had no chance of getting there, so he would have to make do. There was a scrape of metal as the rider drew his long *spatha*. Ferox always winced when he heard the sound, and wondered why the army insisted on a bronze mouth to a scabbard instead of wood, which would not start taking the edge off a blade. Grabbing the shield, he turned. Disturbed by the motion, the wooden sword rolled away and there was no time to reach for it because the horseman was urging his mount into a canter. Someone was shouting and there were figures in armour coming onto the field, but they were fifty paces away and no help for the moment.

Rather than holding the boss, Ferox closed one hand on each of the long sides of the shield and he ran forward shaking it and shrieking. The horseman swerved to come on his left side, sword raised to hack down, and Ferox slammed the heavy shield into the side of the horse's head. The cut came, but it was wild as the animal pulled away, screaming, and the blade bit into the top of the shield. It must have been old, and after the pounding of the training session, the wicker split. Ferox tried to pull the shield back for another swing, but the boss of the bridle ended in a bronze rosette, which had snagged in the shield. He ducked as the sword slashed down again, hands fast on the shield so that he wrenched it down with him. The animal reared again even more wildly and, tightly drawn by the bridle, the rein snapped, so that the rider slammed back against the two horns on the rear of his saddle. Then the beast rolled sideways and the rider was flung free, shield dropping and limbs flailing to land in a clatter of bronze and iron.

'Hercules' balls, what's going on?' A centurion had run up, a dozen soldiers following more warily. They were Tungrians, rather than Batavians, the tops of their helmets bare bronze rather than decorated with fur.

Ferox pushed himself to his feet, struggling for breath. 'That man is a deserter and under arrest.' Rufus, if it was Rufus, lay on his back, absolutely still, and Ferox did not like the angle of his neck and head.

The centurion went over and pulled off the mask from the helmet. 'Yes, I remember this one. Always trouble.' He leaned down and listened. 'Not any more, though. Not ever.' He straightened back up. 'You four, strip this man of equipment and put the body out of the way. You…' he pointed to another '…run to our praetorium and say that the deserter Rufus turned up and is now dead. Ask what they want us to do with him now.' He grinned. 'No one will shed any tears over that bastard.

'You all right, Ferox?'

Ferox just nodded.

V

THE CARRIAGE ROCKED as its wheels skipped over gaps in the road's surface. Crispinus stirred, muttered something, before going back to sleep, resting his head on a pillow jammed up against the back of the seat. Ferox was glad, for when he was awake, the noble tribune seemed utterly incapable of silence. After three days of questions, gossip in which he had no interest, and parades of the young aristocrat's education, wit and insight, a few hours of peace and quiet were a blessed gift from the gods. The prospect of many more days cooped up with the garrulous tribune weighed heavily upon his soul. There was little choice, for they had assured him that he was not yet well enough to ride, at least not as far and fast as they needed to go.

'We are summoned to Londinium, young Ferox,' Crispinus had announced the morning after Rufus' attack. 'So it is a chance to see what passes for civilisation in this land.'

'Do you really need me, my lord? I have work to do up here.'

'Bad news?' The aristocrat was immediately serious. 'Is it that rogue Acco?'

Perhaps it was a lucky guess, but word had come of the old druid. 'Yes, my lord.' Ferox shrugged. 'Probably. And of other signs of trouble to come.'

'Well, that cannot be helped. My uncle, the noble legate, has sent for you.' Crispinus was a small man and had to stand on tiptoe to grab the centurion by the shoulders. 'Note that, Flavius Ferox. He has sent for you by name. One might have thought that his first instinct would be to ask for his nephew, a gallant, dashing young officer of great promise, who constantly displays wisdom beyond his years although no less than would be expected from someone of his distinguished ancestry.

'No, centurion, this time it is not you coming along with me on the vague chance that you might be useful. I am tagging along with you, because this offers a splendid opportunity for seeing my uncle and enjoying his generous hospitality.' He grinned, taking his hands away. 'I am sure my uncle merely forgot to add this instruction to his order.'

'Will II Augusta manage all this time without you, my lord?' Ferox said, staring a few inches over the tribune's head. Crispinus was the senior, senatorial tribune of the legion, his rank marked by the broad reddish band around his cuirass. The legion was stationed at Isca Silurum, back in the homeland of Ferox's people, but since his arrival in Britannia more than two years ago, Crispinus had spent little time with his unit.

'The Second Legion has managed for a hundred years before I arrived, and will no doubt continue to serve its emperor very loyally for a few more months even without my inspiring presence.' The white-haired aristocrat smirked. 'They have coped without your assistance for a great deal longer, have they not?' Ferox had never served with the legion at all, except on a few occasions when he had fought alongside detachments sent to the north. No one had ever shown any enthusiasm for seeking his recall from detached service.

'Well, Ferox, however you feel about it, you are ordered to Londinium and I intend to make sure that you arrive there swiftly and in one piece. Given recent events, that appears enough challenge for any man. Or may I take it that you have never spent enough time down south for anyone there to want to kill you! Sure it won't take you long. So, this Rufus appears seeking vengeance, and simply rides onto the training field as bold as brass. Well, I suppose that is easy enough to do for a former soldier. You have been going there for days so it was a fair bet you would be there today. Surely a risk, though, coming back and hanging around in an inn when there could be soldiers who might recognise him, even with his beard shaved off, as you say. Why go to the trouble?'

'I do not know, my lord.'

'You provoke strong sentiment in others, even if it is not obvious why.' The legate's orders were brief, specific and included no explanation. 'I believe it is not compulsory for the governor of a province to explain his actions at every stage,' Crispinus had said when he showed Ferox the tablet containing the order. It was written by a cornicularius, and added that all military and civil authorities were instructed to assist the centurion and his party in their journey. 'There you are, Ferox, it makes me one of "your" men'.

They set out the next morning, in a four-wheeled *raeda* borrowed from Oppius Niger, with a ten-man escort. Philo insisted that he could not ride in the carriage and was perched on a seat up on the roof, his back to the driver. Fewer men would have been beneath the dignity of a senior tribune, while many more would most likely have slowed them down. Vindex and one of his scouts were part of the escort, along with five Batavian troopers. Ferox had also asked for young Cocceius to join them, and the lad had been given a mount and told that if he did well he might be promoted to *eques* in the cohort. So far he seemed to be managing to handle the horse well enough. The last two members of the escort were the strangest, and each time he looked out of the carriage window, Ferox felt a moment of surprise. When Vindex had come back from Syracuse he had not come alone, but had brought an old friend. Gannascus was a German, a refugee from his homeland across the great grey sea, and now in the service of Tincommius, High King of the Venicones to the far north.

'This big ox had come looking for you,' Vindex explained. 'Not sure they liked the look of him at Syracuse, but thought that if they shut the gate he'd only tear it down.' Gannascus was a giant of a man, almost a head taller than Ferox, with huge limbs and hands that belied his quickness as a fighter. He had brought a papyrus written either by Tincommius, or probably one of his household, the Latin letters large and straight like an inscription rather than the flowing marks of a normal letter, assuring the Romans of his friendship and sending the warrior as proof.

'I help you,' he rumbled, after grabbing Ferox in a hug that almost crushed the life out of him. 'My king sends me.' Even after years with Tincommius the German spoke the language of the Britons slowly and with a thick accent. His companion was a warrior called Sepenestus, who would have been considered huge in any other company, and was clearly a man the big German trusted, although his slim face marked him as a Caledonian rather than a German. Apart from a gladius – perhaps one of the ones Crispinus had arranged to be supplied to the high king – and a small shield, he carried a tall bow of the sort used by some of Gannascus' followers. Ferox had seen the force of the arrows shot by these weapons and was all the happier to have him, for the news in the king's letter was worrying.

'Acco has promised the end of Rome before Samhain comes next year,' Ferox told Crispinus. 'Fire will sweep Rome from Britannia and leave it free forever.' The tribune was dismissive, for such prophecies were nothing new. For the moment he did not say anything about the rest of the king's message, for he needed time to think, and that was hard with the tribune's unending chat.

On the first day they went no further than Coria, Crispinus and Ferox dining with Brocchus, who greeted them with great warmth. 'Shame about that poor fellow,' was his only comment about Narcissus, save to conclude that it was a nasty business. Far more than Cerialis, he was clearly pining in the absence of his wife. Ferox stayed in the praetorium, but no slave girl came to his room in a display of her owner's hospitality and after the jolting ride he was quite happy with this. They kept talking about laying down a proper road over the existing track running west from Coria to Luguvallium, but no one had yet actually done anything.

From Coria they took the great south road, and progress was swifter, even though a fair few stretches had suffered from the weather and were in need of substantial repairs. On the second night they stopped at Longovicium, once a busy fort like Vindolanda, but now maintained by a holding unit. The centurion acting as commander was grudging of his hospitality until he realised who Crispinus was, after which he was transformed into unctuous attention.

Bremesio remained a busy fort surrounded by an extensive vicus, and the prefect in command was readier and far more generous with his hospitality, at least as far as the tribune was concerned. Ferox decided that no one would much mind if he took some exercise in the remaining hours of daylight.

'You up for a ride?'

Vindex rolled his eyes. 'Sits in a cart all day and now he wants to get on a horse. Do I get a choice?'

'The usual. You know where we are?'

'Yes.' The tone was patient, since the question was such an obvious one.

'Want to take a closer look?'

Vindex lifted the wheel of Taranis to his lips. 'Aye, I do.'

Gannascus joined them as they went to the fort gate. 'Too many people,' was all he would say.

Ferox's rank was sufficient to persuade the sentries to let them pass. He had donned his plumed helmet and was holding his *vitis* to make sure that no one could mistake him for anything else. 'We will be back before sunset.'

Ferox was on an old gelding he knew to be well behaved and able to keep going all day. His thigh was still stiff at times, and after the jolting carriage ride, he decided to do without a saddle. Vindex merely shrugged.

'Amazing how Silures think they can ride.'

They walked their horses through the settlement, still busy in the later afternoon.

'Is this Rome?' Gannascus asked.

'No, brother, this place is tiny.'

'The people are small,' the big German conceded, 'but there are a lot of them.'

Men were hard at work fixing the timbers to make a frame for a house near the bridge. A convoy of carts led by *galearii*, the slaves owned by the army, and a few tired and fed-up legionaries were approaching, so they urged their mounts to canter over the planking before it blocked their path. The slave leading the first cart had to hit the oxen and yell to stop them and let the riders past. A legionary screamed at the slave, cuffing him round the head until Ferox glared down. Once he had passed he just caught a string of muttered insults, but decided to ignore them.

There were only a few buildings on the south bank of the river and once they were past they left the road heading east into rolling hills. Ferox had a fair idea of where they were going. His horse, fresher than the others since it had not carried a rider all day, rushed at the first slope and he let it canter freely, heading for the marker at the top of the hill. As he reached it, the animal saw something it did not like in the grass and pulled to the side. Ferox slipped, knew his weight was dragging him down, so grabbed the mane and just managed to loop his left leg up so that he slid down to the ground almost under control.

Gannascus had a big grin, while Vindex simply nodded. 'Guess you wanted a closer look?'

The figure was about four foot high, carved from dark oak and weathered by the years to be almost black. It was roughly human, with stubby arms and legs, and more obvious breasts and the V slit lower down. Such figures had marked the edge of clan and tribal lands for longer than anyone could remember. Some were truly ancient and over the years the carving faded as the wood rotted so that any detail was lost altogether. This one was newer, perhaps half a century old.

Ferox stared at it. They had come less than a mile from the road and yet he felt that the empire was fading away and they were walking into the old world. The Brigantes were the most northerly people to use such markers, keeping them a little away from the stamp of Rome, and it had been a while since he had seen one. He felt its draw, for these were more than simple statues, far more than the perfect yet somehow lifeless bronze and marble images beloved of Greeks and Romans alike. This had power, and he found his hand reaching forward.

'Best not to touch, Silure,' Vindex said with surprising sharpness. Ferox nodded and went over to the gelding.

'Wooden tits not much use,' Gannascus grumbled in a whisper that must have carried a hundred paces.

Ferox led them across the hilltop, down into a valley and up the other side, saw the willow trees by the bank of a stream and headed towards them. They found the stone monument on the far side of the water. It was on a little rise that may have been there forever or may have been crafted by hand. Three rusty spearheads were thrust into the earth around the stone, their shafts almost wholly rotted away apart from little stubs. Fresher were offerings, flowers, newly mown heads of wheat, eggs and little birds, their necks broken. The air was still and warm like a summer's day, the murmur of the flowing brook fading to the very edge of sound.

The pillar was taller even than Gannascus, one of the most expensive tombstones made by a Roman mason anywhere in Britannia. On each of the narrow sides a tiny raven was carved, one with outstretched wings almost like the eagle of Jupiter and the other roosting. On the back was a larger carving of a broad oval with a short handle. The top was fringed with a curving pattern of lines and knots that seemed to cross over and through the oval. Ferox took a moment to see the shape of a mirror, and then could not understand why it had taken so long because it was obvious. On the front, in the very centre of the outlined rectangular panel prepared for a long inscription, was simply the letter C – Cartimandua, Queen of the Brigantes.

Hers had been a long life, coming to an end just seven years ago when she must have been almost eighty. She had been queen when Claudius sent the legions to Britannia and had from the start sought peace and become a loyal ally of Rome. Some called her wise and an oath keeper; others named her craven and traitor. The queen and her first husband never really got on. He was Venutius, the same war leader whose helmet and armour the freedman Vegetus had claimed to have found. There was trouble in Nero's day when they argued and he led his warriors against her followers, attacking the Romans too when they came to help. Somehow there was a reconciliation and brief peace, until the queen took a second husband, a handsome lad from Venutius' household. War broke out again, and once again she lost, until the legions intervened in real force. Cartimandua remained queen in name, although she was made to live in the south for many years, and the Brigantes were brought under the direct rule of the legate of Britannia. Venutius did peace a favour by falling from his horse while drunk and never waking up, and his followers never found another leader to unite them. They went back to bickering with each other, and it was easier to do that if they made friends with Rome so did not have to worry about the army turning up.

'The Carvetii were always the queen's folk, weren't they?' Ferox asked.

'Aye. She was our high queen. Have more than once heard my chief say that Venutius was too clever a man to trust.' That chief was also Vindex's father, but his mother was simply a servant girl, and although he was treated with some favour he had never been acknowledged. It did not appear to bother him. 'The queen was always there. You knew where you stood with her.'

Her name still commanded awe, and was rarely spoken aloud by the Brigantes or their kin. She was Goddess and witch, mother of life and carrion, one who peered into the souls of others to see their weakness and fear. Fifty years ago she had betrayed Caratacus, the greatest leader of the southern tribes in the war with Rome, handing him over as prisoner after she had given him hospitality. Caratacus was a great hero to the Silures, a friend of his grandfather, and Ferox had come to know the old man during his years in Rome. It always surprised him that there was no bitterness. 'You never met her,' Caratacus said when he had dared to ask. 'She was special. You felt like a little boy when you were with her. She just had that power. It would be like hating the moon for its beauty. She just was what she was.'

Ferox realised that he had shaken his head as he remembered the strange words. He turned to Vindex. 'Did you ever see her?'

'My ma always told me that I did,' the scout said, his voice unusually sad and serious. 'But when I asked she said that she lifted me up high to see over the crowd as the queen went past in her chariot. I must have been a bairn and I don't remember a thing. Ma said she was very beautiful, with hair like shining autumn leaves.'

'Is this a tomb?' Gannascus' deep voice broke in.

'Yes and no,' Ferox explained when Vindex obviously did not want to speak. The Brigantes were his close kin. 'It is a place to remember. Her remains are not here, but some of her spirit and power lingers. She died near here.'

The German touched fingers to his lips, then his forehead and then bowed towards the pillar.

'I should like to see the house,' Vindex said. 'If there is time.'

They rode away. It was more than two decades since any Brigantes had fought against Rome and some like their high queen had always been friends. Yet they remained a people apart from the rest of the province, the old ways and old pride just beneath the surface. In her last years the Legate Agricola had allowed Cartimandua to return to live among her people and she had chosen this place. It was a few miles from the great dun where she had held court in the days of glory and wealth, the ramparts now overgrown and only a few small farms dotted around the inside. They had built a home for her here, close enough to Bremesio to be protected by the garrison if need be. As they came over the next rise they saw it, just below them on the flat land where the brook flowed into a larger branch of the river.

The villa was modest by the standards of the south, let alone the grand country residences of the wealthy in Gaul or Italy. Yet it was built of stone, rectangular with two floors and a high roof of red tiles. On each of the long sides of the house was a roofed veranda leading onto a garden with gritted paths, well tended and organised beds of flowers and vegetables. Yet beyond the gardens were wooden fences forming pens for animals, a number of simple timber huts around a big barn. More striking was the other house, close to the Roman-style building, for this was round and thatched and built on a scale befitting the hall of a great chief, perhaps three times the size of the big house in Eburus' farmstead. At the moment half a dozen figures were clustered around it, slapping fresh clay, no doubt to repair damage to the wall.

Half to his own surprise, Ferox nudged the gelding into a canter down the slope towards them. He was not sure why, or really sure why he had come here at all. It simply felt right. One of the little figures ran towards him, waving his arms and shouting. The words were faint, but the tone was not one of welcome.

'You must leave!' the man was still running towards him, close enough now to be understood. He was tall and lean, with a checked tunic, striped trousers and a drooping moustache and long brown hair. Suddenly he stopped and froze, before lowering his arms, and simply waiting for Ferox to reach him.

'Greetings, centurion.' The man must have seen the crested helmet. 'Forgive my rudeness, for you are welcome.' Close up Ferox saw the heavy silver torc around the man's neck, and that his hair was brushed and clothes clean and well woven. Clearly this was a man of some importance. He was also surprised. 'How did you know?'

Ferox introduced himself and then Vindex as the scout caught up.

'Our kin are welcome here,' the man said, before introducing himself as Cunovindus, servant to the old queen and keeper of this place.

His story was simple enough, and did not really come as a surprise for it fitted with everything else. During the night a guard had been struck on the head, knocked unconscious, and then had his throat cut. It looked as if he had heard or seen someone chipping at the wall of the great hall and had gone to investigate. The only other man awake was tending to a flock of sheep at some distance from the house and saw nothing. 'We don't really expect trouble here,' Cunovindus explained. 'Our people would not dare take from us, and the fort protects us from bandits and common thieves.' Yet someone had come, killed the guard and dug their way through the wall. They must have known about the secret chamber in the hall, and not wanted to risk waking anyone inside. 'There were only a handful of old women there, but they were not to realise. They dug through the wall, and into the chamber.' Cunovindus' eyes flicked nervously, but the presence of Vindex appeared to reassure him. 'It was where she passed into the Otherworld, and it has been sealed ever since some of her things were buried there.'

'And these thieves dug up these valuables and took just one thing?' Ferox said softly.

The Brigantian nodded. 'I cannot tell you what it was, for I am bound by an oath. Those who could tell you are not here.'

Ferox did not force the issue. 'You must keep your word.' He was remembering the stone pillar and the carving of the mirror and was sure he knew what had gone. 'Do you wish me to assist you, or send word to the fort?'

'Leave us to deal with our own, my lord.'

'As you wish.'

VI

'SEEN IT BEFORE. It stinks.' Vindex's verdict on Eboracum did not surprise Ferox, who knew that the scout was not fond of towns and cities. The fortress of Legio VIIII Hispana was ten times bigger than Vindolanda and its vicus on the same scale. 'Stinks of shit,' he added later, once Crispinus was not around, since he knew the tribune had learned some of the language of the tribes. With sewers from the fortress opening into the river it was hard to argue at this time of year. No doubt anyone spending a long time here became used to it.

'A lot of people,' Gannascus said over and over again. 'Why would they want to live here?' Ferox tried to explain that many were warriors oathbound to Rome's high king and their families and that he ordered them to be here. This satisfied the big German for the moment.

The *colonia* at Lindum was no more appreciated. 'Stinks of old leather and shit.' There were fewer men in uniform in the city, but a lot of old men who, whatever they wore, carried themselves like the legionaries they had been until a few years ago. Begun under Domitian and officially founded under the far more acceptable Nerva, when the legion was posted away, this place was reborn as a colony for discharged soldiers. The military feel of the place was all the stronger because use had been made of many of the existing buildings. They passed row after row of little houses, obviously built as barracks and now converted so that a family occupied a pair of rooms. At least these each had their own hearth. Ferox wondered who was now living in the big praetorium and the houses once made for tribunes and senior centurions, and wondered how many officers had taken their discharge here to become local worthies. It sometimes must have seemed like the same old service, albeit less crowded. Still, the huge *principia* with its assembly hall made a serviceable basilica for the town council, with space for courts and public records. Among the timber military buildings the newer ones of stone stood out. They were paving a square near the principia and surrounding it with temples – something you never saw in an army base. Statues of Nerva and Trajan were mounted on high plinths in the centre of the square.

'Who are they?' Gannascus asked after he had stared at them for a while. There were stalls set up over much of the open area, traders yelling, customers bartering and all the loafers, idlers, and groups of unruly children you always found in markets such as this. The thieves and whores were there as well, if you knew where to look.

'They are the emperor and his son,' Vindex said, and Ferox was glad that he did not have to answer. 'The high kings of Rome.'

'Is that one a war chief?' the German asked, pointing at Trajan, who was depicted in cuirass with a sword at his hip and pointing as if he was ordering soldiers into battle.

The scout turned to Ferox for help. 'They say he is. A brave one.' Crispinus had confirmed the rumours that the princeps planned to lead a big attack on Dacia next spring. Ferox had fought the Dacians and their allies before, and reckoned it would be a tough task. Depressingly that probably meant more detachments and whole units being withdrawn from Britannia. He hoped that the legate's summons did not mean that his services were required, for he had work to do here.

'Good,' was all the German would say. He seemed distracted, and was clearly aware of all the stares they were attracting. Gannascus stood out anywhere, but especially here. On the other hand it may have been the image of the defied Nerva. Whenever Ferox saw him on statue or coin he was left with the impression of a man thoroughly perplexed by the world around him. He did not relish trying to explain to the German that here was a man chosen as emperor because of his high birth and the feeling that he was insufficiently talented to be too much of a tyrant.

Yet if Gannascus was puzzled it was not at the vagaries of politics. Instead he stared around at the crowd. 'How did all these people reach here before us? Did we miss a quicker path?'

The suspicion that he was seeing the same people over and over again persisted as they travelled south, even though none of the other towns were quite as big. Nothing would convince the big warrior otherwise. 'It's very clever,' was all he would say.

By the second week Ferox was in the saddle as often as riding in the coach. He was feeling a lot better, and even when Crispinus joined them on horseback, the tribune's conversation was less intense and unavoidable than in the cramped confines of the raeda. A lot of the time Philo now travelled inside the carriage while tribune and centurion endured the dust or rain of riding. Vindex found this very funny.

Sometimes, Ferox spoke to the scout and the big German, lagging a little behind so as not to be overheard. He was not ready to tell Crispinus about the theft from Cartimandua's old house. In his letter Tincommius had said that he had been approached by a merchant claiming to act on behalf of powerful men who wished to see a new emperor. This would not be the first time, and he and the king had met because of another plot. The high king claimed that Acco spoke of a great revolt, not simply in the north, but of all the tribes of Britannia. The old druid promised great magic to unite all the tribes and give strength to their swords. Tincommius wondered whether artefacts like Venutius' armour were part of this and Ferox was inclined to agree. The high king believed Acco possessed other objects of power and the lore to understand their uses.

Just a few months ago, Ferox had encountered the druid. They had fought a bitter battle on a far northern island against pirates. Among them was a boy, an especially unpleasant youth whose father had become a wealthy businessman. The son had stabbed his father before he defected and found a welcome among the enemy who knew him as the gifted son of a witch. Ferox had captured him, left the boy under guard, but when the fight was over he had returned to find the boy dead. Acco had come, killed him and taken his head, for everyone knew the skull of a witch held power. It was all beginning to fit together, although Ferox was still not sure what would happen next, and how he might thwart the old man's plans.

Londinium was a lot bigger, twice the size of Eboracum, and had a far more civilian feel and look about it. 'Smells of fish and shit,' Vindex said. Gulls circled noisily above the shallow valley of the river.

Gannascus was even more impressed. 'Faster than us again,' he said as they rode through the thronged streets past the high timber amphitheatre and caught a glimpse of the wide river ahead of them. He stared wistfully at the ships at the jetties and out on the water. The ruins of an old fort were decaying, and in places used for piling rubbish or had shacks built by the very poor. Crispinus explained that there was no longer a fort in the city, and instead substantial numbers of soldiers were billeted in a commandeered area not far from the big house that served as the legate's residence whenever he was here. Another, larger, if less luxurious, house acted as a principia and he led them there to report.

'Something of a novelty,' he announced cheerfully, 'me showing the regionarius and his head scout the way!'

September had gone, and the days were becoming shorter even here in the south so that it was dark by the time they had reported. The soldiers were led away, but on the tribune's instructions Ferox and the others were taken to the same house, lodging high above a pottery. Food was waiting for them, and while it was probably an insult for him not to be given a room of his own, Ferox was content. 'Tonight we stay here. I'll take you around the place tomorrow, but tonight let us simply rest after the journey.' That proved less easy than he hoped, for Gannascus snored as only a great bear of a man could. The others, even Philo, all dropped off one after another, but Ferox struggled hour after hour. He must have slept at some point, but he felt that he had lain awake throughout the night, staring at the beams of the roof overhead.

His orders were to report at the principia by the first hour of the day, and this he did, freshly shaved and so well turned out that even Philo was satisfied. The *beneficiarius* in the entrance hall could not find him on any list.

'I should wait in there, sir,' the man suggested. 'Sure it will be sorted out soon enough. They never tell me anything.' He pointed to a room over to the side, empty save for half a dozen folding chairs. Ferox sat and waited. The walls were bare, the paint faded and with more than a few cracks in the plaster, and offered little to divert him. He heard the trumpets sound the second hour and brief conversations as the beneficiarius outside directed visitors.

It must have been almost the third hour of the day when he heard a familiar voice and went to the door.

'My lord?'

Crispinus turned angrily at the interruption. 'Ferox, where in all Hades have you been? The legate expected you at his house at dawn. I am here to send out men to look for you.'

'I was told to report to the principia, my lord.'

'Which blasted fool told you that?'

'You did, my lord.'

The beneficarius stood rigidly to attention, holding up his ornately headed spear and his face had the expressionless gaze mastered by anyone who meant to get on in the army.

'Did I? Well, I meant the praetorium. The legate wanted to see you straight after the morning *salutatio* was done. You are late, so make sure you apologise.'

'Would you not like to accompany me, my lord?'

'Oh, I have far more important things to do. Now off you go.'

A slave governed admission to the legate's house, and quickly summoned another who led him away down a corridor. Both servants stopped and bowed their heads as a man and a woman walked past.

'Lord, lady,' they echoed. Both were tall, and if there was something about the eyes that marked them as kin, no one could mistake that fiery red hair. The lady wore it plaited and piled on her head, and was in a brilliant white dress, supplemented by a tasteful amount of jewellery. She was pretty, walked with elegance and did not deign to notice the centurion. The man's toga looked faded by comparison, but his left arm carried the folds easily. His face had a hardness about it that robbed it of being truly handsome, although Ferox suspected that it would draw women, each eager to reach an imagined inner softness. For a moment he glanced at the woman and then gave Ferox a wry smile. His eyes still had the softness of flint. Other slaves, presumably their own, appeared from a side room with cloaks and in a moment they were gone. The chamberlain gestured for Ferox to follow the guide.

'Please, my lord, would you wait here.' There were only two chairs this time, high-backed wicker affairs that were a good deal more comfortable, while the walls were decorated with panels of rustic scenes. Tiny farmers ploughed and harvested, shepherds watched their animals, and one lucky one peeked at nymphs bathing.

The house was quiet. After a while he heard a door open, a brief conversation too muffled to catch the words, and then a door closing again. He waited. There was an old army story of a centurion receiving special orders in a base on the Rhine. Before the day was out he was rushed away, carried south by the coaches of the imperial post. They took him over the Alps, down to Puteoli, where a ship was waiting to take him over the Mediterranean to Alexandria. From there it was down the Nile, then into the desert and along the wild roads to the ports on the Red Sea, where traders used the mysterious winds of those waters to fetch silks and spices from the Far East. Reporting to the prefect commanding the garrison there, the man expressed complete surprise. 'Not been told a thing about you or what you are supposed to do here. Did they tell you?'

'No, my lord.'

'Oh well, expect we will work something out in the end.' Depending on who told the story, it took a whole year or even three years before the man was sent back to his legion, with no one any the wiser about what it had all been for.

'Ferox, my dear fellow, you seem deep in thought?' The speaker was short and bald save for a wild fringe of white hair. Quintus Ovidius was a philosopher and poet, a junior member of the Senate and friend of the legate, who had accompanied him to his province.

Ferox smiled broadly. He had always liked the spritely old man, and since Ovidius had accompanied them on their desperate attack on the pirates' stronghold, he had come to respect him as well. 'I fear I was pondering on the nature of the army's administration.'

'Intriguing, no doubt, though probably not satisfying. How are you, my friend?'

They talked for a while, Ovidius explaining that, although the legate was detained, as soon as he had learned that Ferox was in the house, he had rushed to see him. 'Although I fear this reunion is soured by some sad news. Caratacus is dead. Word arrived from Rome nine days ago. I am very sorry.'

'He was old.' Caratacus had been well over ninety, and had been frail the last time Ferox had seen him, some twelve years ago.

'Sadly it was not age that claimed him in the end. He was murdered in the gardens of his villa in the Alban Hills.' Ovidius had only a few details. A woman and two men had appeared late at night asking for shelter. It was some sort of feast day for Caratacus' people, and his custom to walk alone save for a boy in the grounds from midnight until dawn. The boy fled when the guests came for him, blades in their hands, and when the house was turned out they found the old man stabbed to death.

'Did they take his torc?' Ferox knew the answer before Ovidius nodded in surprise. At that moment the slave reappeared, announcing that the legate was ready to see him. Ovidius followed and it was clear that the legate desired his presence as well. They found Neratius Marcellus sitting at a desk, still at work. He was clad only in a pale blue tunic, belt and shoes whose lattice pattern gave glimpses of his blue socks. A slave handed him a succession of open writing tablets, which he signed, said should be added to the pile of other matters that did not demand a swift reply, or rejected by simply scratching a cross with his stylus. 'Tell them no.' He flashed a brief smile to the visitors and urged them to sit. Two folding camp chairs were on either side of a table.

Another slave brought well-watered wine, since it was early in the day.

At long last the batch of correspondence was finished, the slaves left and the legate breathed a sigh of relief. He was a small man, who reminded Ferox of a restless bird, always on the move, and it was strange to see him sitting still. 'It won't be long before Tiro is back with an even higher stack.'

'Perhaps you shouldn't have bought a clerk called Tiro if you did not want to spend your life scribbling,' Ovidius said. The governor glanced at Ferox, watching intently.

'Cicero's trusted freedman was named Tiro,' Ferox explained. 'He prepared the letters for publication after his old master's death. I've always suspected he snipped out a lot that was embarrassing to Atticus.'

They did not nod or show any obvious signs of approval, and paid him the respect of not expressing surprised pleasure.

'There will be two more weeks of this,' Neratius Marcellus went on wearily. 'Then it is almost four months of assizes, here, at Camulodunum, Lindum and a few of the civitas capitals.' He gave a grim laugh. 'The price of office.'

Ovidius showed little sympathy. 'If you had wanted to cling to the City as Cicero advised, you could easily have done so, my friend. We both know that dignified leisure has never really suited you.'

'Neither is it likely to be my fate for several years at the least.' The legate drummed his fingers on the table top. 'Forgive me, Ferox, for not welcoming you with greater warmth, but it is not even noon and I have spent hours returning the morning greeting of visitors, reading or listening to petitions, both formal, and the "while I have your ear, my lord, may I ask…", whether it is about business or justice, favours or little matters such as the leadership of a great tribe. Your failure to arrive kept me listeing to such tedious matters even longer than duty commanded.'

Ferox did not bother to explain. With senior officers there was rarely any point unless they asked a direct question.

'No matter,' the legate continued. 'When I sent for you it was for onc reason, but now I find that I need you for something else, so it is convenient that you are here, for I will keep you busy. I only wish that you had arrived a few days earlier.' The legate sprang to his feet. He was always happier talking while on the move and they made no attempt to rise and join him.

'Something is wrong. I have been in Britannia long enough to sense it in the faces who greet me and come asking for favours. They are nervous. I remember seeing faces like that in the last years of Nero, when I was a mere boy, and again under the unlamented last of the Flavians, when I probably looked much the same. There is fear, a sense that things will change soon, without any clear sign of which way they will change. That was why I wanted you in the first place. I have come to value your instincts, your knowledge of the tribes, and your talent for sniffing out the truth.'

'Although it means inflicting another letter upon you, my lord, I received this from Tincommius, the High King...'

'Of the Venicones and the rest?' Neratius Marcellus grinned. 'I do pay attention, every now and again. Show it to Ovidius, so that he can be useful for a change, and tell me what was in it.'

Ferox told him about Acco's promises and the king's warning about a plot among the Romans.

'Hmm.' The legate paced from one end of the room to the other and back again. 'Yes, I fear that once again some fools in the Senate are restless. For some it will be sheer vanity, for a few probably the belief that they act for the good of Rome, even if that will cost us a civil war. "Where are you rushing to fools…"'

'That's Horace, my lord,' Ferox explained.

Ovidius snorted in amusement. The legate frowned. 'Well, perhaps I deserved that.' He began pacing again, and his arms started to wave, the gestures apparently natural and yet always under control. Many senators were a great loss to the stage.

'It is forty years since Boudicca burned this town to the ground, and others, and slaughtered a hundred thousand or even more. The owner of this house, who graciously loans it to the legate without charge out of duty to the *res publica* – and of course to show what a fine and rich gentleman he is – remembers fleeing with his parents, when Suetonius Paulinus abandoned Londinium to its fate, taking only those who could keep up with his cavalry, and leaving behind by the roadside any who discovered that they could not. It really is not that long ago, and yet all of my senior officers and all the tribal leaders assure me that it would be unthinkable now. The eagerness with which they assert this only makes me more sceptical.' He turned dramatically to face Ferox, who wondered whether performance came so naturally to trained orators that they actually forgot that they were performing. 'What do you think?'

'I can only speak of my region, my lord, and the lands around it. There is discontent and worry. A rebellion is quite possible. Not inevitable though.'

'Hmm. Not, inevitable. Inevitability is too big a question for my mind, and I shall leave such philosophy to idlers like Ovidius.'

'The answer is perhaps,' the old man said. 'It nearly always is perhaps.'

'As wise and unhelpful as ever,' the legate said fondly. 'What is certain is that the leading men in most of the tribes are heavily in debt. Oh, it is probably our fault as much as their own. Since Agricola's day every legate has encouraged them to spend. Get Greek tutors for their children, fine clothes and jewellery, fashionable slaves and carriages for their wives, and to build, always to build. We praise them if they give themselves large houses in the towns or villas in the country. We praise them even more if they pay for temples, basilicas, statues and monuments in the towns, and when they give their fellow tribesmen festivals, races and gladiators. So they borrow to show off to us and each other, and deep down most borrowers believe that they will never have to pay back all that money. Something will turn up and the debt will simply go away.'

Ovidius grinned. 'The voice of experience.'

'The voice of a man who has seen the world. Tell me, Ferox, do you know much about the rebellion in the Rhineland at the start of Vespasian's principate?'

'Something, my lord. I have spent a fair bit of time with the Ninth Cohort at Vindolanda.'

'Of course, my splendid Batavians. Then perhaps you know that its leaders began by telling everyone that they were supporters of Vespasian against the false emperor Vitellius. Perhaps they were sincere. It was only later, as their power grew, that there was talk of an empire of the Gauls. So it seems to me that a plot against Trajan and a rising of the tribes might not be altogether separate. The leaders of the first might well be happy to encourage the second. Rebellion in Britannia would embarrass the princeps, and if it got out of hand it might even finish him. As you have informed us so many, many times, the army in this province is weaker than it has ever been. For all the brilliance of my leadership, we might fail to crush the rebellion before it gathers pace. The princeps is focused on his plans for pacifying Dacia and its king. Could we cope with a crisis here as well as a grand campaign on the Danube?'

'In the end,' Ovidius said. 'We'd win in the end.'

'Yes, Rome is big and they are a lot smaller, although they may not realise it. The empire will always win in the end, but at what cost?

'As I said, Ferox, that is why I summoned you, and not simply because you Silures revel in silence, making you the perfect audience for my thoughts. However, since then events have galloped away with us and added to the tasks I wish you to perform. May I assume friend Ovidius has told you the news about Caratacus?' Ferox nodded. 'Nasty business, thoroughly nasty. I did not know him at all well, but he impressed me by his dignity. His grandson died fighting for us on the Danube. You knew him, did you not?' Another nod. 'Such is fate. But the deliberate killing of an ancient hostage has a viciousness about it that screams out politics. Since he could have no significance at Rome, I would guess his enemies were sent from Britannia. Why after so many years?'

Ferox said nothing.

'That is one question. And then on the Ides of October someone breaks into the Temple of the Divine Vespasian here in Londinium, bludgeoning the watchman to death. By sheer chance a couple of my beneficiarii came to make a vow – in the middle of the night they assure me, and for the moment I will choose to believe them. They saw three hooded figures climbing over the rear wall of the temple precinct and gave chase. The robbers escaped, but they dropped a box. That one over there, in fact. Open it for me, if you will, and show us what is inside.'

Ferox did what he was told. The long iron key was in the lock and turned easily. He raised the lid and saw dark cloth folded. The box was little more than a foot square, but heavily bound with iron edges so that it must have been heavy. He lifted the cloth out, and as he stood up realised that it was a cloak, fringed at the bottom in faded gold. The rest was more dark brown than the bright purple it had surely once been.

'The key was provided for me by the head priest,' the governor explained. 'He tells me that this is the cloak they place around the statue of the divine Claudius when he and the other deified emperors accompany the statues of Vespasian and Titus to the opening of the games. All of the statues have cloaks, and this is the least fine, though perhaps the oldest of them.'

'Ferox knew about the theft of Caratacus' torc before I told him,' Ovidius says.

The legate raised an eyebrow quizzically.

'A guess, my lord, but the answer did not surprise me.' Ferox told them about the thefts in the north, and about Acco. 'It was the torc worn by the kings of the Catuvellauni for generations, even before it belonged to such a famous war leader. If Acco seeks objects of power from among the tribes, that would be a great prize.'

'That villain still up to his tricks, is he? And with a long arm to reach out to Italy. That is worrying, since it would be likely he has influential friends. Still, shouldn't think he cared one way or another who was emperor.'

'No, my lord, but he might well try to use people who did.'

Neratius Marcellus stopped mid-pace and spun around to stare intently at the centurion. 'You really think he is that smart?'

'I know he is, my lord.' Ferox did his best to explain to them about a man's power, and how not only what he did and who he was fed it or weakened it, but also the people and things around him. A man's spirit grew as he took objects touched by the past and perhaps by the gods. At the same time the things themselves became more potent because of the one who possessed them.

'Are we talking magic?' Ovidius asked, genuinely curious.

'Only in a sense,' Ferox said. He knew these men were intelligent, more sympathetic than many Romans, and trying hard, but there were simply not the right words in their tongue, or even in Greek – at least all the Greek Ferox was able to remember. Romans did not think this way. 'Acco is known as the last of the true druids and he is feared accordingly. Gathering these things will add a little to his reputation, but I suspect there is more than that. Druids – and many who would claim to be druids – always wanted to possess things of power. There is more to it than this. Why these things and why now unless he has some definite purpose?'

'Why indeed? And I take it you have no idea of the answer.' Ferox shook his head. 'Ah well.' The governor reached up and stretched like someone waking from sleep. 'Then it seems we shall all be very busy. You and this old fool will begin by searching the archives here. Find anything we have about the objects they have taken or tried to take.' He reached out for the cloak and stared at it as if it might reveal a secret. 'Perhaps there is a connection.' He must have seen the look on Ferox's face. 'And, yes, I realise that perhaps the records of past governors will have little interest or understanding of such matters, but you never know. Perhaps there is something, or even a clue to spark an idea. At the very least we must start with what we have in case there is something there. I also want you to find out all you can at the temple. And you are both dining here this evening.'

Ferox stood up and to attention. 'Yes, my lord. Are we ordered to enjoy ourselves at the dinner?'

The governor glared for a moment, before his face softened. 'I shall not go that far. It may even prove more of an ordeal than searching dusty rows of documents, but there are people you should meet. Before the year is out, we may even have to kill one or two of them. That is if they do not kill us first.' Ferox could not remember hearing the legate sound so gloomy.

VII

LUCIUS SULPICIUS CRASSUS was a couple of inches shorter than Ferox, his hair the colour of fine gold, eyebrows almost pure white, and had a round, face that was handsome in a very Roman way. Ferox disliked him from the first instant, and found this sentiment growing with every moment, in spite of all his efforts.

'Flavius Ferox is a gallant and gifted officer,' Crassus' sister explained, 'and I may say he has more than once placed us in his debt at great risk to his own life.' Sulpicia Lepidina seemed to glow and it was all Ferox could do not to keep staring at her or to reach out to hold her. Her blonde hair was piled high in the simple style she preferred, which only enhanced her beauty. She had pendant earrings, a large necklace and bracelets on each wrist, and a deep blue dress that in places showed the paler blue of her under-tunic. Claudia Severa was in bright red, had more jewellery – if tastefully not too much – and had her thick brown hair arranged in one of the complex styles dictated by fashion. She was an attractive woman, and Ferox had found her to be a decent person, but whenever she stood beside her friend she paled in comparison.

'The centurion is a veteran on the frontier,' Claudia Severa added. 'One might say a legend in those parts.' That was generous, although until a few years ago it was more his drinking that had been legendary. 'And having been born among the tribes he speaks their language and understands the way they think. My husband says that many times his insights have avoided bloodshed.'

Crassus was unimpressed. 'The sword is what matters,' he declared. 'In the end, it is all a barbarian can understand.' He was just five years older than his sister, but was more heavily built, and might soon thicken out and become jowly. Apart from the colouring he had little in common with her. His expression was determined but dull, without any of the wit that sparkled in her gaze. Ferox was not sure whether the remark about barbarians extended to him, suspected that it did, but that the speaker did not consider him sufficiently important to be worth insulting with any vigour. Crassus' eyes darted around, clearly seeking someone more useful to meet. As a senator, only the legate and Ovidius were his peers, and Crispinus and the two other broad-stripe tribunes were at an early stage of the same career. Therefore he hunted for people more worth his condescension, or who might be useful in the few years he would have to spend in this benighted province. Yet for the moment he must observe proprieties, and his sister was here, and had introduced him to these people. Each thought was obvious as it took shape.

'Yes, my dear lady.' Crassus leaned down to kiss Claudia Severa's hand. 'I am sure your husband is a noble fellow who keeps distasteful matters from his conversation whenever he basks in the brightness of your presence, but it will always be the sword. I for one am glad of it, and hope before long to lead my legion into battle, ideally with Aelius Brocchus and his horsemen covering our flanks! That will be a splendid day! Indeed it will, most splendid!'

'You have a campaign planned, my lord?' Ferox asked before he could stop himself. He saw the brief flash of annoyance in Sulpicia Lepidina's eyes. Still, he thought that his tone was innocent enough. She glanced around the room, and used the motion to edge closer to his side.

Crassus did not take offence and merely laughed. 'Ha, eager for the fray as well, are you? You're not one of my lads, though, are you?'

'Legio II Augusta, on detachment as regionarius.'

'Oh, sick of dull routine, I suppose. Don't blame you,' he went on, making it clear he had paid little attention to the earlier conversation. 'Well, we shall have to see. As for plans of campaign, I have only been in the province five days so give me time. I am sure we can scare up a little war somewhere.'

'You have seen a lot of service, my lord?' Ferox felt a sharp jab as Sulpicia Lepidina kicked him on the ankle.

'What? Oh, this and that,' the commander of VIIII Hispana said airily. 'Like a war horse waiting for the trumpet!'

'Well, brother, since trumpets are lacking, let me sound a call. Over there is Claudius Arviragus, likely to be the next king of the Brigantes. Since your legion is based among his people, it would do you no harm to meet him. Let me make the introduction. Please excuse us.' The sister led her brother away like a mother hen towards the red-haired man Ferox had seen that morning leaving the praetorium. He had spotted him in the crowd, the fiery hair very distinctive, but had seen no sign of the woman who had been with him. The pair had looked so Roman that it was a surprise to realise that they were both presumably Brigantes, and from the royal line, descendents of Cartimandua herself. To his surprise he wished that he had gone with Sulpicia Lepidina and her brother.

Instead Ferox asked about Claudia Severa's children, knowing this was always a welcome subject and because he was genuinely interested. 'I suppose it is for the best, moving the families down here for the winter,' she said after a while. 'It can be harsh in the north and children fall sick so easily. Yet I miss my husband. I know that must sound silly when it has only been a month.'

'I saw the prefect only days after you had gone, and it was obvious to all that he was missing you every moment of the day.' He smiled. Gallantry did not come naturally, but he had real affection and respect for Brocchus and his wife. 'I cannot blame him.'

Claudia Severa blushed and gave a smile, and for that moment looked truly beautiful. 'Well, I can partly blame you for all this. You have him worried. All your talk of unrest among the tribes and Rome's weakness. I believe a desire to put us safely out the way lies behind his and Cerialis' plot to send us south.'

'I had no idea. When I saw them we mostly spoke of the...' Murder was probably not a fitting subject for a social gathering at the legate's praetorium. 'The unfortunate incident at Vindolanda,' he finished rather lamely.

'I have not shed any tears for that rogue. Someone who attacks my friends deserves no better.' The bitterness was surprising, and instantly regretted. Before Ferox could react a voice interrupted.

'Severa, my dear, it is good to see you. We Claudias must stick together after all.' Smiling warmly, the red-headed woman came from behind him, stepped up to Claudia Severa and kissed her on both cheeks. 'My name is Claudia, as you may have heard, although in my experience most men rarely listen to anything said by a woman; probably too complicated for their little minds. Claudia Enica to give it in full and avoid confusion with dear Severa here. Or you may prefer red Claudia and green Claudia if that is simpler for you.' A sweeping gesture indicated her own sea-green dress and the other woman's red. 'Though perhaps there may be confusion given the shade of my hair. Not very Roman, is it, although I should guess the Domitii Ahenobarbi had the same affliction or distinction as you prefer. Not Nero, though, dare I mention him, even though he came from that line. Well, sir, if you are still confused, perhaps tall Claudia and short Claudia, or nice Claudia and Claudia with goddess-like beauty – my friend here of course, or should I dare you to choose like Paris? Or shall we stay with the *mos mairum* – our ancestors by adoption if not blood – and stay with Claudia Prima and Secunda?'

Claudia Severa was trying not to giggle. 'Peace, my friend, you must give poor Ferox a chance.'

'Why should I, Prima, my friend?' she said, looking him up and down. 'He does not appear frail.'

Ferox guessed that she was a year or two past twenty, and the hairstyle she had adopted was even more ornate than Claudia Severa's with pearls dotted along the green ribbon arranging the coils of her hair and between some of the ringlets. She was quite tall, long boned like most of her tribe, with a slim face and surprisingly full-lipped mouth. More pearls were in her neat ears. Her eyes were pale, more green than brown, and they continued to inspect him. Her Latin carried no accent, and was precise and sophisticated even as the words galloped out. The dress was of shimmering silk, expensive, although modestly cut with a high neck and, like all the other ladies in the room, no sleeves. Her arms were fashionably white, although lacking the slight hint of plumpness considered perfect in a lady. A Greek sculptor would have wept with joy if he had carved limbs like that on the statue of a growing boy.

'My lady, it is an honour to meet you.'

'I shall not bother to deny the truth,' she replied.

Claudia Severa chuckled, and then remembered where she was. 'You are as mischievous as Cupid, my dear. So to restore decorum I shall formally introduce Flavius Ferox, centurio regionarius, and a friend of mine and of Brocchus, and dear Cerialis and his wife.'

'I have heard of you,' Enica said. 'Still, it may be that the worst stories are not wholly true.'

'They probably are,' he said, and thought he saw delight in her eyes.

'Ferox, yes, now it comes back to me. Your grandfather was Lord of the Hills, or whatever it is you Silures call your greatest chief.'

'He was, my lady.'

'And you do not have kings, only princes and chiefs.'

'Something like that. Now we have Rome and peace, or so I am told.'

'As have we all.' Enica smiled. Her teeth were neat and very white against her rouged lips. She put her head slightly on one side as she looked at him. 'You answer, but you do not ask? Is it then true that Silures simply take whatever they want, not bothering to ask first?'

'We try our best, my lady.'

The legate's chamberlain pounded his staff on the flagstone floor for silence and then announced that dinner was about to be served, inviting guests to take their places. There were three *triclinia*, three sets each of three couches laid in a U-shape, the open side to allow slaves to bring in successive platters. Ferox was unsurprised to find himself with the least prestigious. Arviragus was with Crassus, Sulpicia Lepidina, Ovidius, the three military tribunes and a squat figure he had learned was the procurator of the province. Enica and Claudia Severa were among decurions of Londinium, a number of prefects and a couple more women he did not know. The last group had a couple of senior centurions, neither inclined much to speak, and traders and other local worthies. The wife of one, an elderly lady with a vague expression, was convinced they had met before, and spent most of the meal trying to work out where.

'Were you ever in Colonia Agrippiniensis?'

'I fear not, my lady.'

'Noricum, perhaps. We lived there for a couple of years.'

'Afraid not.'

'Was it here in Londinium, oh, a good thirty years ago it must be.'

'I regret that I was but a child then, my lady.'

'Of course, of course, my apologies, I meant no offence.' Her husband, happy to be relieved of the responsibility of amusing his wife, conversed enthusiastically with another trader on the opposite couch.

Ferox listened politely, stole glances at Sulpicia Lepidina, and now and then at the red-haired Brigantian princess, since that presumably was what she must be. Once he looked to see that she was already watching him. She shook her head like a mother disappointed at a small boy surreptitiously dropping food he did not like.

The dinner ended, and Ferox wondered whether Vindex and Gannascus had got into trouble. He had said that it was fine for them to explore, but did wonder whether they were ready for a big town. Or indeed whether Londinium was ready for them. He hoped that he would not have to go looking for them.

Near the end a slave slipped him a small roll of papyrus, tied tight and sealed with unmarked wax. As servants fussed to bring cloaks and the company prepared to leave, for just a moment Sulpicia Lepidina caught his eye.

To his relief, all of his companions were back at the house, smelling strongly of beer and already snoring away. By the light of a lamp he opened the letter.

I need help. Come when I call.

VIII

THE ARCHIVES WERE housed in several buildings in and around an even older fort than the one they had passed on the way into the city. This one had had its walls and most of its buildings demolished, and the rest converted much like the old base at Lindum. The largest building of the archive was obviously two old barrack blocks knocked together, with numbers painted by the door to each room. Inside were rows of shelves, with just enough space to squeeze between them. Greek letters and Latin numbers were painted on the wood so that each slot had its own identity, and held a single folded wooden tablet. On most the original seal was long since broken, and a piece of ribbon fixed, the colour depending on the year it arrived. A notation on the side of the tablet was made each time its content was amended. In theory this meant that it should be straightforward enough to find any document, if you knew what category it should fall into and when it was written. Which was all fine, if only Ferox had had any clear idea of where to start.

The orders from the legate helped a great deal. A gift of an amphora of wine to the *speculator* responsible for overall supervision of the archives, another slightly smaller one to the beneficiarius who spent most of his days there, and gifts of money to buy a few drinks to the three *exacti* who actually ran the place had done almost as much to oil the wheels of bureaucracy.

'Just like being back in Rome,' Ovidius had said when Ferox suggested that they take this precaution. 'If only the sun would get warm I could feel right at home! By the way, I had a bright idea during the night. Acco says he is the last of the true druids, does he not?' In truth that was what others said, and the priest chose not to deny. 'Well, perhaps I ought to start with the correspondence and especially the reports written by Suetonius Paulinus? After all, he was the fellow who did more than anyone else to crush the cult. Crossed over to destroy their most sacred shrines on Mona – is that how you say it?'

'Yes, it is. And, yes, that is as good a starting place as any. Agricola went back twenty years later, so you may want to take a look at what he said as well.'

'Splendid!' Ovidius seemed genuinely excited by the task. They had decided that the old man would begin searching in the rooms where records on papyrus were kept, since he was more used to such things than the smaller army documents written often on wood and full of the abbreviations and other pieces of obscure military terminology. Ferox suspected that there was slightly more chance of finding something useful among the papyri than in the mundane reports and returns that composed most of the wooden archive. Yet he doubted that they would come across anything. He wished that Ovidius had not mentioned Mona, a dark place even after all these years. A fear had been growing within him that he might have to go there and speaking the name aloud was like hearing the baying of hounds on his trail.

The exactus who guided Ferox was young, but limped and had a scar running across his cheek and onto his mouth, which gave him an odd whistling lisp.

'My cohort was up north two years ago when the legate defeated that mad priest. You were there too, weren't you, sir?'

'I was there.'

The lad was eager and talkative. 'Thought I'd be discharged from the legion for a while, but thank the gods I was passed fit enough, seeing as how I can read and write a good hand. This is a good posting and there's a decent chance of promotion. Guess I'll never do a hard march or cut turf for rampart again, but it's not a bad life all round.'

Ferox began by asking for routine reports from unit commanders back from Suetonius Paulinus' day, feeling that he may as well follow Ovidius' suggestion.

The archive clerk led him to a row of doors. 'Yes, sir. These rooms along here. Look for red tabs that far back, although we've used the colour four times since then. They come around every ten years. Legions in those rooms, by their number. Cohorts and alae in the ones next, in that order and by their numbers and designations. Things a bit confused from those days, though, sir, what with the rebellion and all that. A lot of things were lost.'

'I can imagine,' Ferox said, before realising that irony was not something familiar to the exactus. 'Could you find me all mentions of druids or temples?'

'Sorry, sir. Only filed by unit and date. Begging your pardon, but no call for anything else, sir. Now, sir, shall I help you start with the legions?'

Four hours later and Ferox had learned nothing of value. It was easy to get sucked into following a story. There were several references to his own people, the Silures, and even a mention of his grandfather, the Lord of the Hills being labelled an 'old villain' by the legate of II Augusta. With effort, he did not let himself be distracted, and went back to scanning reports, often handing them back to the clerk for re-shelving within moments as it became obvious that there was nothing worthwhile there. Like the barracks they had once been, the rooms were gloomy, and they needed to refill the pair of lamps they were using a couple of times. At last Ferox gave up, and telling the exactus and the rest of the staff that he would be back tomorrow morning, he set out for the Temple of the Divine Vespasian and a meeting with one of the priests.

It was a grey day, spotting with rain, but that did nothing to deter the crowds thronging the street. Wherever there was space, even on the sides of the little alleys between the blocks of houses, someone set up stall and was trying to sell something. Ferox had to push away two persistent whores who plied their trade in a poorly curtained alcove just around the corner from the archives. As he came onto the major streets things looked both more respectable and more expensive. Ferox was wearing tunic and breeches, boots and a heavy cloak whose hood provided some protection from the rain. He carried his vitis to show that he was a centurion, and if necessary a flick of the cloak would reveal his military belt with gladius and pugio.

Even in the crowd, Gannascus stood out, a head or more taller than those around him, and when he spotted the centurion he let out a deep below of delight. People moved out of the way of his determined progress, and soon Vindex and the others appeared, along with several more big men wearing military cloaks. They were Batavians, led by Longinus, now sporting a thick grey beard.

'We found some friends,' Vindex explained. 'So perhaps you could help me out with some money.'

'What happened to the coins I gave you yesterday? There was enough for ten days.'

'The dice was loaded,' Gannascus boomed.

'And the women were expensive,' Vindex added. 'Everything costs a lot here.' In spite of his recent marriage, the scout's enthusiasm for other women had not slackened.

Ferox dipped into the purse on his belt. 'Try to keep them out of too much trouble,' he asked Longinus. The veteran nodded. 'I'll see if I can join you later on. Where will you be?'

'By the river.' Vindex nodded at the huge German. 'He likes watching the ships.'

Ferox hurried on, crossing the wooden planked bridge over the stream that flowed down into the main river. The press was thicker there, until some burly slaves used threats and some blows of their sticks to clear a path for a pair of litters. His size, as much as the centurion's cane he carried, prevented them from trying to force him out of the way. As the first litter passed he received a far softer greeting.

Claudia Severa peeked out of the gap between the curtains, then turned and said something. A moment later Sulpicia Lepidina's face appeared beside her. There were smiles and greetings, and an invitation to visit them on the next day around noon. 'The House of Verus in the third quarter. You must come,' Claudia Severa urged him. 'The children always love to see you.' Ferox could read nothing in the other woman's face to explain her note, but that did not surprise him.

'I shall surely come,' he said, hoping to reassure Sulpicia Lepidina that he was at her command.

The slaves clearing a path were facing pressure from an impatient crowd. One of the women called out and the litter bearers began carrying it forward again. As the second one passed it too stopped, and another head appeared, this one small, dark skinned and with a mop of blond hair that must be a wig.

'Ugly man,' the little man said in a piercing squeak. 'My mistress has something to say to you.'

'Who is your mistress?' he asked.

'What do you care? By the look of you, you should be grateful for anything. She's easy and already on her back. What more do you want?'

There was the sound of a slap and the dwarf shot back inside. Another slap followed. Ferox turned away.

'Hoy!' The dwarf had reappeared, wig precariously hanging over one eye. 'Please come over or she'll have me beaten again.'

Ferox gave in and went to the curtained compartment. The little man had vanished again, and he opened the curtains enough to see inside. Claudia Enica was stretched out on cushions, her arms back behind her head, showing off a figure swathed again in shimmering silk. Jewels glittered at her throat, at her wrists and in her ornately arranged hair. Her face was heavily made up, managing just to stay on the right side of good taste and fashion.

'You are not easily intrigued,' she said, treating him to a languid smile.

'I am a plain man, and a mere soldier. The ways of princesses are new to me.'

'A princess is still a woman, and you cannot tell me that a rough soldier has no desires. You have such a big sword.' As Ferox leaned in his cloak had parted and the pommel and hilt of his gladius poked out. Before he could answer she went on. 'Do you like my whisperer?' The dwarf was crouched in the far corner of the compartment. 'His name is Achilles and I shall most probably order him beaten tonight to make sure that he is not spoiled. They say that Livia, wife of the divine Augustus, doted on such creatures and she was a Claudian. Her husband hated them, though.' Achilles darted around and stuck out his tongue. 'I must say that I am coming to the same opinion.' Enica lifted a foot and kicked the dwarf with as much force as she could muster, so that her slipper came loose. Then she stuck out her own tongue. 'Little beast.'

Ferox coughed. 'Forgive me, my lady, but I am late for an appointment and must hurry.'

She grabbed his wrist, surprising him with her speed. 'Now that is not courteous from a Roman officer or a prince of the Silures. Or would the Silure in you just slaughter Achilles here and bear me off over your shoulder? Come now, do not be a disappointment. I believe that we shall be friends and good ones at that. What is it they say about the Brigantes?' This time the smile was genuine and less of a pout.

'That they talk too much.' He did not add, much like the Romans.

'We do. But some of what we say is worth hearing, and much of the rest is amusing, and I am also good at listening. I must go now – for you see the lady must end any meeting of this sort. I heard the others extend an invitation. Do come and see us, for I have rented the house and they and their families are my guests. Come at any time, whether they are there or not. I must speak to you about the robbery at my grandmother's house. You were there, were you not? Yes, I thought so. So come. If you like you can always kick Achilles around the floor for amusement. Walk on, you dolts!' The last command was loud and aimed at the bearers.

Ferox walked on, slightly resentful as it half felt he had been given an order along with the slaves, and it was almost a relief not to run into anyone else he knew. A group of urchins surrounded him at one point, one trying to open his purse while another lifted the pugio from its scabbard. He smacked the largest with his palm and waved his cane at the others to drive them off.

The Temple of the Divine Vespasian stood at the corner of two wide streets, behind the high plastered and whitewashed walls of its precinct. A doorman sat cross-legged by the open gate, and simply nodded when Ferox explained who he was. In the courtyard were statues of Vespasian and Titus either side of the steps leading up to the high-roofed temple with its pillared front. On the right were Augustus and Claudius, and on the left Nerva stood alone. Ferox wondered whether the plinth, perhaps even the body of the statue itself, had originally been planned to hold the image of Domitian. That emperor's images had never much resembled the real man, disguising that restless energy and the burning rage that led equally to cold cruelty or outbursts of appalling anger. The face of Augustus here was of a handsome, eager youth, not the old man he had become. It was hard to imagine so serene a face being disturbed by the antics of his wife's dwarfs and other freaks kept for entertainment by the fashionable.

Pretending that their best rulers became gods was one of the odder affectations of the Romans. Even after all these years, Ferox could not tell whether they were serious about it, or if it was yet another piece of flattery that everyone was too polite to question.

Slaves were scrubbing the flagstones near the altar as he passed, and a man was waiting to take him to the priest, who proved to be surprisingly young, with the even more surprising name of Julius Kopros.

'Grandfather was a foundling in Alexandria,' he explained, evidently used to explaining, at least to anyone he judged able to understand Greek. 'He was left on a dunghill, so someone took him as a slave and named him Kopros. Years later he bought his freedom from the profits of making and selling shoes and somehow ended up in Gaul. He got a contract to supply boots for the army as long as he was willing to set up here in Britannia within weeks of Claudius' legions invading. And so we have been here ever since.' The priest had a thin, angular face, a neatly trimmed beard, curly black hair and thick eyebrows over clever brown eyes. 'Grandfather and father are both long gone, but they felt it important to carry on the name. Why hide your past when you have worked to make your own fortune, they would say. Which leaves me running the business, serving the town as priest here in this temple – and putting plenty of my own money into the day-to-day running of the place – and with a name that ought to be swept down a drain and into the river.' He grinned. 'So, how can I be of help?'

In truth there was little more to add to the story, except for a story about the cloak.

'I can tell you that it is old, perhaps very old,' the young priest explained. 'It was originally sent by Claudius himself as a gift to his new colony. Grandfather brought it from the Temple of the Divine Claudius in Camulodunum just days before the colonia was surrounded by Boudicca. He was not a priest, but was asked to bring it out, along with a couple of other pieces, by an old friend who was. Afterwards it took a few years before everything started again, and Londinium dedicated a temple to the cult of the emperors before Camulodunum so he presented them to the priests here. That was the old temple, now gone, but everything in it was moved to this one when they opened it twelve years ago.'

The other pieces he had rescued were a mould for baking sacrificial cakes and an incense burner, and Kopros happily showed them to Ferox. 'They were in a box that the robbers opened, and they must have seen them and not wanted them.'

'Even so I should keep on your guard,' the centurion advised as he left. 'They may not know the legate has the cloak and might try again here.'

'We'll be ready.'

As Ferox left, a spare, elderly man in expensive but sober clothes was asking the doorkeeper to send word to the priest. 'Tell him that Cnaeus Domitius Tullus is here. He will know why.'

There was something about the voice, a hint of the rich inflexion of a well-educated Gaul, that made him turn because it seemed familiar.

'Excuse me, sir, are you from Lugdunum?' he asked. Ferox had spent years in the city being educated as a Roman, but it was more than just the accent that struck a chord. He did not recognise the man, and even though Flora had spoken of a merchant named Domitius it was a common enough name.

The eyes that glared back at him were cold. 'What business is that of yours, soldier? You look more than half a barbarian. Good day to you, sir.' He stalked off towards the temple, his cloak an unusually bright tartan.

'Miserable git,' the doorkeeper muttered. 'Been here three times now and never given a tip for good luck.'

Ferox smiled. 'Sorry, it slipped my mind,' and handed the man a sestercius, suspecting immediately that this was too much. 'Know much about him?'

The doorman glanced about to see that no one was paying them any attention. 'Turned up a few weeks ago. Rumour is he will donate a fair bit of money to the temple, and others here in Londinium. There's always folk like him arriving and trying to buy the connections to do the really big deals.' He spat in contempt. 'Usually they try to be a lot more friendly, though. This one acts as if everyone else is doing him a favour.'

Ferox was hungry, so he stopped at one of the many small bars opening onto a street and ordered posca, some bread and soup. It was simple but filling, and had the owner not kept on trying to sell him oysters he might have stayed longer. For a while he considered searching for Vindex and the others. It would be good to talk to Longinus, if he could get the veteran alone. In the end he decided that he did not have the energy and toyed with the idea of visiting one of the bath-houses. Then in the passing crowd he saw two hooded figures walking with purpose and deep in conversation. He recognised Domitius from his cloak. On a whim, he left coins to settle the bill on the table, waited for a little while and then followed. He had his own hood up, and kept his vitis low, so that it should not be obvious who he was unless someone was paying particular care.

Almost as soon as he started to follow the pair stopped, threw back their hoods and went into the precinct of another temple. Domitius' companion was Julius Kopros. Ferox waited, staying where he was a good seventy paces down the street. A juggler was performing and he joined the half-dozen or so watching the man, while making sure he could see past him to the entrance to the temple. After perhaps half an hour, and another coin to make his interest in the entertainer convincing, he saw them leave. Ferox let them have a head start and then followed. The pair visited more temples, to Minerva, Silvanus and Liber Pater, and the brightly painted shrine to Isis and Serapis where, even outside, the air smelled heavily of rich incense and he could hear the rattles shake as the priests performed one of their rituals. Finally they crossed the long bridge to the smaller section of town south of the river and went to the Temple of Mars Camulos.

Ferox was not sure why he followed at all, other than a sense that something was wrong and the vague familiarity of a voice. On the way back over the bridge he kept his distance, and managed to lose them in the crowd. Then he heard whoops and the big German's bellow as Vindex and the others appeared and dragged him into a bar. The noise in the rest of the tavern was oppressively loud, so that his merry friends had to shout to be heard. Longinus was not there, but three of the Batavians were, and they were just as raucous. Gannascus was playing dice with anyone who was willing. He won a few times, but lost more often, betting wildly. A Roman would no doubt have thought that this was typical of a barbarian. Ferox was still enough of a Silure to understand that a warrior would always be bold. When the huge man came over and said, 'I need more money,' he handed him most of what was left in his purse.

'His luck's bound to change,' Vindex said with approval. There was no sign of it for the next few throws. As a centurion Ferox was well paid and his life at Syracuse rarely cost him much. Still, he wondered how long the coins he had brought would last if they stayed many days in Londinium. Gannascus split the room with a great bellow of triumph as he won.

In one of the rare lulls, Ferox had a quick word with Vindex, explaining that he might suddenly disappear. 'Follow if you can, just in case. But only join me if it looks like real trouble.'

Soon afterwards he left them, needing air, and not wishing to drink too much lest it ease him back into his old ways. The sun was setting, the clouds pink edged with dazzling yellow as he looked down west along the river. He got lost on the way back to their billet, for one street looked so much like another, especially now that many of the stalls and peddlers had packed up for the day. More than once he suspected that he was being followed. Perhaps he was just nervous. After just a few days he was remembering why he did not care much for city life.

Philo had two messages for him. The first had been brought by one of Ovidius' slaves, and said that he thought that he had found something and would explain tomorrow. The second was from another slave, who had said simply that someone would come for him later tonight from S, and he was to go with the guide if he would. The man sounded as if he was a Briton, and there were scars on his face and arms, suggesting he had done a lot of fighting in the past.

Hours passed, and the drinkers did not return. Ferox wondered whether Gannascus had had a run of luck. Either that, or his luck had been bad and he had gambled away their freedom or started a fight. By the third hour of the night there was no sign of them and he started to worry a little as he ate the supper Philo had prepared. A burst of singing in the street outside proved to be another group of drunks and not his friends.

The guide came just as he finished his meal. He had a round, pockmarked face and a head of closely cropped dark hair. Ferox did not recognise him, but followed anyway, leaving his cane behind, but keeping sword and dagger on the belt concealed by his cloak. The guide took him west and then up one of the gentle slopes. Turning a corner he saw the shacks and old fort with the amphitheatre looming behind them. He placed his hand on the guide's arm.

'Where are we going?'

'You follow. I take you to her.' The man's Latin was slow and clumsy, and he did not look like a Briton.

Ferox followed. There were fires among the shacks, and low voices of the people who lived there. As they passed, a voice called out asking whether they wanted a 'clean woman or a nice boy', but the weary tone suggested habit more than any expectation of a reply.

'This way.' The guide took him past the locked sheds outside the arena, past the walls plastered with announcements of old and future games, to one of the small doors of the amphitheatre itself.

'Wait.' Ferox was tired, had drunk more that he should, but none of this felt right.

'She is waiting for you,' the guide said. He licked his lips nervously. 'Ready and eager.'

Ferox grabbed the man by the arms. The guide started, eyes wide in panic, and whether it was chance or he heard or saw a movement, the centurion twisted the man savagely around as he turned to put his own back against the doorway. He felt the force of a blow as the man's body shook once, then a second time and the tip of an arrow burst through the guide's throat. He was choking, spitting blood, and Ferox backed into the doorway. He heard the thrum clearly as another arrow came at him and whisked past his head. The dying man shook again as a fourth missile slammed into his back.

Ferox threw the man aside and fled down the corridor. It was a low arched passageway ending in darkness. Steps led off to the right, climbing and then making a sharp turn, but it was lighter up there, perhaps a glimmer of moonlight. A long scream split the night air and then sank into a bubbling sob. The door behind him slammed closed.

IX

EROX STOPPED, WRAPPED his cloak around his left arm and drew the gladius. Slowly, he began climbing the steps. He paused at the first corner, took a deep breath and then jumped around, sword back, ready to thrust. There was no one there. The stairs went up, turning again. He guessed this must be a small passageway used by staff rather than a route in and out for the audience. The timbers around him smelled damp and mouldy, and he guessed it was not cleaned too often. He stopped, listening, but could hear nothing apart from his own breath. After a moment he started walking up the stairs. The light was brighter now, which meant the cloud had broken and a moon close to full was bathing everything in silver.

Warily, his head emerged from the open trapdoor at the top of the stairs. Towering above him, he could see the dark outlines of the frames that carried the canopy raised over the top of the amphitheatre as shelter from sun and rain. There was no sign of anyone and he kept going until he was standing on the walkway used by the workers who operated the canopies and raised the flags and just kept an eye on the audience. The topmost tier of seats was just below, their backs against a four-foot-high solid fence.

The amphitheatre was silent, with no sign of life. Almost at the centre of the arena's sand was a dark huddled shape. Ferox vaulted over the fence onto the seats. Still no one else moved. Whoever had tried to kill him outside must have known where he could go, so why were they waiting? He edged along past the bare seats, which always looked odd without the cushions the audience brought or hired for the day, and came to the wide stairs leading down towards the better seats and the edge of the arena itself. At least here he could move faster than he could in the narrow path in front of the seating. Slowly, crouching as a poor defence against any more arrows, he walked down towards the arena.

The clap echoed around the amphitheatre, unnaturally loud. Three times someone clapped, and only then did he see the darker shape in the shadows at the back of the box on the far side. On festival days, that was where the president of the games and his guests would watch the slaughter.

'Who are you?' a deep voice called out, the sound echoing even louder than the clapping. The words had a Gallic accent.

'You call yourself Domitius Tullus,' he shouted back.

'Sometimes, but that was not the question. Who are you?'

Ferox glanced down. The arena was a good nine or ten feet below him. He could jump over the wall and drop onto the sand. Perhaps one of the gates onto the arena was open. Or he could take the same wide passageway that the audience would take to leave. Either way there would surely be someone waiting in ambush. He could not see a way to reach the box without giving Domitius plenty of time to escape.

'Are you half-witted, boy? Who are you?'

'Who is that?' The dark shape down on the sand was obviously a corpse. For a moment the horrifying thought came that it was Sulpicia Lepidina, but then he dismissed it. She had not set this trap and he was a fool to have walked into it.

'A man who was no longer of any use. Or just another sacrifice in this temple of blood.' The echo was even louder down here. 'But once again I must ask, who are you?'

'Flavius Ferox, centurio regionarius.' His voice broke as he spoke.

'You do not sound sure.'

Something moved over to his right and behind. Ferox glanced back and saw someone emerge from the stairs over past the next *cuneus* of seating. The shape seemed odd, until the moon glinted off metal and he recognised the outline of one of the high helmets worn by some gladiators. A noise came from the other side and two more armed men were coming up the stairs over in that direction.

'Whom do you serve, boy?'

'The princeps,' he shouted back. The arena seemed the best option as there was still no sign of anyone there. He wanted the three attackers closer, so that when he jumped down they would either follow as a group or have to spread out before they came down. 'I have taken the *sacramentum*,' he called, playing for time.

Domitius clapped again. 'Well done. But which *princeps*? Does that really matter to you? Who is Trajan to you? Another lord could be a good deal more generous?'

'I am listening.' The men on his left were twenty paces away, both bearded and shaggy haired, wearing cloaks. One had a gladius and the other a short spear. The one over to his right was more cautious and his face was covered with the mesh mask of the high-topped gladiator's helmet. He was a Thracian by the look of him, with curved sword and shield.

'What do you most want?' The question surprised Ferox and for a moment he hesitated. Then he put his cloak-wrapped left arm on the top of the fence between two of the decorative wooden pommels.

'Don't!' yelled the Thracian, and it was a woman's voice, but Ferox had already swung up and over. His hand held onto the top of the wall for just a moment, slowing his fall. The landing was harder that he would have liked, and his knees gave and he rolled onto the sand. His cloak had snagged on a pommel and been left behind. He pushed himself up and ran towards the box.

'Kill him!' Domitius' voice boomed around the amphitheatre. With a painful grating of poorly oiled hinges, an iron barred gate opened. Ferox waited, but no rush of armed men appeared. He glanced behind him, but no one had followed him down. In the middle of the arena, he could see the corpse clearly and recognised Kopros, several great wounds to his chest and stomach, although most of the blood had soaked away into the sand.

The growl was low, but rumbled in a way that suggested size and strength. A lion was standing in the open gateway. He could hear it sniffing, no doubt smelling the corpse. It came padding forward, head searching from side to side and shoulders swaying. Steel clashed on steel somewhere up above and there were grunts of effort and pain, but Ferox kept his eyes on the great beast. He stepped back, slowly, wanting the dead Kopros between him and the cat in the hope it might choose the easiest meal.

The lion twisted its head back and growled, louder and even more menacingly this time, and another cat, without a mane appeared beside it. As they came into the arena they spread out, prowling across the sand, one either side.

'Die, pig!' The woman's voice was gruff as she yelled the insult, and for a moment he turned, saw the spear as it flew through the air, going wild and slithering across the sand to stop seven or eight paces short of him. Gladiatrix or not, she could not throw a spear.

Ferox stepped to his right, towards the spear. The lioness roared. She was on that side, closer to the spear than he was, and he had no doubt that she was faster. He was not fond of the games and gladiators, but in his youth he had had a brief passion for the *venatores* and the beast fights. He had seen animals like this in the Flavian amphitheatre in Rome and elsewhere. The Silures called themselves the wolf people, but he was alone, without a pack around him, and lions were far greater killers than wolves.

The lion reached the corpse, sniffed for a while and then reached down and began to tear at his flesh. Before the games, animals like this were all but starved for days and had weeks or months of training to kill humans. Maybe these were new and the next festival some time away, for the lion seemed happy for the moment with this meal. The lioness showed no interest and simply watched him.

Ferox wished that he could reach the spear. Instead he crouched down on one knee, moving slowly in the hope that this would not provoke the beast.

The attack came without warning, as the lioness bounded forward, and he would never know whether he had provoked it or not. Ferox leaned into it, head bowed and left hand folded protectively in front, gladius held out as firmly as he could, the pommel hard against his stomach.

In an instant the animal leaped, and the sheer force and weight was far greater even than he had feared. He was knocked over and back, breath driven from him as the wooden pommel was slammed into his stomach. There was hot blood everywhere, soaking onto his hands, and a burning pain on his face and one shoulder, but his right hand still grasped his sword and he forced it as hard as he could, feeling it tear through muscle. The lioness hissed and then slumped onto him.

With effort, Ferox rolled the animal's dead weight off and staggered to his feet. His tunic was badly torn and not all of the blood came from the cat. The gladius was buried up to the hilt in the carcase, stuck too hard to come free.

The lion paused in its meal to glare at him, but otherwise seemed unmoved. Moving slowly, head still reeling, he edged towards the spear. There was a crack, then another and a man in tunic and boots appeared in the arena, wielding a whip. Two more men came behind him, *murmillones* in big face-covering helmets, and each with a gladius and scutum like a legionary. The whip was swung again, snapping not far from the lion, which turned to roar angrily. Another crack and it grudgingly left its meal. Ferox reached the spear, bent over, almost fainted, and managed to pluck it up and ready it in both hands.

Outside a bell started to ring insistently. The lion remained surly and uncooperative.

'Finish him!' The man with the whip shouted, snapping the whip once more, but failing to make the animal attack.

'Come on then!' Ferox called back, hoping to hurry the gladiators. They ignored his taunting and came on slowly, one cautious step after another, moving apart to take him from two directions just like the lions. He flicked the spearhead to face each man in turn.

There were shouts now from outside. Ferox went back, guessing he had about twelve or fifteen paces before he would be up against the wall with nowhere left to go. His chest hurt with each breath, and he knew he did not have the strength left to rush one of them and kill the man before his comrade could intervene.

Back, still back, the gladiators following cautiously. Neither was as tall as him, but their shoulders were broad and their arms and legs thick like all professionals'. The ornate bronze helmets shone in the moonlight, their faces covered. Behind them the man with the whip watched, while the lion returned to its feast.

'Come on, you bastards!' he yelled, hoping to break their calm. They ignored him.

There was a distant banging followed by a crash. Then there were shouts, which sounded as if they came from another direction although it was hard to be sure down in the arena. Ferox guessed he was a couple of paces from the wall. He sprang forward, pelting at the gladiator on his left. The man stopped, shield up ready, and he skidded and nearly fell as he changed to head for the other man, trying to get on his unshielded right side.

With all his strength he stamped forward and jabbed with the spear, aiming for the man's armpit, but he was moving and instead the spear caught him lower down, grazing his stomach, drawing blood from the bare skin. Then the gladiator had recovered, stepped back and was facing him, body covered by the shield. Ferox started to spin around to face the other one, who was coming on, then with a crack something grabbed his left arm. The man with the whip had him and jerked him off balance, and the one he had wounded punched with his shield, the dome-like boss smacking the centurion in the face and flinging him back. Ferox staggered, falling to his knees, and the other gladiator pounded him on the side of the head and he dropped, face down, on the sand.

An iron door swung back to open with a bang and there were shouts echoing around the arena. Ferox tried to push himself up, but his head was swimming and the best he could do was roll. A sword thrust into the sand an instant after he had moved, and then the gladiator was being forced back, massive blows from a sword taking lumps out of his shield. Gannascus followed, and for a big man his speed and balance were amazing. When the gladiator feinted and jabbed, the German was simply not there, and laughed as he beat the other man's guard and slashed a deep gouge across his chest. Ferox almost felt sorry for the gladiator. He had fought the big man once, when they had first met, and only survived that because help had arrived and Gannascus had decided to leave. Two more blows and the gladiator was on the sand, desperately trying to hold in his bowels.

The other one was already dead, finished by Vindex and one of the Batavians, while Longinus had almost beheaded the man with the whip.

'What in Hercules' name is going on? Who are you?' A stocky man, with a big belly but plenty of muscle, led half a dozen others armed with clubs and spears into the arena. They came from the same tunnel the lions had used. Already angry, he became incandescent when he saw the dead lioness. 'My breeders. Which mongrel got them out of their pen?'

Ferox tried to get up, but was struggling until the grinning German lifted him to his feet. If these were animals kept for breeding rather than fighting, then it helped to explain their reluctance to kill.

'I am a centurion,' he said. 'Acting on the orders of the legatus Augusti himself.'

'Are you? Well, I'm not under your damned orders and you can go and shag yourself blind outside. I'll have you in court.'

It took a moment before he began to calm, helped by the realisation that he was faced with five armed men, one of them huge and the rest big and handy enough. Ferox tried to explain that he was lured here by a guide, then ambushed.

'We got one,' Vindex said at that point. 'The other got away, but I gave a good enough cut to the arm to stop him shooting a bow anytime soon.'

Ferox went on, telling how he came inside and found the murdered Kopros.

'Knew him,' the thickset man said. 'Bit too fancy, but played his part when the statues of the emperors were paraded. Poor bugger.'

When he spoke about Domitius there was also recognition. 'That old sod. He's been sniffing about a few times in the last weeks. First he said he wanted to hire some of my boys, then buy some animals. Nothing came of it.'

'Three gladiators attacked me.' He pointed at the corpses. 'Those two and I guess the one with the whip. The other one was a woman.'

'Woman? What sort of *ludus* do you think I run? No women, no freaks, nothing but the real art of fighting. That's what you get from Sempronius. Only the best.'

'Are these men yours?'

'If they'd been mine, lad, you wouldn't be talking now. No, never seen 'em before. Probably someone's bodyguards or from out of town.'

'Anyone see the woman?' Ferox turned to look at the others, but was greeted by shaking heads. 'Any sign?' he called up to Sepenestus, who with his bow had climbed up among the seats.

'No. Couple of dead men and that's it.' Ferox wondered about that. By the sound of it they were dead before the archer arrived, which meant maybe the woman had killed them. If so, then she really was dangerous, but it would seem she was not working for Domitius.

'What did she look like?' Vindex asked. Even in the moonlight his leer was obvious.

'Like she wanted to kill me. Who knows about her face? She had a Thracian's helmet on.'

'Sounds a good woman.' Gannascus slapped him hard on the back and he almost fell over.

'No women fighters,' Sempronius repeated. 'Not here, not ever. Go to the east if you want that sort of skin show. Or Rome in the old days, but not in Londinium.'

The sky to the south was glowing. 'That's a fire,' Sempronius said without any obvious emotion. 'Well, we can leave my formal complaint at turning the amphitheatre into a private battleground until tomorrow. You clear off, and we'll clear up. I can think about that formal complaint in the morning.'

'My name is Flavius Ferox of Legio II Augusta.'

'I heard the name the first time, and the legion don't matter. This is still a small town, sonny boy. If I want to find you, I'll find you.'

'Do you need a surgeon?' Longinus asked as they left, having waited for the archer to come down and join them in the same tunnel Ferox had used to enter the place. It was hard to tell how long ago that was.

'No, Philo can fix me up.'

'He was the one who sent us,' Vindex explained. 'Said I was to follow if you slipped away. There was no sign of us, so he followed on his own, saw you were coming here, and by the time he got back we were just coming in. By the way, we may need some more money.'

'Dice were crooked,' Gannascus said, as if pained by the evil in the world. 'Still, fight was good. I like it here,' he added with an air of finality.

As they came outside and went past the buildings they could see the glow of at least three fires in different parts of the town.

'That doesn't look like an accident,' Longinus said. 'You sure you will be all right?'

'Yes. Help me back to the billet. And thank you all. You saved me,' he said, and meant it.

'We all make mistakes,' Vindex said, and the German roared with laughter.

X

THE TEMPLE OF the Divine Vespasian was burned almost to the ground, and the fire had spread to a warehouse that backed on to it and was storing olive oil, among other things. By the time parties of soldiers and gangs of locals had managed to knock down enough buildings to make a fire break half a dozen houses and shops were reduced to ashes. Fortunately there had been no wind, or the damage would surely have been a lot worse, but people had died and others were scorched and overcome by smoke. The shrines of Liber Pater and Mars Camulos were almost destroyed, but there the fires had not spread and only a nightwatchman had died in Mars' temple. The head priest suspected the man was too drunk to wake in time. The keepers of Minerva's house were fortunately holding an overnight vigil and were not disturbed. Less surprisingly, the always active priests of Isis saw intruders with torches, and by banging their gongs and clashing cymbals chased them away and roused the neighbourhood. A woman initiate had been stabbed in the scuffle and the injury was said to be serious, but they had caught one of the attackers and torn him limb from limb.

'Before he could talk, of course,' Crispinus said. 'Rather a pity really.'

'Did anything happen at the Temple of Silvanus?' Ferox asked. He had been summoned to the praetorium the next morning, and then ushered into a waiting room while the legate went through the formalities of morning salutations. The young tribune had joined him soon afterwards, brimming with news.

'No. At least nothing has been reported. Why do you ask?'

The door opened and Ovidius was ushered in, his tufts of hair wilder even than usual.

'The legate's apologies, but it will be a while before he is done. The worthies of Londinium are nervous and need reassurance.'

'I don't blame 'em.' Crispinus was even more full of cheerful self-assurance than usual. Perhaps it was being in a town after so long or enjoyment of the crisis, or both, but he even stood a little taller. 'But, noble Ferox, you were about to explain your question. Why Silvanus and not any of the other shrines dotted around the place? Come on, man, speak up.'

Ferox told them about Domitius and Kopros, and how he had followed them on their tour. Then he spoke about the ambush last night, not saying why he had believed the messenger or making any mention of Sulpicia Lepidina.

At the end of it all Crispinus let out a low whistle. 'And there was I too polite to mention that Philo had made a pig's ear of shaving you this morning!' Ferox sensed that much of his story was already known to the young tribune, who liked to play these little games, always exploring others' openness and trust. He knew there were bruises and scratches on his face. The cuts were light and would soon heal, but the bruises and broken ribs would take longer.

'You killed a lion, single-handed?' Ovidius was impressed. He patted Ferox on the arm and then looked guilty as the centurion winced. His whole body was sore.

Crispinus laughed. 'Sounds as if inspiration for a work art is forming as we speak. A five-book epic perhaps?'

'At least, my boy, at the very least. Why, this is a feat for Hercules himself!' said Ovidius.

'It was not a very big lion, my lords, and I was lucky, very lucky.' That was true and he knew it. Chance had made the animal land at just the right angle, impaling itself on his sword, its own weight driving the blade deep. 'The poor thing was a female, part of their stock, and not an animal trained to kill.'

Ovidius beamed at him. 'You really do need a poet to tell your tale, friend Ferox!' he said. 'You wish to hide your glory. Why, I could make you a new Achilles.'

'Well, he's taller and better looking than Claudia's whisperer.' Crispinus grinned. 'Well, in a good light, at least. Shall I call a slave and see if we can find a good enough light?' He slapped the centurion hard on the back and with great effort Ferox managed not to react. 'Splendid, splendid. Now, let us return to Silvanus. Do you think his house was spared because the god is from Britannia?'

'What about Mars Camulos?' Ovidius asked. 'He sounds rather local.'

'He comes from Gaul,' Crispinus replied, not taking his eyes off Ferox. 'A god of the Remi, I believe.' He smiled when Ferox gave a slight nod. 'Unlike Silvanus Vinotonus.' He paused. 'At this point a flood of praise for my knowledge would be nice. No? Oh well, in truth the explanation is simple, and more than the blind chance that Archimedes would tell us will eventually mean that even I can be right now and again. I've hunted enough with Cerialis to know the north's god of the chase. But to return to the point. Was Silvanus deliberately spared?'

'I believe so,' Ferox said. 'But it may have more to do w the billeting of some of the legate's mounted *singulares* i. the next street. No soldiers live as close to any of the other shrines.'

'Hmm. We shall have to check, but that sounds plausible Well done. We must assume they did not want a general conflagration, since that would have been easy enough to arrange, even in this damp weather. Kopros is dead, and since that is unlikely to have been his objective, we must consider what this Domitius wants.'

'Nervous people,' Ovidius said, in the tone of a schoolmaster impatient for a pupil to get to the point. 'No one likes the houses of the gods destroyed. They see it as a sign of displeasure, and an omen of worse to come. You could see it in the faces of half the legate's callers this morning. Speaking of which, I will go and see whether he is ready for us. If you will both excuse me.'

After the old man had hurried away, Crispinus chuckled fondly. 'Well, he came with the legate because his life was dull. We have done a good job of changing that!'

'He is a good man, my lord.'

'Yes, he is. And a good friend to my uncle. No, I do believe he is thriving in his new life.' The tribune chuckled again. 'And how about you, centurion? Are you truly all right?'

Ferox shrugged and wished he had not as his body complained. 'I'm alive, my lord.'

'And what do you want from this life, my friend? You know the legate thinks most highly of you. We all do.'

The sudden change of topic caught Ferox by surprise. 'I do my job, my lord,' he said for want of anything better.

'Such devotion is admirable, and deserves reward. No doubt promotion will come, but as well as a loyal officer of the princeps you are a prince of your own tribe. Do you ever think of going back?'

'Doubt I'd be welcome, my lord.' Ferox still found the conversation baffling. 'Reckon I'll just keep on serving. Be good to get back to my region.'

The tribune ignored the hint. 'Then do you ever think of marriage?'

'Marriage?' Ferox repeated the word before he could stop himself.

'Well, perhaps you should think on it. From all I understand, being mauled by a lion would be considered admirable practice for that hallowed bond between man and woman!'

The door swung open and Ovidius' head appeared. 'Time to go.'

'You should think on it,' Crispinus said quietly as Ferox stood to let him leave the room first. 'Might be time to settle down.'

Neratius Marcellus, the legatus Augusti of the province of Britannia, was still, which was never a good sign. He stood behind a chair, gripping the back so hard that his knuckles were white. The room was large, with the wall panels painted in cityscapes and the wooden floor of well-laid and highly polished timbers.

'About time,' he snapped, as they were announced. 'Centurion, you look a mess.'

'You should see the lion,' Crispinus whispered.

Philo had done his best, but an accident had left Ferox with most of a plate of porridge over his best tunic. In its place he now wore the same garment he had worn yesterday, hastily darned and cleaned as well as the short time had allowed. The blood stains remained obvious.

'Never mind, sit down, all of you.'

Cornelius Fuscus watched with obvious amusement. The procurator was around fifty, his hair kept black with dye, eyebrows neatly plucked and tunic, toga and shoes immaculate and obviously expensive. His face was very large and flat, the nose crooked from an ancient break, a scar on his chin, the skin leathery and lined, and it did not fit the clothes. His hands were massive, on short, obviously powerful arms. Ferox thought he looked more like a short gladiator or wrestler than the emperor's chief financial representative in the province.

'Are you sure about this, my dear Cornelius?' the legate asked.

'Yes, my lord. Word came two hours ago. Two days ago there were fires in Camulodunum. The temples of Mars Ultor, of Diana, and of the Divine Claudius were all destroyed. It is unlikely to be a coincidence. It makes a man question whether the destruction of the temple of Mars at Verulamium last week was mere accident, as was first thought.'

The legate grunted.

'I am sure I have no need to remind my lord that all three places were razed to the ground by Boudicca.'

Ferox wondered whether the wooden top of the chair was going to snap. After a moment, Neratius Marcellus managed a smile. 'Indeed you do not. Thank you for expressing your concerns with such rare frankness. I should not detain you any longer, procurator.'

Fuscus stood up. He could only have been a few inches taller than the legate. That did not reduce the sense of immense physical power about the man. 'Thank you for your time, my lord. I shall report that matters are in your safe hands.'

The legate's smile became broader. 'That is kind.'

'Please know that I am sincere in my belief that there is considerable discontent throughout much of Britannia at present. The tribes complain of debt and struggle to pay their taxes.'

'Which I am sure are collected with the utmost tact and kindness by your staff, who do everything in their power to make the burden as light as possible.'

Neratius Marcellus watched the procurator swagger across the polished plank floor. 'Fat-arsed little shit,' he muttered once the doors had closed behind the procurator and his attendants. 'Hopefully one of you has news for me that will help roast the little pimp over a fire. No? Nothing?' He sighed. 'To business then.'

Crispinus gave a full report about the fires, by the end of which the legate was more himself, walking up and down as he interrupted with short, always pertinent, questions. Ferox went next, prompting amusement as well as interest in his description of the fight.

'Somebody wants you dead! Splendid, splendid.' The legate stopped pacing to roar with laughter. 'Then we must be doing something right!'

At the end Ovidius repeated what was known about Domitius. 'Very little, I am afraid. He appears to be an eques from Gaul, has considerable funds, interests in many businesses, is very free making loans, and brings impressive letters of recommendation with him. He has not been in Londinium long, but some of the merchants say they have run into him in other towns in the last month or so. Perhaps he is the Domitius whom Ferox heard about at Vindolanda. Perhaps not. Most likely he is the agent of a senator or senators, doing their work. The priests claim to be unable to remember the names on the letters he carried. One suspects all are in his debt in one way or another, and of course he is not yet openly accused of anything.'

'Facts, gentlemen, facts are what we need. All of this merely assures us that we are right to be suspicious. There is some connection, I am sure, between all or most of what has happened and we need to understand it. But where are the facts?' He stopped mid-stride and spun around. 'How goes the search in our archives?'

'I believed that I was onto something, but am not now so sure,' Ovidius began, running a hand through the remnants of his hair as he scratched his head. 'The Emperor Claudius sent a cloak to the temple set up in his honour in Colonia Camulodunum. Not only had he worn it in his triumph over Britannia, but it had been worn by Pompey Magnus in one of his triumphs. He brought it back from Asia and it was said to have once belonged to Alexander. For a while I thought it might have been our cloak, but the trail ran cold, as I believe you trackers say.' He smiled at Ferox, who for the first time smiled in return.

'It is our cloak. Kopros told me that it was rescued from Camulodunum before it fell to the rebels and eventually taken to the temple here. He only knew that it once belonged to the divine Claudius.'

'The cloak of Alexander!' Neratius Marcellus was grinning like a schoolboy given a tray of sweet cakes. 'Here of all places. Shame it would be sacrilege to wear it.'

'Who would know?' Ovidius asked, but was silenced by the look of the legate. 'Pity.'

Neratius Marcellus walked slowly to the chair and sat down. It was almost as if he was proving his self control to his own satisfaction. 'A better question would be whether or not this Acco would know of Alexander?'

Ferox rubbed his chin, a scab from the night before feeling very large. 'Probably.'

'But would he value something the king of Macedon had possessed? Or the Emperor Claudius, for that matter.'

'Hard to say. Perhaps.'

'Well, earn your pay, and work it out. It is time you went back to the archives. You too, old friend.'

The old man stopped halfway towards the door and turned back. 'Do I get paid as well?'

'Only by my continuing patience, and I dread to think how much that costs. Now leave us. We must now consider again the question of Brigantia, and who will rule there. I understand you have an idea, nephew. Out with it, man.'

'It occurred to me that the choice may be genuine after all...' Ferox and Ovidius were outside and the double doors closed behind them before he could hear any more.

'That is not a decision I envy making,' the old man said as they walked down one of the long corridors. 'To choose whether brother or sister should become high king – or high queen, I suppose, of one of the most populous tribes on this island. You have met Claudia, I believe.'

'Claudia Enica? I have.'

Ovidius peered up at him. 'Your silence speaks volumes. I take it you were not too impressed. Have you met her brother?'

Ferox shook his head.

'He has charm, some intelligence, considerably more confidence, but his judgement…'

'Enough eloquence, too little wisdom?'

'Sallust? You continue to surprise me. Whether or not he is a Catiline, I do not know, but there are some people I find I just cannot trust, even when I do not really know them.'

'You are turning barbarian in your old age, my lord, to trust instincts over reason.'

'Oh I do hope so,' Ovidius said happily. 'Let us just put it this way. When you meet the brother, your esteem for the sister tends to grow. Sometimes I wonder whether she is a great loss to the theatre.'

Ferox wondered whether the mime was more fitting, with its dances and simple stories.

XI

T HE MORNING PASSED slowly, sitting on an uncomfortable stool in the archives, his sides, arms and back aching, sifting through the tablets brought by the clerk, who was enjoying himself.

'Thought you might like these,' he would say, 'once you have finished with that lot.' Soon there were stacks of tablets neatly laid out on and underneath the table, awaiting his attention. Ferox ploughed on, hour after hour, and saw nothing out of the ordinary. It was amazing just how dull reports written weeks or even days either side of battles and other great moments often were. That was the army for you, and sometimes he wondered whether its real purpose was to create these mountains of records, a task occasionally interrupted by having to fight someone.

By noon he was hungry. An hour later he was hungry, in some pain and fed up. Then he saw a simple entry in a strength return which the overeager exactus had brought him after a foolish comment about that being the last place to look.

escort to Prasto   28 including 2 centurions

He glanced at the top of the page. This was an entry in the return for Cohors IV Batavorum on the Ides of August in the consulship of Nero and Cossus Cornelius Lentulus. It was an odd thought that only in military archives did no one bother to erase the name of an emperor whose memory had been formally damned by the Senate. The army needed to keep its records straight and clear, politics or no politics.

Prasto? He had seen the name before, noted it as odd, but passed on without thinking any more about it. It was Celtic, and likely enough he was a Briton, but that was too early for Britons to be serving in the army, especially in a rank that warranted an escort. Two centurions was a lot for so few soldiers, but twenty-eight was more than most of the procurator's staff or other officials would get.

Ferox realised that he was drumming his fingers on the table. He had heard the name before somewhere. It was not common. Then he remembered a boy a few years older than him at his grandfather's dun all those years ago. A lean, fair-haired youth taken as a captive on a raid and raised as one of their own. He never quite fitted in among the dark Silures, but was always willing to follow someone else's lead and beat up anyone who was smaller. In one of his visits, Acco the druid had dubbed the lad Prasto and the name had stuck. His grandfather used to make a sign to ward off evil whenever he heard the name spoken, but Acco was Acco, even then when he could not really have been so ancient. He had heard whispers, no more, about a druid who had aided the Romans.

'Fetch me back the returns for ala Petriana for the same year,' he said to the exactus. 'And of all the Thracian *cohortes equitatae* for the consulship of Novius Priscus and Commodus.' The clerk limped away, a happy expression on his face as he carried tablets to re-shelve and went in search of more.

Ferox was close to giving up when he found another mention of Prasto, this time given twenty horsemen from an ala as escort. After a while he found the name again, in the first year of Agricola's term as legate, when he fought the Ordovices and crossed to Mona. A Prasto was there, guarded by a decurion from a mixed cohort and seventeen troopers.

'Have you a fresh tablet?' he asked the clerk. Surprisingly in this building packed with documents, a blank writing tablet took a while to be found, and Ferox was toying with the idea of warming his stylus and melting the wax on the book he was using to make notes. Just then the clerk returned, with a folding page, slightly battered on the edge, but good enough. Ferox wrote a note to Ovidius, explaining what he had found and asking him to search in the reports of Suetonius Paulinus and Agricola for mentions of a Prasto, perhaps a renegade druid. Slipping the exactus the price of another few drinks for carrying this to the old man, Ferox got up. If he did not hurry now he would be late.

It took a while to get anywhere in Londinium, at least in the daytime. In Rome there were more people, ten or even twenty times more, but the main streets were wider and there were more restrictions on where stallholders could set up. Today was a market day, even busier than usual, as some of the harvests had only just come in. The stalls overflowed with vegetables, sacks of grain, and cages with poultry squawking or hares staring round-eyed through the bars. The larger livestock were in pens, and he avoided the streets behind the basilica where they were being auctioned, but the signs of their passage were everywhere, the earth of the alleys and side streets churned up into clinging mud, and great piles of dung even on the main roads. Today, Londinium smelled like a farmyard, and he wondered if that would make Vindex feel more at home. The scout kept complaining about the reek of the town, so Ferox had told him and the others that he would take them all to a bath-house later today. Much to his surprise, they had agreed.

The exactus had told him about a short cut through the courtyard of the basilica, and Ferox found it, for the moment leaving behind the shouts of the market traders and replacing them with the shouts of petitioners and the grander merchants, yelling at each other. He had never fully understood how commerce functioned, but it clearly required a lot of shouting regardless of the scale. Up on his tribunal, under a canopy in case the weather turned poor, he saw a stone-faced Neratius Marcellus, sitting on his chair of office, listening to a tall, lanky man making a speech. No doubt he was asking for some favour or other, and had dressed up in a toga for the occasion, although he was clearly unfamiliar with the garment because twice it slipped off his left arm.

Ferox went through an arch into one of the halls, then out towards the main entrance. In the shadows by the gate he saw the short red hair of Arviragus, talking to a tubby figure in a dark tunic and Greek cloak. As he passed he recognised Vegetus, the freedman whose cart had been attacked by Rufus and the others what seemed like an age ago in another land. A big slave cleared a path through the crowd, and he glimpsed the stocky figure of the procurator joining the two men.

The house was on one of the hills, some way back from the river. There was more space up here, where the air was a little clearer, and the houses were big and surrounded by substantial, well, groomed gardens, some containing big trees whose leaves were just beginning to turn brown. Ferox was trying to get more sense of the layout of the town, so took a route he had not used before and soon got lost. Streets that appeared straight never quite seemed to lead where he expected, and so many of the buildings looked alike. There was less noise here, and the roads less muddied by wheels and hoofs, but the belief that if he kept climbing he was going in the wrong direction soon proved false when he reached the top of the wrong hill, occupied by a few workshops and some larger fields and open spaces. He gave up and asked the way, and ten minutes later was in the right place.

A slave he did not know answered his knocking, but as he was led into the house he saw a maid he knew, and as he was led through into an inner garden heard the familiar raised voices of the children at play. When excited, young Brocchus had a shriek as shrill as any girl's, while Cerialis' oldest son was given to loud howls of uncontrollable laughter. They were playing catch, dropping more than they took, the younger ones bustling around their feet, and they all sent up a delighted cry when they saw Ferox, and then threw the ball at him. He caught it, pretended that the force sent him staggering back and spun around before finally slumping to the ground. In a moment the children were battling each other to climb all over him. His bruises and broken ribs complained, but Ferox did not really mind.

'You are a bad influence, Flavius Ferox,' Sulpicia Lepidina said.

'Atrocious,' Claudia Severa agreed, looking up a moment from her knitting. The two friends sat in high-backed chairs. In front of them, Marcus rolled and gurgled to himself on a spread blanket.

'Men are just children at heart,' Claudia Enica declared. She sat a little apart, under a parasol held by a slave, even though that side of the garden was shaded by the buildings. She was carding wool, working with two boards, but not putting in enough effort to achieve very much. Once again she was in silk, this time coloured sea green, and matching stockings showed through the patterned tops of her shoes.

'Of course they are, my dear,' Sulpicia Lepidina explained, 'that is why we let them have their politics and their wars to keep them amused, while we get on with the important things in life.'

Enica struggled to free the carding combs, which had become stuck fast. 'That does not sound very fair,' she said, pressing her teeth against her lower lip as she tried to pull them apart.

'It isn't, dear.' The other Claudia spoke in a stage whisper. 'So we have to be careful not to let them know.'

The red-headed Brigantian chattered away, frowning as she battled with the wooden combs. Ferox did not really listen, for it was talk of clothes and colours and jewellery, subjects on which he had few opinions. Apart from that, the children were trying to roll him across the grass, and he pretended to resist, while helping them in their task. While they drew back and gathered their forces, he undid the clasp on his belt so that in the next roll it came free and he left it and his weapons behind. Much to his surprise, it was obvious that the friendship between the three women was genuine, however unlikely. Sulpicia Lepidina had a sharp, incisive mind, and if Claudia Severa was not the brightest, she was nobody's fool, and yet they chuckled and smiled at the rapid flow of trivial conversation pouring from their companion.

'Away from the water!' Claudia Severa barked the command as forcefully as any centurion, and Ferox realised that he was getting close to the edge of a sunken pond. 'You have all got soaked once already today, and that is quite enough. Leave our guest alone.'

'Yes, the poor fellow was attacked by a lion yesterday,' Sulpicia Lepidina said. 'We don't want you finishing him off! Now help him up.'

Ferox wondered how she had heard about that, and guessed that Crispinus had called. The children took his arms and he started to sit up and then roared like a lion and pulled them down onto him again amid plenty of giggling and shrieks of delight.

'You really are worse than they are.' Sulpicia Lepidina had walked to stand over him, arms on her hips as she smiled down at them. She was in pale blue, a colour she often wore, and with her golden hair she was like the serene statue of a goddess. His fevered dream flashed into his mind, and part of him wanted to pull her down as well. Instead he eased the children off and sat up.

'I try my best, lady.' Little Flavia was sticking her tongue out at him. He cupped his hands around his mouth and roared again.

Enica was shaking her head. 'And the emperor pays you a generous wage. Extraordinary.'

'He does indeed, and it is worth every last coin.' Claudia Severa came alongside her friend and grabbed the little girl by the arm. She grinned at Ferox. 'Looks really can be deceiving.'

'That's true,' the Brigantian allowed. 'One of my tutors once said that I would grow up to be wise like a philosopher.' She sniffed back a laugh. 'Silly old fool.'

Sulpicia Lepidina had grabbed the smaller Flavius, but turned. 'There's still time, my dear, if you ever do grow up.'

'Oh, I hope not!'

The mothers led the children away, asking Enica to watch the baby for a moment, and leaving a slave woman, waiting discreetly in the shadows in case there was need. 'Perhaps you can take care of our guest for a few moments? We shall not be long, but these urchins need to be cleaned and prepared for their meal,' Claudia Severa said.

Enica finally abandoned her combs and dropped them on the sleeping Achilles. He stirred, and when his mistress gave a flicking gesture with one hand he scampered away.

'Well, centurion, how shall I take care of you?' She stood, the silk dress shimmering with every movement. It was high necked, with short sleeves and although it hinted at the outlines of her figure, it was nowhere near as sheer as the dresses that had caused such a scandal in Nero's day. Her hair was carefully arranged, if a little less ornately than when he had last seen her and apart from a pair of small earrings and a couple of rings she wore no other ornament.

'Shall I dance?' She walked past him towards the infant. 'Or sing? You would be better off asking dear Lepidina in that case, for she has a true gift.'

'Yes, my lady. I have had the honour of hearing the prefect's wife play and sing.'

'So what's this about a lion? Does the army make a habit of battling with beasts? Or is this how you occupy your time when off duty? Oh, do not worry,' she went on before he could answer. 'I am sure you had good reason. The tribune said it was a lioness. Seems cruel to pick on a girl, and you such a big fellow.' She frowned. 'You know, you are not easily teased, prince of the Silures.'

'I'm just a centurion, my lady. Haven't seen my tribe for twenty years and probably won't for another twenty. And as to teasing, I should say that you are doing a good job.'

'Of course I am, for I am of the blood of Cartimandua – and what's more, I am also a Roman lady so must occupy my time somehow or other. Have you met my brother?'

'No, lady.'

'He is even more of a Roman, as solemn as a Cato when he needs to be. Has served as a prefect of a cohort, as narrow-stripe tribune with a legion, and in the last few years has commanded the royal guard for our late father.' She stooped down and scooped up little Marcus. The baby gave the briefest of protests at being disturbed, but then nestled contentedly against her. Enica was wearing less makeup this morning, although her lips were still rouged. She pursed them now, blowing noisy kisses to the baby and shaking her head from side to side.

Ferox stared at the son he could not acknowledge, longing to hold him, but not knowing any decent way to suggest it.

'Huh, he's a weight,' Enica said. For the first time Ferox thought she looked both natural and happy, which made him wonder whether Ovidius was right and maybe this was another act. 'Still, his father is a big man, a brave and handsome soldier, so we should not be surprised. I hear he resembles him a good deal.'

'The prefect is a fine man,' Ferox said, trying to judge whether or not she was hinting at the truth, for the baby had a mop of black hair just like his.

'I have not had the pleasure of meeting him as yet.' That seemed to settle the matter, until she went on. 'Dear Lepidina has a picture, of course, and in that I am afraid I cannot see the likeness. Still, often art robs the life from someone's face.' Enica glanced at him just once, before gazing back down at the baby. She started to let him grab at her fingers. 'Lepidina and Claudia both speak very highly of you, do you know that? Much of it is surprising, some rather hard to believe. Have you really saved Lepidina so many times and others too?'

'They exaggerate, my lady. Perhaps a couple of times I have helped. Others were there as well.'

'A modest hero? Well, that is something new indeed. Men usually brag about anything, and the boldest surely have something truly glorious to brag about. It would be like expecting me to be modest about my beauty and charm.' Her eyes darted up to watch his reaction, her face briefly glaring in mock annoyance. 'That was your signal to say something about the radiance of my beauty and how it must be praised at every opportunity! Hmmm. For a man who has spent time in Rome you lack many of the graces.'

'I am merely a centurion, and was there for less than a year, training with the praetorians and the horse guards before I was sent to a legion. Before that I was four years in Lugdunum.'

'Oh, that hole. It was such a joy to be taken from there to Rome. Still, the people were welcoming. I stayed with the Fulvii, do you know them?' Before he could reply, the baby was beginning to nuzzle against her, lips starting to suck with enthusiasm. 'Oh dear, I fear he wishes for something I am unable to give. Take him for a moment, while I fetch the nurse.' The baby was thrust into his hands and he took him, amazed at his lightness. Marcus was still making earnest attempts to suckle, and Ferox gave him his finger and felt the surprisingly strong suction. His eyes started to prickle.

'I will do my very best for him.' The voice was soft, little more than a whisper. He had not noticed Sulpicia Lepidina return. 'And so will Cerialis. He is a good man.'

'Is he well?' Ferox knew the child had had some bouts of sickness.

'Strong as an ox, and greedy with it.' She smiled and pressed his arm. Ferox felt he was in a dream as impossible as his encounter with the bathing goddess. Here he stood, under the afternoon sun, with his son in his arms and this beautiful, beloved woman beside him. Yet she was as unattainable as a goddess, even if she had been free, for a senator's daughter might deign to wed an equestrian, but never someone of his lowly rank. What they had done put them both in danger, for the law was severe and the emperor known for his strictness in adhering to it.

The lady glanced quickly to make sure that the garden was empty. 'I am sorry about what happened. It was not my doing.' The words were so faint he could only just hear them. 'But I do need your help. My brother is in trouble and may ruin us all. He is playing foolish games and has not even been discreet.'

'You know you have only to ask.'

'It may mean a death,' she whispered, just as Enica and Claudia reappeared, the wet nurse following.

The Brigantian laughed to see him holding the child. 'Be careful, he will drain you dry! And being a soldier no doubt your blood is more wine than anything else and we shall have a drunken infant on our hands!'

Ferox handed Marcus to the nurse, who had already removed a brooch so that one breast was exposed. He gave the slightest of nods, hoping that Sulpicia Lepidina would see and understand. Somehow the expectation that he would kill for her did not surprise him. All along he had known that their love was as absurd as it was impossible. She was not some slut of an aristocrat, of the type he had seen hanging around the training grounds in Rome, watching the guardsmen and foreign youths like him at the exercises, or drooling over the gladiators in their *ludi*. He thought that she loved him, but she was clarissima femina, her duty to her family greater than anything else in life. Probably she knew that her brother was a pompous halfwit, but he remained her brother and honour and family were everything. Now Ferox could be useful and she expected him to do her bidding. The price for loving a goddess was never cheap. For some reason he imagined what Vindex would say. 'So I get to hump her and all I have to do is kill some poor bugger! Is there a queue?' Ferox guessed that he would do what she asked, but for the moment all he could do was wait.

It was time to go, and he made his farewells and was forced to promise to pay another visit, tomorrow or the next day at the latest.

'Yes, you absolutely must, my modest hero,' Enica declared. 'If you do not come then I shall send Achilles to hunt you down. He may be small, but he is implacable – and he can bite in some truly unpleasant places! Oh do not frown like that, dear Claudia, none of the children are in earshot and it was merely a jest. How do you know I was not talking about his knees anyway?'

'Do not shock our guest,' Claudia Severa said, trying her best not to smile.

'I should feel a great sense of achievement if I managed to shock a centurion of the legions. Especially this one.'

Ferox gave a slight bow. As he left he saw Longinus and three other Batavians arrive, one of them Cocceius and all carrying packs and tools. The one-eyed veteran explained that they were planning to build a little fort and pitch a tent inside for the children.

'Will it be to keep us out or keep them in?' Ferox joked. He talked to them for a while, but was once again late, so he invited them to join the party going to the baths. The three soldiers were obviously enthusiastic.

'We'll see,' the veteran said. 'Work to do first.'

Ferox left and started off downhill towards the river. The streets were barely less crowded than earlier, and soon he was surrounded by bustle and noise, as people talked and yelled in half the languages of the empire. Almost at once, he sensed that he was being followed. He carried on, as if he had noticed nothing, hoping the pursuer would draw close. His cloak was tight around him again, and he kept his hand around the handle of the pugio, a handier weapon than the sword in such a crowd. Nothing happened, but once he turned suddenly and was sure he saw the face of the slave who had brought the message the night before. The man blinked, realised he had been seen and vanished into the crowd.

'Alms for an old soldier.' A man missing a leg and supporting himself on crutches stood in front of him. 'Please, sir, for the sake of the *aquila*.'

Ferox gave the man a couple of coins. So many beggars claimed to be old soldiers and more than half were probably lying, but this man had the air of a former soldier about him.

'Which legion?'

'Hispana, sir. Fifteen years until I lost this.'

'Good luck to you, legionary.'

'Thank you, sir. Best fortune to you for your kindness.'

There was no sign of the scarred slave, and the press was too thick for there to be much hope of finding him. Ferox went on, soon reaching the streets nearer the quayside, where the scent of fish filled the air.

The others were waiting by the main bridge, as they had promised.

'Time to introduce you to civilisation and cleanliness,' he said.

Vindex rubbed his chin. 'Are you sure this is a good idea?'

XII

Ovidius was so excited that his words tumbled out almost as fast as Claudia Enica in full flow. He had worked on in the archives until the third hour of the night, a special order from the legate forcing a few of the staff to stay with him, do as they were bid, and make sure the old fool remembered to drink and have something to eat. The next morning they again waited on Neratius Marcellus, and while they did Ovidius scarcely paused to draw breath as he told his story. Ferox listened with patience, and because the only way to have interrupted would have been to grab the old man and shake him bodily.

Did Ferox know that Agricola was a broad-stripe tribune under Suetonius Paulinus? Yes, of course he did. And that the legate took a shine to the diligent young officer and kept him with him throughout the expedition to Mona and when they turned around to meet Boudicca? Perhaps not. He trusted him with activities that were not generally made public, and one was to deal with this Prasto, who had been captured by chance a year before and decided that his hide was more precious than his cult. Agricola was tasked with keeping a close eye on the man and with learning as much as they could. There had been rumours of captives kept alive by the druids for years, including at least one narrow-stripe tribune, and the governor was keen to discover whether or not there was any truth in this. If there was, their rescue came second only to destroying the cult.

'And as far as I can see, Prasto took with relish to the task,' Ovidius went on. 'It turns out that he was in dispute with many of his fellow druids, something to do with seniority, which he felt had been unfairly denied to him. So he was happy to see his old colleagues put to the sword, and the sacred groves cut down or burned. A man of strong passions, it seems! Yes, yes. More murderous in revenge than his fellow priests were in their grim religion. Led the Romans to Mona, and then guided them so they knew just where to strike and who needed to be caught and killed. Helped a lot in dealing with the rebels too, because he knew Boudicca and most of the chieftains quite well. The gods only know what they thought of him! Still, if he was a traitor, he was our traitor, and very useful too, more than justifying the reward of a plush villa by the sea and enough gold and silver to live in comfort. Agricola remembered him when he came back, and employed him again, and one of the results was this!' The old man brandished a scroll.

The usher had to raise his voice and repeat his message before the oration ceased and Ovidius realised that they were summoned. Ferox and the slave both had to hurry to keep up as the old man almost danced along the corridors.

'No luck, I see,' the legate said as his friend bounced into the office. Crispinus grinned. He was the only other person in the room once the slave closed the doors behind them.

Ovidius went back to the beginning, starting with getting the note from Ferox, and then went through his search, the false starts, growing despair at another trail apparently leading nowhere, and then the thrill when he saw the name. Neratius Marcellus listened with patience and growing interest. 'And when can we expect the first reading of the poem about this great quest?' he said when the old man finally stopped and slumped down exhausted. 'What about you, Ferox, anything to add?'

'Only a little, my lord. I found a Batavian whose father had served and been one of Prasto's escorts.' In fact, Longinus was his source, speaking a little more freely than usual the night before as the wine had flowed. There was something about Gannascus' huge and merry presence that made other men relax. After several hours in the baths they had gone to some bars, and spent a long time watching the dancers in one tavern, the lithe girls in skimpy leather costumes.

'I must be getting old,' Longinus said as he joined Ferox in a quieter corner. After a while he coaxed the story from the veteran. He had served in cohors IV Batavorum, one of the old units disbanded after the rebellion that Longinus-Civilis had led. 'In those days they used to send us noblemen to serve as a trooper for a year or two before they made us prefect. Good system, since you got knocked about a bit – but not too much because they knew you would come back very senior – and at least knew a bit about soldiering when they made you prefect.' He remembered the turncoat druid. 'That bastard. An animal or worse. Never forget him even if I tried. I've met some wrong 'uns in my time – well, I knew Nero and Vitellius – but that sod didn't even try to hide it. Wish I could forget.' Ferox knew how the veteran felt, for now that he had heard what had happened he half wished he could forget.

'Prasto was vicious,' he told the legate, 'even more than the noble Ovidius has told us. He tortured and killed with such glee that even the legionaries were sickened, and you probably know how much they loathed the druids, especially once the stories came out of what Boudicca's warriors were doing. Prasto hated and desired many of the women who were part of the cult.'

'I did not know that there were women druids,' Crispinus said. The legate gave him a quizzical look. 'Sorry, I am just trying to understand.'

'There were not, my lord, although these days I have heard of women claiming to be druids. In the old days women acted as seers and performed some of the rituals, but they were not druids and did not have their learning. Some were old, and these Prasto had killed, usually through some inventive torture. The younger he took and toyed with, taking pleasures as he willed. I am assuming the details are unnecessary.'

'Well...' Crispinus began, before his uncle silenced him with a gesture of his hand.

'Most he killed in the end,' Ferox went on, 'or they took their own lives if they had the chance, and the survivors he kept as slaves.'

Neratius Marcellus sighed and stood up. Ferox had been impressed at how long he had kept still listening to his friend. 'Bad business, but those were grim years, and if he was a dirty tool for us to use, he did serve a purpose. Now, where does this take us in our present need? I am not sure...'

'Oh, I forgot about this!' Ovidius bounded to his feet again, waving the scroll. The legate smiled and nodded for him to continue. 'It was written for Agricola after he had gone to Mona and was preparing his drive to the north. He asked Prasto to record a good deal of the lore of the druids, in case the cult sprang up again. And the greatest was this list.' Ovidius unrolled the scroll, coughed and began. 'The Treasures of Britannia! Prasto calls them artefacts of great potency and symbolism – perhaps what friend Ferox here would call power?' The centurion nodded.

'Some will be all too familiar to us. Here we have the armour of Venutius, the mirror of Cartimandua, the cloak of Claudius – odd, that, but I suppose even the enemy has power. The torc of the high king of the Catuvellauni. Oh dear, that was what they took from poor Caratacus, I suppose. The Spear of Camulos and the cauldron of Morrigan. Not heard of those so far, and he says that they are hidden in the cavern of the three-faced god. The shield of Boudicca, but he says that was buried with her corpse and no man knows where her grave was made. After that it is not so much specific items as objects with power, the blood of kings and queens, the tears of the gods – I wonder how you collect those for he does not say – and the skull of a witch or druid.'

'Is this Prasto still alive?' the legate asked. 'I confess that I never heard his name until today, which makes me suspect that he is dead. Can we check?'

Ovidius beamed. 'Vanished at sea five years ago. He was a very old man, but liked to go out fishing in a little boat along with some of his almost as elderly slaves. One day the weather was bad and they did not come back. The body of one of the slaves and timbers from the boat washed up. One of the procurator's men sent in a report about it because the emperor was heir to all his estate.'

'Generous, since we'd given it to him in the first place,' Crispinus said.

'Do I take it you had to request this information from the procurator's office?' the legate asked, paying no attention to his nephew. 'Yes, I thought so. Ah well, probably cannot do any harm.'

'I invented a legal case involving property in the area,' Ovidius replied. 'And gave the usual sort of gift to encourage the efforts of the freedman.'

'Fair enough, and it cannot be helped.' Neratius Marcellus set off on one of his walks. 'Let us assume Prasto is dead. Let us also assume that someone, probably Acco, has taken the cuirass, the torc and the mirror. The shield may be lost forever, and we have the cloak. What about this spear and... what was it?'

'A cauldron.'

'Truly?' The legate paused to shake his head and then turned to pace in the opposite direction. 'Does not seem so very dramatic, but there it is. Any idea where they can be found?'

Ovidius shook his head. 'The beneficiarius assures me that there is another scroll associated with this one. He reckons it was put back in the wrong place, but has set his men to searching. Perhaps there is something in there.'

Neratius turned to Ferox.

'Mona would be the most likely place, my lord.' Ferox wished he had another answer, and part of him wanted to pretend that he had no idea because he feared to go there and could sense what would come next. He was also sceptical that Prasto was right about everything, or that the Romans really understood. Acco's own power grew as he acquired each treasure. He doubted that all were needed, and the druid might already have enough for his purposes.

'Very well. If we have learned nothing more certain by the end of tomorrow you will set out for the island at dawn on the next day. See what you can find.'

'My lord.'

'Good. You must make the most of the remainder of your time here. Have you heard about the statue? No. At least someone has not. This morning a statue of the princeps fell off its mounting on the wall of the basilica. The head broke off and has not been found.'

'The work on the pedestal was very poor,' Crispinus said. 'It is no surprise that the mortar crumbled and the thing fell down.'

'That does not explain the theft of the head. It is not as if it was bronze and could be melted down by a sacrilegious thief. And accident or not, people see it as another bad omen. Rumours are spreading that the princeps is ill and not long for this world.'

'I haven't heard that.' Crispinus' surprise seemed genuine.

'Then perhaps you should spend more time around the docks!' The legate's pacing meant that he was standing behind his nephew and he reached down and grabbed his shoulders. 'As far as I am aware, it is not true, but it is repeated and some will believe. Nothing has been seen or heard of that rogue Domitius, and that is also worrying.' The legate paused and faced the double doors. 'I always know when my *accensus* is impatient!' The doors opened slowly. 'Off you all go. We have already spent too long and I shall be late convening today's first case.'

Ferox thought the tribune wanted to speak to him, but Ovidius took the young aristocrat by the arm and led him away. That was a relief, because he wanted to go to the principia and preferred to go on his own. Once there he sought out the office of the *frumentarii*, the soldiers detached from their units to help organise the supply of grain and other bulky essentials to the army in the province. They were a privileged group, who spent a lot of time on the move, as likely as not travelling to Rome to liaise with their counterparts there. An idle remark by the exactus had made him wonder whether he knew the centurion in charge, one Valerius Maximus who for a while had served as regionarius to the east of his own patch.

Thankfully, he was right, and although he had to wait a good hour before the man returned to his office, it gave him the chance to call in a few favours. The most important was to ask for help. Frumentarii heard a lot of things in their job, especially in the markets, inns and harbours, and since many people wanted to secure contracts to help the army they were usually well treated. Ferox wanted to know if they had picked up any rumours about Domitius. Maximus was a sensible man, honourable enough in his way, so he risked a few hints about plots.

'I'll do my best, *contubernalis*.' Maximus had lost all the fingers on his left hand and his lonely thumb tended to twitch when he was thinking. His other hand closed around it and grinned. 'I thought you said last time that you would never ask me another favour.'

'Sorry. Still, it got you this posting and you never really liked it up north.'

Declining an offer of dinner, Ferox went to the office of the procurator and asked to see the freedman Vegetus.

'Why?' The deep voice came from behind him, and he turned to see Cornelius Fuscus standing in the doorway. His head jutted forward so that he resembled a small and angry bullock.

'My lord.' Ferox stood to attention and raised his arm in salute. He was not sure whether the procurator had a right to this courtesy, but felt that it could not do any harm. 'My name is Flavius Ferox, centurio regionarius. A short while ago a wagon owned by Vegetus was attacked, two of his slaves killed, another abducted and his property stolen. Although I have punished the bandits responsible, the property has not been recovered and I was hoping to learn more to help me to find it.'

The procurator glared at him. His eyes were pale and watery, without any hint of softness. For a long time he was silent, and Ferox was not sure whether he was trying to think of a reason to refuse the request or simply wanted to display his power before he agreed.

'I have seen you,' Fuscus said at last. 'And now I recall your name. You are the one who failed to discover who murdered Narcissus at Vindolanda. You do not seem very good at finding anything.'

'Sir.' Ferox remained at attention and stared over the procurator's head. If the man wanted to revel in his rank then let him.

'Why should I help you, centurion? Tell me that. My staff are busy.'

Ferox said nothing. The procurator walked around him. He stayed as he was, staring straight ahead. A warrior of the Silures took pride in his outward calm. Still, a warrior of the Silures might easily have slit the stocky man's throat for such an insult. At least all these years in the army made it easy to ignore the obnoxious behaviour of those protected by rank.

'You are a dull sort of fellow, aren't you. Most officers have shit for brains.' He was back in front of Ferox again, glaring up, and so close that flecks of spittle pattered onto Ferox's chin. 'They are useful to kill and be killed, but for little else.' The procurator slapped him a stinging blow across the face, and then stepped back a pace. Ferox remained rigidly at attention. 'Hmm. At least you are not provoked easily. I shall let you bother Vegetus. See to it.' The last words were to the clerk at the desk.

'At once, my lord.'

Again Ferox had to wait, but only for a short time and then he was taken into a side office and found Vegetus slumped in a chair behind a desk, piles of tablets in front of him. It was the first time he had glimpsed the freedman at work and he was impressed by the surprising energy of this obese man.

Ferox did not expect a warm welcome and was not disappointed. The gaze was cold, although harder to tell whether he was most blamed for the horrible death of his wife Fortunata two years ago or the more recent loss of his prized antiques. He said little that Ferox did not already know. Still, he had not appreciated the bitterness of the dislike the man felt for Narcissus, which was clearly more than merely the rivalry of two collectors.

'Nasty bugger.' Vegetus almost spat the words. 'Always listening, learning secrets. He liked to hurt people and make them crawl. A plotter too.' Vegetus realised his hatred had carried him away, but he could not turn back. 'I had reason to doubt his loyalty.'

'Did you report this?'

'Of course.' Which meant that the procurator knew and had not told the legate.

'Do you know who killed him?'

Vegetus screwed his face into a grimace. 'How should I know? I wasn't there. Some friend of our lord Trajan perhaps? Or just someone he had pushed too far. Who hasn't got secrets they would rather no one else knew? I cannot lament the loss of such a worthless life. Now, is that all?' Without waiting for an answer, he opened the next tablet in the pile and reached for his stylus.

'Thank you. Yes, that is all.'

Ferox wondered whether anyone had liked Narcissus. Mention of his name to Longinus the night before had prompted a snort of disgust and a simple 'Little bastard got what he deserved, didn't he? I'd shake the hand of the man who did it – well, as long as he's washed since then! Give it another month and he will be forgotten. Nobody cares even now.'

A couple of Batavians were with Vindex and the others when Ferox joined them a little later. The one-eyed veteran was not there, but Cocceius was. They were all sitting in the benches on one side of the amphitheatre. There were no games today, but men from the ludus were practising and now and then fighting mock bouts. Gannascus had been asking about the place ever since the fight, so Ferox had told them to bring him. The German watched every move, at least when his attention could be prised away from the girl sitting on his lap. She looked about sixteen, dark skinned and with long black hair that shone like silk. An easterner certainly, perhaps a Parthian or even an Indian, her face with the soft features that made you understand why the

Greeks said the Persians were the most perfectly beautiful people in the world. She wore a threadbare, faded tunic and plain sandals, but it did not really matter for she looked like a princess until she spoke in a jarringly harsh voice.

'He won her, didn't he,' Vindex explained.

'With my money?'

'Maybe. He's lost and won back so many times that it's hard to say.' There was a bruise on the scout's cheek, which he rubbed now and again. 'Her owner wasn't so keen on his taking his winnings, though. We had a bit of an argument.'

'Anyone dead?'

Vindex thought for a while. 'Probably not. No one likely to have important friends, anyway. You should have come with us after the bath. It was a good night.'

'Couldn't get used to you being clean,' Ferox said. To his great surprise the others had enjoyed the bath-house, especially when they found one section where women were allowed to bathe with the men. That led to one fight, but the sheer size of the German helped to keep the peace. 'We'll probably be moving day after tomorrow. Make sure everyone is ready and check on the horses.'

'Where?'

'You wouldn't like it if I told you.'

'Humped again, are we?' Vindex reached for his wheel of Taranis, but his fingers closed on nothing. He sighed. 'Forgot. Some bitch stole it last night.' He grinned. 'I was busy at the time, and happy too, I'll give her that.'

'Heard any rumours?' They were far away from Vindex's homeland, and he did not know towns and cities, but Ferox had long come to value the scout's instincts, almost as much as his own.

Vindex curled his lips, his big teeth sticking out. 'Lot of talk of rebellion,' he said after a while. 'Not from those who want one, but those who fear one. The temples and that statue haven't helped. Making people nervous. Seen the tribune about a lot, talking to all sorts. He's playing some sort of game.'

'He usually is.' Ferox remained puzzled by Crispinus' suggestion that he marry. 'Think some of it has to do with the successor to the old high king. Who do you think it should be?'

'Me! I don't exactly move in such circles.'

'You're Carvetii, though.'

'Aye, I am, but if I was a great chief I wouldn't be hanging around with the likes of you, now would I? Course not. So what I think don't matter spit. What I hear is that it's between the two children, and most likely the brother, whose older, said to be a great warrior and a hero. The sister is younger. Nice tits, so I hear.' Ferox snorted in surprise. 'It was a chieftain who told me. So what, she may be royal, but she's still a woman and there's no harm in admiring from a distance. The Romans will chose the lad because they like kings over queens. That doesn't really matter to us, or the Brigantes. Depends how much of their grandmother is in the lass.'

'So tits aren't everything?'

Vindex considered this. 'Dumb question. They're a lot, course they are…' He lapsed into silence for a while, studying the girl on Gannascus' lap, who was giggling and whispering in the big man's ear. 'Bit small,' he said after a while. 'Nice, though. She's a dancer, worth a fortune according to her former owner, but he was desperate and had run out of coin.

'No, I reckon it will be a new king rather than a queen. That's the way the Romans think. Still, maybe it doesn't matter. From all that's said, brother and sister are more Roman than anything else, and you know what they're like.'

'Bastards every one of them,' Titus Flavius Ferox agreed. He noticed Sempronius the *lanista* was down in the arena and kept glaring up at him.

'You always make so many friends, don't you?' Vindex said. 'It really is a gift.'

Ferox stood up. 'Tell Gannascus that the girl cannot come with us. So he can either sell her back or find someone to take care of her while we are away, although I cannot promise that we will return to Londinium.'

'Where are you off now?'

'Work.' Ferox did not tell his friend that the work in question meant visiting several brothels, otherwise he knew it would be even harder work stopping the scout from coming along. For a married man, Vindex had a lot of energy. Armed with letters written by Flora, he was calling by appointment on three of their owners. It was business, not pleasure, and he hoped to find out things it would be hard to learn another way.

Three hours later as the sun was setting, he found Longinus waiting at his lodgings. The others were out, apart from Philo. 'He's been here for a long time,' the boy said in explanation.

'Promised to give you this in person,' the veteran said, standing up and handing over a closed and sealed tablet. 'Make sure it isn't left lying around. Right, I'll be off.'

Ferox told the slave to fetch a lamp and light it. The boy looked surprised, for the room was still fairly light, but did as he was told. Once he had gone, Ferox broke the seal and opened the letter. The wooden frame was thick, for this was the sort with a heavy layer of wax on them and someone had scored the letters deeply.

I need not say who I am, but I remember a bath and a tower far away. C whose name is hated and mocked in Parthia is in trouble. CF lures him into conspiracy for his position is one where there is plenty of wealth. He has letters that I thought gone where C wrote foolish and disloyal things and threatens to show them if C does not do what he asks. CF is cruel and does not threaten idly. Help me, please, for love, friendship and for another most precious to us both.

When the slave returned Ferox held the stylus over the lamp's flame until even the handle became hot. Then he rubbed it over the surface of the tablet, melting the wax to erase the writing. It took a while, for the wax was hard and the pen soon cooled, but in the end he was satisfied.

'I'm going out,' he said. 'I may send word. If I do, the others are to come with all speed.'

XIII

THE BOARDS CREAKED as Ferox edged towards the light. He stopped, his breath sounding terribly loud, and waited. The low murmur of conversation did not change, and after a while he started to crawl again. There was dust and chaff all over the floor and his throat started to prickle. It had made sense to leave his weapons' belt behind, and certainly he could not have crawled so easily with it on, but he still felt naked and unprotected. Slowly the edge came nearer. The light was a lamp, dim enough in such a big warehouse, and, whenever the conspirators gathered around it moved, they cast weird tall shadows. Conspirators they must be, to meet in secret so late at night, but whether or not they had anything to do with his business, he did not yet know.

One of the brothel keepers, a woman of the shape conjured up by Flora's laugh, but who spoke surprisingly pure Attic Greek as well as polished Latin, had given him the tip, and one of the others had helped explain how he could get there. There were two groups meeting in secret most nights, each in a different building that ought to have been locked shut at that time of night. Prominent men met in this way, at least so it was claimed by freedmen and slaves from their households who liked to tell secrets to the girls when they visited. The whores told their owners, and for Flora's sake they were willing to tell him.

Getting there was not easy. Ferox started in one of the brothels not far from the wharfs on the river. He climbed to the top of the house, passing some of the thriftier or poorer clients who paid for no more than a coupling in an alcove off the stairs or corridor. Some did not have curtains, so his walk was accompanied by moans, sighs, screams and glimpses of writhing flesh. Half to his surprise he did not see Vindex or anyone else he knew. The slave who led him must have seen all this and more so many times that he paid no heed, and eventually they reached a ladder that took him to a hatch that opened onto the roof. From there, the man pointed out the backs of the two taller buildings, and showed how he could get in. An alley separated them from the row of warehouses, but the jump was not too far. Even so, Ferox eyed it for a while as the rain pattered down. The shingle roofs were slick and getting slicker by the minute, and he could feel his tunic and breeches getting steadily wetter. A cloak would be too cumbersome for what he had in mind.

Taking a deep breath, Ferox leaped, slamming hard into the opposite roof and only sliding a little before he got a firm hold. The first one was the easiest, and just a few paces away there was a hatch similar to the one on the other side. He felt around the edges, found a catch and was surprised to find that it lifted easily. Once he clambered through and dropped down onto the top of a big barrel, he could understand why. No one could have sneaked in through the roof and made off with anything so bulky and no doubt heavy. The upper floor was crowded with similar barrels, the light too poor to read any markings on them. It took a while to find the gap around a trapdoor leading downwards. Ferox eased himself down from a barrel taller than he was, and sneaked to the open trapdoor. The light from below was bright, and at first there was silence. Then people, dozens of people by the sound of it, began to sing a long, repetitive song, and many of the words were in a language he did not understand. After that, a man spoke for a while, then another voice took over.

Ferox edged to peak through the open trapdoor, and saw the speaker, arms stretched out on either side, head bare and looking up, but with closed eyes. He spoke of blood, flesh and sacrifice, and much of what he said seemed to be quotations that Ferox did not recognise, although presumably the audience did. Most were in a similar pose, and it was odd to see people praying with their heads uncovered, apart from one woman who wore a scarf. She was the only woman he could see, but there must have been more people out of view. This was no conspiracy, at least not one to bother him, and as they began to sing once more, he went back up the way he had come. The new song was in Greek, and spoke a lot of love for others and of the god. Presumably this was a cult frowned upon by the authorities, unless its rituals were secret for the sake of being mysterious. A lot of what they said reminded him of Philo, and he wondered if this was some Jewish sect for he knew that there were many. Since the great rebellion against Nero, Jews had to pay a special tax, but as far as he could tell they had once again become reasonably loyal to the empire.

The rain was a lot worse by the time he was back up on the roof, and he slipped a couple of times on the shingles as he made his way all along the row of buildings. Each warehouse pretty much butted onto the next, so only once did he have to make another leap. The one he wanted was almost at the far end, and once he was close he could see the crane sticking out from its wall. According to the slave, all he had to do was lower himself off the roof, swing and grab onto the crane, turn and then use one foot to lift the catch closing the loading door, hook it around the edge, open the door and swing in. The man claimed to have done it a fair few times on business of his mistress. Ferox thought it better not to ask what such business might have been, neither did he ask if the fellow had ever done it in this sort of weather.

He wiped the rain out of his eyes. The alley was a good twenty-five feet below so he might not be killed outright if he missed his jump and fell. Someone had left a cart full of hay that must be getting very wet, but selfishly they had left it too far for him to reach if it went wrong.

Ferox jumped, for an instant thought he would be too short, then the crane was there and he grabbed it, body complaining of this fresh mistreatment. Whether the catch was stiff or his feet in his boots less agile than the slave's, it took a while to get the doors open. Finally he was inside, on an almost empty platform covering two-thirds of the space in the building. There was the dim light of a lamp from down below. Closing the door behind him as gently as he could, he waited. There was a series of muffled greetings. No one sounded agitated, so he lay down and crawled towards the edge.

'I'm sure I was followed,' a voice said. It was faint, and he had to strain to catch the words.

'Imagination. They may be suspicious, but they can know nothing for certain.' The second voice sounded more excited than afraid, and clearly had no fondness for his companion. 'At least, as long as all of us remain true to our oath.'

'For my part. I cannot speak of the others.' The first voice sounded even more nervous.

A door opened. There were greetings, too low to catch, and Ferox doubted any names were used, but at least two more conspirators had arrived.

'What news?' It was the first man again, and his voice cracked as he spoke, so that he had to repeat his words. 'What news?'

'Matters are going well, my lords.' That was Domitius, no doubt about it, and sounding mightily pleased with himself.

'The centurion escaped.' This was a new voice, brusque and sounding vaguely familiar. Ferox edged a little closer, wondering whether he would be able to see over the edge without them noticing.

'A small matter. He is of no consequence.'

'Indeed.'

'But surely he may find out?' It was the first voice again. 'We are taking too many risks. To kill him was bad enough, but to botch it… Unforgivable.'

There was silence and Ferox imagined the cold stare before Domitius replied. 'The risks were always there, but the prize is almost within our grasp. The fires worried people. The fall of the statue frightened them. Tomorrow we shall terrify them. It is the same in the other towns and cities.'

'So you say.' The second man did not sound convinced. 'How can we know?'

'I know,' the brusque one cut in. 'I get regular reports from all over the province. That at least is working. Everyone talks of bad omens and trouble coming.'

'But the legate must realise this is not chance.' The nervous man was almost pleading for his fears to be confirmed.

'Perhaps, perhaps not, but what can he do about it?' Ferox almost snapped his fingers as he realised that the brusque voice was the procurator. 'No one has broken their faith, so our secret is safe. If not, I would know and I would not be here – or if I was it would only be to make sure none of you ever left this building.' Ferox could imagine the face jutting forward, the pale eyes glaring around as the threat was made. 'Most of our august governor's officers have shit for brains. Even if they are suspicious they would not know what to do.'

'Well, we have people frightened.' Ferox wondered whether the second man glanced at the first as he spoke. 'That is something, but will not matter if the risings do not occur. Will they?'

'As soon as the word is sent,' Domitius answered. 'It is almost time.'

'And who will rise?' Cornelius Fuscus was as rude as ever. 'They must know the cost of failure.'

'There are men in half the tribes of the south,' Domitius declared. 'Among the Durotriges, Dobuni, Atrebates and Corietauvi. Others will join soon enough if it prospers, from the Catuvellauni, and even the Iceni.'

'What of the western peoples?' the second man cut in. 'The Silures and Ordovices have been peaceful for less time than all of those others.'

'Your answer?' Fuscus demanded when no reply came.

'The Silures will never follow anyone else's lead. Who knows what they will do?' Ferox smiled with pride at this judgement on his kin, and with some relief for he was glad they were not involved. 'The Ordovices are still cowed by defeat, and their chieftains not bold enough to have run up the debts that make so many others eager for change. They are a little people, of no account.' Ferox knew he was grinning broadly. The Silures held their northern neighbours and traditional enemies in contempt.

Fuscus did not sound impressed. 'You mention many tribes, but not the one we all know matters the most.'

'The Brigantes will rise.' Domitius remained unruffled. 'Some of them at first, and then more and more. You have sent the grain?'

'Yes, Two-thirds lies in ships already within the mouth of the Abus. The rest is travelling north, or already stored in villas and towns. I am still waiting for full payment.' The first man's voice did not squeak when he spoke of money.

Ferox reached the edge of the floor. The conspirators were closer than he expected, little more than eight feet below. They stood in a circle, only heads visible behind ranks of big amphorae. He saw Fuscus nod to Domitius.

'You will be paid in full by sunset tomorrow,' the merchant said.

A sturdy, broad-shouldered man with a thick black beard nodded. Ferox had not expected the nervous one to look like this.

'Who will lead the Brigantes?' Fuscus demanded. 'That is still uncertain, and...' They all went silent and heads snapped around as they heard a door open. There was a whistle, obviously a signal, and they relaxed.

'He is here then,' Fuscus said. He shook his head. 'Shit for brains, all of them.'

Ferox craned to see the new arrival, saw the hooded figure, then someone was shouting and the bearded man was pointing.

'There! Upstairs!' Ferox just glimpsed the new arrival, saw the hood of his cloak fall back as he was startled, then he pushed himself to his feet and ran for the loading door. As he reached it, he heard someone pounding up the rungs of the ladder. The door came open and he leaped for the arm of the crane, narrowly missing hitting his head on a heavy wooden block hanging just underneath.

'Kill him!' That sounded like Fuscus.

Ferox got one elbow on top of the arm, hauled and swung until he managed to get onto it. Someone grabbed at his foot and he stamped back as hard as he could.

'Bastard!' the man hissed.

Ferox was up, facing the wrong way, and the crane juddered as a man jumped out, missing the arm, but grabbing onto the dangling rope. Rather than try to turn, Ferox leaped across the alleyway, saw the roof opposite coming at him, knew he was low and then his waist slammed into the edge of the curved tiles. He grabbed, felt one loose tile give way and fall to shatter noisily below, but his other hand fastened around the ridged top of another tile. The rain was driving down, soaking through his tunic and breeches, and the baked clay slippery. His fingers closed around a higher tile and he pulled. This time the tile held and he climbed, swung up one leg, slipped, swung again and this time gripped. There were cuts on his hands, and even more bruises, but he was up and risked a glance behind. The man who had caught the rope was struggling to get up onto the arm of the crane. Another man, the bearded merchant who was supplying the rebels with grain, was in the doorway, a wild look in his eyes.

Leaning, one hand often pressed against the sloping roof, Ferox started to work his way along, heading back towards the brothel. That must be four buildings away at least. His pursuer was up on the crane. With hair so close cropped he was almost bald, he was not one of the main conspirators so presumably was a bodyguard or servant. He wore a drab tunic, closed boots and had a knife tucked into his belt.

'Go on!' shouted the merchant. The other one looked back, then at the gap and hesitated for only a moment. He took two steps along the top of the crane and flung himself across, landing higher than Ferox, and hardly slipped at all. Behind him the merchant leaped and grabbed onto the rope.

The next building was higher by a good few feet, and Ferox managed to haul himself up, helped because this too had ridged tiles and they were easier to grip. By the time he was up the merchant was on the arm of the crane and jumped. He landed badly, scrabbling for a hold until the slave steadied him.

Ferox worked his way along and went higher up the roof, wanting to have a good chance of stopping his fall should he slip. He reached the top, felt around and found what he wanted so stopped, sitting astride the apex. Two of the tiles were loose, and one had a crack he could feel. He got the tips of his fingers underneath the first, prised it up and propped it against his thigh. The next one broke apart as he worked at it, and left him with two handier sized chunks.

'There he is!' The merchant's voice cracked again as he pointed. He and the slave were peering over the edge of the roof. Perhaps the slave was surprised to see their quarry waiting for them, and it was the master who first climbed up, working his way across and upwards, using his hands just like Ferox had done. The slave followed, going slowly and carefully as the rain hammered down even heavier than before.

Ferox waited until he was four or five paces away and threw the first lump of tile. It was about the size of his hand, and a clumsy missile that flew past the merchant's shoulder. He ducked, slipped a few inches and recovered just as the second fragment, almost as big as the first and more pointed, struck him in the face. If he gasped the noise was lost in the rain, and the involuntary jerk as his head snapped back unbalanced him and he was falling, sliding across the tiles. The slave was reaching for him, mouth wide in a noiseless cry, but he was too far away and the bearded man shot down and vanished over the lip of the roof.

'You don't have to die!' Ferox shouted, trying to be heard over the rain.

The slave did not hear him or did not care, and advanced steadily, now coming as straight as he could towards the perched centurion.

'I'll see you're well treated.' Still the man came on, saying nothing. Ferox tried to grab another fragment of tile, but the only one that came away was too small to be of use. He lifted the whole piece and slammed it down on the beam underneath. It refused to break. Taking it with both hands, he hurled it at the oncoming slave. The man flung himself upwards, gripping the top of the roof as it flew past, smashing impressively when it landed, and breaking some of the tiles there. His knife must have slipped, for it rolled down until it too dropped into the alley.

'What is your name?' Ferox was trying to loosen the closest tiles. He wondered about attacking while the slave was scrabbling up, but did not trust the slippery tiles and still hoped to make the man give in, so that he could at least find out his master's name. 'I can help you.'

The slave was on the apex and he stood, his balance impressive on the narrow ridge covering the edges of the tiles. He started walking forward, arms out on either side for balance, going faster and faster. Ferox crouched down, hunching his back, his left arm protectively in front and the right poised to punch. He knew the timing would be crucial, and he still could not believe that the man had not fallen, then the slave hurled himself at the Roman, his arms out in front ready to grab. Ferox punched, felt a good blow connect with the side of the man's neck, but his weight bore him on and they were both falling, rolling over and over as they sped towards the plunge down. Tiles came loose and slipped away as the struggling men struck them. Ferox butted hard with his head and the man's grip loosened, then they were at the edge and he just managed to close his fingers around the ridge of a tile, then grasp the top of another, standing proud because the one above had slid away. He jerked to a halt, belly pressed against the edge of the roof, and an awful weight around his legs as the slave clung on. Ferox kicked, and writhed, trying to loosen the hold. The rain helped, for his trousers were soaking and he felt the grip slide down, until the man was hanging with both hands around one of his feet. He slammed the other boot down, felt the impact as the hobnailed sole smashed into the slave's head. With a wrench that felt as if his other foot was being yanked off, the left boot snapped apart and suddenly the weight was gone. He was not sure whether he imagined the thump of the slave hitting the floor of the alley.

Breathing hard, he managed to get back up onto the roof. He could dimly see two dark shapes down below and neither was moving. There was no sign of anyone else. Much to his surprise, he realised he still had his sock on, and the wool tore several times as he made his way along the roofs. The slave was waiting for him at the hatch in the roof of the brothel. Once again, his face betrayed no surprise even when Ferox climbed inside, lacking a boot, drenched to the skin, and his face scratched and fingers showing numerous cuts. The slave led him down, and then others tended to him and provided him with dry clothes and a pair of shoes, roughly his size. Once he had his weapons on again and a cloak around him, he was ready to leave, profusely thanking the proprietor of the establishment.

'I didn't do it for you,' she said. 'I just owe Flora. Sure you are not stopping? This is the best in town. No? Please yourself.'

The rain had stopped, but the cloud was thick and the night dark. Ferox wondered about going back and asking for a lantern and then decided against it. Both men still lay in the alley, but someone was stooping over the merchant. It was hard to see, but the figure was not big and when it stood he saw the sweep of long hair. The woman saw him and ran. Without thinking, he gave chase. There was a little light spilled from the badly closed shutters of a bar in the next street and her shape was obvious in the short tunic and high boots – the same worn by the woman gladiator. He could only see the back of her head, but she had long hair that looked dark in this light. She was also fast, and he was not gaining. She swerved into an alley, and he followed, but once inside it was so dark he could no longer see her. There was a noise behind him and he turned too slowly. Something slammed into the back of his head and he felt the vomit coming as he dropped. Then there was only darkness.

XIV

FEROX OPENED HIS eyes and still saw nothing, for there was a bindfold tied fast around his face. He was lying on his side, hands pulled hard behind his back and held there, his feet bound together. His cloak had gone, so had his weapons and belt. The floor was wood, so he was indoors and it did not feel very different from the floors of the warehouses he had been in earlier. It felt as if he was in a small room, but whether that was true or he was among stacked goods was hard to say. There was a faint smell of beer and decaying fruit.

The back of his head throbbed and his mouth was full of bile. Memories came back and he could not believe his own stupidity. No one had known where he had gone even before he went chasing fleeing women down dark alleyways. He ought at least to have sent word to Vindex before he went charging off. The scout was a decent enough tracker out in the wilds, but it was too much to hope that he would somehow scent danger and come to the rescue. If he did he would laugh his head off at the thought of his friend being lured into a trap by a woman.

Ferox tried to move his hands, seeing if the knots were loose, and failed. His legs were just as securely bound and there was nothing left to do but wait for whatever fate his captors had in store. The woman had been a fleeting shape in the night and although he was sure it was the one from the arena that did not much help. Probably she served Domitius, and perhaps a woman was a useful killer because few would suspect danger until it was too late. The bearded merchant had not died in the fall and someone, presumably the woman who had been bending over him, had slit his throat. The smell of the blood had been strong and fresh as he had run past in chase.

Ferox had not cared for Cornelius Fuscus. In truth his feelings towards senior officials mattered very little in the great sweep of things and there were plenty in the emperor's service who seemed cruel, dishonest and half-witted, and often all of those things. It was still a shock to know that someone so highly placed was encouraging rebellion, presumably in the hope that the resulting chaos would discredit the emperor and help another to seize power. That must be the goal, not throwing off the rule of Rome, and he wondered whether the chieftains among the tribes understood this or were being used.

The Romans would win in the end. Even if the garrison of the province was defeated, more legions would come and in the end the Romans would crush all those who stood against them. Before the inevitable end there would be death and destruction, perhaps as bad as in the days of Boudicca, and the coldness with which the conspirators had spoken of this provoked a deep anger. It would have been useful to talk to the merchant, but he felt no regret about the man's death. He had served his purpose, and was badly injured, so his throat had been slit to prevent him talking. That was a small cruelty compared to what would happen if the conspirators raised their rebellion.

Fuscus had broken his oath to the princeps, that was clear, and at least that might make his service to Sulpicia Lepidina easier. If it was shown that the man was a traitor then killing him became a duty, not a crime. Ferox was less sure about the one who had arrived just as he was discovered. There had been no mistaking that shock of prematurely white hair, or the face that refused to lose its calm even when people were shouting about being seen and betrayed. Crispinus was there, no doubt about it, and would make a powerful ally. Two years ago Ferox had wondered whether the young aristocrat was part of another plot against Trajan and was still not sure that he was altogether innocent. Neratius Marcellus had once said that he was confident his nephew would always emerge on the winning side. Was he working for the governor now or making sure of his own future one way or another? His instincts told him that the legate was loyal to Trajan, but instinct was not always right and ambition stirred in many an unlikely heart.

A new smell reached him. Ferox had once tried to explain to Crispinus that Romans and Britons smelled different. The tribune had curled his lip as if dirt was so natural to barbarians that this should occasion no surprise. You could often tell a man's trade by his scent, and not just the obvious ones of tanners and butchers. There was also a different scent to a tribesman, or at least one who lived mostly in the old ways, a faint smell that was somehow earthy, even damp. Crispinus had claimed to be deeply offended when Ferox told him that many Romans were followed by a vague odour of olive oil, sour wine and onions. Even with his nose covered Ferox could tell that there was a Briton or Britons in the room and that seemed strange, for the conspirators' allies sounded like chieftains who lived in the Roman way these days.

A far more powerful stink overwhelmed everything else, and Ferox felt something warm and rough rubbing his chin, lifting the cloth slightly. He knew that smell and the scruffy dog that dwelt in its midst, even if he had never thought to meet them here. Suddenly the animal yelped and was jerked away, no doubt kicked by its master.

'Well, boy, will you thank me for keeping you alive this far?' Acco rarely shouted or even raised his voice, and yet when he spoke men fell silent around him. There was menace in his soft words, a barely veiled power that made warriors and kings blanch.

'Thank you,' Ferox said. 'For this far.'

'Good, at least your few wits have not been knocked out of you. Not yet. So tell me why I should let you live any longer?'

'Your dog likes me.'

Acco's laugh was more of a cackle, louder than anything he ever said. 'So who speaks to me this night? Is this the Roman centurion or the prince of the Silures? Do you even remember your own kin any more?'

'I remember.' It was hard to speak through the cloth bound around his face, for the dog had only shifted it a little. 'I remember my oath too.'

The druid spat, although Ferox did not feel any land on him. 'Oath to a Roman? Why should I care if one man or another wears the purple?' That meant that Acco knew about the conspiracy, must even have known what Ferox had been doing. It was not really a surprise. Acco always seemed to know everything and his understanding of Rome and the empire never dented his loathing for them. 'See how they plot and betray each other so readily. They are filth and pollution on our lands, and it is almost time to scour them away.

'Would you not wish to be part of it, to see your people strong again, the wolf folk, living free and fearing no one? You could lead them, boy. Your cousins are weak fools, so jealous of each other that they fawn on the Romans for the slightest favour. At least you are a true warrior, even in a bad cause. You could become Lord of the Hills, just like your grandfather, even now, even after all these years and all you have done.'

Ferox heard the scrape of a sword being drawn from its scabbard. A moment later the cold metal tip touched his arm and then his throat.

'This is a good sword you have.' Acco took the blade away and there was a thrumming as he dealt strokes to the air. 'The smith who forged it knew some of the old lore and not just the skills of Rome. How many have you slain with it?'

'Too many to count,' Ferox said. When young he had thought that he would always remember the men he faced and killed and feared their faces would haunt his dreams. Some did, but as the years passed most faded from memory. It was better that way, although he wondered whether part of his own soul died each time and followed them to the Otherworld.

'You are a true warrior.' It was a statement of truth and the druid did not seem to judge one way or the other. 'Killing is natural for you, even more than your kin and they are the wolf people. Do you know the story of this sword? It is a long one and took many lives before you saw it, let alone learned to wield it.'

'My grandfather took it from a Roman officer,' Ferox said. 'And gave it to me when I was not yet strong enough to hold it steady.'

'He did, and I was the one who told him to do it, though in truth he needed little urging for you were his favourite, more even than your father, the son he lost in his prime.'

Ferox flexed his legs, bending them at the knee, for they were starting to feel numb. Acco did nothing to stop him. 'I felt his hand often enough,' Ferox said after a while. 'And he was a stern lord and sterner still with me.'

'That is because he loved you. I remember your birth, seeing your mother's whole spirit spent as it gave life and power to you. I was the one who gave you your name, your true name, that I will not speak. Did you know that?'

'No.' A man's name was a sacred, secret key to his soul, hidden from all save the closest family. Ferox had never known his mother and was barely walking when his father fell in battle against the Romans. Acco had appeared at times while he was a child, like a harsh wind that blew for a few days and then vanished. The Lord of the Hills took guidance from the druid as he did from no other man – save, it was said, Caratacus in the old days.

'I know your name, boy, and it is not Flavius or Ferox, or even Comus as the boys called you. With your true name and a little of your blood I could make you do my bidding, but the cost would be high for your soul and I will not destroy you in that way. I see inside you, boy, I have always seen inside you and I know your destiny.' There was another swish as the sword slashed through the air. 'This sword was meant for you, but it was not made for you. The day we took it I spoke to that Roman before he died. He was a prisoner and a brave man, refusing to bow or beg for mercy as many of the others did. They knew the skill of your kin in inflicting pain and so did he, but it did not unman him. I really think he understood.

'That blade was forged by a smith from Avaricum, a man famous throughout the tribes of Gaul. Caesar's men had stormed the town, slaughtering everyone in their hatred, but a prefect of cavalry sought out the smith and ringed his forge with soldiers who were sober and still obeyed his will. The prefect was from Narbo, his mother of the Allobroges, and he knew of the sword-maker's renown. Amid the screams as a town died, he offered the smith protection at the price of making the finest sword he had ever made. So he worked, putting all his skill and essence into that blade, mouthing spells to make it strong, yet flexible, keen and yet light, and hammering at the iron to save his life and keep his daughter from violation.'

'Were you there?' Ferox asked flippantly, and received a violent kick in the stomach.

'When the task was done the town was in ruin and the smith wept because he knew that he would never again make anything so perfect, and he melted his hammer and other tools in the fire knowing that he would not wield them again. In the days that had passed his daughter and the tribune became lovers and married, and a year later she was made a Roman. Caesar was generous to his followers, and with that sword in his hand the prefect led charge after charge. At Alesia he slew two kings, and when Romans turned on Romans he cut down many of the famous men who dared to oppose Caesar. Later he went back to Gaul, became a great man in the new province, and his son and grandson each in turn buckled on the sword and served Augustus, Drusus, Tiberius, Germanicus and a host of lesser commanders, until the great-grandson came to Britannia. With this sword he slew your father on the shore, and it was not that day your kin caught him, but only after many stern fights.

'All this he told me, and for all that he was Roman the blood of Gaul still flowed in his veins. The others the wolf people killed, slowly as only they know how, but I took the tribune with me to Mona.'

'Did his blood flow there?' Ferox gasped as he was kicked again. How much of this was true? His father had died years after Suetonius Paulinus went to Mona.

'Fool. We talked a good deal on that journey, and he called me brother and willingly bowed for the knife by the end. There, between the two lakes where only a thin sapling grew where once there had been a hundred sacred oaks, I killed him as an offering to the gods. A quick death and one with meaning, and I have no doubt that one day he shall greet me again as brother in the Otherworld.'

Ferox heard another thrum as the blade cut through air and even though he could not see, he could sense the long tip was close to his face. 'Tell me, boy, do you deserve a quick death?'

'I no longer know what I deserve.'

Acco cackled. 'That is something, at least. This is a fine blade, a killing blade, and it does not care whose hand wields it. I am old, but have no doubt that I could drive this through your eye. It might need both hands and my weight behind it. Yet, for your grandfather's sake and yours, I should prefer to let you live. Will you join me? Become Comus instead of Ferox, a prince of the Silures and no mere centurion, and lead your people to freedom? I will help you at every stage, help you to find the true power within you and draw strength from your ancestors back to the first man.'

'Why do you want me?' Ferox expected another kick, but instead there was silence. He sensed the sword was withdrawn.

'For many reasons, and because it is your destiny. I read the signs when you were born and have never seen the like. Your story is a strange one, great and not great, true to your soul and not true, and you are fated to do something no one else could do. It came to me in a dream that night after you were born, a message from the gods as clear as any I have ever heard. It is your fate to kill me.' The cackle was louder this time. 'Who am I to question the will of the gods, strange though it may seem? I will fall by your hand – perhaps even by this very blade. So be it, that is the prophecy, but if my death is to have meaning I should die at the hand of one who is true to his blood, a leader of his people and not a lackey of Rome.'

Ferox lay there, unable to see or move his limbs, and unsure what to believe. He wondered whether to pretend to agree, in the hope of escape. Yet Acco would know the truth, of that he had no doubt. Perhaps if he spoke the truth about the prophecy then it would not end here. The dog returned, slobbering over his chin for a moment. Then it drew back, but he felt the warm, wet spray on his tunic as it urinated over his chest. It seemed to go on for a very long time before he heard the animal pant as it wandered away.

'Come, boy, what is your answer?'

'I have sworn an oath.'

Ferox was not quite sure whether or not he heard a sigh.

'So be it,' the old man said.

There were footsteps of two or three people and what smelled like a burning torch.

'It is done.' A woman spoke in Latin, with an odd accent he did not recognise.

'Good. Then give me the torch.' To Ferox's surprise it was Domitius who replied. Did the merchant know who Acco really was or fear him as he should? The man was a Gaul, but all the Gauls had been peaceful provinces for many years. He did not sound or look like anyone's fool, so perhaps there was profit for him in raising rebellion, or he was confident of controlling the druid so that all served the purpose of creating a new emperor. 'Did you have to kill anyone?'

'Two, and one more who will most likely die.'

'You should have finished him,' Domitius snapped. 'He may talk.'

The woman did not sound overawed. 'What can he say and what harm will it do now? We have brought what you wanted and have our payment.'

'Then go.' There was no warmth in the merchant's voice. 'If you are wise you will be on the ship and leave before dawn. In case he does talk and they are looking for you. Go. We will deal with this one.'

Footsteps departed and for a while there was only silence.

'I will leave your sword here on the floor,' Acco said. 'You may manage to reach it and cut your bonds or you may not.

Soon this place will be on fire. The timbers will burn slowly, but when the amphorae start to crack the oil inside them will…' The soft voice trailed off. Ferox heard the sword drop and knew it was not close.

'You have chosen your path, boy, and the gods will decide. Farewell.'

'What of your prophecy?' Ferox tried to inch across the floor.

'It was a dream,' the druid said. 'Dreams can be wrong.'

Ferox heard the dog whimper as it was kicked and the tread of the druid as he left, by the sound of it climbing down creaking wooden stairs. He tried rolling over and that moved him a little more until he was on his front. He shifted his shoulders to turn again, managed to do it, but it was awkward now that his hands were under him. Halfway through the next roll his knees hit something hard and solid. There was a box or barrel in the way. He caught the scent of smoke. Pushing hard failed to shift whatever was blocking his path. Ferox rolled back and then brought up his knees and shifted his weight to edge clear. It took a while, and then finally he rolled again and this time it worked. Then his head struck another crate.

It was getting warmer and through his blindfold he saw a faint glow. As he rolled again it grew stronger and he coughed because smoke was filling the room. Two more rolls and he felt a shape digging into his chest. It was the pommel of his sword. He rolled away, so that his tied hands were towards it, and then shifted his weight again and again to edge back towards it. He felt the wooden pommel, wriggled with his fingers, trying to get them around the grip. Instead the sword moved away from him. He tried again, ever more desperate because the glow of the fire was stronger and he could hear the flames roaring below. He felt the sword, but it skidded and banged as it fell down the stairs.

Someone else coughed and he froze, then realised the folly of that so shouted. 'Help! Up here!' More coughing, a hint of a shape against the orange glow of the flames and cold steel brushing his ankles and a weight on his feet. A boot was planted on him to hold the rope steady as it was cut. It seemed to take an age.

'Thank you,' he gasped, but the only response was more coughing. His legs were free at last and he tried to stand, but would not have managed if his rescuer had not helped lift him. 'My hands,' he begged. 'Please, cut the rope.' The smoke was worse now that he was standing, and although the cloth over his head was a shield he began to cough and could not stop.

A hand took his shoulder, turned him, so that he must have had his back to the stairs and gently pulled him backwards. He followed the lead, almost slipping on the first step, but thankfully they were wide. They were both coughing and the heat was like a furnace, bright even through the blindfold. If it reached the olive oil then all of this would be for nothing. Sparks fell on him, and then they were down. The hand turned him, it seemed to push him towards the heart of the fire, but he decided to trust and ran straight ahead. His boot hit a beam on the dirt floor, and that was lucky because something bigger crashed down just in front. He was shoved again, to the right this time and he ran and suddenly the air was colder and the smoke starting to thin.

'Thank you,' Ferox gasped, and was hit hard in the middle of the back with what felt like the pommel of his own sword. He staggered, struggling for breath, and sank down onto to his knees in the mud. Somehow he managed to stand and ran, pelting across an alley until he slammed into a wall. With a great roar the fire burst up through the roof of the warehouse behind him and a hot wave of air pushed him against the wall. There were shouts now and he ran towards them, until someone grabbed him by the arm.

'Watch yourself, sir.' He heard the clink of sword and decorated belt that surely meant a soldier. 'Been playing games, have we?' The cloth hood was yanked off his head and he saw a round, leathery face staring at him.

'Let me free. I am Flavius Ferox, centurion of II Augusta.'

'Well, I'm buggered,' the soldier said. 'Hear that, Celsus? This is the one we've just been ordered to arrest.'

XV

THE SUN ROSE as they led him through the streets, which were already filling up and noisy. They took him to the principia, and that was something because if they had been attached to the procurator's staff and under his orders then they would surely have held him at his offices. He did not think that any of the conspirators would have got a good enough glimpse to recognise him, but it was hard to be sure and he had seen Crispinus clearly and the tribune knew him well.

The older soldier was a speculator, a name that had once signified a scout or even a spy, but these days was just another title for a man who spent most of his time reading and writing reports as part of the governor's headquarters. Celsus was a legionary and young, a big fellow chosen for size rather than brains or experience. They were both kind enough, but firm, and had no explanation.

'No idea, sir. Orders came through in the fourth hour of the night. You were to be detained and taken under guard.'

'What if I refused?' They had cut the bonds on his wrists and life was slowly coming back to his arms.

The speculator tapped the hilt of his gladius. 'Best you come along, sir.'

Ferox did not have the strength to argue and let himself be led. Prince Arviragus rode past him, accompanied by two troopers and a heavily tanned warrior whose nose had been bent and flattened years before. The prince noticed Ferox enough to sneer.

'Should have seen that bugger fight,' the older soldier said after the riders had passed. 'The ugly one. They used to call him Brigantus in the arena. That was before the prince there bought him. Fastest man I've ever seen with a gladius.'

At the principia all was bustle, far more than was normal, and no one on duty had any idea why he was wanted or what to do with him. In the end, a beneficiarius had him locked in one of the side rooms. There was some light from a little window too small to climb through and a stool, so he sat and waited, or sometimes paced up and down and waited. Trumpets sounded the start of the second and third hours of the day and still no one came. Ferox was hungry, sore and so weary that he was tempted to lie on the cold floor and try to sleep.

At last the door opened. A legionary he did not know appeared. 'You are to come with us, sir.' Two others were waiting outside.

Ferox did as he was told and again there was no explanation. The soldiers led him out of the principia, which was worrying, until he realised that they were going to the praetorium. Even better was the sight of Vindex, Gannascus and the others, waiting near the entrance, fully equipped and standing by their horses.

'What's up?' the scout asked.

'I'm under arrest.' Ferox tried to sound cheerful.

'About time.' Vindex nodded to the legionaries. 'Chain him up, lads.'

There were more armed men than usual standing outside, and guards in the main corridors of the house. None of them saluted as he passed, but neither did they try to stop the escort leading him through. Even more to his surprise they went to the back of the house, which was residential rather than official, where even the corridors were finely painted and had mosaic floors. As they approached a door a slave appeared, his tunic of good quality and his manner suggesting that the legate trusted him with considerable authority. 'You're to go right in, sir,' he said. 'You will not be needed, soldiers.'

The legionary in charge stared at the slave for a while, just to show that he was only obeying because he chose to do so, and then led his men off.

'Ah, Ferox, my dear fellow, it seems we have both been in the wars.' Ovidius was propped up in bed, his face pale, almost grey, in the lamplight. The legate's own physician, an Alexandrian whose fame almost equalled his self-esteem, worked at a table mixing something in a bowl.

'The bastards stabbed him.' Ferox had not seen Crispinus sitting on a stool and working alongside a clerk at a table they had somehow crammed into the room.

'No need for vulgarity,' Ovidius said. He coughed and winced because the movement obviously caused him a lot of pain.

'They stuck a knife in you, old friend,' the tribune said softly. 'And murdered two of my uncle's slaves.'

'Did they?' Ovidius frowned with the effort of thought. 'Yes, of course they did. Bastards.'

Crispinus smiled, but his face betrayed his worry. It was the first time Ferox had seen the tribune with stubble on his chin and a tunic that look crumpled and dirty.

'And where the hell have you been?' Crispinus glared at the centurion. 'The legate wanted you last night and you were nowhere to be found.' The story came out quickly. A report had arrived of a large band of rebels or bandits threatening the roads near Verulamium and even the town itself. Neratius Marcellus had taken most of his mounted singulares, supplementing these picked men with any other horsemen who could be rounded up and issued supplies in a matter of hours, and ridden off to see what was going on. 'He wanted you with him, but no one could find you.'

After the legate had gone, someone had broken into the praetorium, getting in by prising open the shutters on one of the top windows. 'There's building going on behind the house, so we reckon they took a ladder from there. We do not know who they were or how many.'

'There were three,' Ovidius cut in. 'Two men and a woman.'

'Do not tire yourself,' the doctor said without looking up from his work. 'And do not put strain on those stitches. I refuse to let my patients die until I say so.'

Ovidius managed to laugh. 'This is important, good doctor, and soon I trust that your potion will give me blissful sleep.

'I was on my way to the legate's room. He had taken one of the documents I have found and I needed to check something. There were voices, a man and woman talking, though I could not catch the words. I called out, thinking it must be some of his household and not wanting to alarm them by appearing suddenly. Slaves can be nervous if you surprise them when they are doing something they should not, so it is always better to warn of your approach. Then the woman started screaming for help. I ran in…'

'Of course, our aged Hector.' Crispinus was grinning.

'Well, I ran in. Saw a man, his arm raised to strike a cowering woman, and I punched him. I'd forgotten I had a stylus in my hand and the point was sharp enough to draw blood. He yelped and jumped in the air, then another one came at me and as I turned to face him, I was struck in the side. The woman had stabbed me.' The old man sounded truly puzzled.

'What did they look like?' Ferox asked.

Ovidius shook his head. His skin seemed even paler apart from the dark rings around his eyes, but there was a proud defiance in his face. 'I do not really know. It was dark in there, and everything happened so fast. Their clothes were drab. The one I stabbed had a shaven head, the other dark hair. The woman was pretty, I think, quite tall and full figured.'

Crispinus smirked. 'You are not that old then.'

'What colour hair did she have?' Ferox asked.

'Dark, probably. I think so anyway. There was not much light, and it is hard to say. I am sorry, but what matters is that they stole the cloak. The chest was in that room, and they prised it open.'

'Was that all?'

'Yes. Well, apart from a scroll that was on the table. It was written by Prasto, but I believe would not be much use unless you already had a good understanding of this matter. But you know what this means?'

Ferox nodded. Someone close to the legate must have told the thieves what to take and where to find it. 'Acco is in Londinium.'

Crispinus gasped, and then recovered his poise almost immediately. 'Here. Are you sure?'

'He tried to burn me to death last night.'

'That sounds definite.' Ovidius laughed and it did not seem to cause him pain. 'Well, we are glad he failed in his attempt. Are we not, noble Crispinus?'

'Fairly glad.' The white haired young aristocrat was grinning broadly. If he had recognised Ferox at the warehouse then he was hiding it well.

'Quiet, all of you.' The doctor had come over to the bed and was holding a bowl. 'That is enough.'

'Not yet, doctor, I pray you.' Ovidius pushed himself to sit up a little more. 'This is important. The legate left orders for the centurion, but I must explain some of them.' He was struggling for breath, but waved the doctor back.

'We are to go to Mona,' Crispinus said. 'We will take your men and an escort of Batavians, but we must go within the hour. If Acco was in Londinium a few hours ago then we may have a chance to beat him there. The legate wants us to find the last of these treasures and keep them safe or destroy them. He has written our orders, and we are just making up the passes and letters instructing all garrisons to aid us.'

'I have made notes, some from memory.' Ovidius winced and closed his eyes The pain was obviously growing, but he struggled on. 'Prasto returned to the island when Agricola attacked. He describes an old shrine and I am sure he believed that items of the greatest value were buried or somehow hidden there. It is the best I can manage, I am afraid, but hopefully will guide you.' He was gasping for breath.

'That is enough.' The doctor was a small man, yet somehow managed to loom over the room. He crouched beside the old man and held a small bowl to his lips. 'Drink this. It will help.'

There was the sound of shouting from outside and the door was flung open. Crassus stood in the doorway, his face red. He saw the doctor and the injured man and sagged a little, but then noticed Ferox and the anger returned.

'This man is a murderer. He should be under guard until the trial and punishment can be arranged. Hercules' balls, why is he here and not in a cell?'

Ferox stiffened to attention. The young tribune stood up, and Crassus flinched slightly because he had not seen him in the corner of the room. 'Noble Crassus, it is good to see you.' The tribune smiled warmly. 'I shall personally ensure that the centurion is kept under close watch, but for the moment the legate has need of him, and so do I.'

'Neratius Marcellus is no longer here, and left before the crime was known. I am now senior, and thus in charge until the governor returns. I shall take full responsibility.' Ferox got the impression that Crassus did not much care for the younger man. 'He is to be locked in a cell and that is an end to it.'

'I have written orders, if you would care to read them, signed and sealed by my uncle. He requires Ferox for a special task, the importance of which overrides everything else – at least for the moment.'

'What task?'

'I am sure that in due course the governor will confide in his senior and trusted subordinates.'

'Not good enough. Not good enough at all, dear Crispinus. This is too delicate a matter for me to take a risk, surely you must see that. I have authority and I have made the decision.'

'Servilius.' Ovidius croaked the word. He had pushed himself up, glassy eyes fixed on Crassus. 'Servilius,' he said again.

Ferox was close enough to see Crassus blink several times. He had no idea who Servilius was, but the power of the name was obvious.

'The legate's orders are specific and in writing.' Crispinus was holding up the tablet. 'There are copies here so that there can be no doubt that you act according to his instructions.' He stepped closer. 'Come, obeying them is the prudent course. Time is pressing and the legate will not take kindly to needless delay.'

'Very well. But make sure this rogue does not escape.'

'You have my oath on that, my dear Crassus. Justice will be served.' There was a hard edge to the tribune's voice. Ferox still wondered how much he knew or suspected, and whose side the young aristocrat was really on. 'Let me call a couple of soldiers to watch this fellow while he returns to his quarters to collect a few things.'

'This is a risk, though,' Crassus said. 'A great risk.'

'And one the governor is taking, not us.'

'In my experience blame spreads a long way. I want it on record that I am against this course of action.'

'It shall be set down.' Crispinus turned to the clerk. 'See to it.'

Less than a hour later, they started to make their way through the streets on their way out of the town. Seventeen horsemen, most heavily armed, and led by the tribune in his polished cuirass and high plumed helmet, ought to have been sufficiently impressive to clear the path, but Londinium was Londinium and trade was trade, and the stall holders yelled and haggled, and there was no quick way through the crowds. Some people watched them with suspicion. The legate had left late at night, taking almost half the soldiers in the town with him, and there were rumours of war and rebellion. Another senior officer riding away was not encouraging, and it added to the nervousness all could feel. Even sadder was Gannascus' slave girl, who walked with them to the edge of the town, weeping and kissing the big warrior's boot and leg as he rode. Philo walked beside her, and he would take charge of her while they were away. Crispinus had been clear that the boy was not to go with them, for they would be riding hard into who knew what perils, and they could not take care of him. Ferox was glad that he had not had to give the order, and at least there had been time for the lad to shave him before they set out.

'Must be love.' Ferox rode with Crispinus at the head of the little column and the tribune was his usual talkative self. The sight of the slave girl following the big German amused him. 'And you say he won her at dice? I've only ever won money – and lost more often than I would like. Pretty thing, though, very pretty. Although you cannot beat a true lady.' They had turned a corner, and to his surprise he saw Sulpicia Lepidina and the two Claudias with their maids looking at material in one of the stalls, and discussing it in great detail. He had heard her say that the best buys were often found away from the expensive, fashionable shops near the basilica. 'Well,' the tribune continued, 'the old laws say a husband can beat his wife or a father his daughter, and there's one or two out there who'll let a man whip them and thrill to it, but you know what I mean.'

Claudia Enica noticed them, gave a broad smile and waved. The other two were a little more restrained, Sulpicia Lepidina favouring them with a simple nod. Achilles scampered out from behind the stall, a piece of red silk draped over his shoulder, and he must have made some tart comment because his mistress slapped him around the ear.

'Fine-looking woman, and of royal blood as well.' With all the hubbub of the crowd, Crispinus spoke without worrying that the ladies would hear. 'Much to my surprise I am rather taken with that red hair of hers. Striking, although one wonders whether it speaks of a fiery temper. Must be twenty, though, or even older. Needs a husband.' He smiled at Ferox, who was baffled until realisation set in and then he was simply aghast. 'No need to look like that. Probably missed the chance now.'

When they passed the ladies, Ferox had not recovered from so bizarre a suggestion. Crispinus made formal greeting, and he simply nodded and gave as much of a smile as he could muster. Enica stared up at him, head on one side almost in the same way as she examined goods on the stall. Claudia Severa wished them luck on their journey. Sulpicia Lepidina was stiff and formal, but then she was in public. Ferox could not stop himself from glancing back after they had passed. The others had returned to their shopping, but she was watching them and when she saw him turn mouthed, 'I'm sorry.'

'Do you think he will take her back home with him?' Crispinus interrupted his thoughts. After a last burst of sobbing, Philo had led the slave girl away.

'No idea.'

'Of course not, you never have an opinion on anything, do you, centurion? Eh? Well, you must have some thoughts on the task at hand.'

'Mona is a big place, my lord. I have not yet seen my lord Ovidius' discoveries, so cannot judge how easy it will be to find these things.'

'You really do not want to go there, do you?'

Ferox sighed. 'No.'

'Surely it is a place like any other.'

Ferox said nothing.

'Talkative as ever.' Crispinus lowered his voice. They were almost at the gate and a handful of bored auxiliaries stood guard. 'You will feel better when you have a sword at your side. Have to keep up appearances while we're here for the sake of that fool Crassus. Once we are properly clear we can forget about all this arrest nonsense.' Ferox was wearing his mail and helmet with its feathered, transverse crest, but under his cloak he had a belt bare of any weapons. His old felt hat was lost, and he knew that he would miss it as the journey went on. There was a borrowed sword on one of the four pack ponies they were taking with them. He had not hefted the weapon yet, but it was bound to be a poor thing after his own sword. He wondered whether that was melted inside the ashes of the warehouse or stolen by whoever it was who had led him out and then vanished.

'So can I go where I like once we are outside?'

'Ferox, you are a centurion under orders and will obey. The orders say you are going to Mona. After that, who knows, but there will be new orders and fresh tasks. From all I can see, we are going to be busy.'

'Perhaps you should have applied to return to Rome, my lord? Your service has already been long.'

'What, and miss your sparkling company?'

A trooper trotted forward, informed the sentry who they were and they were waved through. The gateway was built of stone, with two low towers, and joined onto the timber and earth ramparts surrounding the greater part of the town. It was not much of a defence, and Ferox hoped that it would never be tested. Outside were more houses and taverns, for the wall had been built thirty years ago and was now too small for the town. It was a good quarter of a mile before the buildings were replaced by gardens and graveyards. Mourners were shrieking and priests and priestesses of Isis wailing and swinging rattles as a woman's corpse was laid on a pyre.

'So who did I kill?'

'Curiosity at last. Most men arrested and charged with murder would have asked at least a few questions.'

'I'm under orders, my lord. I speak when I'm spoken to.' More priests joined in the noise, clashing cymbals. Ferox wondered whether the woman had been the one caught up in the attack on the temple. That was only a few days ago, even though it seemed like an age. A torch was put to the piled wood and the flames shot up from the oil in which the pyre was drenched. He shuddered. 'So who did I kill?'

Crispinus studied him for a while. The noise of the funeral rose to a crescendo and then stopped abruptly. 'You really do not know, do you?' he said in the sudden silence. The mourners sent up a great shriek and his horse stirred, its ears twisting back and head flicking up. He patted its neck. Ferox was riding a docile animal that did not seem to care.

'You still have not told me the answer, my lord. Last night I fought with men on a rooftop, and hurled them to their deaths without ever knowing their names. That does not sound like murder to me. Afterwards I was knocked unconscious, trussed up and held for who knows how long, threatened by Acco who set the place on fire with me in it. I'm still not sure who helped me out.'

Crispinus threw his head back to laugh. The horse, used to its rider's strange ways, did not flinch at all. 'Urban life really does not suit you, does it? My dear fellow, you have been busier even than I guessed. No lions this time? Pity.

'Cornelius Fuscus is dead. Ah, that does appear to startle you. I doubt that it is from fondness for the man. Indeed I am almost disappointed that you did not kill our procurator because I would most likely have shaken you by the hand in congratulation. A brute, if ever I met one, and I have good reason to suspect that he was plotting treason. However, as far as we can tell that was not why someone stabbed him to death sometime last night. That someone left your dagger in the man, and that battered old hat of yours on the floor. Now perhaps you have an idea why suspicion has fallen on you! Add to that you were seen arguing with the man shortly before, exchanging blows, and a letter found on him claimed to have evidence that would bring ruin to you, as well as other things. There was a lot of blood on it and it is not easy to read, especially after I put the papyrus in the fire.'

'Thank you, my lord.' There seemed little point in saying that Fuscus had hit him, but that he had not responded.

'You sound sincere. That makes a change. Better that it is gone, as it complicates matters. The whole thing smells wrong. You might murder a man if you had cause, but I'm reluctant to believe that I have friendship with a man so stupid as to leave incriminating evidence on the corpse.'

'Thank you again, my lord.'

'Flavius Ferox, I have lost count of the number of times I have urged you to trust me. I do not know what will happen in the long run. Unless Fuscus' treason can be proved then someone will have to pay for his death, and you will be too busy to find out who did it in the weeks to come. The man was a rogue, but he was the emperor's own man and if we were concerned about that freedman up at Vindolanda, this is a hundred times more serious. For the moment the news will be kept as secret, that is if Crassus can keep his mouth shut. A murdered procurator is not likely to spread calm when people are already frightened. The legate fears that the trouble in Verulamium is just the start. Still, he will deal with that and we play a different part. 'I have been thinking. If Acco knew where these treasures were hidden then would he not have retrieved them long ago?'

'Perhaps, perhaps not, if he did not need them until now. That is always assuming he does not already have them.'

'Cheerful and suspicious as ever.' Crispinus glanced back at the column and smiled. Faces turned expectantly. Apart from the odd building and a few travellers, they were alone. 'Let's not worry for the moment. The horses are warmed up. Let's give them a run and shake off the dust and crowds! Come on!' The tribune's horse leaped forward, hoofs pounding into a canter. Ferox and the others followed. Vindex whooped for sheer joy and the Batavians grunted their approval.

XVI

THE WEATHER WAS good for the first week, crisp in the mornings and overnight, and bright and clear in the daytime. They took the north-west road, following the same route as the legate and his cavalry, whose passage was marked by more piles of horse dung than was usual from trade. Before they caught up, Crispinus ordered them to leave the main road and follow farm tracks heading westwards over the rolling hills. It was a well-trodden route, the going good after a dry summer, and if the tribune wished to avoid the legate then that was his business.

They went quickly, sometimes riding, sometimes leading the horses, past tilled fields, cattle fat from summer grass, and plenty of farms, almost all the buildings rectangular and built in Roman style, whether of timber or stone. Large posts stood at the boundaries of clan lands and larger ones at the edge of tribal territory, each bearing a carved Latin inscription of ownership. This was good land, territory of the Atrebates, a people who had thrived as part of the province. It was hard to see any hint of brooding rebellion, and the farmers and their families were friendly, welcoming them with food and drink when they camped near their houses.

On the second day, Ferox saw the riders following them, mere spots in the distance, keeping more than a mile back, and sometimes all he saw was a little plume of dust from the hoofs. Yet they were always there, and the same was true the next day. By then Vindex had spotted them, and showed it by a quick glance at Ferox, who shook his head as a sign that he was to say nothing yet. Longinus must have noticed, for he hung back behind the column and stared for a long time, hand cupped over his one eye to shield it. Ferox doubted he saw anything, but it did not take great imagination to guess what they had been looking at. That night they were given shelter at a villa owned by a local chieftain, a man clearly eager to prove how Roman he was, and thrilled beyond measure to have a senator's son as his guest.

The morning brought thick fog, and if their host had not obliged them by acting as guide they might well have got lost, for it did not lift until noon. Ferox saw no sign of pursuers that day or the one after, and the fog returned for the next few days. More than once they got lost, even when guided by locals, and spent a lot of time travelling in circles, until they came to a river and followed it. The nights were damp now, and they were glad of their tents, and gladder still when they were offered shelter indoors. They had reached the lands of the Dobuni, the dreaming folk, who seemed part of the land itself. In the old days the Silures had often raided them, for the Dobuni were never renowned as warriors, although stubborn and brave enough, and the Lord of the Hills used to joke that they were his herd to do with as he wished. Some of them still dwelt in round houses, although the bigger farms and barns were after the Roman fashion. Carved figures, vaguely human in shape, stood as markers, and at times Ferox felt that he could have been in northern Gaul.

'We're not taking you home,' Crispinus announced. 'Not this time.' They were only a few days' ride from the borders of the Silures. Ferox was relieved. He was no longer sure that it was his home. There would certainly be no welcome for him, and he could expect only malice from his cousins, however much Acco had dismissed them. They had supplanted him and would never trust him because of it. Besides, it was surely better to keep the memories of childhood and not sour them by seeing places now.

Before they reached Corinium they went north, and the weather turned dull and cold, with a sharp wind. As they had gone further and further west the trees they passed had browner leaves, and now their horses' feet crunched through mounds of fallen leaves. Crispinus continued to avoid garrisons and towns, but had plenty of coin to buy provisions from the farms. Some of the locals were not keen, for people in these parts had less need of silver or bronze than elsewhere, but the presence of armed men and the obvious importance of the tribune usually tipped the balance. One of the ponies had gone lame, an injury that ought to heal well enough in time, and they bartered him for beer, bread and strips of salted beef.

The pursuers had caught up with them, for the trail was not a hard one to follow. They came a bit closer now, so that a few times Ferox glimpsed them. They were both hooded and cloaked, riding greys. Later in the day he saw a blur, much further away, like a shadow on the hills, though moving against the wind, of several dozen horsemen at least. Otherwise they mostly saw shepherds leading their flocks down from the high pastures, and drovers with herds, many of the animals destined for slaughter to feed the tribe through the winter months.

Drizzle grew stronger and turned into driving rain as they reached the lands of the Cornovii, and the bad weather persisted day after day. Some of the Batavians muttered when Crispinus told them that they were not stopping at Viroconium. Longinus' face was expressionless, although later that evening he followed Ferox when he left the camp and wandered down near the stream. Each man carried a *dolabra* and after making a suitable hole in the ground they lowered their trousers and squatted. Ferox smiled at the thought that it was just like being in a fort, until the sour memory of the filthy corpse at Vindolanda came to mind.

'You reckon he knows?' the one-eyed veteran asked.

The rain meant Ferox had not seen any of their pursuers for days, but he guessed what Longinus meant. 'Hasn't said anything, and you know how he talks. Maybe he's guessed?'

'So either he isn't surprised, isn't worried, or reckons he can keep ahead.'

'Aye, that's how I see it.'

'The ones behind are cavalry, no doubt about it.' Longinus sensed some surprise at his tone of certainty. 'I may only have one eye, but I can see straight. It's the way they move. Army or close enough. Not sure about the others. Our lad Arcanus isn't the brightest and not one to speak out of turn to a nobleman, but he's spotted them and bound to say something soon.' Arcanus was the *duplicarius* or 'double-pay' soldier in charge of the detachment of Batavians. He was neat, reasonably efficient and obligingly willing to obey any command. Other than that, he was not a man to be noticed in a crowd. From the start Ferox had wondered why they did not have a decurion in charge. Still, with the flap on and the legate charging off to Verulamium, there may not have been any available. That was the straightforward answer and he suspected it was wrong.

Longinus whistled softly, one of those army songs as old as the legions, and for a while this was the only sound. 'Reckon a couple of us could hang back and scrag them?' the veteran said at last.

'Reckon I could.'

'Are you going to?'

'I'm a prisoner. It's not up to me.' Ferox finished and picked up some of the leaves he had gathered.

'You didn't kill him, though, did you?'

Ferox said nothing.

'Little shit deserved it.' He glanced around to make sure they were alone. 'She told you about the trouble he was causing her. Did she say what he wanted?'

Ferox shrugged. 'Money, I guess.'

'Oh, that, yes, he did, but he wanted more.' The one eye was hard as flint. 'What else does a man want from a woman? He wanted to take it soon, but wanted to enjoy her fear and hate first.'

Ferox froze as he was fastening his belt. For a while he stared at nothing. His hands clenched until the knuckles went white. 'Wish I had killed him,' he said softly.

'Well, someone beat you to it. If he was trying it on with her there were probably others. That's the way I see it. One of them got to him. *Thetatus.*' Longinus drew a finger across his throat. Army clerks when they updated a unit's rolls marked the names of dead men with the letter theta. It was not long before soldiers turned that into a slang word for died.

They heard Crispinus calling for Ferox. 'Better go.'

'Aye.' Longinus grunted as he stood up and shook his head. 'I'm too old to be living like this. Maybe too old for living. What was it Caesar said, "I have lived long enough for either nature or glory"? These days I know how he felt.'

'Better than being dead.'

'Maybe. Sometimes it feels more like punishment.' The veteran grinned. 'If it is then I'd better commit some more crimes to make it worthwhile.'

'You could always start another rebellion.'

'Nah, done that before, my lad. No future in it.' He finished cleaning himself and hitched up his trousers. 'And by the sound of things they don't need me. Perhaps I'll just look for whichever god keeps raining on us and try and kill him.'

Crispinus shouted again, the voice a bit nearer. 'I'd better see what he wants,' Ferox said as he swilled his hands in the brook. The tribune appeared, trailing the duplicarius.

'Ah, there you are. Been looking for you. Carry on, trooper.' Longinus was holding his dolabra and still had filthy leaves in the other hand, so he gave the tribune a respectful nod. 'You too, Arcanus.' The duplicarius was lean for a Batavian, although far taller than the diminutive tribune. 'Back to camp and tell everyone we will set out two hours before dawn.'

'Sir.' There was great no enthusiasm in Arcanus' voice.

Longinus washed his hands and then sauntered back to camp.

'Cerialis thinks very highly of that man,' the tribune said once they were out of earshot. 'And we know he can fight, but

I do wonder whether he was the right choice for a journey like this. There's something about him that isn't right. Oh well, no matter.' Ferox doubted that the young aristocrat knew who the one-eyed trooper really was, although it was hard to be sure. 'The duplicarius strikes me as steady enough, and wholly lacking in imagination, so eminently suitable for the task at hand. But it does make me think that he may be right in his belief that we are being followed. That would not surprise me, and since you appear unmoved, I am guessing that he is right.'

Ferox told the tribune what he had seen.

'And it did not occur to you to say something, centurion?'

'Sir?'

'Never mind. You are not sure whether the pair of riders scout for the others?'

'Do you wish me to find out, my lord?'

Crispinus sniffed. 'Not yet. We shall hope to lose them in the mountains.'

'Mountains, my lord? I understood we were heading for Mediolanum and then Deva.'

'No longer. If Acco is on our trail then we must make haste. You shall find us a route through the mountains as straight as you can. It's only the third day after the Kalends of October, so we should not have much trouble with the weather. I have great faith in your skills as tracker and guide and we can seek help from the locals.'

'The Ordovices?' Ferox tried and failed to keep the contempt from his voice. 'They are not generous folk or trustworthy.'

Crispinus was dismissive. 'Agricola taught them a hard lesson and they have not made much trouble since then.

It is the fastest and most stealthy route. If we can reach Segontium before anyone knows where we are going then I'll be much happier.'

'I'm sure Acco will be pleased once he realises we are going this way.' Ferox hesitated for a moment before he added, 'My lord.'

'Captivity has made you even more surly, Flavius Ferox. My hope is that he will not realise until it is too late. While we might get help in a town or from Legio XX at Deva, we might get delays as well, and gossip. At the moment it is hard to know who to trust, so I shall rely on my own wits – and your skill and knowledge as well. This is my decision.'

'I'm sure that will be a great consolation if the Ordovices cut off our balls, my lord.'

For an instant Crispinus' eyes flashed with anger before the charming, impassive face of the politician reasserted itself. 'Carry on, centurion.'

'Sir.'

They turned north west, riding over hills and through valleys of thick woodland that at least gave some shelter from the driving rain. Late in the next day they passed one of the Cornovii's boundary markers. Half a mile on stood another post, carved with a fat body and round head and obviously, even abundantly, male.

Gannascus' booming laughter echoed around the dell.

'The symbol of the Ordovices,' Longinus said when the German finally stopped.

Ferox shook his head. 'They are a little people, braggards who lie about everything, break their oaths and are foul of habits and speech.'

'Sound a lot like much of the Senate,' Crispinus said happily, and ordered a halt. They camped next to the marker, and inevitably someone hung a helmet on the wooden phallus. Ferox insisted that they post four sentries, relieved every two hours, and ignored the groan as the order was conveyed. Up until now they had made do with just two, so that most of them had an undisturbed night at least every other day. Crispinus looked as if he was about to countermand the order and then nodded.

As if to show their blessing of the tribune's choice, the next day the sun rose bright and they made good progress towards the mountains. Longinus acted as guide.

'Spent two years here, back in the days of Frontinus and then with Agricola,' he explained. 'Hasn't changed much in twenty years.'

Crispinus frowned when the veteran made this announcement, but since asking why the man had not mentioned this before had invited an unhelpful response, he smiled broadly, clapping the old soldier on the back. 'Splendid.'

For a few days Ferox did not spot their pursuers. Now and again warriors stood on the high ground and watched them. They passed only one farm built in Roman fashion, and everyone else lived in round houses, small even by the standards of Ferox's region and the other lands to the north. As they climbed higher there were fewer farmsteads. Then Longinus began leading them along valley floors and there were more people living in these. Twice chieftains came to greet the strangers. Neither were important men, the first accompanied by four warriors, and the second by just two. Only the chieftains had swords, just one wore a battered bronze helmet and neither they nor their warriors wore any other armour. At Ferox's prompting, Crispinus presented each chief with a gift of one of the light javelins the Batavians carried in a long quiver suspended from the right rear horn of the saddle.

The tribune had been doubtful at first. 'If your fears are right, won't we need every weapon we can muster?'

'If my fears are right, my lord, it really won't matter.'

The gifts were accepted with grunted thanks, the closest the Ordovices ever came to cheering. Ferox hoped that he looked just like any other Roman centurion, for he had little doubt that the folk here would remember the Lord of the Hills and have no love for his kin. Even so he caught the chieftains staring at him closely and could not make up his mind whether they gave as much attention to the rest of the party. Gannascus was hard not to notice, for the Ordovices were small and slight, and although their hair was often fair or reddish it was usually smeared with mud to make it spiky or simply so filthy that it seemed the colour of the dark earth. They stared up at the tall Batavians, and were in awe of the German giant. Ferox noticed Cocceius watching the warriors with that mixture of fear and longing for battle so common in young soldiers. He hoped the boy's curiosity would not be satisfied, at least until they were through the mountains. For all his contempt for the Ordovices, he knew that they were fierce enough in their way, and could easily massacre a party as small as this.

There was a reminder the next day, when Longinus reined in as they came to a ford across the stream bubbling along the bottom of a valley. 'This is where the last of ala Indiana died,' he said, solemnly. 'There were nearly two hundred of them when they started, maybe ten miles that way.' He pointed in the direction they were heading towards high peaks on either side of an ever-narrowing vale. 'The prefect was hit in the face with a sling stone early on. The Gauls tried to carry him, and got him halfway here, but were losing horses and men every few paces. And if a man lost his horse, thetatus. Must have been thousands of warriors, nibbling away. They'd flee at each charge, but this is not cavalry country, and they always came back, throwing javelins, slinging stones, in some places just rolling boulders down from the heights. We found about twenty bodies on the far side of the stream. They were the ones who had kept together. None had horses by this time, and there had been fifty troopers when they started marching in an orb from that hillock over yonder. The rest of the Gauls didn't make it. Maybe they were too tired to go on, maybe the stream was too high with winter rain, but they stopped and they died here. We found the bodies a week later. These ones by the stream were the only ones the Ordovices hadn't mutilated. Even left them their heads and just stripped them naked and left them near enough where they had fallen.'

Crispinus curled his lip up at the corner. 'A cheerful story, and no doubt an inspirational reminder of discipline and loyalty.'

'Begging your pardon, my lord, it's a reminder of what happens when a bastard procurator gets too greedy and ramps up the levy from a tribe for no reason. He wasn't here, was he? Course he wasn't. Fat bugger was a hundred miles away in Deva, surrounded by walls and half a legion. Useless prick. Fine to order other poor sods to do the dirty work and die.' Ferox noticed that Longinus spoke more like an old sweat than usual and wondered whether he was determined the tribune should never guess at his past as an eques and prefect of auxilia, let alone as leader of the Batavian revolt.

Arcanus nodded. 'Procurators, I've shit 'em,' he muttered, and then realised that he was beside a senior officer. 'Sorry, sir, didn't mean anything.'

Crispinus smiled. 'Well, the past is the past. Agricola avenged them all – with your help, Longinus.'

'Aye, my lord. A lot of them died for what happened here. Some more of our lads too, to get it done. And all because one man got greedy.'

'They make a desolation and call it peace.' Crispinus intoned the words as if they were a quote, although it was not one Ferox recognised. 'The consularis Publius Cornelius Tacitus has lately written a book about his father-in-law.' Seeing Ferox's blank expression, the tribune explained. 'Agricola himself. You should keep a closer eye on the breeding arrangements of the senatorial class, you really should. Anyway he gives those words to Calgacus, commander of the Caledonii at Mons Graupius.'

'We killed a lot there as well,' Longinus said in a low voice.

'Indeed you did, most gallantly, and in loyal service to the empire.' Crispinus kept his tone flat. 'Well, let us hope we can get on for the moment without any more killing or making desolations.'

At noon the next day they reached the top of a high pass. It had taken hours to climb the slope, in the end leading the horses and ponies by hand and going single file, Ferox, Vindex and Longinus finding the best path. They rested and ate a little at the top. Ahead and behind the views were magnificent, a few clouds in the blue sky casting shadows over the grey and purple mountains. Down in the valley behind Ferox spotted two tiny white-grey dots. Some way behind, at the very edge of vision, he half saw, half sensed the bigger group.

XVII

THE BRIDGE GAVE way slowly, the rotting main beams breaking under the weight so that the rest sank down into the roaring torrent. It was roughly made, wide enough for one man or beast at a time, and spanned the high chasm over the stream, the waters brimming over from yesterday's storm. They had crossed slowly, a man at a time, each leading a horse, warily taking each step, unable to hear the creaking over the noise of the rushing water, but feeling every sag in the timbers underfoot.

Crispinus had gone first. 'All right for him,' Longinus had shouted into Vindex's ear, 'look how light he is.' The Batavians followed, one by one, and then Sepenestus. Gannascus hesitated, and no one could blame him. Sepenestus came back and offered to lead over the other man's mount. The giant shook his head, so the archer took a pony over instead. As soon as they were across Gannascus spat for luck and strode onto the bridge. The rest watched, at once horrified, fascinated and a little amused. Halfway across a piece of wood broke away and fell, and they waited for more, but it did not come, and then with half a dozen more steps the warrior reached the bank, his horse following. Some of the Batavians clashed their spears against their shields in approval, and the German shook his fist at the stream. The scout went next, got his horse over without trouble and then came back for the pony.

Vindex did not see any sign until the bridge began to collapse. The last pony reared and screamed, until the planks lurched down and it slid into the water.

'Let go!' Vindex screamed at the scout who was leading the animal. The man gaped, and must have wound the lead around his arm as he had tried to drag the skittish beast over the widely spaced planks of the little bridge. As the pony fell he was yanked down after it. Both disappeared into the foam. A couple of times Vindex glimpsed the head of man or beast as they were whisked away, slamming into boulders, until they vanished over the top of the waterfall a long bowshot away.

Ferox heard the shout and galloped down to the bank.

'Poor bugger,' Vindex said as he arrived. They were the only ones still on this side, Crispinus having ordered the centurion as next most senior officer to bring up the rear of the little column. He had also suggested that perhaps Ferox might disguise their tracks, in the hope of throwing off pursuit. There had been little point in explaining the impossibility of hiding the passage of so many heavy riders across spongy soil thoroughly soaked in the storm.

'Can you hear me?' The tribune had cupped his hands around his mouth and was yelling across the chasm.

Ferox raised his thumb and shouted that he could.

'Longinus thinks there should be another way across about three miles to the south, and maybe twice that to the north! You know where we are going! Catch up when you can! Understand?'

Ferox raised his thumb again.

'Simple as that.' Vindex spoke loudly and Ferox was beside him, but still strained to hear. 'Humped again.'

They headed south. The land dropped sharply, making it a difficult route, so they led their horses down little paths clinging to the mountainside or along rocky defiles. It drizzled, making the ground even more slippery, and they went slowly. If one of the animals fell and broke a leg then they would be in even more trouble.

After three hours they had gone less than a mile from the bridge as the raven flew. They kept close to the stream, not in any hope of finding the scout alive; at best they would see his corpse and Vindex could say words over it. It might be a small comfort to the man's wife and parents. They found a path above a thirty-foot fall. It got ever steeper as it led down until it reached the narrow gap between two bluffs. There were piles of sheep droppings in the little track winding along, all hard so weeks old at least, and once Ferox saw the print of a boot that was more recent, although at least a few days old. People came here, even if it was hard to know why.

'That's that, then,' Vindex said as they stared at the fallen rocks blocking the defile. There was no way around. 'Looks fresh.'

'Probably yesterday. Oh well, back we go.' It took even longer retracing their steps, for they were getting tired, and they were halfway back to where they had started by the time they stopped and rested. This was also the first good path heading away from the ravine once crossed by the broken bridge.

'Come on.' It was Vindex who urged them to move, for Ferox was enjoying the freedom of being away from the others. Still, there was another hour or two before this gloomy day would turn to night and he knew they must go. So far the Ordovices had been wary of seventeen well-armed Roman cavalry. They might not prove so cautious when it came to two riders on their own, although the pair on the greys seemed to have got away with it. By now those two could be at the bridge, perhaps even starting to follow them south.

He got up. 'Follow me then.' Both men wore mail and Vindex wore his old-fashioned helmet. Ferox left his crested helmet tied to the back of his saddle and in spite of the drizzle he kept his hood down to see and hear better. The sword at his side was a regulation gladius, slimmer and with a shorter point than his own lost blade. It would serve, although as he tapped the oval pommel he once again missed the feel of his own weapon. He had given up wondering how much of what Acco had said was nonsense, but the druid was right in one thing. It was a true killer's sword, and lucky with it. Vindex had a spear light enough to throw if he needed and a small round shield, the dark blue paint on it so faded it looked black and the white figure of a galloping horse only visible if you stared hard. The locals would think them well worth killing to steal such equipment, apart from wanton malice.

Ferox led his horse and did not hurry as they followed the path away from the stream. After half an hour they came across another shepherd's track, looping as it went up a hard rocky slope. He took them up it, the horses needing to be coaxed and threatened. The top of the hill was long and low, with outcrops of dark rock at either end, and he remembered looking up at it from the far side as they had climbed towards the bridge that morning. On the far side the valley was shallower.

Vindex muttered curses all the way up, and when they were near the top Ferox raised his hand to halt.

'Wait,' he said, handing the other man the reins of his horse. The centurion went up on foot, moving carefully and crouching as he got nearer. As he went he imagined warriors squatting among the rocks, hefting javelins, waiting for the fool to come close so they could spit him with ease. He was almost at the crest now, and flinched when a black shape leaped out into the air. Wings flapped and a harsh voice called as the raven brushed against his hair. Ferox was breathing hard with more than the exertion of the climb. The Morrigan's bird was here, watching the world with its black, beady eyes, and in his heart he knew that warriors would soon spill their blood.

No tribesmen waited for him at the top, but they had been here, not long ago at all, at least three of them from the prints. Perhaps they had watched as the Romans rode past early that day, and then sometime later they had jogged off towards the bridge. Ferox kept low and went to the far end of the hilltop, where the land sloped down and even on this gloomy day you could see for a couple of miles. There was no sign of the main body of cavalry, and even from up here he would have seen their tracks in the valley below if they had already passed.

Ferox went back to help Vindex with the horses. 'A few warriors were up there,' he explained. 'They've gone now, but could be they are following those boys riding the grey horses. I've a mind to take a look.'

'Just look?'

'We'll see.' The raven circled above them and gave another cry. Vindex grimaced.

They crossed down into the valley. Ferox did not want to risk leaving the horses, at least not yet, and they could not be led along the top of the crest. Down on the main path the prints of two small horses were clear and fresh, overlying the marks of Crispinus and the rest of them.

'So by now they're at the bridge,' Vindex said. 'Can't go on, but how about they follow the two idiots who went south, and the Ordovices follow them, and then we come up behind. Do you see we might end up going in circles for days!' There was no response. 'Well, it will keep us all amused.'

The thin rain stopped and there was a glimpse of the sun as it came under the clouds, bathing the mountains in warm light and setting the sky afire in reds and pinks. Ferox tried to picture the land ahead and work out what each group was most likely to do.

'Do you remember that hollow not far from the bridge?'

Vindex sucked on his long teeth for a moment. 'Aye, rock behind you, a few in front to give shelter from the wind, and space for the horses behind those bushes. Decent campsite, only the tribune wanted to push on. Bit big for two, though, if that's what you're thinking. Anyone could get above you with a couple of men. You'd be easy meat for a man with a good eye and a handful of javelins. And with a few friends to box you in from the front. Thetatus.' Vindex had heard Longinus and liked the sound of the word. 'These two have been smart enough to follow and stay alive so far. Why should they turn dumb now?'

'Only a thought. Hold a minute.' Ferox stared at the ground until he was sure. 'Five of them or maybe six. All

Ordovices.' He could tell that from the shape of their boot prints. 'Came down from up there and crossed the path.' He followed for a few paces. 'Two went on up the far side. The other three, no, I'm right, four, kept going along the path. An hour ago, give or take. Come on, hurry.' He swung up into the saddle and prodded the horse into a trot.

'Oh bugger,' Vindex moaned, and then vaulted onto his bay and followed.

The path wound around a corner and for a good half-mile the slope rose gently and, weary or not, the horses surged up it joyfully. After that it became more difficult and they slowed back to a walk. Ferox patted the neck of his gelding. He had never seen the animal until they left Londinium, and had only grown fond of it on the journey. A little further on and he needed only a slight tug on the reins to halt. He gave it another pat.

'We leave them here,' he said. 'Hobble them and hope for the best.'

'Trust to luck? On a day a bridge fell down in front of us.'

'Well, how can it get worse after that?'

Vindex undid the chin strap of his helmet and pushed his fingers over his face to rub his eyes. 'Dying springs to mind.'

'Acco tells me I'm destined to kill him,' Ferox said. It was the first time he had told anyone else and oddly enough speaking the words made it all seem possible. 'Haven't done that yet, so I'm all right.'

'Oh, thank you very much.' Vindex lifted off the helmet and shook his long hair, then carefully donned the helmet again. 'Truly?'

'That is what he said.'

Vindex whistled. 'Could be a weight on a man's soul, something like that. Even with what he is and what he's done. Might bring a whole storm of bad luck.'

Ferox laughed. 'Or it might explain why my life has been like this up to now!' He remembered Longinus saying something about needing to do the deeds to earn the punishments he'd suffered. Something else was fighting for attention in his thoughts, but there was not time now. 'You know you don't have to come.'

'One day, I won't, you old bastard.'

'Dumb after all,' Vindex whispered.

Ferox put his fingers to his lips. Sound carried so easily at night, which was why the Silures were schooled from childhood to cherish silence. Use the quiet, use the darkness, they were taught, and wait, wait, wait for the right moment. Yet he had to admit that the two riders had been most unwise. They were in the hollow just as he had thought they might be. That much was obvious, even in the darkness, for they had lit a fire, and their two pale horses cast flickering shadows against the rocks of the cliff. Neither of the men was on guard, and he could plainly see all of one dark shape asleep by the warmth of the fire and glimpse the end of the other. At this distance he could not see whether it was the head or the feet.

Their two pursuers were either very foolish or this was a trap, although probably not for them. Ferox had led them up the slopes on the opposite side of the valley, and then close to the chasm, going slowly and often stopping to listen. The thick cloud meant that it was a dark night, but after a while his eyes became used to it. Vindex sounded like a cavalry charge following behind, even though he knew the scout moved stealthily enough. It was just that he was not a Silure. For a while they were so close to the stream that its unceasing roar covered any noise they could make. Once near the posts where the bridge had stood, it was easy enough, keeping the track on their right and crouching, then crawling pace by slow pace over the folds in the ground. It led them to a couple of boulders where they rested and watched. He could sense Vindex getting restless as at least an hour passed and nothing happened.

Ferox tapped the scout on the shoulder and pointed up to the bluff above the camp. The firelight was dying down with no one awake to feed it, and its light did not reach so high. Even so, the crest was darker than the sky, and he had spotted a shape moving on top. Vindex shifted slightly, nodding to show that he had seen, and then Ferox pointed again, this time at a less clear figure near the other one. He started to scan the ground in front of the camp, and happened to be staring at the spot just as a warrior stood up. The man had a spear and shield, the weapon held up ready to throw or thrust. Again Ferox tapped the scout and pointed, wondering why it was that his friend needed help to spot things in the dark. Another of the Ordovices rose from the tussocky grass, to the right of the first man, no more than twenty paces from the camp. Ferox looked to the left and one, then a second man appeared, all armed like the first. Spear points glinted faintly red in the firelight. Without a sound the four warriors started walking forward, closing in on the sleepers.

Vindex moved to get up, but Ferox pressed his hand on the scout's shoulder to wait. Another dark shape appeared, indistinct in the shadows because it was between them and the warrior on the far left. Ferox smiled.

A javelin flickered as it was thrown down from the bluffs and struck the fire, scattering sparks high. The four warriors yelled and dashed forward, but neither of the sleeping forms stirred. Behind them, the fifth, darkest figure strode silently after them, but none turned to see it. Before they reached the camp another missile came from above, driving into one of the sleeping shapes.

Run now, Ferox thought, but knew they would not and he tapped Vindex. 'Come on,' he whispered, and stood, drawing his sword. The Ordovices were in the camp, jabbing with their spears and then one shouted, yanking back the blankets and then tipping up the log they concealed. One of the men on the bluffs screamed and fell, limbs thrashing like a speared fish and the shaft sticking out of his back. The four warriors in the camp yelped and scattered to avoid him.

The dark figure behind them threw off his dark hooded cloak and in the same gesture raised a sword in one hand and a curved blade in the other. The steel gleamed, as did the polished helmet he wore. He started to run. There were shouts from the top of the cliff.

Then the man in the helmet shrieked an unearthly cry, high-pitched and appallingly loud even over the distant roaring of the water. Ferox drew his sword as he ran and heard Vindex tramping across the grass beside him. He had explained the plan at length. Deal with the Ordovices first, then try to get at least one of their pursuers alive and find out who they were. 'So whose side are we on?' the scout had asked.

'Our own, of course. Don't kill either of them unless we have to. Not until we know why they have followed.'

The warriors spun as the awful shriek echoed around the dell, but the man in the helmet was fast and the nearest one seemed frozen with surprise. He feebly thrust out his spear as the man came at him. The curved blade hooked the spearshaft aside, the man spun with the motion and drove the gladius in his right hand into the warrior's throat. Thetatus, as Longinus and now Vindex would say. The man in the helmet spun again, moving fast with the grace of a dancer and dodging the enemy's attacks, even though he was now in the middle of the three of them, no longer shrieking as he faced each in turn. His face shone, and Ferox realised that he wore a cavalry helmet with a face mask. Apart from the helmet he had no armour and wore a short tunic, his bare arms and legs pale.

Ferox went to the left, Vindex to the right, and one of the tribesmen must have seen them because he shouted a warning. Two of the men turned to face them, leaving the other to fight the man in the helmet, who jumped nimbly back, avoiding a spearshaft swung like a club. A cry of pure fear came from up above and Ferox saw two men falling, locked together, one with his arms around the other's neck. They slammed into the fire itself, flinging burning branches as well as sparks. The man in the helmet was closest and stumbled back, only just managing to block a savage swing from the spear at the price of losing his curved *sica*, which clattered against the cliff face. He grabbed his other wrist to add strength to the gladius. Then Ferox realised that he was a she, wearing high Thracian boots just like the woman in the arena.

The shock nearly cost him dear as a warrior stamped forward and jabbed with his spear. Ferox had no shield, something he kept meaning to acquire, and leaped back, but slipped and fell. Vindex was busy with his opponent, and before he could get up the spear point thrust again, and he rolled to dodge it, losing grip of his sword. He rolled again, pushed with both hands and bounded up, but the warrior was standing over the lost sword, teeth bared in a grin. Ferox ripped off the brooch holding his cloak and swung the garment, the wool heavy from all the rain. The warrior kept his distance, watching and waiting for the right moment.

The warrior facing the gladiatrix threw his spear. She batted it away with her sword, and it struck sparks off the rock behind her, but the man had flung himself at her and with a clang and a weird, distorted cry, she was driven against the cliff. She pounded the top of his skull with the pommel on her gladius, striking again and again and drawing blood, and yet still he clung to her, trying to wrestle her to the ground. Ferox swung the cloak again, snapping it with the motion, and hoped the man facing him would throw his spear for that might give him a chance. Instead the next time he swung the cloak the man tried to catch it on his shield and pull it away.

Vindex drove his spear through his opponent's stomach. At the same time the one struggling with the woman succumbed to repeated blows to the head and collapsed, one hand still gripping her tunic which tore away as he fell, exposing her breasts.

'Bugger me!' Vindex's amazement was clear, but not enough to distract Ferox's opponent, who lost his shield in the process, but plucked the cloak free from the Roman's grip. The man grimaced again and thrust. Ferox grabbed the shaft, but his fingers slipped over the damp wood and came loose. Vindex was transfixed, and it was the woman who moved first, running as lightly as at the start of the fight, even with the front of her tunic hanging down over her belt. The warrior realised she was coming, must have been surprised when he turned his head and saw a silver mask and bare breasts, and Ferox grabbed his spear firmly this time. A moment later, the woman stabbed the long point of her gladius into the man's eye. She twisted the blade, slipping it free as the warrior dropped forward onto his knees, and then she danced back a few places, glancing down at the two men who had landed in the fire. They were both obviously dead.

Ferox still had hold of the spear and spun it around so that the point was towards her. Vindex, breaking free of his happy stupor, drew his sword.

'I don't want to kill you.' The woman's voice was distorted by the small mouthpiece in the mask. She spoke in the language of the tribes.

'That's nice,' Vindex said. 'Can we be friends?'

'Why are you following us?' Ferox asked. 'What do you want?'

'To help.' She stood, balanced perfectly on the balls of her feet, ready to take her sword against either of them. 'I could have managed all four if you hadn't shown up.' It was hard to tell her tone because of the mask, but she sounded matter-of-fact. Ferox saw a small darker mark on the skin between her breasts.

'All four?' Vindex asked mockingly.

'They were only men.' She was slim, fairly tall and had dark hair tied in a ponytail hanging down from the back of her helmet. It swung every time she switched her guard to face the other man.

'Did the Mother send you?' Ferox asked. He had seen that mark before, just this summer, a little scar between the breasts, a sign that a woman was one of the initiates of a cult of fighters who lived far away on a tiny island off the Caledonian coast. Boys and young women from Hibernia and the northern tribes went there for three years or more to be taught by the Mother, a woman who had been a skilled warrior, but was now sworn not to kill or to lie with a man and instead devoted her life to training her charges. A few months ago he had seen one Mother killed and another take her place.

'No.'

'That's my sword.' Ferox had just realised that she was carrying his gladius.

The woman swung the blade so that it hummed through the air. 'It's a good one,' the oddly muffled voice conceded.

Ferox lowered his spear, though not so much that he could not easily bring it up to parry or attack. 'Take off your helmet and tell us your name.'

'No.'

'Come on, love.' Vindex gave the leering smile that was his only smile. 'Let us see you. Judging from your tits you must be a rare beauty.'

The woman used her left hand to snatch up the torn front of her tunic.

'Pity,' Vindex said.

There was an odd noise. Ferox wondered whether she had tried to spit in contempt, forgetting that she was wearing the mask.

'Drop the sword,' he said. 'Let's talk.'

'Yes, come on, love. There's two of us and one of you. The odds aren't good.'

'Do you want me to wait for another ten to join you?'

Vindex snorted with laughter. 'I like her. But look, lass, we did just save your life.' He took a pace closer. The woman darted forward, thrusting the sword so that the point was at eye level. Vindex jumped back, tripping over the corpse of the man he had killed and sprawling onto his back. 'Bugger!' he gasped as he landed. The woman turned back, sword facing Ferox.

'I have saved your life twice, centurion. So we are still not even.'

'You saved me from the fire,' he said, and it all seemed so obvious now. 'And stole my sword. That's once.'

'In the amphitheatre. I threw the spear down to you.' She had switched to Latin, the words fluent and vaguely familiar, although it was hard to be sure.

'I thought you threw it at me.'

'If I had, we would not be having this conversation. You offer a big mark. I would not need to be Camilla to strike you at that distance. Your frame is a large one.' The words were precise, well chosen and correct, so that the mention of the Volscian warrior maid from the *Aeneid* sounded entirely natural.

'Fat arse,' Vindex said softly, and started to laugh.

'Show some respect,' Ferox said, and thrust his spear into the ground. He raised his hands to show that they were empty. 'This lass might well be your next high queen.'

'*Salve*, Flavius Ferox.' She reached up with her left hand, letting the front of her tunic flap down.

'Lovely,' Vindex said.

She fumbled with the straps to undo one side of the face mask, the first time any motion had been clumsy, but it was a hard thing to do one handed. Persisting, it came loose and the chin strap followed. There was more of her usual grace as she plucked mask and helmet off with one motion and let it fall onto the grass. Claudia Enica smiled. 'You have taken a while to work that one out.' Hand now free, she covered her chest again with her torn tunic. She took a step towards him, until the tip of her sword pressed lightly against his mail shirt. He did not move back. 'You really did. You were almost a disappointment, Flavius Ferox, after all that I had heard. And would not that be terrible, disappointing a lady. Of course it would.' Her voice changed, and even in the firelight so did her face, and it was easy to imagine the ornate hairstyle and heavy makeup of Claudia, the Brigantian princess raised as a Roman noblewoman.

'Oh shit,' Vindex said, the truth sinking in and no doubt remembering what he had just said.

'Why are you here, lady?' Ferox used one arm to nudge the sword away from his stomach. 'What is it you want?'

'Blunt as ever.' Her voice took on a harsher air and she switched back to the language of the tribes. 'And still slow to catch up. Try not to disappoint me again after all the trouble I have gone to. Well, among other things, I am trying to stop a war.' She stepped closer, staring up at him challengingly. 'Is that enough for the moment?'

Vindex sat up and sucked in his breath. 'Sounds like we're hum…' He stopped, remembering whose presence he was in. '*Omnes ad stercus*,' he said instead. 'I mean,' he spluttered, realising that the lady spoke Latin. 'I mean to say, that is… We are at your service, my lady.' He stood and bowed. 'My sword is yours, my life at your service.' It was an old oath among the Brigantes and their neighbours.

'Thank you, Carvetian. Your service is accepted.' She did not turn and kept her eyes staring straight at Ferox. 'And I suspect you are right. We probably are humped.'

Vindex laughed so much he had to sit down again.

XVIII

ENICA RODE WELL.
'She's Brigantian,' Vindex said, as if that should be clear to anyone. 'Of the royal house, granddaughter of Cartimandua and Venutius – of course she can ride. Bet she can drive a chariot too. They say Cartimandua was better than any man, rivalling the heroes of legend. The women of that line are special.' Ferox had never heard his friend speak in such admiring tones of anything, let alone anyone.

She did not dress for the journey like a Brigantian or a Roman. After sending Vindex to fetch their horses and telling Ferox to drag the body of her servant out of the fire and carry him to the chasm, she had vanished behind the rocks. When she joined him by the river she was wearing baggy trousers and a long-sleeved tunic, with another short-sleeved one over the top. She had kept her felt boots, and girded the tunics with a wide leather belt.

'I suppose you had better have this back,' she said as she handed him his sword in its scabbard. She had the sica on her left hip and a plainer gladius on the right.

'Thank you.' If she had the blade, then she must either have been in the warehouse and led him out or known who did. Ferox nodded at the corpse. He had rolled the man up in a blanket, leaving only his face exposed. 'I have seen him before.' It was the scarred man who had brought the first message that night he had been ambushed in the amphitheatre.

'I know.'

'We should talk.'

'Later.' Enica put two fingers to her lips and kissed them, then leaned over and pressed them to the dead man's forehead. 'Give him to the river. It is the best we can do.'

Ferox obeyed, lifting the body and walking over to the brink of the chasm. He let the man fall, saw him vanish into the foam, and part of him half expected the woman to step up behind and push him over as well. When he turned he saw that she was already on her way back to the camp. As soon as Vindex returned with their mounts, they set out, riding north for an hour before they made a cold camp. They left the Ordovices to lie and hoped no others would appear seeking revenge. Before dawn they woke and set out once more.

Enica dressed like a Parthian and rode like one as well, her grey seeming to respond to her merest thought without need for any gesture. At times she did not even hold the reins, merely looping them round one of the pommels on her saddle. Before she swathed herself in a hooded cloak the next morning, Ferox saw that her trousers were russet, her tunics a pale blue, and all of them from silk.

'Any fool can be uncomfortable,' Enica told him, noticing his surprise. 'Lice don't seem to like it, which means it's also the best way to keep free of them.' Ferox wondered whether that was true. Vermin were simply a fact of life. You could cull them now and again, smoke them out if you did not mind your clothes reeking of charcoal for a month, but only really be free of them if you lived close to a good bath-house, used it often, and changed every day. Otherwise, lice were like the weather, sometimes a torment but usually bearable.

'It makes you conspicuous,' he said. He guessed that with the silks, the princely grey horses, the young woman was probably wandering around with the equivalent of a hundred years' pay for a legionary.

She gestured with her hand, splaying the fingers like a fan as she passed by her face. 'I am conspicuous.'

'That you are, lady,' Vindex said admiringly.

She smiled at him. 'The Carvetii are a courteous folk. Sadly, the Silures mistake silence for wit.'

The tracks to the north were hard to find, and they got lost more than once or came to a dead end beyond which the horses could not pass. At first they said little, although Vindex sang softly for much of the way. He did not have a pleasant voice, but he sang stories of the old days, of the proud kings and magical queens of the Brigantes, of feasts and rivalries, contests and battles. Enica smiled at him often. Now and again she caught Ferox's eye and then she would screw her face up in a scowl, mocking him.

Twice Ferox saw a warrior up on the peaks above them, squatting beside a boulder, watching as they passed. He was not sure, but thought that it was the same man each time, and a nimble man on foot could easily have kept pace along the heights, given how slow and winding were the paths they took. At noon they reached a bridge, much like the other one, save that it had been deliberately broken. There were tracks of around thirty or forty horses; the mud was too churned up to be more precise. The horses were heavily laden and all much the same size, and the prints left by the men who had dismounted showed hobnailed *caligae*. Cavalry had come here, crossed over and then ripped up the planks, piling them neatly on the far bank.

'I'm guessing you are not with them,' Ferox said.

'I am with you, centurion, hadn't you noticed?'

Ferox ignored Vindex's chuckle. 'Then who are they? They cannot have been far behind you all this time.'

'Is it my fault if men follow me?' The voice was pure Claudia, in spite of the Parthian rig and swords at her belt. She sighed. 'You can be rather dull, do you know that? I had always understood the Silures could look at tracks and tell you what colour eyes the wife of the rider's cousin has. No? Pity.

'They are Brigantes, since your art fails you so lamentably. Men from the royal ala, and led by my brother.'

'And what does he want?' An arched eyebrow prompted him to add, 'My lady.'

'At last, a tiny piece of courtesy. Maybe there is hope for you after all, Flavius Ferox. My brother does not want what I want. He never really has, since the days when I followed him around and his pride took daily insults because his little sister was better than him at everything.'

'Apart perhaps from modesty?'

'That is merely a fancy way of telling lies. Why should I deny the truth? I thought that at least was something Silures understood?'

'You need to tell me what is going on, my lady.'

'Do I?' She gave him a coy look. 'Do I really? Perhaps later.'

'I could make you,' he said, growing tired.

'You could try.' She walked her horse away from the river. 'Had not we better move on? As we climb nearer the source of the stream there is bound to be a spot narrow enough to cross. Come along.'

'I am not your whisperer, lady.'

'Indeed not, Achilles can be amusing. He is also one of the finest bookkeepers in all the lands. Vindex?'

'Yes, lady.'

'If this fellow insults me again, will you be kind enough to kill him?'

The scout gave a broad grin. 'Happily, lady.'

'If he is a only little rude, just chop something off.'

'Happy to oblige.' He rode after Claudia Enica. Ferox stayed where he was, and after a moment Vindex turned back and leered. 'You don't have to come.'

Soon they were leading the animals more often than riding. Claudia Enica kept pace and showed no sign of being more tired than either of the men. They kept climbing and eventually reached a wide plateau. The stream was smaller there, chuckling along at the bottom of a gully. After a search they found a spot where it was only a few yards across, and the banks looked firm on either side. Vindex insisted on going first, and whispered in his horse's ears before he put her at the jump. The mare sailed over, landing well. Before Ferox could offer to help, Enica took both her greys over at the same time, riding one and leading the other on a long rein. They were superb animals, smaller than Frost and Snow, a pair of matched greys given to Ferox by King Tincommius, but alike in many ways. He wished he had either of those mounts with him now, but one was lost and the other still recovering from a wound.

Ferox came last, and his gelding was not keen at all. Twice it refused, and he had to slap it hard on the rump several times. First it bucked, then it shot forward and bounded over the gap so suddenly that he almost lost his seat. The others watched with amusement.

The afternoon wore on as they began to follow the stream and go down to where they could hope to find a better path. As the sun started to set, Vindex cantered ahead to look for somewhere to camp for the night.

'I suppose you expect to share my food,' Enica said as she watched him vanish into a dell.

'We have some.' In truth they had little left, for most of the provisions were on the pack animals with the main party – or scattered in the chasm and down the flowing stream in the case of the lost pony. 'And are used to going without. I am sure you are too. The Mother teaches hard lessons to her sons and daughters.'

'She does.'

'When I met Claudia Enica in Londinium I would never have imagined you now, or fighting with those warriors. She – well, you – seemed so…' He sought for the right word, sensing that all the time she was testing him and that so far he had not done well.

'Soft,' she said. 'Weak and silly.'

'No.' In truth that was just what he had thought. 'But precious, like a glass vase. Beautiful and perfect, and so fragile that it must ever be wrapped in silk and kept safe.' He felt he was getting it right. 'I fought alongside the sons and daughters not long ago. The sons were not far into their training. The daughters were good, although not as good as you. You reminded me of the Mother.'

'You were with her when she died.'

How did she know that? Ferox had been the only Roman in that desperate fight on the clifftop. Vindex had arrived later, and not really known who the Mother was. Ferox had never said much to anyone about the woman and her pupils. He was not quite sure why; it just felt as if their world should remain secret, a living memory of the old world of heroes, before the Romans came. 'I was,' he said at last. 'We were losing. There were just too many of them and they kept coming. She knew the price of breaking her oath, but did it for her children, and it saved them.' That was only half-true. Vindex, Longinus and the others had come to their aid and the main force of Romans was on its way. Some of them might have lasted until that help arrived. 'She killed and died because of it.'

'She was special, even among the long line of Mothers back to the beginning.' Enica's voice had a reverence Ferox had not heard before. 'Brigita of Hibernia may be another.' The solemn face broke into a smile. 'You are surprised? The whispers of the Mother reach her children wherever they are. For our whole lives we are bound to her and each other.

'Brigita was coming to the end of her time of training there when I arrived. An older one is given as a guide to the newcomer, and I was bound to her. She was…'

'A tough bitch.' There was enough sheer admiration in his tone for her to nod. A queen of a Hiberian tribe, Brigita had been abducted by a band of deserters from the army, the same ones who had taken Sulpicia Lepidina. Ferox led the rescue, and then watched as the queen fought alongside his men. When it was over, she turned her back on her tribe and homeland to become the new Mother.

'She was hard on me, very hard, and so I learned well.' She lifted up her right leg and spun so that she was sitting in the saddle as if it was a chair, facing him. The horse did not stir and her balance was perfect. 'You don't often swear, do you? I hear that is the way with Silures.'

'Waste of good anger. But these days I seem to curse a lot more.' He snorted with laughter. 'I must be turning into more of a Roman.'

'To live in two worlds at once.'

Ferox nodded. 'I guess in that we are alike. You are young, though, and I know you were educated in Gaul, so how did you find the time to go north?'

'My mother – my real mother – decided, and father did as he was told. They sent me to Lugdunum when I was eight and then later Massilia to improve my Greek and gain understanding of the philosophers.' She shook her head. 'Very dull old men, most of whom have never lived and will never live, but love to talk.'

'Unlike the Brigantes.'

'We talk, it is true. You Silures should try it sometime. It is very freeing. So I learned, and they condescended to say that I was quite bright for a little girl. So I smiled as if I was proud, and made a joke about Epicurus, but made sure to get the details of the story slightly wrong so that they could feel secure in their wisdom. Soon I was nearly fourteen and it was clear I would not be a girl for much longer. The features your friend so admires appeared overnight. Well, began to show anyway. My tutor sent word home, and my parents whisked me away less I be debauched by fellow pupils or master. As if any of those fools had a chance! Pigs and apes the lot of them, and all so very stupid. They brought me home and then sent me to the Mother, to learn and to stay chaste. A son and daughter are not permitted to lie together,' she explained. 'Three years on and the Mother told me that I was ready to go back. I knew it too, although I feared being made to take a husband on my return.

'Thankfully, my parents sent me to Rome instead, to "complete my education".' She snorted scornfully, and the grey horse shook its head in surprise. Without shifting from her awkward, sideways posture, she cooed to the animal and it calmed. She even crossed her legs and somehow remained balanced. 'What a place. You have been there, I know. So many people, so many temptations and vices. Thus Claudia was born. Yet I had a guide and she steered me through. What is it Caesar said, like a helmsman avoiding a reef. Though if I recall he was speaking of oratory.'

'So I understand.'

'Do you, or are you just pretending? Half of life seems to be about pretending, doesn't it? Not making others feel uncomfortable. In the old tales the heroes boast all the time and parade their prowess. I sometimes wonder whether wisdom is about hiding who you really are and what you are capable of doing.'

'Yesterday you killed two men. At the amphitheatre you killed two more. From the ease with which you did it I doubt that they are the first. Now you ride like a centaur and speak of hiding your skills.'

She stuck her tongue out at him like a child. 'Half of life, I said. And here there is no one to see, apart from you. Even so, those are just a few of my talents. There are lots of others.

I can stand on one hand with my feet straight up in the air, but I hardly ever do. Especially when I'm wearing a dress. And if Vindex were here he would no doubt have muttered "Pity" at that point. And I can juggle.' She frowned. 'Your seriousness can be a bore, do you know that? Try acting as if you are entranced by my wit. I well see that my beauty stirs you.' She glanced down, and before he knew it he did the same. There was nothing to see, as he should have known. 'Got you,' she said, and stuck out her tongue again.

'Who was your helmsman?'

'Oh, back to business. Can't you guess? I thought you were supposed to be good at rooting out the truth.' He said nothing. 'Then perhaps if I say that my family's old friendships and the emperor's favour recommended me to the house of the Sulpicii?'

Ferox laughed and once he started he could not stop. Claudia Enica watched him with the expression of an indulgent parent. For a while they rode side by side, until she hooked her right leg back over the saddle, then pushed on the horns and jumped, placing her boots on the saddle. She stood upright, arms straight out on either side. The grey walked on, apparently oblivious.

'Clever.'

'Not really. Clever would be if the horse could stand on my back. Still, at least it has brought an end to your yokel-like merriment. As you have guessed, I met Sulpicia Lepidina four years ago and we got on from the start. I think she found it a pleasant change from conversation with the buffoons in her family. She was not married then, and her brother was busy getting exiled, while her father drank too much, made unwise investments and generally wasted the family's wealth.

Frankly she needed company. She took me in hand, refined my manners, we talked for days about clothes and then went shopping, came home and talked even more. Better yet she sneaked me into the local ludus. Of course they thought two noblewomen were only there for a bit of rough. You know what some are like. Personally, I could not see anything very appealing about muscle-bound and scarred heavies, but each to his own. One tried it on, so I slid his knife out of its sheath, gave him a cut on the arm and then had the point at his throat ready to press. After that they were all lambs, and they let me train and taught me the curved sword and more than a few tricks of the arena.'

'Sulpicia Lepidina did not join you?' For all his surprise, Ferox found the story all too easy to believe. The lady was never one to be bound by convention and clever enough to hide it. Still, the thought of her handling a sword was unlikely.

'She just watched. I made her laugh, you see. She did not have much to cheer her in those days. She kept a couple of the bigger household slaves with us in case of trouble, but there wasn't any need. She charmed them. You know how she can, and I amused them, and they could see that I was good. The lanista even wanted me to be in a show fight at the games!' She slid down, smacking into the saddle and making the grey bound forward. 'Good boy,' she said, stroking its ears.

Vindex appeared and raised an arm to show that he had found somewhere suitable. The ground was too uneven and broken by little gullies to risk a canter, so they walked towards him.

'She loves you very much,' Enica said softly. 'And the boy is everything to her. You have given her glimpses of happiness. There can never be more, for that is not fated, but never doubt that her love was real.'

'I do not know what you mean.'

She leaned over and patted his arm. 'Aren't Silures supposed to be good at lying? I told you, we are close friends and friends talk. Unlike Claudia Severa I am not shocked. It gave Lepidina pleasure to live the moments again in the telling and I was the only one to trust. I've shocked you. Well, that is something.'

He sighed 'I have more questions.'

'Is this the vanity of man?'

'Not about that.'

'Sshh. Later.' Vindex was close now. 'Another time.'

The scout chattered away happily, joking with the lady, while always keeping his humour just this side of Brigantian courtesy. She responded, with the greater licence permitted to someone of her rank. They spoke about his father, and she surprised Ferox by also knowing the name, if no more, of his mother, a servant at his homestead who had caught the young chieftain's eye.

'I am more like him,' Vindex admitted. 'They say she was a beauty, although I do not really remember her face as I was little when the fever took her. The chief has been good to me.' Vindex never used the word father when speaking of his lord.

After that they spoke for hours about horses, and a little about chariots. Ferox admired both, and could watch them or try them out for as long as anyone. Talking about them always seemed a waste of breath and effort. He had never met a silent Brigantian. More than any other tribe they prattled away, whether or not they had anything worth saying, as fond of their own voices as any sophist. Sometimes they spoke over each other, and he was baffled because they still seemed to follow what everyone else was saying. Claudia, the fashionable Roman woman, had barely stopped for breath. During the rest of the day and the evening Enica the princess of the Brigantes did not appear to need to pause at all.

Ferox left them, saying he would take the first watch. At least they had the sense to keep their voices low, although now and again Vindex brayed with laughter, making Ferox wince. It was a clear, still night, and the sound would carry a long way. He went a fair distance from the camp until he could barely hear them, and then kept moving, circling the walled sheep pen they had settled down in, stopping often and listening. There was no sign of anyone out there. They were still high up, where no one lived in winter, and although the cold and snows would most likely hold off for another month or so, already the high pastures were almost empty.

Eventually Vindex came to relieve him. Back at the camp, Ferox found Claudia Enica soundly asleep. There had been no later for them to talk, and there were still so many questions. Often silence and stillness cleared his mind. He could never remember working out a problem, yet somehow afterwards answers came clearly. That had not happened tonight, and instead he still had mysteries and suspicions. Claudia Enica was a skilled warrior, and he guessed Ovidius was right and she was almost as skilled an actress. Vindex worshipped her, and not simply because he had been raised to be loyal to her family. She was beautiful and charming, and it was hard not to like her.

Many years ago, Caratacus had told him that Silures were always wary of charm because they did not have any of their own. The old man had said it as a compliment, for he admired Ferox's people and always said that if he had stayed with them instead of trying to rally the Ordovices, then he would still have been free and fighting into his old age. Caratacus had charm, but the Lord of the Hills trusted him because he had seen the man fight. His grandfather had told him that sometimes in life you met someone who truly was as amiable, capable and trustworthy as they seemed, and the danger was that you would miss the chance of making a true friend because you were too suspicious.

Enica claimed to have saved his life twice and he believed that, albeit at the arena he had had to survive the first attack for her help to have mattered. He believed her too when she claimed close friendship of Sulpicia Lepidina, for there was no other way she could have known so much. Ferox's life was pledged to the mother of his child, a woman who had reawakened feelings he had thought long dead with his first lost love. Sulpicia Lepidina was also the wife of another man, daughter of a senator, and intrigue and politics were in her blood. Someone had tried to arrange his death in the arena, that night when Enica's dead servant had come to him, and he wished that he could be sure it was not Lepidina. If it was Enica, then she had changed her mind, and if it was all Domitius' plan, then how had Enica known about it?

She was a killer. He had seen that now. Caratacus was dead these long months past, and they said the killers were led by a woman, and presumably a woman familiar enough with the ways of Rome and Italia to pass without notice. Another woman, bold and quick thinking enough to bluff the soldier who stumbled upon her, had been there when Narcissus died, and had ridden off on horseback afterwards. Ferox tried hard to remember the voice of the woman paid off by Acco and Domitius while he was their prisoner. He did not think she had sounded like the young woman softly sighing in her sleep just a few feet away. Yet if Claudia the Roman and Enica the Brigantian were themselves performances, then perhaps there were other parts she could play just as convincingly. Cartimandua had betrayed Caratacus. Had her granddaughter murdered him?

Ferox had never fought a woman. The closest he had come had been when he and Vindex faced the masked Enica and that had never become serious. He feared having to kill her or any woman. The Silures did not kill women, or children for that matter, for it was seen as unlucky. They took captives on the raids, and the women suffered and became slaves or sometimes wives. It was not the softest of lives, but over time many became as much part of the tribe as those of the blood. That was if they realised that being of the Silures was to be of the finest people in the world, the only true people.

His instincts revolted at the thought that he might have to kill a woman, or hand her over to let someone else do the job since that was simply a cowardly way of doing the same thing. All boys born to his tribe were bound by bans against doing certain things. These were secret, known only to them and whoever had prophesied their fortune after their birth. He was bound never to harm a woman, child or creature from the deep sea. His soul, his very essence and certainly his power as a man would decay and crumble if he violated any of these taboos. The one about the sea creatures was easy enough, and the others fitted the beliefs of the Silures, although he suspected these were rare as he had never heard of any past warrior of his tribe bound in the same way. He wondered whether Acco was the one who had given him such a strange fate. After so many years as a Roman, Ferox should probably have dismissed all this as mere superstition. Yet not long ago he had seen the Mother break her oath and die moments later. There was so much about the world the Romans – or even the Greeks with all their cleverness – could simply not understand.

He must have slept in the end, for Vindex's snoring woke him with a start. The sky was clear, the stars beginning to fade, and dawn not far off. Enica was gone, so he rose and went to find her. It was good to move to shake off the chill and stiffness of the night. He found her easily, standing straight, her heavy cloak pulled tightly around her. For a moment he thought of one of those statuettes of Ephesian Artemis that he had seen many Romans from the east carry with them. She was staring out across the valley at the high peaks in the far distance. Some still had snow on them from the last winter.

Enica smiled. 'You came at my summons. Good.'

'I just woke up, my lady. Vindex's snores would wake a stone.'

'Just chance, you think.' She had coiled her pigtail and piled it on top of her head, making her almost as tall as him. It was a style he remembered Brigita using. 'Have you become so much the Roman?'

He did not answer.

'You know who my grandmother was, and you know of her power. Do you know of her grandmother? No. She was

Mandua, daughter of Manubracius, King of the Trinovantes, at least until Cunobelinus defeated him. You know of him, at least, the father of Caratacus, although from all I hear the son was the greater of the two, though the father was great enough. I liked Caratacus, although of course I only met him when he was very old. We spoke of Britannia and he liked that, and I joked with him and he told me I was a naughty child and that next time if I did not behave he would spank me.' She laughed. 'I was so sorry to hear that he had passed.'

That could mean anything and nothing, and Ferox let her talk.

'Mandubracius was ally of Julius Caesar in his war against Cassivellaunus. Heard of them?' She pulled a face that was pure Claudia the Roman. 'At least you must have heard of Caesar?'

'I have.'

'Silures.' She shook her head. 'My family say that Caesar took a shine to Mandua. That was his way, they say, and of course she was a beauty because all the women in my family are beauties. Soon afterwards she was sent north to marry the high king of the Brigantes – he was only a man so his name matters little – and at the end of the year she gave birth to a daughter.

'My brother believes that the girl was the daughter of Caesar and not Mandua's husband, so that we are of the line of Caesar himself.'

'And what do you believe?'

'I do not believe; I know. Some of Mandua and Cartimandua is reborn in me, each of us a different part of the same soul, and we see things that others do not. Caesar was my ancestor, and that is honourable enough, if of little consequence compared to being part of them.' She reached up and plucked two pins from her hair, letting the ponytail drop down behind her back. 'I know other things as well.'

'We ought to rouse that snoring ox and tend to the horses. It will be time to leave very soon.'

'You are mine.' Enica took hold of her braided hair and toyed with it. 'You are mine, prince of the Silures and centurion of Rome, as surely as if I were to tie you with my hair. It is the will of the gods. Your soul kneels to mine. I shall have to think what to do with you, shan't I?'

Ferox was in no mood for more games. For all the confidence in her voice, this woman had seen just twenty-one summers. 'Shall we go?'

Enica shook her head again. 'Silures. So used to hiding the truth that they often cannot see it when it stares them in the face. Very well, let us go. But do not forget what I have said.'

Ferox bent his knees as if to kneel, then stopped and shrugged. He strode away and did not look back.

XIX

'Two,' VINDEX SAID softly, giving a big smile. 'One on either side.'

Ferox rubbed his face and grinned in return. 'Five. Two on the left, one high up on the right and the other two behind those boulders near the base. Three have been following us since dawn.'

Vindex patted his horse's neck. 'What colour eyes have they got?'

Claudia Enica stared at the narrow defile. The setting sun sparkled for a moment on something metal in the heather up on the right. Hours before they had come across the track left by her brother's men. It was almost a day old. They had followed because for a while it offered the easiest route down. For two miles they had gone along a valley that grew narrower and narrower until it came to this gap, with steep, heather and rock covered slopes on either side. It was an obvious place for an ambush, so obvious that Ferox doubted even a Silurian child would use it, but the Ordovices were not the wolf people.

'Only five,' she said after a while. 'Are you sure they are waiting for us?'

'We have good horses, weapons, and you,' Ferox said. 'They will want all of those. The Ordovices are not kind to women.'

Enica sighed. 'So do you two want to wait while I kill them?'

'I think we should go back and find another path.' There were too many birds in the sky beyond the defile. Most were too far away to recognise, but something was wrong. 'If they follow us, you can always kill them later.'

A figure leaped up from the heather on the right, closely followed by another. They pushed their way through the fronds, climbing higher up. Then the man on the left did the same. A horseman appeared in the gap, his oval green shield uncovered, and the top of his bronze helmet dark with fur. He trotted through, almost casually deflected a thrown spear with his shield, threw his own javelin in reply, spitting a warrior just as the man stood up from the boulder. Another tribesman scrambled up and ran. The horse went into a canter, the rider drew his sword, came alongside the fleeing warrior and cut back just once. Blood spurted high as the corpse dropped, head hanging to the neck by little more than a thread. The Batavian brought his horse to a dead halt and raised his dripping blade in triumph. Even from this distance, Ferox could see the empty eye socket as Longinus waved to them.

'Come on!' he shouted.

'We should run,' Ferox said, and was not quite sure why. Vindex frowned.

'It's Longinus,' Claudia Enica said. 'I trust him.' She set off at a smooth trot, leading the second grey. Vindex's horse stirred and he let it follow. Ferox hesitated for a moment and then gave in.

Longinus was beaming. Ferox had never seen the old man smile as broadly, but then perhaps he had never seen him welcome Claudia Enica. As she approached, the veteran wheeled around and set off to lead the way through the defile. It proved longer than Ferox had expected, and curved to the left so that they blinked as they rode straight towards the burning red sunset. Suddenly they came out into a wide pasture.

Horsemen waited in a semi-circle, spears held ready and shields up. In the centre was a tall man, wearing an ornately crested helmet with a gilded face mask. Crispinus was behind them, looking awkward, and then Ferox realised that his hands were tied behind his back. A cavalryman with a blue shield and tartan cloak stood his horse next to the tribune, a naked blade in his hand. There was movement on either side, and Ferox looked up to see dismounted troopers on the slopes on either side of him. He dragged at the reins to pull his horse around.

'Move and she dies!' The leader with the face mask had his spear point inches from Claudia Enica's chest.

Ferox jerked the reins hard, and his gelding reared and fell. He pushed out of the saddle, hurling himself away as far as he could and striking the rocky side of the defile.

Vindex dropped his spear. 'No trouble, lord. No trouble.'

Ferox managed to push himself up and like the scout he raised his hands in the air. A dismounted trooper came behind him and undid his belt and took it along with his sword. Longinus had turned and was bringing his horse back.

The leader slowly raised his spear and then held it out until one of his men took it. Ferox saw Batavians among the blue shielded men, and they did not look happy. He could not see Gannascus or Sepenestus. The men with blue shields looked much like ordinary troopers, save each wore matching shirts of scale, with silvered and gilded pieces alternating, and even in the wilds they were polished so that they flickered whenever a man shifted and caught the light of the setting sun. Their helmets were tinned, scabbards, belts, and harness fittings more ornate than the wealthiest, most ostentatious soldier in an ala, and their horses taller and finer. Most sported long moustaches and their lean faces reminded him of Vindex. These must be the royal ala of the Brigantes, many of them sons of chieftains. A vicious, flat-nosed man he remembered as Brigantus, former gladiator and now the prince's bodyguard, swung down from his horse and strode towards Ferox. By now Longinus had turned and was walking his horse back.

With an easy gesture, their leader flicked up the face mask, which was hinged and rigid enough to stay open. Arviragus smiled. 'Did you really think I would kill my own sister?' Claudia Enica laughed, a sweet sound even when it mocked him. Ferox took a step forward, the rage brimming up inside him, as much at his own stupidity as anything else. The bodyguard drew his sword, but Ferox did not stop.

'Don't be a fool!' Crispinus yelled.

Longinus kicked his horse on and swung the flat of his sword, pounding it against the side of Ferox's head and the darkness engulfed him again.

Ferox doubted that he was unconscious for long, and awoke draped over a horse, wrists and ankles tied and a sack over his head. Soon afterwards they stopped, and someone pitched him off onto the turf.

'Shall I cut him free?' The voice sounded like young Cocceius.

'No. Drag him over there with the others. He can have his hands free to eat, but tie them again until you're told otherwise. They say he's dangerous.' Someone kicked him hard in the side and he groaned as the pain shot through his bruised and battered body. 'Doubt it myself.' Ferox rolled up into a ball. 'See, can't take it. Southerners are all the same.'

Ferox was lifted rather than dragged, which suggested that the Batavians were the ones doing the work, and set down on the ground. The sack was pulled away. It was dark, but he saw the big shape of Gannascus, someone else behind him and Vindex on the other side.

'Bit of a bugger, this,' the scout muttered.

'Sir,' Cocceius whispered by his ear. The young soldier was leaning down, pretending that part of the sack had caught on the shoulder buckle of Ferox's mail shirt. 'Think she's the one, sir.' He glanced nervously to either side, then dropped the sack and cupped both his hands over his chest. 'Do you get me?'

Ferox gave a tiny nod.

'Not sure, but reckon it is,' the lad went on. 'Could do with another look.'

Brigantus glared down at them, fingers hooked in his belt. 'Clear off , lad. These prisoners are not to talk to each other or anyone else without my say so. Wait here. Be silent.' His voice was a whisper, as if his throat had once been badly hurt.

A little later they were brought bread and some weak beer, but instead of freeing Ferox's arms, the bodyguard sliced through the ropes on his legs. 'The prince wants to talk to you.'

He was led to a leather tent, one of the larger ones normally given to centurions on campaign. He had noticed that the Brigantes had half a dozen mules to carry their baggage. The bodyguard lifted the flap and gestured for him to go in.

The air was heavy with the smell of stale oil burning in a little lamp and making too much smoke. Arviragus sat on a camp stool, as did Crispinus, his hands no longer tied. Claudia Enica sat cross-legged on a blanket behind them, her baggy clothes and boots giving her the air of a Sarmatian or another of the wandering races as much as a Parthian. They had all just finished a meal, the odour of a fine stew competing with the smoke.

Arviragus smiled and got to his feet, offering his hand, then realising that Ferox was still tied. 'There is no need for bonds,' he said, and glanced around.

'Here.' Crispinus held out a clasp knife.

The Brigantian prince flicked the blade out and cut the rope. Ferox wondered why neither the prince nor his henchman bothered simply to untie a knot.

'This afternoon was a regrettable mistake,' he said. His smile was broad, showing his perfect teeth, but did not extend to his eyes. 'In days like these we must all be careful, and you have the reputation of a dangerous man, perhaps even an impulsive one. Now that I have had time to speak at length with the noble Crispinus, I believe I understand better.' He held out his hand once more. Ferox massaged his fingers for a moment and then shook it.

'Good. Please sit. I fear we do not have another stool. Unless you are stiff and prefer to stand for a while?' Ferox sat down on his haunches, after the manner of his tribe.

'Like you,' Crispinus said, 'it seems I too am a prisoner.'

'You may as well explain,' the prince agreed, taking his seat again. 'Are you hungry, centurion? I can send for food? No? In a moment then.'

'No doubt the whole matter will soon be cleared up,' the tribune said airily. 'Indeed by the sound of it your innocence is well on its way to being established.'

'One of Fuscus' people produced documents implicating him in treasonous plots,' Arviragus interrupted.

Crispinus smiled. 'Indeed he did. Our old friend Vegetus, no less. Which would mean that even if you killed the little swine you were doing the res publica a favour.'

Arviragus interrupted once more. 'Sadly, some of the letters could be interpreted by a malign judgement also to implicate the noble Crispinus. Obviously mistaken or deliberate fraud, of course, but I was sent to take him into custody.'

'By whom, my lord?' Ferox was sitting straight-backed, trying to be as formal as possible. 'If you will forgive my curiosity.'

He was not sure whether there was a flicker of anger before the smile reasserted itself. 'Of course. And I understand your meaning. No, the legate had not returned. This was early morning of the day after you left. In his absence my orders were given to me by the Lord Crassus. Most of the mounted soldiers in Londinium had gone with the legate or were needed, which meant my men were best suited for the task. I obeyed as was my duty.

'However, since the legate had confided in me something of your mission and its importance, I judged it prudent to follow at a discreet distance. Only when you went into the mountains did I begin to worry that I might lose you.

Prudence dictated that I catch up, and then decide how best to proceed. Unfortunately we came on each other rather more suddenly than I had anticipated, and suspicion led to blows. That German knocked down three of my men with his bare hands, and had to be restrained. At first I had to threaten the tribune until he ordered his soldiers to obey me. It was all deeply unfortunate, but thankfully no serious harm was done.

'Now, since we have had time to consider the matter, the noble Crispinus has convinced me that we must do our best to accomplish his task on Mona. He has agreed to place himself in my charge until this is done, and then until I bring him to the legate and other matters can be investigated properly. Will you now give me your word to do the same?'

Crispinus nodded encouragingly.

'What of my men?'

'They will all be free, as long as you stand surety for them. Come, centurion, let us all serve the legate and our princeps. I have heard that you are a great warrior, and my sister tells me that you treated her with... what was it you said?' He turned around to stare down at Enica.

'Surly respect,' she said.

Crispinus nodded. 'Sounds about right.'

Arviragus laughed. 'Well, knowing my sister, I dare say there was a good deal of patience as well.'

'Indeed, my lord, that was the longest I have known the lady go without speaking.'

The laugh became a great roar.

'Why is the lady here, my lord?'

'My sister goes where she wills. If she has not explained her purpose, then I fear I cannot. No matter. We shall all go on this quest together.'

'That is the will of the gods,' she said flatly.

'Of course it is, my dear,' her brother said like an indulgent parent, 'so let us not disappoint them. Do I have your word, Flavius Ferox?'

Crispinus leaned forward eagerly. Enica was staring at the floor, apparently paying no heed.

Ferox nodded. 'Yes, my lord.'

XX

SEGONTIUM WAS MUCH like Vindolanda and the many forts dotted around the provinces, so familiar that any slight differences were oddly jarring. Built to house a cohors milliaria of some eight hundred men, there were barely half that number there at the moment, even though winter was approaching and many detachments had returned to barracks. They had missed the prefect by only a few days, for he had left to take up a post as narrow-stripe tribune with a legion in Syria, and his replacement had not yet arrived. The senior centurion in charge was welcoming, especially after he had read the letters Crispinus carried signed by the legate himself, although the news he passed on was bad. Neratius Marcellus had crushed a group of several hundred bandits near Verulamium, but had been wounded. The centurion did not know how badly. He had heard rumours of banditry and rebellion among several tribes, although so far the Ordovices and Deceangli were quiet enough.

The garrison maintained several boats, big enough to carry a dozen men and fitted with oars and a sail, and the centurion was willing to put one at their disposal if it would be useful. The main group would need to use the ferry or swim their horses across the straits.

'It's a little late in the year,' the centurion conceded, 'and there won't be many more cattle coming across that way until next spring, but you should be all right. Batavians know what they're doing on water, don't they?'

Arviragus and Crispinus decided on the ferry and Ferox was glad. His own mount was tired after weeks of travel, and as he looked across at the far shore it seemed a long way. Yet to his surprise the island appeared innocuous enough from this distance, although he could not see a single house. Somehow he had expected mist and sinister shadows, and instead there was sunshine, which was warm as long as you were sheltered from the gusty wind.

The ferry was shallow-bottomed, rowed by four big sweeps on either side and steered by a rudder. Half a dozen men and horses could squeeze onto it, so the crossing would take a long time, especially as the current tended to take them over to the right, and it was hard work to bring it back to the jetty on the return trip. Yet the soldiers operating it were cheerful for this was a break from routine and the unit's tradition meant that they would be given a pass to stay out in the vicus as long as they returned when the fort gates opened at dawn. Until then they were free to drink, gamble, whore, or do whatever they liked away from their officers. The same applied to the soldiers in the boat, who shadowed the ferry in case of accidents, although they would have to wait for their orders were to stay with the expedition until it returned. There were no other detachments on the island and no permanent outposts there.

'We don't have enough men,' the centurion explained. 'Wouldn't really be worth it even if we had. There's really not many people over there, and they don't make trouble.

Besides, no one ever really wants to stay there. Too many dark memories. I've seen things over there. Maybe they were *lemures* or other unquiet spirits and maybe they were just my mind playing tricks. This side of the island is the worst. Up north its bleaker and just empty. Here there are patches of scorched grass where the groves once stood. You'd think after forty years there would be no mark, but there is. They should send a legion and give it a year to burn everything, every tree, every bush, every blade of grass, and then in a hundred years the whole place might be clean.' He smiled. 'Sorry, been here too long and a man gets to brooding. You will be fine. Just don't let your minds play tricks. Be careful with the current, sometimes the sea misbehaves. The boat will stay with you in case anything happens. If it does, then the horses will only make it if they swim, but maybe we can catch any of you before you drown.'

Ferox was glad that he was not on the first few trips. Arviragus led, standing tall at the front of the wooden ferry, with Crispinus looking tiny by his side. The next boats took an equal number of Batavians and Brigantes. The prince had given orders that Ferox and his men were each to go separately, and flat-nosed Brigantus decided that he would wait for the final crossing, so kept Ferox with him.

'I shall cross with you as well,' Claudia Enica declared.

'As you wish, lady.' The bodyguard did not sound happy.

In the event Longinus accompanied them, and that was all, for they had the lady's two horses and a skittish pack pony that did not want to go up the ramp onto the ferry. Longinus tried and failed to calm the animal, and then Enica came to it, whispering soothingly, smoothing its ears.

'She's special, that one,' the veteran said softly to Ferox as they leaned on the rail above the rowers. The two Brigantes were on the far side of the ferry, the animals in between.

'Did you swim it last time, when you came with Agricola?' Ferox asked, not wanting to discuss the lady.

'Yes. And the first time with Paulinus as well. We were Batavians, so had to show off.'

'Was it a hard fight?'

Longinus unbuckled his helmet and took it off, hanging it on the corner post of the ferry. He rubbed his grey hair. 'Hard? Not really in the end. They were waiting on the beach over there.' He pointed and then waved his hand along the shore. 'Up to the headland there, you see it? They were silent at first, and that's uncanny among the tribes. Then we got closer and saw them. Old men with robes to their feet and hair and beards almost as long. Women in black waving torches, and some naked as a babe, but writhing in a wild dance. There were warriors too, behind the rest, although only a few thousand. They had lines of our lads shackled. Men they'd taken in fights, some of them years ago. The old sweat riding his horse in the surf next to me saw an old mate of his they'd lost three years before. Once we were close enough to see them then the chanting picked up, and druids ran forward to curse and scream their magic.

'One went along the lines of prisoners. He was all in red, the only one like it on that whole beach. Even his face was painted red and his hair dyed that colour. A couple of others pushed a prisoner to his knees, then the red boy put his hand on the poor devil's head. After that the women took over. Sometimes they cut the throat. Sometimes they ran at him and drove a big spear right through and then watched him writhe. They even castrated a few of them. Then all of a sudden, silence again until red boy whines this song in Latin if you please, and the words didn't seem to go together, but it was full of magic and hate.

'The army stopped. Men at the oars just stopped. Never seen anything like it before or since. We were lagging behind by this stage. I mean the cavalry. Look at it. It's a hell of a way to swim a horse and the tide was getting stronger. Seemed to be holding us back, and even the old sweat said it was magic and red boy was pushing us away.

'You've read Caesar, haven't you. First time he came, his lads balked when they saw the Britons waiting on the beach for them. Then the *aquilifer* of Legio X jumps over the side and shames the rest into following.' Longinus had been holding fast onto the rail, lost in his memories. He let go and gave a grim laugh. 'Caesar doesn't give the fellow a name. Always wondered about that. Makes me think he was one of those soldiers who was very useful in a fight and a humping nuisance the rest of the time. Or maybe he was just some peasant whose name no one back in Italy would know or care about.' He sighed. 'Like those poor sods on the beach. As our whole army hesitated, the shouting burst out again, and one by one they killed the rest of the prisoners. We watched.

'It wasn't a standard-bearer or a centurion or anyone else who should have given a lead. One eager tribune was trying to urge them on, but even he faltered. Words wouldn't make them go on. And it wasn't vengeance either, not then. My horse seemed faster than the rest. She was a good one, could keep running all day. Swam quickly too and soon I was ahead of the rest of the *turma* and alongside one of the barges full of legionaries. I could see their faces. They were pale, teeth clenched. As the last prisoner died it went quiet again and red boy strode towards the surf. Two of the women came with him, both naked and pretty enough if you don't mind crazy. Red boy raised his arms and opened his mouth to curse us again, and it was as if even the waves were deathly quiet.

'Then someone on the barge farted.'

Ferox laughed. 'What?'

'I'm telling the truth. It was like thunder and went on and on. This lad broke wind. You know what army bread is like, especially on campaign. Red boy stopped. Maybe he heard it too or maybe it was greater magic than his. 'Longinus, you mongrel,' someone said. Men groaned, and then they laughed. It broke the spell. I don't know why or how, but it did. 'Now they know we're coming!' someone said, and they laughed again. There was noise again, our noise – the clank of armour, the little jokes and curses the lads make when they're nervous. I didn't hear any order, but the rowers started to pull again on that barge, and when they saw it go so did the others. Then the whole army was moving and I felt the current pulling me and the horse into the shore. Red boy turned and ran. The rest didn't and started shrieking again, but even they did not sound so convinced. I reckon they really believed their magic would stop us, turn us into smoke or something. When it didn't they couldn't quite believe as hard and as we splashed ashore they just stood there yelling. That was when the rage for vengeance really started. Only time I saw anything like it was weeks later when we smashed Boudicca. The lads just wanted to kill. At least Boudicca's warriors fought back hard. These lads, and those mad lasses too, they just died. We hardly lost anyone in the fight – that day or in the nine days we were on Mona. Warriors would ambush us, then seem to give up and let themselves be slaughtered.'

'Longinus?'

'I reckoned it was as good a name as any when I needed a new one. That lad's bowels did the empire a service, but you won't find it in Paulinus' report or any history. You won't find red boy either. He ran fast and we didn't catch him, that day or afterwards. Some of the lads were saying he was a Roman who'd joined them. I guess because he spoke Latin. Still, you know that there are more rumours in a camp than flies buzzing around the horse lines.'

They were almost at the far shore. Ferox realised that Claudia Enica had gone to reassure one of her greys so must have heard most of the story. She noticed his gaze and winked.

'Ever thought you would come back here, Longinus?' she asked.

'No, lady, but life's like that. You rarely get what you expect.'

The ferry ground onto the shingle of the beach. The boat did not come quite so far in, and one of its occupants splashed through the water to reach the shore. He was to guide them to a campsite further along the coast, and the boat would pull up on the beach near there.

Some of the Batavians helped shove the ferry off. Ferox watched it go. The mainland was clear, little plumes of smoke from farmsteads and a bigger cloud where Segontium lay out of sight. Over all stood the mountains, the sides dark with shadow, the edge of a different world.'

'Yes, I know.' Vindex had appeared beside him. 'Back when we were in the tower I didn't feel so cut off.'

'Come on, centurion. We have work to do.' Crispinus was eager as he sat on his horse next to Arviragus. 'May as well take a look around while the rest make camp.'

Mona was bigger even than Ferox had expected and they did not stray far that first day. They came across the patches of scorched ground the centurion had spoken of very soon. There was a lot of woodland, every few miles a hut or two. The inhabitants were small as a rule, the men with beards, which was a rare thing among the tribes. Their dialect was odd, so that the Brigantes understood very little of what they said and even Ferox struggled.

For two days they spent most of the time in the saddle, as Ferox tried to make sense of the descriptions left by Prasto. They went inland to the higher ground, which helped, although there were so many folds and little valleys that he knew that he was missing a good deal. There were also few tracks and a lot of trees as well as thick, thorny hedges that criss-crossed the country and seemed to make little sense as field boundaries. Since it was almost the end of October, the days were getting short, which gave them less time to search. The fourth day began with driving rain. The prince and the tribune insisted that they keep searching. That was the only day Claudia Enica did not ride with them, and instead she stayed in the little tent set aside for her. The next day was the same, with no reward for long hours of suffering. Two of the Batavians and one of the Brigantes developed a fever overnight.

'The prince is worried that you are not really trying,' Crispinus told Ferox as they ate a cold meal. 'We seem to be getting nowhere.'

'What would you have me do, my lord?'

'Find a way, Ferox, as you have done before. Get lucky if that is what it needs.'

'This is not a place for good luck, my lord. And I have little to go on.'

Crispinus took a spoonful of stew and then wrinkled his nose in distaste. He stood up, short enough to do so without crouching, and went to the door of the tent to empty the rest of the bowl outside. Coming back, he patted Ferox on the shoulder. 'Do what you need to do. But know that this matters more than I can say. The price of failure will be high. Not just for you, but for the one you care about most. Think on it. Now, I must brave the elements to answer a call of nature.'

The sun shone the next morning, although a high wind kept driving rain clouds across the island. For a while there would be a deluge, then clear blue skies before the next one came in. Ferox led them to marshland covering miles. The soldiers from Segontium said that they had never been in there, although they did know that the boggy country stretched to the sea. A shepherd was no more informative.

'We don't go in,' he said through his wild beard. 'If a sheep strays we leave her, for it means that the gods demanded payment.'

'Ask him about the old days.' Arviragus was leaning down from his horse, looming over the small man. 'Was this a holy place?'

Ferox tried, but could sense that the man's fear of speaking far outstripped any fear for his life. That meant that the place was special, and it could fit with Prasto's description – as could half a dozen other spots they had seen already. Would it match what Acco had said? 'I don't think he can tell us any more, my lord,' Ferox said, looking up at the prince.

'Soon find out.' Arviragus gestured to his bodyguard and another Brigantian. 'Persuade this fellow to talk. When he is ready, call us and we'll come and ask questions.'

Ferox watched glumly as they dragged the man into the trees. 'We won't learn anything we don't already know, my lord.'

'We shall see. May as well eat while we are waiting.' The soldiers gathered wood to make a fire.

Ferox went over to sit beside Vindex. The scout was unimpressed. 'Useless bastard,' he muttered. 'Give me the sister anytime.' Once again the lady had remained in their camp.

'She kills people,' Ferox said.

'If they deserve it.'

A scream split the air. 'Come on, let's take a look up there!' He nodded towards a conical hill about a mile away, its top covered in trees. They walked, and the only one to see them was Cocceius who grinned and made a show of turning the other way.

'How are you at tree climbing?' Ferox asked as they neared the top. He saw the expression. 'Fine, stay here and I'll go.'

The oak was bare of all but a few shrivelled leaves and looked bigger than all the trees around it. Vindex crouched and made a cup for the centurion to put his foot in and Ferox managed to swing up onto the first big branch. For a while it was easy, the boughs solid and conveniently spaced, even though the rain had left them slippery. Ferox could not remember when he had last climbed a tree, and found that he enjoyed it far more than he expected. It was like being a child again. So far there was nothing to see save more trees and a squirrel that eyed him suspiciously. He pressed on, taking a while to choose his path. The little red-brown creature kept ahead of him, watching closely with its black eyes, and he fought the urge to throw something at it.

Ferox could not reach the next branch, even with his foot on a well-placed fork. He put all his weight on it, lifting the other boot in the air and gathering himself for a leap. As he jumped, the sole of his boot slipped. Fingers brushed against the branch above, but could not grasp it and he was falling, dropping five or six feet and landing astride another bough.

'You all right?' Vindex sounded distant, although he had obviously heard his friend's yelp. The squirrel raised its front paws and scrutinised him. Then it bounded upwards, until it vanished.

'Easy for you,' he muttered.

'You there yet?'

'Yes!' he shouted, and could not think of anything witty to add. After getting his breath back, he started again, finding a different way. Soon there were no more trees on either side, and he worked his way out wider until he could see properly. The branch bent under his weight, going lower and lower until he decided not to risk any more.

It took a while to get his bearings, although the camp and its smoking fire helped. That was sloppy, and he had found the Brigantes to be casual even by army standards when it came to concealing their presence. Beyond them, closer than he expected, although it was partly an illusion, was the rich blue of the sea. The mainland was so clear he could tell rain was coming without having to look at the brooding clouds rushing in from the west. To the left of the camp was the marsh, a richer green than the fields around about, but otherwise hard to tell apart until it turned into the pale brown of tall reeds. Deeper in there were glints of sunlight off water, perhaps from ponds or streams, then broader patches of blue free of reeds. There were two lakes, each a couple of hundred paces across and in between a spit of land rising into a low hill. A single tree stood at the highest point, and perhaps it had been the sapling Acco had mentioned. Three low stone huts stood a little apart, but there was no sign of life.

Ferox took a long time climbing down, ignoring Vindex's increasingly impatient shouts. All the while he wondered whether to tell what he had learned. Crispinus' threat might be a guess or mean that he had evidence for his affair with Sulpicia Lepidina; enough to humiliate and ruin her.

'Oh, you haven't gone,' the scout said as he jumped to the floor. Vindex saw his expression. 'Bad as that, is it?'

'You know what tomorrow night is?'

'Aye.' It would be a day before the Kalends of November, but that was not what Ferox meant.

'And do you want to be here then?'

'I don't want to be here at all. Still, we need to protect the lady.'

'Who'll protect us from her?'

The shepherd lay moaning on the grass when they returned. He was badly bruised all over his face and chest left bare by his torn tunic. They had carried him off to one side and dumped him there.

'Where have you been?' Crispinus barked angrily as he saw them.

'Doing my job, my lord. I take it the prince learned all he needed to know.'

Arviragus appeared from behind a bush, straightening his trousers. One of his guards stood by holding his armour. 'Don't be insolent, centurion. And remember that you are a prisoner.' He glanced at the shepherd and then back at Ferox. 'So what have you learned?'

'We will need the boat,' Ferox said, and began to explain. An hour and a half later he sat in the prow as the soldiers rowed. Crispinus was behind him, as well as Cocceius. 'In case we need a good swimmer,' he had told the boy, who had almost burst with pride to be chosen. They headed around the coast to the east. First there were cliffs, then another beach, before rounding a headland they came to the edge of the marsh. They went in closer, looking for streams to take them inland. After a while they found one and followed it until in ended in reeds too thick to push through. The second one got them a little further before the keel hit mud, and then one of the soldiers remembered seeing something that might give them a chance over on the far side. Another cloudburst came in, drenching them afresh, but they found the mouth of the stream and although it wound back and forth it was wide and deep enough for them to keep going. On either bank were reeds so high that they could not see out. Ferox struggled to judge how far they had gone in a straight line, but although it became narrow and they had to paddle rather than row, they were still moving, ever deeper inside.

'We need to turn around,' the senior soldier said. 'Otherwise be dark before we get back to sea.'

'Just a little more,' Ferox said, and Crispinus nodded his approval. They turned another bend and the reeds were sparse ahead of them. Ferox took a spear and thrust down into the water. It was only a couple of feet deep, but the mud below was loose. He tried again and hit something far more solid.

'Ready, lad?' he asked Cocceius. The boy grinned. Both men stripped off their clothes. Neither had come in armour. Ferox went first, dropping over the side. The shock of the cold water was appalling, but his boots sank only a little into mud before they stopped. He reached up for the spear, and prodded down through the water in front of him. As he took his first step, Cocceius came into the water behind him.

They waded on, the Batavian close behind. After a few paces the water deepened again and reached their chests. Ferox could feel the flow plucking at his legs and running out the way they had come. Mud sucked at his feet each time he lifted one, and he leaned on his spear to pull himself out. Another step and the water was at his chin, but the spear prodded and it was shallower ahead. He warned Cocceius, who grinned again, and pushed ahead. Then he was climbing, for there was almost a bank under the reeds, and as he pulled himself up, slipped, breaking the reed he was holding, and recovered, he suddenly saw it. The lake was smooth as glass and dark as night, and beyond it was the low hill and the tree. The huts must have been on the far side of the hill because he could not see them. Still, this was surely where Acco claimed to have sacrificed the man who had once carried Ferox's sword, and his instincts told him that this too was the most sacred place Prasto had searched for and never found. If they were to find what they were looking for then it would be here.

'Can we swim it?' he asked the young Batavian.

The lad gave another big grin. 'In our sleep.'

'We need to go,' Crispinus called. 'Now, centurion, before we lose the light. If you have found what we want we shall return tomorrow.'

Ferox sighed, for he had known all along what would happen. For the Romans tomorrow was merely the last day of October. Yet here, and among all the tribes, it was Samhain, the night when the gates to the Otherworld opened and the dead walked abroad. Nowhere on Mona would be a good place to be when the sun set tomorrow, but who knew what horrors would come here, where once a sacred and very secret grove had stood and bloody sacrifices taken place.

XXI

'WE SHALL NEED another boat,' the tribune decided, and the prince readily agreed, but the wind had picked up as they had battled their way against the tide, and the senior soldier refused to try going to Segontium during the hours of darkness.

'Not in this weather, sir, begging your pardon.'

Ferox sensed Arviragus was itching to send them anyway, but for once the tribune stood up to his 'captor' and talked him round. The storm that blew in an hour later proved that this was the right decision, and the wind did not drop until the third hour of the day. Ferox sensed the inevitability of it all, since this meant at least a couple of hours before they returned with the second boat, and hopefully with a small punt he had requested. By the time the rowers had taken a little rest and parties been organised, the afternoon was well advanced. If they got there in daylight they would be lucky, and he knew they would not get back.

At least the delay gave him a chance to have a quiet word with Vindex and Gannascus, for it was no surprise that none of his men were to accompany him. Only Brigantian guards would go, apart from Crispinus, young Cocceius and the soldiers needed to row the boats, although half of these were replaced by the prince's men. As they were getting ready to leave, Claudia Enica appeared, swathed in her heavy cloak, and strode towards the boats. The bodyguard looked questioningly at Arviragus, who just nodded and then held out his hand to his sister

'As you wish, my lord.'

Enica did not acknowledge him in any way. Neither did she even glance at her brother, but instead waded to where Ferox sat in the other boat and reached out her hand. He took it, and helped her aboard. She was barefoot, and as her cloak parted he saw that she was wearing a tunic much like the one she had worn to fight. Cocceius stared wide-eyed at her legs as they came over the side. Once she was in, she took her boots from where they had been tied round her neck and pulled them on.

'Thank you,' she said. They were the only words she spoke during the journey, and the rest of the time she stared fixedly out to sea, watching the gulls as they swooped and dived. Ferox found her uncharacteristic stillness and silence vaguely unnerving. Cocceius spent the trip in smiling worship, perhaps helped along by memories of their first encounter back at Vindolanda.

There was much more of a swell today, and before long all the Brigantes were suffering, faces deathly pale or touched with green, so that the soldiers cursed them whenever they missed a stroke. Arviragus sat next to Crispinus in the other boat, and although he did his best to look unconcerned, his hand gripped the side of the boat tightly. Cocceius grinned as he so often did, at least whenever he could prise his eyes away from the lady, for now and then the wind parted her cloak and showed off her legs. Then his gaze reminded Ferox of the squirrel. The lady paid no heed to anyone, and showed no sign of any sickness.

Ferox's boat led the way upstream, towing the punt. As they went between the reeds, they entered a world of shadows, for the later afternoon sun was already low in the sky. They went quicker across the smooth water, winding round a path they knew. Ferox had made sure that his was the same boat with the same steersman and some of the rowers who had made the journey yesterday. At times the second craft struggled to follow.

The light lasted, if barely, and they reached the thin line of reeds between the stream and the lake. Ferox and Cocceius stripped again, the boy self conscious and blushing this time because the lady was there. She ignored them. The two men waded back to the punt and unfastened it. With some effort, and the help of two Brigantes who had joined them in the water, they managed to drag it up and through the reeds onto the lake.

Claudia Enica pulled off her boots and then stood up, still paying no attention to the men around her. She unfastened her cloak and dropped it, undid her belt with its weapons and then pulled the tunic off over her head. Cocceius gasped, eyes wide and mouth gaping. Underneath she wore a wide calfskin breast band and two soft leather triangles tied together with thongs around her hips. Ferox had seen outfits like this on the beach at Baiae, and sometimes even in the baths, but they appeared a revelation to the young Batavian, although it was hard to tell whether or not he was disappointed or thrilled that she was not quite naked. He blushed a violent red and crouched, then turned and dived into the lake. Ferox laughed and did the same.

'You should cross with us, lady,' Crispinus called.

'Or wait for the second trip,' her brother suggested.

Enica's only answer was to hand the bundle she had made by wrapping her things up in her cloak to one of the guards. 'Have them take this across for me.'

The punt was long enough for five, but one needed to take it back again for the next party, so it would carry the tribune, the prince and two of his guards across on the first trip. With some reluctance Ferox let them take his sword, belt and boots as well. Cocceius had brought an old shield, and they piled their clothes and a dry blanket on top. The lad exaggeratedly showed the hilt of the pugio he had slipped in at Ferox's request. Thankfully the two Brigantes were too busy watching Enica as she climbed over the bank and then dived gracefully into the water. Without waiting for the others, she swam straight out towards the hill ahead of them.

'Come on, boy,' Ferox said and they followed.

They were halfway across the lake before the punt set out, although it had nearly caught them up by the time they reached the far shore. Enica was first, striding up from the waves like Venus. The gracefulness of her movements truly was remarkable, and Ferox felt like some ungainly aquatic monster as he waded ashore. Cocceius was beside him; he rather felt the boy had been polite and kept to his pace, for the Batavians tended to be superb swimmers. They used the blanket to dry themselves a little and then started to dress.

'Don't on my account,' the lady told them. Cocceius' blush spread again, almost as pink as the clouds around the setting sun. Ferox shaded his eyes against its light. Night was coming. He shivered.

Arviragus bounded off the punt and came rushing up the slope. Crispinus trailed behind with the two guards, one carrying the lady's bundle.

'So, where now, centurion?' The prince was brimming with enthusiasm.

He pointed to the tree. 'Up there, then the huts on the far side,' he said, even though he had no real idea what to expect. My lord, has one of your men brought my sword and boots?'

The prince did not bother to ask. 'Sorry, Ferox. Got left on the boat. They'll bring it with the next trip.' The punt was already a fair way out from the shore.

Ferox led them to the tree. Close up, he was no longer sure that this was a hill, for it had an even look, like one of the mounds left by the forgotten people, the users of flint and the makers of the stone circles.

'I see a yew tree,' the prince said. 'I am assuming there must be more.'

They could see the huts now and walked down to them. Enica caught up, dressed again in tunic and boots and with her gladius and curved sica at her belt. The huts were strange, even the roofs made from stone, reminding Ferox of the houses built by the folk in the far north of Caledonia. Perhaps that was no surprise, since by sea Mona was not so very far away. It was often said that the people who lived there were more akin to the northerners and the Hibernians than they were to their neighbours the Ordovices.

The huts were in poor repair, gaping holes in their roofs and walls, but there were tracks by the doors of each one and some of them were fresh, no more than a few hours old. He could not say more in this light and decided not to mention it. None of this felt right. Ferox bent down to go through the door into one. It was dim and all he saw was broken pots and rotting pieces of wood.

'Be dark soon,' he said. 'We will need light. Did you bring the torches?' The Brigantes had remembered this and when the prince snapped his fingers they set about using a flint to light some kindling.

The second hut had even less inside it. Set in the stone were a number of thick rings, the iron heavily rusted. They might have been meant to tether animals rather than people, but Ferox doubted it. The third hut stank and was full of old sacks, bones and dung. There was a dead fox, belly burst open and covered in maggots, and no doubt the source of the worst smell. Arviragus ducked his head in after Ferox and then pulled back, face screwed up in distaste.

'Nothing here,' he said.

'I need a light,' Ferox said. 'And a spear. Come on.' He kicked at some of the rubbish to clear it. There was no reason for all this to be here unless it was hiding something. Arviragus took a torch from one of his men and came back inside.

'You,' Crispinus commanded the other guard. 'Your spear, man.'

Ferox used the shaft to drag aside some of the filth and debris. There seemed to be bare earth underneath. Then he tapped the butt of the spear down. It did not have a spike and the wood hit the floor and threw up dust.

'Hollow?' The tribune crouched down to see better. 'Hercules' balls. It is hollow!'

Turning the spear around, Ferox used the head to dig into the earth and scrape it away. It was loose, not packed hard, which made him think that it had not lain very long. He scraped again, and this time it was so easy to push the muck out of the way that he wondered whether it had only been there a few hours. 'Post a sentry.'

'Yes, I see,' Crispinus said. 'If someone has covered this over they may be around outside somewhere.'

The prince thought, nodded, and gave the order. Four more of his guards had joined them.

'Have they seen anything?' Ferox asked.

The Brigantes claimed to have seen nothing untoward, so he kept on clearing the earth and debris aside until the wooden trapdoor was uncovered. It was about two feet square, of thick pieces with almost no gap between them, and with a large iron ring.

'Stand back,' he ordered, and used the spearhead to hook under the ring. It needed very little force to lift, confirming his suspicion that they were not the first to come here. As it opened, all he could see below was darkness. 'Let's have some light.' Crispinus came up, holding a torch, and Ferox could see that there was a drop of some four feet to a mud floor of what looked like a long tunnel. There were prints of several people. 'Someone's been here within the last day, perhaps even within a few hours, my lords,' he said, just in case they all continued to ignore the obvious signs.

'Acco?' Crispinus suggested. Neither he nor the prince seemed surprised. 'Has he beaten us to it?' The tribune frowned. 'Then why hide this tunnel?'

'We've come this far, my lord, so we may as well find out. I need my sword and a torch,' Ferox said. 'This spear will be no use down there. And my boots.'

The footwear was readily provided.

'We'll pass the rest down to you, centurion.' Crispinus grinned. 'For a moment I was worried you would suggest the shortest of us should go first.'

Ferox sat on the edge and them jumped. Crouching, he stared into the darkness and reckoned that the tunnel was heading underneath the mound. Stories told of ancient tombs filled with gold and gems, but protected by monsters and terrible spells. At least he would not be the first to visit. He reached up and the tribune gave him a torch. 'Just the blade, my lord,' he said, when Arviragus appeared, holding out his belt and scabbarded sword from one of the guards. The tunnel might get smaller, and it was better to carry the gladius in his hand than wear it.

The prince of the Brigantes slid the blade out. He felt it, hefting the sword, and flexing his wrist. His eyes glinted in the torchlight.

'Beautiful,' he said, and Ferox sensed a reluctance to hand it down, but if there was, then the prince swiftly got over it. The centurion's fingers closed around the familiar bone handgrip. He did not trust any of the others, and was sure this was a trap of some sort. He had not expected to be given a weapon, least of all his own sword. Somehow the gesture made him even more suspicious. 'Wait here until I take a look.' Hoping they would obey, he ducked his head, thrust the torch ahead of him and walked on.

The floor was soft mud, the passage little more than a foot and a half wide, and so many booted and bare feet had passed along it that it was hard to make out individual tracks. The walls were flecked with stone and slate, and in places carved out of more solid rock. There was a harsh smell faint behind the damp, musty odour.

There was a soft thud as someone jumped down behind him.

'You should wait, lady,' he said without looking around.

'What?' Claudia Enica tried to make her voice as deep and manly as possible, and Ferox was glad he had guessed correctly. No one else followed her.

'Come on then.'

The passage went straight for ten paces, then turned left, making a long curve, before turning back to the right. It was higher now, just high enough for him to stand almost upright and only now and then brush his hair against the roof. Just around the first bend a skull grinned at him from a niche carved into the wall. He waited, hoping for a nervous gasp when the lady came around the corner. In the event, it was barely more than a soft hiss of surprise, but he smiled to himself anyway. After the next turn there was another skull. This time he heard no hint of surprise. The smell was getting stronger. He coughed, for it stuck in the throat, like smoke, yet it tasted bitter. Ferox was not sure whether he saw dust or smoke or both in the air. Water dripped from the roof.

It grew narrower, and at times he had to turn sideways and edge along. His torch was in front of him and when he glanced back Enica was a faint shape. Still, he suspected Vindex would have made some comment about it being too narrow for her.

'Do you want me to go first?' she said as he paused for just a moment.

'Wait.' The floor in front of him was smooth, unbroken by any footprint. With difficulty he swapped his torch and sword. Leaning over, he prodded the earth with the long tip of the gladius. He sidestepped forward and then did it again. The third time the point drove through the thin straw and mud covering a small pit. In the centre was a stake, perhaps no more than six or seven inches, but sharpened to a point and no doubt smeared with filth. The army called a trap like this a *lillia*, after the vague resemblance to the lily flower. For the Silures they were gnat's bites. They did not kill, at least not quickly, but a man with a hurt foot was slower and made others cautious.

'Watch where you tread,' he whispered.

Ferox found three more lilies, the last where the narrow passage made another sharp turn, but then grew wider before another abrupt corner. He still had the torch behind him and the sword in front. Even with his body masking a lot of the light he could see that there were footprints on the earth; a clear trail, one person walking towards them. Enica stepped over the last of the little stakes and was only just behind him. He glanced back. Her skin seemed very pale in the torchlight and her face was eager.

'What now?' she asked.

'Hold my sword.'

'What here? Now?' Sometimes the sense of humour of the Brigantes was tiresome, although he could imagine Vindex cackling at this, especially since such vulgarity was surprising in a lady.

With difficulty and a few grazes he brought his right hand back and held the sword for her to take. She leaned forward, brushing against his left arm as it held the torch.

Then he eased that forward and lowered it close to the floor in front of him. There was nothing to see. Ferox edged forward, feeling exposed in the wider passage. He kept the torch low, inching along. The Lord of the Hills always said that to set a trap or escape one you had to outthink the other man. They had just come past the lilies into a passage that was wider and easier. He doubted the philosophers with their logic ever considered such a problem, but to him it was natural to expect them to feel relieved and relax their guard.

There it was. Just before the next corner a cord was stretched across barely an inch off the ground, where someone holding a torch at normal height was unlikely to see it. He knelt down next to it and beckoned to her.

'Tread lightly, lady, and where I point. First tread in the prints.'

Enica glared at him with the assurance of a noblewoman who gave rather than received orders. Then she obeyed. Although wider than before, the passage was still little more than two feet broad so that she would have to squeeze along. Enica was just behind him now. She thrust his sword into the earth so that he could take it back when ready.

'Step high, and watch my hand.' He half expected another joke, but there was none and the lady did as she was told. The torch was in front of him, over the cord and he waved it until Enica nodded to show that she had seen the danger. He arched his hand over to point to where she must tread. She was close, the hem of her tunic brushing against his face. Her hands held her two swords up high to stop them snagging, and she lifted her leg up and across to plant it firmly beyond the cord. So close, it was hard not to admire her legs and Ferox had to bite back a comment. He must have spent too much time with Vindex.

'Now very carefully,' he said, and gently touched her other leg. She shivered, and that surprised him, but they both needed to concentrate. Foolish though it sounded, it was so easy to set off a trap like this by relaxing too soon. Enica stepped forward and he steered her other leg across, pushing a little so that she kept it higher for just a little longer. 'There,' he said. A moment later he took his hand away. The air was growing thicker, and she coughed.

'Thank you,' she said. 'I would have walked into this.'

Ferox retrieved his sword and with great care stepped over the cord. On the wall around the corner was a heavy frame of wood mounting long spikes. He saw ropes and guessed the cord was connected to them, intended to shift the big stone used as a counterweight and swing out with force to strike anyone in the passage. Although it looked old, someone had taken care to repair it and he had little doubt that it would have worked.

It was getting harder to breathe and the air felt thick. The dripping was louder, almost like voices coming from the rows of skulls set into both walls. Ferox blinked. It was getting harder to see clearly, as if they were walking through a cloud. He went in front, searching the ground, but raising the torch to look at the walls and ceiling as well. The floor was once again a mass of prints, which was encouraging. The passage wound and twisted, and they turned sharp corners, going slowly and carefully. He started to feel that the skulls were mocking him. They must have passed hundreds of them by now and the power of this place was growing so great that he feared it would crush him.

There was light ahead, and as they came closer he saw faint clouds of vapour drifting in it. The stench was overwhelming and he wondered whether he would ever be free of the taste. Enica stumbled beside him, and when he lifted her he swayed.

'Come on,' she said, her words slurred. She pushed him aside and rushed towards the light.

'Wait!' Ferox wanted to shout, but it came out as a croak. He went after her, almost panicking because he feared she would vanish. The skulls laughed louder. He ran, and then burst into a large chamber, with doors opening in the walls and a floor made from little stones pressed into the earth. In the centre a fire burned, giving off the vapour. Enica was on her knees in front of it, panting hard. As he came in the smoke almost choked him. He staggered, but pushed on and dropped the torch to grab her by the shoulder, dragging her away from the fire. It felt cooler to the side, the air clearer, and although she tried to push him away, he pulled her hard, sliding her across the floor until they were both on the far side. Then he fell beside her, struggling for breath. The air was fresher and he managed to push himself up on his arms.

The old man moaned. There were manacles on his arms and a slave chain around his neck, although neither were really needed. He was naked apart from a dirty loin cloth, and had no feet, just stumps, the wounds clumsily closed with fire not long ago. Ferox stared at him for a long time, his thoughts grinding slowly and with difficulty into place at first. The old man did not look back, because his eyes were gone, the wounds older than those on his legs. There were scars all over his face, body and limbs, some fresh and some healed.

'Who are you?' Enica gasped.

The old man muttered something that did not sound like words. Ferox managed to stand. His mind was clearing. When they had opened the trapdoor the raught had sucked the smoke from whatever was burning down along the passage. Now he was behind the fire he was breathing more easily. Beyond the fire, laid out in a circle around the tortured man, were objects. There was a cauldron, its sides decorated with scenes of war and sacrifice, and a spear lying on the ground to point at the man. Next to it was a skull, then a torc, a shield, a mirror and a helmet placed on top of a scale cuirass. Above them all, set in the wall, was a stone carved so that the three projecting sides each had a face. The Treasures of Britannia, and as the memory came he realised who the old man was.

'Prasto?' he asked.

The man stirred, making an odd gurgling sound.

'Well done, centurion.' Domitius came out of one of the inner chambers. Ferox blinked because he had not expected the trader. 'It is indeed what is left of the druid who joined the Romans. Well, the one who did it openly, at least. But he cannot answer, because he has no tongue any more.'

Ferox picked up his sword, but as he leaned forward his head started to swim again. Standing straight, he went for the man until his knees gave way beneath him.

Domitius laughed. 'It will take a while for you to recover.'

A scream echoed from behind them down the passage and the merchant laughed again. 'It seems we shall soon welcome our other guests.'

The smell was less strong here, and then another stale odour replaced it, as a scruffy little dog trotted out to stand by the merchant's feet. Ferox stared at the animal as he began to realise what a fool he had been.

Domitius did not appear to move, and yet somehow his face and posture were different. Acco laughed. 'Welcome, prince of the Silures. Welcome, princess and queen of the Brigantes. You are both most welcome.' There was a flint knife in his hand. He strode past Ferox, ignoring a feeble attempt to stop him, and entered the circle. Four warriors appeared. One was small and wiry with dirty red hair, carrying a torch in one hand and a club in the other. The others were not local, for they were taller, their hair stiffened into spikes with lime and their faces and bare torsos covered in tattoos. Two went to the cauldron, lifted it with some effort and then poured out water over the fire, which hissed and threw up a last thick plume of smoke.

The other two went to Ferox and one was carrying manacles like the ones binding Prasto's arms. He scrabbled for his sword until they kicked it out of his reach. Then they kicked him twice, knocking him down as he tried to rise. He rolled away, and as he lay on his chest a boot pressed hard down onto his back. His arms were wrenched back behind him, making him grunt with pain. He felt the weight of the manacles and heard the snaps as they closed shut. The man standing on him pressed down harder, grinding his face into the floor.

'Enough!' Acco barked, and the boot was lifted away. Ferox struggled to breathe. Beside him he saw that Enica was trying to sit up, but her limbs lacked strength and she kept slipping. A warrior appeared on either side of her and she was dragged to her feet, arms pinned behind her back. Her belt was unclasped and it and the two swords clattered onto the floor.

'Sit him up.' Ferox was turned over and then lifted. His head was clearing and it was getting easier to see and think again. Enica's head kept nodding and her eyes blinked again and again. She did little to resist when one of the men produced a rope and tied her hands behind her back. The same man then tied Ferox's ankles together.

'You must think I am very dangerous,' he croaked. The warrior ignored him.

Acco knelt beside the blinded and mutilated Prasto. 'Did you ever think that you could escape punishment? Was it just jealousy?' He spoke softly, his tone was that of a parent disappointed in a child who kept on failing. 'You know it was not, don't you? This was your fate. You just thought that you were being clever. Yet for all your wealth you were never free, for in the end you had to suffer. You know that, don't you? You cannot betray the gods and escape. This is merely the start, for the curse will follow your soul in the Otherworld. Sightless and footless, you will crawl along and all will know what you did.'

The druid stood up, knife ready. There was a shout and one of the Brigantes leaped into the chamber. He carried no shield, but his slim spatha was held low, ready to thrust. Arviragus came behind him, blood spattered on his face.

'Stay!' he shouted. He lifted his own sword, as his eyes flicked around the chamber. Crispinus came next. A warrior held a blade to Enica's neck and the men went still.

'It is true,' the prince said, staring at the circle of objects.

Acco ran his hand through the old man's thin and dirty hair, the gesture surprisingly tender. He neither looked up nor answered the prince. His fingers touched the empty eye sockets and the scars on the man's face.

'Drop your swords!' Arviragus shouted. None of the warriors moved.

'Your story in this world is over,' the druid said to Prasto, and cut his throat. Blood gushed. For all his wounds the old man still had plenty and it splashed over him and onto the floor. His mouth opened and closed without sound, until he slumped down.

At last Acco deigned to notice the new arrivals. 'You are welcome here, prince of the Brigantes.'

Arviragus took a step forward, pushing past his guard. 'Tell your warriors to lay down their arms.' Another Brigantian trooper came into the chamber, with Cocceius following. The lad's eyes were wide with fear, but Ferox felt it was the Brigantes who were even more nervous, fearing Acco and his power.

'That is not necessary.' The druid wiped the flint knife on his clothes and tucked it into his belt. 'Neither is that.' He nodded to the warrior threatening Claudia Enica. The man lowered his sword. 'You have no power here to match mine.'

'We have five swords.' Crispinus did not sound confident. 'Even if you slay us you will pay a high price.' He spoke in the language of the tribes, the words slow, but clear enough.

'You do not understand, Roman.' Acco's soft voice somehow carried around the chamber more powerfully than anyone else's. 'But let me speak in a way you will understand.' He had switched to Latin. 'There are thirty warriors outside. I am guessing you saw them and that is how you found the courage to follow these two.' He gestured at Enica and Ferox. 'That is what you will think at least. For the truth is that I summoned you all. You know this, do you not, prince?'

'Ferox, is there another way out?' the tribune asked.

'I do not think so.' Ferox's throat felt thick and it was difficult to talk. The draught had taken the fumes up the tunnel, which meant that it was the only way in, unless another door was sealed tight. He had seen no sign of another entrance when he had searched above the mound.

Acco paid them no attention, and instead walked towards the Romans. 'Come, prince. I have what I need. Will you take what you want and go? The warriors outside will not hinder you unless I order it.'

Arviragus sheathed his sword.

'Can you trust him?' Crispinus' whisper came out louder than he had intended.

The druid spun around slowly, waving his hand around the circle, then turned and walked away. Arviragus licked his lips and took a pace towards it. 'This is why we came,' he said. The next step was a little more confident. He rubbed his hands together nervously.

'You may make two choices, prince,' Acco said. 'Just as we agreed.'

Enica frowned, her thoughts still clouded. 'What is he saying?'

Her brother stared at the circle of objects and did not even glance towards her. 'It is meant to be. There is no other way.' He knelt beside the helmet and cuirass. For a moment he hesitated, then he touched them with the tenderness of a lover. He smiled and lifted them. 'Take these,' he told the nearest of his guards.

'One more, prince. Two souls for two things. That is the bargain.'

'What?' Enica almost spat out the word. 'What have you done, brother?' Ferox guessed that he and the lady were the druid's price.

Still he did not face her. 'It is the price of glory.' For a while he held his hand over the mirror, until he shook his head. Next he stared for a long time at the neatly folded cloak of Claudius and Alexander. 'No,' he said in the end. 'It must be this.' No longer hesitant he strode over and snatched the torc of Caratacus and the high kings of the south.

'So be it.' Acco almost shouted the words and they echoed around the chamber.

'Have I been wise?' Arviragus asked as the sounds died away.

'That is for you to discover. Now you must leave. You will not be harmed.'

'What about them?' Crispinus asked. 'My centurion and the lady should come with us.'

Acco said nothing.

'They stay,' Arviragus said after a moment. 'Let us go quickly.'

Acco nodded to the small warrior. 'He will guide you and see that you come to no harm. Leave and live with your choices.'

The prince frowned. He was holding the torc and bent it back so that he could slip it around his neck. He swelled visibly as if it gave him strength. 'Come on,' he said.

'We can't leave them.' Cocceius stood in the doorway and raised his sword. 'They must come with us, sir. They just must.' The lad sounded confused, but very determined.

'Out of my way, boy!' Arviragus yelled.

Crispinus shrugged. 'Best obey, lad. Or we all die.'

'It's wrong, sir, and you know it.' The young soldier sounded surprised at his own defiance.

Arviragus half turned back. 'What do you think, my Lord Crispinus?' Suddenly he plucked a sword from one of the guards, shifted his hand onto the grip and drove it into the lad's belly, grabbing him by the shoulder to pull him further onto the blade. Cocceius was wide-eyed in surprise, gasping, but the prince merely threw him down. He ripped the sword free and stabbed down again. Cocceius went still. 'Come on,' the prince said, tossing the bloodied blade back to his guard.

Acco laughed softly. 'Blood of king, blood of queen,' he whispered as they left. Crispinus turned as if he had heard. 'Do you remember those words, Flavius Ferox? The one who said them was wrong and yet right for the hour has come. Rest a while, before you both set out on a new path.'

Again the druid laughed.

XXII

'WHAT ARE YOU doing?' Claudia Enica's voice broke the long silence, even though she spoke in a whisper. They were in one of the side rooms off the main chamber, the roof so low that Ferox felt his hair brushing the stones if ever he sat up straight. He could see nothing at all, for without any light they were surrounded by a blackness deeper than any night.

'What are you doing?' she repeated, her tone angry. They had been placed on the damp floor, back to back and a little apart, before Acco's men left and took the torch with them. Ferox had listened for what seemed a long while until he was sure they had gone, before sitting up and shuffling towards her. There was no way to unlock the manacles, but they allowed him a little freedom to move his hands and he wondered whether he could untie Enica's wrists. His fingers felt smooth warm skin. She shuddered, saying nothing at first, and he eased along, pushing up the hem of her tunic until he found a knot. It felt too small, although maybe that was because his fingers were clumsy.

'Trying to get us free,' he whispered.

'Huh!' No one could express disgust quite like the Brigantes. To display the same passion as a Roman Claudia would have had to spit on the floor in public. She was silent for a moment. 'Would you like me to bring my arms to your hands?'

Ferox remembered the slim thongs tying the young woman's little bathing pants. 'Sorry.'

'So are you planning on taking your hands off my arse?'

'Sorry.' Ferox drew back and with some wriggling Enica thrust her tied arms so that they brushed against his hands. He searched for the knot, found something much larger and felt for an end to the cord.

'Can you tell the difference now?'

'I am sorry.' There was a piece of rope sticking out of the knot, but it was so tight that at first he could not move it at all.

'Does he mean to kill us?' Enica asked. 'The talk of blood was not encouraging. Though I am not yet a queen and you are certainly not a king.'

'Silures don't have kings. Not really. And I am just a centurion.'

'My brother means to be king. And more in time. He sees his road leading to the Senate and even beyond to the imperial purple. Acco appeared when he was born, or so he claims. Grandmother would not have wanted him, but she was ill, and father always sought to learn about the future. My brother claims that the druid said his destiny was to rise like a burning star in the night sky, climbing higher than any of his ancestors. Big brother believes that includes Caesar himself.' She shifted slightly and Ferox wondered whether she was shaking her head. 'He is not very bright. Takes after father.'

'Acco told me that it is my destiny to kill him.'

She chuckled. 'Well, it might help us out. He does mean to kill us, doesn't he?'

'Probably.' Blood of king, blood of queen. The Stallion and his men had chanted the phrase and used it in their incantations, planning to make a royal sacrifice on Samhain two years ago. 'Did Lepidina tell you about the attempts to abduct her?' Her husband was a king of the Batavians as well as prefect of Rome, which meant that the priest had considered her to be a queen. Ferox had managed to protect her, but had failed to save Vegetus' wife who was mistakenly taken instead.

'A little. Thank you for not hiding the truth.' She chuckled again, and soon the chuckle became a laugh. 'Poor brother, he thinks he has the armour of our grandfather.'

Ferox had managed to loosen the knot slightly. 'He does not, because you have.' He felt her stiffen. 'You paid Rufus and the others for them, and then watched as they rode off with the girl.'

'It was unfortunate, but I saw no other way.' Her voice was soft.

'Then you were the one who met them and rode off carrying the spoils. And who ambushed the two men I sent after you.'

'I did not know who they were and could not take a chance. Domitius wanted the helmet and the mail. Some folk loyal to me were in debt to him and to Narcissus. They were to be payment for this year and the next and would give time to gather enough to pay the rest.' She laughed again, grimly this time. 'I knew who he really is, but that only made it more important to help my people. The faith of the Brigantes.' She shrugged as well as their bonds allowed. 'I switched the helm and armour with the ones brother is now carrying away. The real helmet is a lot plainer. I thought it odd at the time that Acco did not realise the trick. Now I guess he knew all along.'

'Perhaps he did not care?' Ferox suggested. 'Do you have them still?'

'They are safe. You have stopped work, centurion. Have you given up, or are you poised to grope me again?' Ferox resumed his task. 'Good. We may not have much chance of getting out, but any chance is better than none.

'Narcissus had promised to give me the only record of one loan made to a chieftain and to cancel the debt. In return I had some trinkets belonging to grandmother that he wanted. Nothing very interesting or valuable, but they were what he wanted.'

'And you met him at Vindolanda and found him already dead,' Ferox interrupted. The knot refused to come free and almost felt tighter again. 'He was stuffed in the latrine, and you, noble lady and princess of the Brigantes, jumped down into the filth and searched the corpse.'

'You have worked it out, then? Yes, I wanted that papyrus. And found it as well, so for all his greed he had at least been honest about that. One of my people is released from a great burden.'

'And you heard Cocceius coming, so ripped open your tunic and flashed your breasts at him to make sure he did not look closely at your face.' Slowly, Ferox felt the end of the rope work free.

'Was it that poor boy?' Enica was not much older than the dead Batavian soldier, but easily assumed a superiority.

'I wondered why he kept staring at me. Still, most men do – even the ones who don't think I notice, centurion!' She sighed. 'Poor, poor fellow. He remembered, I suppose, and that is how you know.'

'Did you kill Caratacus?' She pulled her arms away. 'Don't be foolish. This is no time to argue. I merely asked a question.' She relaxed, and painfully slowly he started to pull the knot until it began to loosen.

'No.' Enica spoke loudly. 'I did not, neither would I have done save at direst need. I liked him, and did not know he was in danger until news came of his murder. I am not the only woman in the world, although I dare say by comparison the rest must fade away.' Her heart did not sound as if it was in the self-mockery. 'It was another who killed and stole at Bremesio, and another who went to Rome, murdered the old king, and then brought the torc to Domitius. She and her thugs served him and were well paid. Her name was Achillea.'

'Was?'

'We had a disagreement,' she said mildly. 'It was after I had saved you from the fire. A worthless deed, since it has brought me no thanks, and I wonder now why I bothered. After that I found her on a ship in the harbour. She died. One of her men joined her. The other dived into the river and so escaped.'

Part of Ferox felt revulsion at the thought of a woman killed by the sword, until he wondered whether it was so unlucky if another woman did the killing. Given that Enica now lay captive and likely to be sacrificed in the next few hours, then perhaps it was.

The thread came loose, but the knot was double and all that meant was that he had to start work on the next one.

'Your man was the one of the ones who helped lure me to the amphitheatre. Was that on your orders?'

'No. It was not. He did that for another, although if she had asked I would have told him to obey her.'

A truth he had long fled forced itself upon him at last. Sulpicia Lepidina had sent word for him that night, knowing that because she had asked for his help he would go without question. The woman he loved had sent him into a trap where he ought to have died.

'Lepidina.' He said the name softly, as if he still did not want to believe the truth.

Enica leaped to the defence of her friend. 'She did not have any choice. Fuscus had letters implicating her brother in fresh conspiracy. At first she hoped that you could kill him, but then he said that he had more evidence, enough to convict her of adultery with you. The procurator said he had statements from witnesses, and that they would swear Marcus was your child. You know the price of that? The child declared a bastard, disowned and even killed. Fuscus offered to let her have the statements, but his price was your death, and probably more later, although she did not say what. Neither did she understand why you had become important.'

'Lepidina.' He spoke as a man might about a goddess, beautiful, wonderful and implacable.

'I was not at the house when the word came, but arrived after she had sent my man to you. She told me what she had done, saying that she believed it was a price you would willingly pay for the boy. Perhaps even for her.'

Ferox nodded in the darkness. He had always known that she was a clarissima femina, a senator's daughter whose sense of duty and honour would come before her feelings for him. She felt affection, even love for him, that was real, but never as real or important as her duty. Ultimately he was expendable.

'I agreed,' Enica said. 'She did what she had to do, and did not expect forgiveness. Then I did what I had to do and I followed you and helped, wearing the helmet in the hope that Domitius would not realise Claudia Enica could be the Thracian gladiatrix.'

'I did not realise then.' Acco spoke from the darkness, making Ferox jump and bang his head on the roof. The druid chuckled. He must have been there a long time, perhaps from the very start, waiting behind in the darkness as his men left and listening. 'My eyes are not as good as they were,' he explained, 'especially at night. But when I realised it amused me. You do not disappoint, child.'

'What do you want of us?' she asked.

'For you to fulfil your destinies.' The faint glimmer of flame seemed like the rising sun and made Ferox blink. Warriors appeared, some of them carrying torches, and he had to turn away because it was so dazzling.

Acco said no more as a pair of warriors gently lifted Enica out of the small room and into the main chamber. Two more brought Ferox out, far less gently. The bonds on their legs were cut, and both of them swayed to stand upright on stiff and lifeless limbs. A blade was pressed to his throat as they undid one manacle and brought his hands round in front before they clicked it shut again. All of the objects had gone, but Cocceius still lay near the door, eyes staring up at nothing. As he passed, the druid reached down and closed them with something akin to tenderness. They were led along the winding passage, and saw one of the prince's guards impaled on the stakes of the trap.

Outside it was well past midnight and very cold after the close atmosphere of the barrow. Ferox tried not to shiver, for he did not wish to seem afraid. Slowly life was returning to his legs and they were no longer so stiff as he walked. Around twenty warriors stood in silence on the grass, most of them the small men of the island, their club-carrying leader in the centre. One handed the druid Ferox's sword as he passed and the old man swished at the long grass as he walked. Ahead of them the artefacts were laid out in a circle next to the lake, with a big fire blazing high in the centre. The druid led them to stand in the front of the blaze in the vey midst of the powerful objects. The heat was scorching, the pyre taller than he was, and Ferox wondered whether their fate was to burn.

'You cannot escape,' Acco told them, 'so do not try. Raise your arms out, child,' he commanded Enica, who obeyed. The druid walked behind her and, using his other hand to steady them, he sliced through the rope. She brought her arms around, rubbing her hands on them with pleasure, as the druid came round and stood in front of Ferox. 'You shall not be released. You are too much of a fool for me to take that risk. Few Silures know when to lie down. Yet you should kiss my feet in thanks, because I am about to give you a gift that other men will envy.'

The druid held up the rope that had tied the lady's arm. 'Enica of the Brigantes, granddaughter of Cartimandua, the caster of spells and weaver of enchantments, you did not know, but I was there when you were born and saw your destiny written in the stars and whispered on the winds. There was never any doubt.' He flicked the sword hard so that it spun and sank its point into the earth. 'You must be queen of your people and for that you must have a consort.'

'I know.' Enica's voice was faint. She turned her head and gave Ferox a pitying smile. 'I know,' she repeated firmly.

'Blood of king, blood of queen,' Ferox mouthed the words, not that it made any difference now. He wondered whether he could swing the manacles and knock down the old man and then dive into the lake before the warriors slaughtered him. He would not be able to swim, so must drown. Simple pins held the metal bracelets closed. Could she move fast enough to free him? Would she? To his amazement she looked almost happy, perhaps believing that this was her fate.

'Give me your arm, child.'

Enica stretched her right arm out towards the druid.

'You too, boy.'

Ferox did not move. Acco gestured at one of his own warriors. Gingerly the man stepped into the circle and went over to the centurion. He grabbed him firmly by the arms and raised them up.

'Thank you,' Acco said, and bound Enica's right arm to Ferox's left with the same rope that had bound her. 'So the gods make two into one,' he intoned, and began a long prayer calling upon gods and goddesses by name to bless this union. Ferox did not really listen, although the thought came to him that Crispinus had once suggested this unlikely alliance. The tribune was helping Arviragus, although it was hard to say how willing his assistance was, and what the young aristocrat really intended. At present it really made little difference, much as it did not seem to matter whether he died married or still on his own. Hazy cloud veiled most of the stars, and he could do no more than guess that it was around the fourth hour of the night. Acco did not seem to be in a hurry to complete his ritual.

The prayer ended. 'Kneel.' Enica did as she was told, arm held up awkwardly because Ferox stayed as he was. He had not been listening, so one of the warriors hit him hard in the back of the knees, using the flat of his long sword. Ferox knelt. Enica smiled again.

'Greetings, husband.' Her smile was broad, her eyes glinting in the firelight. He wondered whether she thought this marriage was all the druid wanted from them. One of the warriors undid the cord binding them.

'Huh,' she whispered. 'Is that take your things and go?' Ferox could not help smiling at the traditional Roman formula for a divorce.

'Begin,' Acco told his warriors. Two of them went to the stone head with its three faces and lifted it. They were tall, strong-looking men, and yet they struggled, walking slowly to the edge of the water. Once there they stopped, glancing back. Acco nodded. The men swung the head once, twice and then flung it into the lake, the splash soaking them since it did not go far. 'This is the end and the beginning,' Acco intoned.

Next they took the Spear of Camulos, and one snapped the shaft across his knee. Then the other took the part with the head and hammered the iron until it was bent. Again they faced the druid and again Acco nodded. The two fragments of the broken spear flew further before they sank into the dark mere. The skull of the witch was shattered with the hammer and tossed into the water. When they came to the cloak, they threw it into the fire.

Ferox wondered whether he could reach the gladius stuck in the ground. It was not much more than a yard away, so the chances were good and if he would not be able to wield it properly with these manacles, at least it would give him a chance to take one or two of them with him. Should he kill Acco first? For all that the man wanted to kill him and the woman beside him, he shrank from the deed. It was Samhain still, and he felt as if his ancestors watched him from the shadows of the night. The druid's power was growing almost visibly as the heat of the fire stirred his hair and made it stand on end. Killing these artefacts one by one, sending them down through fire or water into the Otherworld, fed Acco's spirit and his magic. Would the iron even bite if Ferox got the chance? Instead of acting, he watched and waited.

The mirror of Cartimandua was next.

'Please, no.' Enica sounded like a child, so unlike her usual confidence, let alone the chatter of Claudia.

'It is just a mirror, child,' Acco told her. A warrior struck the bronze back with the hammer, bending it. Another took it and threw it far into the lake.

'They say the cauldron of the Morrigan can raise the dead,' Acco said. Ferox wondered why he was taking so long to do everything. Perhaps that was the nature of magic. Unlike the Stallion, Acco had patience. 'Place a corpse inside the bowl, say the right words, and he will leap out, able to run, fight, make love, in fact do anything, except he cannot speak.

'I never saw it done. There were plenty killed when I came to Mona that first time. My comrades, my *commilitones* if you will, died one by one.'

'Domitius,' Ferox said, as the last pieces slid into place, and he knew the old druid had once been a Roman and Gaul, and an officer in the legions.

'You understand at last. You should, you know, for like both of you I have two lives intertwined. I was born Cnaeus Domitius Tullus of Lugdunum and can become him again when need be. That ... ' He glanced at the sword sticking in the grass and Ferox felt the druid saw into his mind. 'That sword was the sword of my family, although for some reason my father did not give it to me when I went to serve as a tribune here in Britannia and was captured by the Silures, who sent me to Mona with their other prisoners.

'The gods shaped their plans and I followed the path set me. Truth can speak to the right mind. My comrades died one by one. Some were brave and cursed back, and some died screaming or begging for mercy. Days passed and they did not come for me. They hung me up by my arms from that tree and sliced at me with knives, and I made no sound at all. That was not why they let me live. The truth came to me and they knew it, for they were old druids, men who knew the true ways of the gods. Now and again they found a pupil who had not come willingly, and found that he learned faster and more deeply than those who chose themselves. They saw that I was such a one, and I saw at last that Rome was a poison, but that here in Britannia Rome did not have to win, not in the end.' He nodded to the warriors and they took the cauldron and sent it into the lake.

'It is almost time.' Acco walked round behind them, raising the flint knife he had used to kill Prasto. He stood there, both arms above his head. A warrior came and stood in front of him, his long sword held low and blocking the path to his gladius. Still Acco waited. At least they were not to go into the fire, and a cut throat would be quick. Yet it was strange that they were to be spared the triple death of sacrifice, for the druid was not in a hurry. They should have eaten the grain and beans with their slow poison, have the cords at their throat ready to tighten, and suffered the death blow with knife or club just before their last breath left them.

'It is the last day,' Acco screamed at the night sky. 'The end of the past.'

Ferox waited. In a moment he would spring up, knocking into the warrior and then hoping to break free and reach his sword. If Enica was quick she might get away. Her arms and legs were free and she was a good swimmer. She could cross the lake and then… ? The boats were surely gone and even the best swimmer would struggle to cross the sea to safety. The most he could hope for was to let her live a little longer and perhaps by some miracle find a way out. That was all he could do for his new 'wife'.

'The last breath is spent,' Acco wailed at the heavens. The little warriors started clashing spears against their shields, going faster and faster. The moment was coming. He could not wait any longer, for his plan had obviously failed. Then a warrior a few paces away sprouted a long shafted arrow from his face and spun around. Ferox flung himself forward, struck the man in front just below the waist and knocked him down. He raised his arms and slammed them down. It was a small blow, but the weight of the iron manacles gave it force and the man's nose broke in bloody ruin. Enica tried to bound forward, then snapped back with a hiss. The warrior standing behind her had whipped a rope around her neck and was pulling hard. Acco raised his knife.

'Morrigan!' he screamed. One of the warriors by the lake was knocked over as an arrow buried itself deep in his chest. The islanders had stopped clashing their weapons and instead there were screams and grunts as a line of Batavians charged into them. Gannascus was in the centre, towering over the little men, his blade carving down through bone, muscle and flesh. Blood jetted high as he beheaded the chieftain.

Ferox pushed up, his knee hard on the warrior's chest, winding him. He reached the sword, pulled it free and was up. Enica's eyes were bulging, hands grasping at the rope as it tightened. Acco stepped towards her. The flint knife was ready to thrust down.

'Lugh, take this soul!'

Ferox stamped forward and thrust awkwardly into the druid's back. The long triangular point of the gladius slid into the old man's body, and if the blow was poorly aimed there was the power of both hands and all his hate behind it, driving the iron so hard that it burst out of Acco's stomach. The old man arched his back, limbs flailing, and the knife flew through the air.

The warrior behind Enica gaped at the dying druid, and must have loosened his grip for she slipped free and slumped to her knees. Ferox left the sword in the old man and ran at the warrior, screaming in rage. He swung his manacled arms at the warrior's face and he fell. Ferox pounced on top of him. Enica was gasping for breath. Ferox slammed the bracelets and his fists into the warrior's face again and again until there was only a bloody ruin.

Gannascus slashed his way through the line of islanders. Vindex was on one side and Longinus on the other. Their chieftain dead and the druid cut down, the little men broke, dropping spears and shields in their flight. There was nowhere for them to go and they were slaughtered one by one.

Ferox kept hammering the warrior's face, but he no longer moved. A hand touched his shoulder.

'He's dead,' Enica croaked. There was a livid mark around her neck, but she was breathing more naturally again.

Ferox stopped. His hands and the manacles were filthy with blood, pieces of flesh and bone. He stood up, panting.

'Sorry it took so long to find you,' Vindex said, as he wiped his sword on the hem of his tunic. Ferox went over to the druid. Acco was on his side, face pale, his white tunic dark with his own blood. The druid looked up, and Ferox was sure he smiled.

'The beginning,' he gasped, and died.

XXIII

CRASSUS' HORSE FLINCHED as its rider slapped its neck repeatedly. The legate of VIIII Hispana did not appear aware of what he was doing and just as unconsciously shifted in his seat and calmed the animal. Like his sister, Crassus was a fine horseman. Yet there the similarities ended, for it was hard to imagine her face so alight with sheer joy of destruction as he watched the villa's roof collapse and send up a great gout of smoke and dust. Ferox sensed that the legate was not really listening to his report.

It was the second day after the Ides of November, and the villa belonged to a Brigantian nobleman believed to have joined Arviragus in rebellion. Ferox was not sure whether this was true, and it was clear no one at the farm had resisted. Two men had still died because they had held farm tools in a threatening way – at least, that was according to the cavalrymen who had first reached this place. The remaining score or so of workers, men, women and children, sat and watched as their home burned and took most of their few possessions with them. No one seemed interested in what they had to say about their absent lord and his family.

'You appear to have dawdled, centurion.' Crassus did not bother to look down. More of the roof fell in and a wave of heat washed over them, reminding Ferox of the bonfire on Mona, and the druid praying, knife held aloft. That was fifteen days ago and the journey since then had not been easy. If Vindex and the others had not arrived just in time, then there would have been no journey at all. Before the prince had set out, Ferox had spoken quietly to the scout and the big German. He did not trust Arviragus or Crispinus – and was far from sure about the prince's sister. So he asked them to wait until they were sure the boats were well away and then to overpower the Brigantes still with them. Once they were secure, leave as small a guard as possible for the prisoners and the horses, and lead the rest into the swamp. Gannascus' homeland was a place of marshes and bogs, and he had trusted the warrior to find a path through to the island between the lakes. The German had managed it, prodding with a long pole, wading where he could, and even swimming where it was safe. It had taken many hours, doubling back on themselves half a dozen times, but in the end he had led them all through. Smeared with mud, they had arrived and saved them. At least, that was the simplest explanation. Ferox wondered whether Acco had guessed what he would try and had delayed to give help plenty of time to arrive.

Leaving Mona was harder than he had hoped. Following the same path, they had gone back to the camp to find the Brigantes gone, the two Batavians and the rest of the soldiers from Segontium dead, and the horses killed or driven off. Only two hours after dawn did they find one of the pack ponies cropping the grass a couple of miles away. A Batavian volunteered to swim the animal across the straits. No one was keen on staying longer on Mona than necessary, for the local warriors might be small, but they were bound to want vengeance for the slaughter of their chief and his men. Even so, the pony was small, its rider big, and the rest of the Batavians placed bets on whether both would drown as they watched him ride into the sea. The odds against them making it started out very good and soared when he fell into the water. Yet somehow he kept hold of the mane and clung to the animal, swimming beside it. Longinus scooped most of the bets as they saw the man and pony clamber up onto the far shore.

'Don't worry, boys. Forget about it,' he told them.

Eventually boats came from the fort and took them off. A merchant ship had stopped at Segontium the day before, and then come and carried away the prince and his men. The liburnian based at the fort was away, and when it arrived late in the day the rowers needed rest. Thus it was not until the next morning that they set sail, a gusting westerly wind at least in their favour. Ferox stared at the beaches and cliffs as they passed Mona, still puzzled by Acco's intentions. It was almost as if he had wanted to be killed and for them to escape.

When the wind shifted, the liburnian lowered sail and the rowers took over, heading steadily east, until a storm rolled in and they had to work their way out from the shore. The night was grim, but the optio in charge knew what he was doing and kept them safe until the weather cleared. Late on the next day he landed them on the coast. After that they walked to Bremetennacum, and found only the rump of the cavalry ala normally stationed there. The prefect was away, and a decurion in charge of the barely one hundred men present. Ferox's rank impressed him less than Claudia

Enica's connections and charm, and eventually convinced him to loan them some of his horses.

The news he gave them was not good, adding to all the stories they had heard since landing. 'Rumour, the swiftest of all evils' as Claudia Enica called it, quoting the *Aeneid* again, had flown across the land. People said that Trajan was dead, although while some said that fever had taken him, others spoke of assassins' knives. The decurion had heard nothing official, but said that a trader passing through had been sure that it was true. Neratius Marcellus remained crippled by his wound. Yet it was said that he had proclaimed himself princeps and that II Augusta had already declared its support and it was likely the other two legions would soon copy that. Arviragus was the only one to oppose him in public, declaring himself for the true emperor, who would be recognised by the Senate, and was rallying forces to fight if necessary.

In the farms, the Brigantes told everything in their own way. Arviragus was to be high king and lead his tribe and all their neighbours to victory. His sister and her consort had gone into the Otherworld to speak for him and rally all the souls of the dead to spread terror into his enemies. Who was emperor mattered little as men prepared for winter and its hardships. Glory for the tribe was good, plenty far better, and that was what he would bring after a struggle. In whispers men spoke of Acco, the last of the true druids, who had worked great magic at the most sacred lake on Mona. Paying with his own life, the old man had brought an end to one age like a season. Much would wither and die in the months to come, as so many things perished in winter, but spring would renew the world.

Rumour ran faster even than Ferox had expected, each story growing with every re-telling. They stayed in farms and more than once saw shields freshly painted, spears and even some swords cleaned and sharpened. He did not think their owners were sure why they did this.

'They are frightened,' Enica said. 'Change is coming and strife with it. They remember past wrongs, whoever did them, and soon they would fight anyone who appeared.' Their welcome was always greater once folk realised who she was. One or two of them even asked her about the Otherworld and what she had learned on her journey. 'That my brother will die soon, and that I am to be queen,' she told them, and Ferox wondered whether that story would take on a life of its own. Sometimes she introduced him as her consort, a prince of the Silures and friend of Rome, something all good Brigantes should be.

It was the only time she spoke of their marriage. At the start of the journey, any talk pained her, for her neck was swollen and tender, and she spent days in uncharacteristic silence. Later they were all so tired and never alone. Gannascus thought it hilarious. Vindex was amused, if a little envious. 'It will be hard to show you respect. I mean, I know you too well,' he said.

Rain and wind ensured their long rides were tests of endurance that left little energy for talk. At Verbeia they found fresh mounts and the news that the Brigantian royal guard had acclaimed Arviragus as king, that a few chieftains had already joined him with their followers. Some army detachments were said to be obeying him as well, so that already he had several thousand men under his command.

Crassus, lately arrived from Londinium, had reached Lindum and gathered an army to crush the rebel, for that was what the prince undoubtedly was – at least unless he won. The bulk of Legio VIIII was at Eboracum, gathering supplies in case it needed to take the field and waiting for orders. 'Crassus is marching north along the road,' the prefect at Verbeia told them. He had received no orders to move as yet, and was keeping a wary eye on the hills in the distance. Patrols reported little bands of horsemen watching them. 'I've barely three hundred fit men, and not enough mules to carry tents for half of them. It's been quiet here for years, apart from the odd bandit. No one expected this.' He was cautious about their plan to ride to join Crassus. 'Your funeral,' he said. 'The lady ought to stay here, though, where she is safe.'

'I go where my husband commands,' Claudia Enica assured him, and almost sounded convincing.

Riders shadowed them, but the only time a petty chief and twenty warriors barred their path, he quickly bowed to the lady and helped them with a guide. They came down from the hills a few miles behind Crassus' column as it approached Danum. Ferox started to worry when they got very close before a couple of cavalrymen confronted them. He announced who he was, saying that he needed to see the legate straight away and that his companions needed food and fodder for the animals.

'I should come too,' Enica said, her voice almost back to normal.

Ferox grinned. 'Obey me, wife.' He leaned across the neck of his horse to whisper, 'Crassus is less likely to take advice if he thinks it comes from a woman.'

She frowned, and then nodded.

As he rode along the side of the road, passing the main column, Ferox felt his concerns growing. The decurion who led the escort guiding him to the commander was young and eager, but his answers only added to the worry. Crassus' army amounted to fewer than fourteen hundred men, plus a few hundred *lixae*. Just over half the fighting strength came from a vexillation of VIIII Hispana, which for eighteen months had been undertaking construction work in and around Lindum, and before that most of the men had worked on the road. It was a long time since they had been soldiers, able to drill and train for war. They marched reluctantly, obviously feeling the weight of shields, armour and the packs hanging from the pole over each shoulder. He spotted a fair few who did not have a pilum, and who marched with a javelin instead, and even a couple without helmets. Crassus can have given them little time to get ready for a campaign.

The seventy men from XX Valeria Victrix stood out, even though they marched behind an optio and did not have any standard. They were veterans still with the colours, serving the last few years of their twenty-five years under the oath, and until recently in garrison at Lindum. Older by far than most of the work party, they almost swaggered along, crests mounted on their helmets, all equipment as it should be, but worn or carried comfortably.

As well as his legionaries, Crassus had mustered some three hundred auxiliary infantry from several different cohorts, and two hundred and twenty cavalrymen, again small detachments and strays from three alae and four cohortes equitatae. Most looked in better shape than the

Hispana, but it was never a good thing to ask men to fight alongside strangers and under officers they did not know. If Arviragus really had a force of thousands, at least some of them disciplined and well equipped, then this was not many to face them. Whatever the Roman column did it would have to do quickly. Judging from the score of wagons and several hundred mules and ponies, the Romans were carrying food for little more than a week.

'The legate is confident the towns along the road will supply us until we can reach the granaries at Eboracum,' the decurion said loyally, when Ferox made a comment. 'And we have confiscated cattle from the enemy.'

Ferox was not sure who the enemy was. Plumes of smoke rose from three clusters of huts to the right of the road, and he wondered what they had done to deserve this punishment. There was no sign of a people in rebellion as yet.

None of this appeared to bother Crassus, who brimmed with confidence and even seemed pleased to see Ferox. 'Come in for the kill, have you, Ferox? Splendid. Must make a change from killing procurators!' The nobleman threw his head back and roared with laughter. 'Turns out that fellow was plotting rebellion after all, so we shan't say any more about arrest, at least for the moment anyway.' Crassus slapped him heartily on the back and laughed for a good long while. 'You may even get a reward, for it turns out he was part of a conspiracy with this Arviragus.' He pointed at the burning buildings. 'This will send him a message and scare anyone foolish enough to think of joining him.' The legate revelled in the destruction as his men burned the main villa and barns and huts around it. It was easy enough to understand. Twice disgraced, the man had come to Britannia and then found himself perfectly placed to crush a rebellion, winning glory and proving his loyalty to the princeps. The latter, at least according to the legate, was most certainly alive and well.

'So the scoundrel is saying Trajan is dead, is he? Damned fool. And the noble Neratius Marcellus too. I can assure you our noble legate is recovering. Be up on his feet soon enough.' That helped to explain Crassus' haste to confront the enemy and win the war before the governor arrived to take charge.

'Do you have a good idea of Arviragus' numbers, my lord?'

'Doesn't matter too much. Rabble mostly. Those tribal guards are fine for parading around, but have never fought a battle. The rest will be a mob of half-naked barbarians. The only hard part will be to find him and make him fight. Doesn't matter where as long as it is soon. My biggest fear is that he will run.'

Ferox reported what he had heard, and what he knew of the prince and the prestige he might gain from the blessing of Acco and wearing what he claimed was the armour of Venutius and the torc of Caratacus. Crassus watched the burning villa exultantly and showed little interest. 'Good, I want him puffed up with pride, then he will come to me and I can kill him.'

'He has the tribune Crispinus,' Ferox added.

'Prisoner or ally?'

'I am not sure, my lord.'

The main column was close now. A centurion saluted the legate and asked what he was to do with the people from the villa.

'Spoils of war,' Crassus said, condemning the prisoners to slavery. 'Just like the cattle.' As the decurion had said, the force was gathering a fair herd of cattle, which at least meant they would have meat for a while. The seventy or so head from the villa swelled the numbers again.

A trooper galloped up, splashing across the muddy yard behind the ruined villa and reining to a halt beside the legate.

'Decurion Simplex's compliments, my lord. He has seen two hundred head of cattle three miles away. He asks whether he is to confiscate them, and if so, could he have another turma to support his men.'

Crassus slapped Ferox again. 'Hear that man, more beef for our bellies! Tell Simplex to snap them up as soon as he is reinforced.'

'Do we know whose herd it is, my lord?' Ferox asked. 'Should we not be careful to make sure that the owner is a rebel before punishing him? And cautious that this is not an ambush?'

'Caution is for cowards!' Crassus snapped, face red with anger, until he managed to control himself. He gave a little laugh, although his eyes stayed hard. 'I have enough men to march through all the lands of the Brigantes and kill anyone who tries to stop me! The people here have not come in to submit and show their loyalty. I will treat them all as enemies unless they do that.'

'But, my lord, is that not the way to create rebels where there are none.' The face was flushing red again, and Ferox knew there was no point saying more, but could not stop himself. 'People are frightened and do not know what is happening, there is a danger...'

Crassus had raised his riding whip above his head, ready to strike. 'You forget yourself!' he yelled, frightening his horse again. 'I gave you a chance, centurion, but I shall not be lectured by you. You could have shared a little of the glory and cleared your name, but you are too arrogant to see my clemency. Decurion?'

'Sir.'

'Place this officer under guard. He is to be watched at all times and go nowhere without my permission.'

'Yes, my lord.'

XXIV

'So, am I married to a criminal?' That night Enica came to the tent where Ferox was held. Longinus was with her, but even so a legionary came inside to watch them. Under her cloak she wore a dress rather than her travelling clothes. 'A gift from the legate,' she added, seeing him notice. 'Plunder from the villa, I expect, and a little vulgar. And not silk, more's the pity. I feel alive with vermin.' Rain pattered against the roof of the tent as they spoke.

'Are we even married?'

She placed her hands over her heart and feigned a sob. 'How can you say that?'

'Did the cavalry come back?' he asked. 'The ones sent after the herd?'

Longinus shook his head. 'Two turmae gone.'

'Crassus expects them to return by dawn. Probably had to go further than expected, he says.' Enica kept her tone flat. The legionary was young and seemed nervous. 'There is no need to panic over so small a matter.' She sighed. 'Of course, I asked Crassus to release you. I think he was shocked to hear of our wedding. Seemed best not to say anything about the ceremony. As far as he is concerned, we are both citizens, lawfully and properly wed, even though he clearly feels I have married beneath me. That is quite something given that I am sure he feels I am half-barbarian still.'

'Well, he has a point.'

'Legionary,' she commanded, 'I think you should kick the prisoner for insolence.'

'My lady?' The soldier was confused.

'Never mind. Let us just say that I begged that he show leniency for my sake and the sake of my friendship with his sister, that he must excuse your atrocious manners and that you were a highly experienced officer who could be very useful.

'He told me not to worry my pretty head about such matters, that he knew best, and then he put his hand on my leg. In Londinium more than once I caught him looking at me. It was not any great compliment, as he leered at anything with breasts.'

'What did you do?'

'Perhaps you should kick him, Longinus, as a favour to me.'

'An honour, lady.' The veteran did not move.

'I behaved with dignity and left. I did not even kill him. He is brother to my dear friend, after all.' The legionary gaped at her. 'And such as he is, he is the only man with the rank to command here.'

'How will your brother fight?'

'He is not clever, but neither is he a fool. He must win or no one else will join him and he is doomed. Tomorrow perhaps, or the day after. I cannot see his patience lasting longer.

'Now, we must go. Soldier, do your orders permit a wife to kiss her husband?'

The legionary was uncertain. 'I was told you are not to touch at all, lady. I am sorry.'

'Then how would it be if I was to kiss you and you passed the kiss onto my husband's lips?'

The legionary blushed.

'Try it, lad, and I'll throttle you,' Ferox said.

'So be it. Farewell, husband.'

The next morning, Enica's judgement of her brother was borne out. In the second hour of a short November day, the leading horsemen saw the enemy. They were waiting where the road climbed a gentle hill, armour and weapons gleaming in the bright sunshine that had finally broken through the clouds.

Crassus was delighted, so much so that he ordered Ferox brought to him and even permitted him to have his sword. Claudia Enica was there, escorted by a pair of Batavians. The dress had gone, and she was once again in travelling gear, the familiar boots joined by breeches and two heavy tunics so that she wore her cloak open, and Ferox could see the hilt of a borrowed gladius. Before he left the camp, Ferox had managed to have a word with Vindex, so that the scout and the others ought to be riding out to the west, making sure that the prince had not sent a force to come in behind Crassus. As far as he could tell, the legate of Legio VIIII Hispana was not worried about such things. Indeed he was joviality itself, holding out a hand in welcome. 'Ah, Ferox, I trust yesterday's reproof has sobered you, and that you will remember the proper way for an officer to behave.'

Enica glared at him warningly.

'My lord,' Ferox said, hoping the aristocrat would take this as obedient contrition.

'Good man.' They were on a hillock beside the road, watching the column deploying into a battle line. Crassus swept his arm along the ridge ahead of them. 'There are the rebels. I make their numbers little more than ours.' A mounted vexillarius carried the square red flag marking the commander's position.

That seemed about right, though only if he believed the entire enemy force was visible. In the centre, formed across the road itself, were the dark blue shields of around three hundred men of the Brigantian royal cohort. From this distance they looked the same as their own auxiliaries, for they wore mail, bronze helmets in the regulation pattern, and each carried a spear and a lighter javelin, as well as having a gladius on their right hip. They were drilled and trained like Roman soldiers, and if they were anything like the horsemen who had accompanied Arviragus, they ought to be pretty good. Their line was broken a little by the ditch on either side of the road, but otherwise their formation was neat. More to the point they waited in silence, keeping in their ranks and watching as Crassus' men formed up to attack.

On each flank a body of two hundred mounted guards sat on their horses, the gaps between each turma visible even at this distance. Ferox presumed the men he had got to know a little on their journey to Mona were among them. At this distance they could easily have been a regular ala, and a good one at that, each turma mounted on horses of a distinct colour. For some reason the Brigantes had always had a fondness for chestnuts, and more than half of the troops rode them.

Next to each detachment of cavalry was a loose swarm of horsemen, tribesmen armed and ready to fight in the traditional way. Ferox could make out a couple of mail-clad leaders in front of the warriors on the enemy left and three on the right, and judged that there were over a hundred riders in each group. Between them and the foot guards were clumps of warriors. They were not in neat ranks and there was a lot of movement as men milled around, some sitting or standing, and, no doubt, being Brigantes, all of them talking. They would close up before the fight, but were not soldiers and saw no reason to act like them. There were some three hundred and fifty on either side of the royal cohort.

'How many men serve in the royal guard, lady?' Ferox asked the question loudly enough for Crassus to hear.

'Nearly eight hundred infantry in the cohort,' she explained. 'My Lord Crassus, is there not a name for a regiment of that size?'

'Indeed there is, my dear Claudia. It is a cohors milliaria. The royal ala is of standard size.' Crassus gave her an indulgent smile. 'It is much to the credit of your fellow tribesmen that so many of them have refused to join the rebels. As so often, rumour has exaggerated the army of your treacherous brother.'

Ferox was about to suggest the obvious alternative, when another fierce stare from Enica warned him off. On the enemy right the ground rose steeply up towards the hills, which meant that the Romans could not try to envelop them. On their left was a wood, straggling on for miles away from the road. Plenty of men could be waiting there in concealment. More could be behind the low crest of the ridge.

Crassus had deployed his own men to match the frontage of the enemy. The turmae sent on the cattle raid had not returned, and with so few horsemen left, there were around ninety on each flank and a turma of twenty-eight stationed near the commander. These, along with the veterans, were his only reserve. The legionaries of VIIII Hispana stood as two improvised cohorts in the centre, the men standing in three ranks. That was fine for steady, confident troops, but Ferox wondered whether it was deep enough. One cohort was led by only two centurions, the other by three, and there were barely more optiones and other leaders standing behind the formation to keep the men in ranks. The auxiliary infantry on either side of the legionaries were six deep, a far more prudent formation that made it easier to control the men. A tenth of all the infantry were still at the camp, some four and half miles to the rear, guarding the baggage.

'Time to temper the steel,' Crassus announced, and rode towards the battle line. 'Soldiers!' His voice surged to the power of a trained orator. 'Before us we see traitors to the lord Trajan. He is our emperor! To him you swore your sacramentum! To him we look to steer the res publica onwards to peace and prosperity!'

Ovidius had said he thought Claudia Enica to be a great actress. For Ferox, all that meant was that she was a wealthy and educated Roman, for they all performed at every opportunity. Crassus must have read in histories of the great orations delivered by famous commanders before a victory. He could sense the man revelling in the occasion, perhaps imagining how a writer would phrase what he said. Enica shrugged and trotted her horse after the commander, and Ferox followed.

'Arviragus who leads that rabble over there took the same oath! He has broken it! None but the vilest of worms would commit such an impiety. The gods will punish him and all who follow him and we are their instruments.'

Ferox lagged behind, so that he heard muttered comments from the legionaries.

'Hear that, we're gods!'

'Can't be, gods don't fart! You might be a humping goddess.'

'Promises, promises.'

At least they sounded in good spirits. A soldier with the energy to moan was not too worried to do his job.

'Traitors will suffer eternal torment in the Underworld. Think of Sisyphus...' Crassus seemed to have forgotten his audience and began to invoke a schoolboy's list of famous traitors and others suffering punishment in Hades. The legionaries lost interest and began to joke and bitch about other things. It was better than thinking.

'Buggers had to be uphill, didn't they', 'You're a lazy bastard, Servius', and so on and so on. Crassus was walking his horse further and further away, right arm flailing in all the gestures of an orator.

'Look, lads!' Ferox raised his voice so that he got their attention. 'Brigantes can't fight, but they're all rich. So go up there and slaughter the bastards and shag their women!'

Someone laughed and then started to cheer, and the shout rippled along the line. Crassus spun his horse around on a denarius, delighted at the enthusiasm his words had provoked. Enica flicked her hand against his thigh in reproof.

He shrugged. 'Best to keep it simple,' he whispered.

Sadly, that also appeared to be Crassus' approach to tactics. 'The army is to advance!' he shouted. 'Keep in your ranks, follow your orders, and the day is ours!' He drew a sword with an ornate handle shaped like an eagle's head and pointed it towards the centre of the ridge. 'Forward!'

Officers repeated the order and the line stepped out. The enemy were half a mile away, and for the moment the ground was flat. Part of Hispana had the same problem with the ditches as the royal cohort, but they coped well and kept the separate sections of the cohort in line. The enemy watched, the warriors shuffling and pushing into a closer formation so that soon they had a front rank of men standing in line, shields ready. Most of the boards were painted blue, the favourite colour of the tribe when it went to war.

Crassus came back and they fell in with his staff.

Ferox knew he had to speak and did his best to find the right words. 'My lord, barbarians are naturally devious, and the Brigantes worse than most.' He suspected Enica's eyes were boring holes into his back. 'That wood on their left is a likely place for a treacherous ambush.'

Crassus was still buoyed up by the cheering. 'Yes, I have thought the same thing,' he replied, 'and wondered whether anyone else would spot the danger.'

'Perhaps if we refused our right, my lord? Then if they come at us from the wood, we can hit them hard once they are in the open.'

'Serve 'em right too.' Crassus smiled. 'That is exactly what I was planning. Send orders for the cavalry and auxilia to hold back a little.' A galloper rushed off with the message.

The Brigantes were singing, the sound still too faint to make out the words. Ferox did not recognise the tune, but beside him Enica stiffened. She reached out, clasping his wrist tightly. 'Oh the raven! Oh the wolf.' The words were in the language of the tribes. 'Come to me and I will give you flesh!' Her eyes were glassy. 'It is the old battle song of my people. I never thought that I would hear it. Still less from an enemy.'

Ferox leaned over and kissed her, and wrapping his arm around her back held her for a little while. He was as surprised as she was, and when the moment passed they pulled apart, embarrassed.

Crassus laughed. 'Time for that later! Ah, good, they are obeying.' On the Roman right the cavalry halted. The auxiliary infantry went a little further and then stopped. Ferox saw an optio on the far right of Hispana's line stand and stare at them. Crassus had not explained his plan to the rest of his force. The far end of the legionary cohort seemed to stagger, men confused and nervous, before shouts and blows got them back moving again. A moment later, the auxiliary horse and foot started advancing again, so that the right flank of the army was stepped back.

'Come to me and I will give you flesh!' Ferox caught the words now, for they were less than a quarter of a mile away. The Carvetii were kin to the Brigantes, but he had never heard Vindex or any of his warriors raise this chant. The tune was gentle, almost mournful, and yet the words held a deep menace. He saw a lone figure on a grey riding up and down in front of the Brigantian line. At this distance the face was unclear, and he could not hear the lone voice shouting, so imagined Arviragus bellowing at his warriors to keep in line. There were always youngsters eager to show off or too scared to wait, let alone the men drunk to the fill and brimming over with the courage it sometimes gave. If a few surged forward, more would follow, and the prince was doing everything to control his men and make them fight as one.

A narrow ditch, unseen until the last moment because of the long grass, caused confusion among the left cohort of Hispana. Some men jumped it, others slipped in or chose to wade through the foot or so of water in the bottom, and there was much shouting and jostling before the ranks were restored. The Romans marched on in silence, until some of the auxiliary infantry began their own chant. It sounded like an angry grunt, repeated over and over again.

'Tell them to be silent and stay in their ranks,' Crassus barked at a decurion, who rode off to give the order. 'Discipline wins battles, not shouts and bravado.'

'Oh the raven! Oh the wolf!'

Arviragus' horse reared up and he flourished his sword in a great circle over his head. Ferox could see that he was wearing the helmet and armour he had brought from Mona. Perhaps he had told his men that the spirit of Venutius was with them. If so, then little of the old war leader's cunning was on show, for the prince pointed his blade at the Romans and set his horse into a gallop straight at them.

The singing turned into a roar and the warriors followed, streaming down the slope. The royal guards hesitated for just an instant, and then they too charged, ranks quickly becoming ragged. Horsemen rapidly outpaced the men on foot.

'No patience,' Enica said softly.

'Barbarians,' Crassus said with contempt.

Hundreds of men were pouring from the woods as well, some in the full panoply of the royal cohort and even more warriors. The Roman cavalry charged to meet them, some of them whooping as loudly as their foes. Seeing them pass, the auxiliary infantry jogged forward, banging the shafts of their spears against their shields.

'What are they doing?' Crassus gasped. 'Discipline.' Kicking his horse, he galloped towards the legionaries, yelling, 'Halt! Halt there!' His standard-bearer and two troopers followed.

The right-hand cohort of VIIII Hispana heard first and shuddered to a halt. The other went on another twenty paces before the centurions screamed at the soldiers to stop. Optiones ran up and down behind the rear rank, shoving men back into place.

'Pila!' Crassus' voice carried. The leading warriors were fifty paces from the Roman line, Arviragus riding among them. Legionaries in the front rank raised their heavy javelins, poised to throw.

'Steady now!' The commander almost shrieked the words, and whether his words were not clear or too many men were nervous, someone hurled his pilum, the slim shank flashing as it caught the light. The missile sailed up and then came down striking the ground and sliding through the grass some way in front of the enemy. Another pilum was thrown, then another, and whole front rank joined in.

'Stop! Stop, you fools!' Crassus implored them, and centurions were yelling. Most of the second rank threw before they understood. One pilum spitted a warrior as he bounded forward, shield held too wide. The impact flung him back and knocked down another man. That was the only missile to strike home and the rest pattered to earth harmlessly.

A legionary in the third rank turned and tried to run. An optio was there, blocking his path with his *hastile*, the staff showing his rank. Then the man next to the first fled, dodging past. More followed. The line rippled like a long ribbon blowing in the wind.

'Go!' Ferox told Enica. Find Vindex and the others, and I'll find you.'

She stared, then nodded. 'What about you?'

'I am still bound to the fool's sister, so will try to get him out of this. Keep her safe,' he told the Batavians. 'Now go!'

Ferox walked his horse over to the turma of cavalry. 'We're going to save the legate. Will you follow me, decurion?'

The man gulped. 'Yes, sir.' He looked relieved to have the decision made for him.

'Optio.' Ferox called to the man in charge of the veterans. 'Form an orb. We may have to fight our way out. Right, boys,' he said to the cavalry. 'Follow me,' He drew his sword.

Crassus was riding among the legionaries, calling for order. 'Pila!' he bellowed. Some responded. The Brigantes were close now, barely ten or twelve paces away, and the few missiles thrown punched through shields and armour into flesh. Warriors dropped, or spun around, shield pinned to their arm or body. It was not enough to check the onslaught.

The legionaries broke. One moment there were two ragged lines facing the enemy, and then there were just hundreds of men running away. Some threw down shields and raced ahead of the rest. Others were still confused, searching for someone to tell them what to do, but fleeing in the meantime because everyone else was. A few knots of men clustered together, walking backwards, still ready to fight, and in a moment they were islands washed around by a wave of enemies. Crassus and his little escort came back with the crowd.

'Halt, damn you! Re-form!' No one listened to the legate. On the left the auxiliary infantry charged with a shout and it was the Brigantes who gave way. The cavalry on their flank attacked alongside them, but at the last minute wheeled their horses round and fled. On the right the Roman horsemen burst into the mass of attacking warriors, cutting them down. Numbers were against them. The charge lost momentum, and the troopers were in the middle of a crowd of enemies. Horses were speared, riders dragged down and slashed as they lay.

Ferox eased his horse into a trot. The fugitives were a hundred yards away, some of the enemy among them. He could see Crassus, mouth open as he screamed at the legionaries. His vexillarius was beside him and one of the troopers. Ferox could no longer see the other one. Crassus slashed down, and he wondered whether the legate had lost his temper and was now attacking his own men. Then the vexillum fell, and the standard-bearer slumped forward onto his horse's neck, a javelin sticking out of his back.

'With me!' Ferox shouted, raising his gladius. His horse stretched into a canter.

Legionaries, faces pale and mouths open, were fleeing past them. 'Rally on the veterans!' Ferox yelled, without much hope that they would obey. Crassus was alone above the crowd, for the other trooper vanished.

'Save the legate!' Ferox yelled, driving his horse forward. The fugitives were splitting to run around the oncoming horsemen, and only a few came straight on, too terrified to reason. One barged into the shoulder of Ferox's horse and was knocked down. He could see Crassus, four enemy warriors around him. Arviragus was thirty paces away, trying to reach the commander, but his own men and the fleeing Romans were in the way.

Ferox saw a warrior raising his spear. He edged the mare to the left, pushed the shaft of the weapon aside, and was past him before there was time to cut down. Ahead of him, Crassus sliced deep into a warrior's skull, but his blade stuck in the dead man. A spear point drove into the side of his horse, and the animal screamed, collapsing. Crassus pushed against its neck, flinging himself off, landing on one of his attackers. Both men fell, but the legate no longer had a sword. Another warrior tried to get past the thrashing hoofs of the wounded horse to stab the aristocrat in the back.

'You!' Arviragus had seen the centurion.

Ferox ignored him. He was alongside Crassus, and cut down, slashing into a warrior's neck. Blood spurted high as the man dropped his own sword and made a futile attempt to staunch the wound with his hands. Ferox sawed on his reins, making the mare rear. Its front hoofs knocked one man back and made the rest wary. He slashed to the other side, striking a shield with a dull thump. Then the turma arrived, spearing warriors, scattering them, driving into the crowd.

Crassus head butted the warrior he was grappling with, leaving his forehead bloody. Ferox had not expected an aristocrat to fight in such a way and could not help grinning.

'Come, my lord! Behind me.' He switched his sword to the left hand and held out his right. Crassus was swaying, stunned. 'Move!' Ferox screamed, and that prompted anger and then realisation. The legate took his hand and jumped up behind him.

'Retire!' Ferox shouted the order as loud as he could. A space had cleared around the turma. Two horses were down, a trooper dead and the other jumping up behind a comrade just as the legate was doing.

'Fight me!' Arviragus still struggled to force his way through the mass of his own men. 'Ferox, fight me now!'

The troopers were falling back, ranks long vanished, but keeping together. Ferox was tempted to pass Crassus to another rider and meet the challenge.

'Give me your sword,' the legate said. 'I'll kill him.'

'Don't be an idiot, sir,' he whispered back, and then raised his voice to shout. 'The queen sends you her greetings! She is well, prince, and will soon lead her people!' Ferox slapped his horse's rump with the flat of his sword. 'Come on, girl!' She bucked, flinging the legate up until he came down hard against her spine, then she turned and cantered away after the turma. A javelin whizzed as it passed over Ferox's head. Crassus had his arms around the centurion to stay on, the motion of the running horse bouncing him up and down with every step, while the rear horns of the saddle jabbed into him.

The few knots of legionaries to resist had been cut down and the survivors were still running. On the left, the auxiliary infantry gave way more slowly, the Brigantes keeping at a wary distance, until some of the mounted guards came in behind them. Someone kept the men in hand, and the auxiliaries formed into a circle, not quite as neat as the defensive orb of the drill book, but good enough. Javelins showered down on them. The entire right of the Roman force had collapsed.

Fortunately most of the Brigantes either chased the fugitives or surrounded the circle of auxiliaries. Only a few hundred, mostly from the royal cohort, were forming to advance against the veterans, and the prince was doing his best to marshal them into ranks. Ferox realised that the optio had not obeyed his order. The old soldiers were in a dense cuneus, a block ten broad and seven deep. At the order they marched forward, forcing the retreating turma to split and go on either side. The optio nodded affably to Ferox.

Arviragus was still mounted among all the men on foot. The front rank was ready, oval shields with dark blue fields almost touching, spears raised to thrust over them.

'Come on, boys! Let them hear you!' The Brigantes yelled defiance. The veterans ignored them, marching forward in silence apart from the bump of shields and rattle of armour and belts. Some of the Britons threw javelins. One fell short, another stuck fast in a scutum and the rest bounced off the big curving shields.

'Pila!' The optio had a voice as harsh as a raven's.

'Charge!' Arviragus screamed, and the Brigantes joined in the shout as they rushed forward.

'Front rank!' the optio cawed. With a ripple ten pila were thrown, spinning through the air. One of the guardsmen was hit in the face, the small, pyramid-shaped head of the missile smashing into the bridge of his nose. Another caught the man beside him in the neck. Two more punched through shields, and slid on breaking rings on mail shirts to reach flesh.

'Second rank!' Ten more pila followed, devastating the ranks immediately in front of the cuneus. Arviragus' horse fell, and he was pitched off to fall among his men. A dozen others were wounded or dead, the charge halted in its tracks and the men clustering together.

'Third rank!' This time the pila struck a huddle of shields, their owners packing tight and trying to shrink to make themselves as small as possible. One of the heavy javelins pierced two overlapping oval shields, pinning them together.

Ferox reined in to watch, and felt the legate's weight slip away. 'They're my men,' he said, striding away to join the cuneus.

'Charge!' As soon as each man had thrown his pilum, he had grasped the handle of his gladius. Pushing forward and down, the short blades slid easily from their scabbards, ready in hand as the order came to attack. The veterans broke into a run and raised a shout that drowned out all the other noise on the battlefield. Ahead of them, the huddle of shields split apart as the Brigantes ran. Not a man stayed to meet the Romans sword to sword.

'That's how it's done,' Ferox said, half to himself. He looked among the bodies and could see no sign of Arviragus, although his horse lay dead. For the moment the Britons were running in this part of the field.

'Halt.' The veterans stopped. 'Retire!' The detachment from Legio XX about faced and marched smartly back the way they had come. Crassus fell in beside the optio on the right at the end of the front rank. 'Well done, boys. Now we shall go back a little way and then face them again. That's if they dare.' The veterans marched steadily on. They had done this before.

Ferox saw the Brigantes reforming two hundred paces away. There were more of them this time, although he could not see the prince. He looked behind and saw a trail of dead legionaries. Some of the horsemen had found easy pickings among the fugitives, but the ones he saw were scattered as they chased the rest. There was no sign of any group under control and likely to turn back to face the legate and his little band. Sixty auxiliaries came to join them, the only formed remnants of the whole right.

A trumpet sounded, a Roman trumpet, and although that did not mean much with the royal ala present, he was relieved to see two turmae who had rallied and now attacked the horsemen pursuing the fugitives. The Brigantes were scattered, horses weary, so were almost as helpless a prey as the panicking legionaries had been not long ago. Over on the other flank the circle of auxiliaries held out, but the organised bands of the enemy were focusing most of their attention on them and Crassus simply did not have the men to reach them. They must either fight their way free or fall where they stood, and Ferox suspected that it would be the latter.

He decided to leave. Crassus had a good chance of withdrawing with what was left of his army, for there was no sense of purpose to the enemy now. He wondered whether the prince was injured or whether he was too inexperienced to know what to do. In the centre, the main mass watched the veterans retreat without making any effort to push them. If Crassus did not do anything too foolish, then he ought to get away. He had lost his first battle and seen his dreams of glory shattered, but at least the man was acting as a senator should, refusing to give in, saving whatever men he could and preparing to fight again another day. That was what the aristocracy preached. Ferox had read that the consul Varro lost fifty thousand legionaries in an afternoon, and then got a vote of thanks from the Senate for not despairing of the republic because he refused to accept the enemy's overtures of peace.

This was a small disaster, very small by comparison, but fortunately both commanders were almost as inept as each other. If Arviragus could have held his men in place for longer, then he would surely have rolled up the Roman line and inflicted even greater loss. Even so, it was a victory, and that was what the leader of a rebellion needed more than anything else. He had drawn first blood, facing the might of the empire and routing it. People would hear the news and wonder whether Rome was as powerful as they had thought. Only the truly desperate or determined joined a cause without hope, but as hope grew they would wonder and more and more would take the risk. News of this victory would surely at least double Arviragus' numbers before the end of the month. If he won again, then all of the Brigantes might rise, and if they did, so would other tribes. The conspirators had spoken of indebted chieftains throughout the province, men with little left to lose. They might declare themselves for some true emperor, or speak of freedom. That did not matter, for all that it really meant was fire and sword throughout the lands. However many years it took, the Romans would win in the end, so it was really just about how many had to die.

Crassus had given Arviragus a chance, and unless he was badly hurt, the prince was the sort of man to seize it with both hands. As high king his words would carry even more weight, and there was only one thing left that stood in his way. Ferox rode off to find his wife.

XXV

THE CLANS ASSEMBLED at Brigantum in fields around the sacred grove of the goddess some called Brigantia, but most knew by other names never to be spoken aloud. Thirty days before the solstice, the chiefs of all the tribe and their kin were called to gather here for council, to discuss the matters of the day, reaffirm their oaths of friendship and service, and make sacrifices. In the old days, when Rome was a distant friend and not a presence in the north, the meeting went on for days, with feasts and warriors fighting duels to settle disputes that could not be agreed in any other way. Then all had come, unless too infirm to travel and then they had sent someone to speak for them. Lately so many chose not to attend that some of the chiefs there spoke on behalf of a dozen others. Usually they had little to decide, for Roman courts dealt with more and more matters each year. This time there was the question of naming a new leader for the tribe, even before Arviragus had announced that the emperor was dead and it was time to support his true successor.

'They are all here,' Vindex said wonderingly, before bowing to an old man with a thin face whose long moustache drooped far down past his chin.

'I'd never realised how much you look alike.' Ferox had never before seen the scout's father at so close a distance. As one of the main chiefs of the Carvetii, Audagus was accompanied by a dozen warriors. Lesser men had fewer, while the heads of the main Brigantian clans each had a score or more

'Always thought I was prettier.'

'Prettier than what?' Longinus wondered. The Batavian and the scout were the only escort allowed to Ferox, and Gannascus and the others were forced to camp outside the meeting place for the council. Enica was attended by thirty warriors, although Ferox could not help noticing that most of them were elderly. 'Their words will count for more in council,' she assured him, 'and this is a place where wisdom matters more than swords.' Ferox had heard similar pronouncements too often in too many places to find them very convincing. He tapped the pommel of his gladius for reassurance.

The journey here had been difficult, dodging bands of horsemen in case they were loyal to her brother. They had gone through the hills, along paths rarely taken at this time of year, and as the days passed the rain turned to sleet, and the icy wind cut through them. They slept in shepherds' huts abandoned for the winter and once just jammed together around a fire, sharing each other's warmth. There were few army posts along these roads, and they avoided the ones there were in case of awkward questions. Ferox even feared a few of the garrisons might have joined the prince.

'Happens quicker than you think,' Longinus had told him one day when they rode ahead along the heights and found themselves above the dark shape of a fort. 'Once one or two take the plunge others follow. Fools like company. I know I did.' He gave a grim laugh. 'You just think it's bound to turn out all right because it's you and you're the hero. Then once you've taken that first step you cannot turn back. If I was Arviragus I'd be sending riders out to all the praesidia, telling them that Trajan really is dead and there will soon be a new emperor, but it won't be Neratius Marcellus and anyone who obeys him will soon be in hot water. Then if he turns up with a thousand men and they get the choice between joining him and standing siege in some bleak place where help may never come, well, sacramentum or not, it's no more than a flip of a coin. Some will spit in his eye and dare him to fight, but others will believe because they're afraid and they'll march out and hail him as their leader. Seen it before. In fact, I've done it before. They're not joining a rebel, you see. He will be a Roman in their eyes, an eques and a former prefect, who speaks their language and knows how to flatter them.

'I'm droning on. Thought all those days were a distant memory, until folk started raking it up. Now it's like seeing it all play out again before my eyes. Actors on a stage, but real, and me in the chorus.'

'Who raked it up?'

The single eye had stared at him for a long while. 'Does not matter now,' Longinus said eventually.

The veteran was silent for most of the rest of journey, saying only what was necessary. The one patrol they stumbled across late one afternoon consisted of three troopers, none of whom wanted to challenge a man who said he was a centurion. When they came closer to Brigantum, it was Enica's name that got them through. A few of the chiefs and their warriors fell in with them, although most were reluctant to commit themselves at this stage and merely bowed and let them pass.

'Pity I have been away for so many years,' Enica said sadly, after yet another nobleman had excused himself from joining them.

'Have you become too Roman?' Ferox asked.

'I fear that they have.' The chief who had refused her was around thirty, clean shaven, with short hair, so that even though he was dressed in tartan trousers, a heavy tunic and wore a checked cloak, he looked as if he would be more comfortable in a villa or even a city than the round houses arranged in a circle outside the grove. There were twenty of them, the two in the centre facing each other much bigger than the rest. 'Those are for the king and queen,' she explained, and after they had dismounted she led them to the one on the south side of the circle. Inside it smelled damp and musty, for these houses were occupied only for this festival, even though the nearest tribesmen followed tradition and kept them all in good repair.

The other large hut was empty. 'My brother is not here yet.' Most of the other houses were occupied, although a few clans were still arriving. The sleet had stopped, but an icy wind buffeted them as Ferox and Vindex took a look around.

'Why do this at this time of year?' Ferox complained.

'We're northerners,' the scout replied.

Enica spent the rest of the day seated beside the fire, as in turn the chiefs came to greet her. 'I wish I had the mirror,' she said before the first arrived. For want of anything else, she was wearing the dress Crassus had given her, but had her hair unbraided so that it fell past her shoulders. A rider had come bringing her a package, and from it she had produced a slim gold torc, bracelets, and a brooch shaped like a galloping horse. There were more bulky objects wrapped in the cloth, but for the moment she left them there. The man had also brought a long sword, its handle shaped like a man and with a blunt tip. 'Clumsy,' Enica said as she drew it and gave a few cuts. 'More like reaping barley.'

'Have you ever done that, wife?'

'Be quiet, husband. This sword was carried by my great-great-grandfather in the battle where he fell.'

'Encouraging.'

On the next day the chieftains met around a fire in the centre of the circle. Enica stayed in the house. 'It is the tradition,' she explained. 'First they must decide that the tribe needs a high queen.'

'Or king?'

'Now why would they want that, husband?'

'Romans fear powerful women, and these men grow more Roman by the day. They've even had latrine pits dug.'

'We are not Silures,' Enica said, wrinkling her nose, 'and do not live like swine.' She sighed. 'But you are right. The old ways are dying, and the leadership of mystical women is one of the old ways. If they are good Romans they may not want a queen any more.'

'The Carvetii will,' Vindex said firmly. 'Audagus is for you, lady, and he is a tough old bird. Not Roman where it really counts.'

'I know. Your father is a good man, but the rest... Tell me, husband, why are men such fools?'

'Practice,' Ferox suggested.

Longinus snorted with amusement. 'Aye, true enough. Why is your brother not here, lady?'

'Arviragus likes to be dramatic. He must be here by sunset to make a claim, so he will come at sunset or slightly before, just when the chieftains are wondering whether or not he will come at all.'

A dozen horsemen arrived just as the sun started to slip beneath the hills to the west. The prince was at their head, armour and helmet gleaming, riding a dark horse with a white star on its forehead. His red cloak streamed out as he cantered towards the ring of chiefs. Beside him one of the royal guards carried a standard with a bronze figure of a rearing horse on top. The other ten all had spears, each one with a severed head driven onto the point. More heads dangled from their horses' manes. Each trophy had a yellow, waxy look, and some were missing eyes or showed other scars from the beaks of carrion fowl. Arviragus himself held up a chain in one hand, and behind his horse ran a scruffy, white-haired and bearded figure in a tinned cuirass.

'Dramatic,' Enica said as she peeked through the doorway. 'Even a stallion with the same mark as Venutius' favourite. And he led a tribune in chains just as he now has Crispinus.'

They rode round the seated chieftains three times. Then the escort peeled away and the prince walked his mount over to the remaining royal house, accompanied only by his standard-bearer and his captive. Some of the chiefs cheered.

'Vindex.'

'Yes, lady.'

'Go to the chieftains and tell them that this night they shall come and share my meal. Tell my brother, as well.' She noticed their questioning looks. 'It is the custom. A royal lady must feed the gathering. Servants from the royal house will come soon with wine, beer, bowls and platters, and with some provisions. It is up to us to make the meal.' Just for once the lady looked uncertain. 'Can any of you cook?'

In the end Longinus took over, after swearing that Ferox would poison them all if he was not careful. The old veteran made a stew in a cauldron brought by the servants, and it certainly smelled appealing, which at least was something. Three wooden chairs with high, intricately carved backs were brought and placed on one side of the iron guard around the central fire.

'You will sit on my left, husband, and you will wear these.' Enica had unwrapped the bundle to produce a helmet and armour. The cuirass was simple mail, but obvious repairs with slightly smaller rings showed where rents had been made in past fights. The helmet was even older, perhaps centuries old, bronze, with triangular cheek pieces, a shallow neck, and high dome topped by a tall diamond-shaped plate. There were dents in the metal, and one of the cheek pieces was held on by wire, but both were surprisingly light and comfortable for all their age and hard use.

'Venutius was a warrior,' his granddaughter said, 'and so are you. Sit beside me and keep silent unless you have no other choice. A Silure should be good at that.'

'May I scowl at them?'

'By all means.' Enica sat in the central chair, having made sure that it stood on a pile of turves so that she would be higher than anyone else. Ferox felt oddly proud as he sat beside her. At times she was magnificent, and he was finding that part of him dreamed that this marriage was not a sham. Another part of him wondered whether any of them would leave here alive.

Audagus was the first to arrive, clad in cloak, tunic and trousers, and with a sword at his belt.

'Greetings to the Carvetii,' Enica said. 'Come, sit, and dine with me.' The old man bowed. A warrior was with him, his face strikingly similar to Vindex's, and probably another son and perhaps legitiame. The chief unclasped his belt and handed it and his sword to his attendant.

As the chief took his seat, the warrior stepped back to stand by the wall. Enica leaned down to whisper to Ferox. 'Bet I know what he's thinking, the old devil. Look at her, nice ti—' Another chieftain appeared, and she jerked upright. 'Greetings to the Setantii. Come, sit, and dine with me.'

So it went on, each man greeted by his clan and not his name. The house soon became very full, the air growing warmer by the minute. When the last had taken his seat, there was just a narrow lane left between the sitting men, leading to the open space closest to the fire. No one spoke. Ferox noticed that Enica was flexing the fingers of her right hand as they rested on the arm of the chair. That was the only sign of impatience.

Arviragus appeared last, and unlike the chieftains, he too wore armour and helmet, as well as the gold torc brought from Mona. He led in Crispinus, still chained around the neck, and strode past the chieftains. In the space by the fire, he dropped the chain. 'Sit,' he commanded the tribune, who obeyed, eyes fixed on the floor. The prince turned to Enica.

'Sister.'

'Brother,' she replied.

Arviragus stared for a moment at the central chair, then strutted across to the empty one on her right and sat down. 'I have news,' he announced. 'Wondrous news that the council must know in full. Do I have your leave to speak?'

'Aye,' chorused the ring of chieftains.

'Brigantia is at war and must fight. Trajan is dead without an heir. Neratius Marcellus falsely claims the purple, but is doomed to defeat once the Senate chooses the real princeps. We cannot declare for a traitor, and because I defied him he sent a legion against us. I met this legion and scattered them as doves flee the hawk. This man is Crispinus, tribune of II Augusta and nephew of Marcellus. He will tell you. Speak, worm!'

There was silence. The chieftains must have known about the battle already, and as yet they were not ready to acclaim or condemn him.

'I said, speak.'

Crispinus staggered to his feet. 'It is as he says,' he said, eyes still staring down. Ferox could see none of the aristocrat's usual restless confidence. 'The prince is at war.'

'Sit, dog.' Arviragus swept the room with his gaze. 'There is more. For months, there have been omens of war and chaos. The priests here have seen them.' Several men nodded. 'You others have heard of them.' He reached for a cord around his neck, squeezing fingers past the torc, and pulled out a small pendant, shaped like an egg. Two of the chieftains gasped for this was a charm of the sort made by the druids. None doubted its potency, but all knew that to wear such a thing broke the laws of the emperors. Arviragus had their attention. 'You all know of the last druid – the last true druid.' Ferox saw a man frame the word 'Acco'. They knew, even the most Roman of them, of the survivor of the old days, the one man who knew the old wisdom. 'Acco gave me this armour and helm.' There were louder gasps at the mention of the name. Arviragus raised a hand. 'I speak of Acco, because now it is permitted. He gave me this torc, once worn by Cunobelinus, father of Caratacus. Acco spoke of the end of all that was past and the beginning of all that is new. Acco is dead.'

There was silence, until Audagus spoke. 'You know this for certain?'

'I know this, although I was not there. I am guessing my sister was there and saw it.'

Enica nodded.

'You ask what this means?' Arviragus shouted over the nervous questions. 'The last druid has passed into the Otherworld. Such a thing cannot happen without unleashing a great magic – his magic. The old will perish and the new will rise. The new world ordained by the gods. We can resist and wither, or embrace the storms of change and fly on their wings.' He snapped the cord of the pendant, raised it high, hesitated and then flung it into the fire. Something flared into bright green flame before it vanished. 'This is old magic and now it must do its work.

'War has come, whether you wished it or not. I bring this captive and other trophies. This son of a senator and nephew of a traitor will wait on us, the lords of Brigantia, as we decide what to do. I am Arviragus, grandson of Venutius who won battles against Rome and forced them to settle with him. I wear his helm and his armour for he is reborn in me, to lead us in this hour. Need I say more?'

'You have said and done enough, brother.' Enica's voice was calm, and she did not shout, and perhaps it was the higher pitch that made the council fall silent. Or perhaps she truly had some of the power of her grandmother. Ferox thought of how Acco's soft words had carried so far and swept over his hearers.

'The war has come because you wished it. Tell me, noble Crispinus, who is it says that Trajan is dead? Tell me that.'

The tribune managed to meet her gaze. 'I do not know, lady.'

'It is a story and nothing more. Stories often lie, and we know this in our hearts even if we love to believe them. Stand, husband.' She gestured with her left hand. Ferox stood, doing his best to scowl as requested. 'This is Flavius Ferox, my consort. He is a prince of the Silures, grandson of the Lord of the Hills. He is a famous warrior, who has served the emperors and won so many decorations for valour that even he cannot remember how many there are.

'Acco married us. At Samhain, on Mona, by the holy lake. The last druid did this. He told us that he would offer us both to the gods, and yet here we are.' There were protests, but she stilled them merely by raising her other hand. 'I do not speak impiety, since I speak only the truth. Acco knew. Before he broke the mirror of Cartimandua, I saw into his old heart. He spoke of the end because he knew that it had come. The druids have passed away. He was the last, and he could not send us into the Otherworld no matter how hard he tried. My husband slew Acco with the sword he wears tonight.' They stared at him with a mix of fear and hatred. Several produced wheels of Taranis or other totems and kissed them to ward off evil.

'Some of you here knew Venutius. I see before me faces of bold warriors whose chariots raced alongside my grandfather's. See now the mail he wore and the marks of the wounds he suffered leading our people. See that helm with its high crest, and remember the days he slaughtered Selgovae, Parisi and even Romans. This is the true armour of Venutius, is it not?'

'Aye, lady.' One of the oldest men spoke. 'I do not know what your brother wears.'

Arviragus glared hatred at the old man. 'These came to me from Acco himself,' he shouted.

'Peace, brother. There is so much you do not know.' Enica nodded to Ferox. 'Sit, husband.' Ferox tapped the pommel of his sword, gave the room another smouldering glare and did as he was told.

'The druids are gone forever and with them the world they understood. Rome is here. Rome gives us peace and plenty. Rome means we do not steal each other's cattle, rape each other's women, or take the heads of each other's warriors. You know all of this. Who truly wants to go back to the old days? Who wishes to challenge Trajan on a mere rumour?

'War is here? My brother speaks the truth in this matter. Thus you must choose. Cleave to him and you will die. Tomorrow, next month, next year, it will not matter in the end. Cleave to me and I will lead you to life.

'By dawn you must decide. You know the customs. Those of you with eyes will know whose spirit burns within me.

Those of you with sense will know that I speak wisdom. By tomorrow eve you must all choose. Will you seek death or life? As my brother said – need I say more? You are the elders of our people. It is for you to decide what is best for them. That is all.' She seemed to shrink a little in her seat as the speech was done, and she reached her left hand back towards Ferox. He took it and held it tight.

'Come, brother,' she said, and there was genuine fondness alongside the sadness in her smile. 'Let us take a drink.'

'Worm!' Arviragus barked the word at the tribune. Crispinus rose, coming close as the prince beckoned. Arviragus pulled the bolt securing the chain, so that it fell, leaving the tribune solely with the iron collar around his neck. 'Serve us each a cup of wine.'

'I would be so grateful to you,' Enica added softly.

Crispinus bowed to her, and then more stiffly to the prince. Two servants waited, one holding a silver cup in each hand and the other an amphora. The tribune poured out the wine, the sound loud in a room otherwise silent apart from the crackling of the fire. He reached out and spread a hand over the wide top of each cup to take them, then lifting them high, before he lowered them. Ferox gripped the lady's hand hard, his senses telling him something was wrong, but her fingers slipped free as she and her brother stood to take the offered cups

The prince searched the faces.

'Latenses, drink with me.' A chieftain rose and walked forward.

Enica smiled warmly at Vindex's father. 'Carvetii, drink with me.'

Ferox was watching Crispinus. The tribune's face hung down, but his eyes watched the scene unfold with an intensity that had not been there a moment ago. Then it changed to surprise, even panic.

The chieftains drank deeply. Ferox sprang to his feet, rushed forward and grabbed for the cups, spilling them both to the floor. Audagus' mouth opened in a yell of rage, the prince was screaming something about treachery, and then Vindex's father began to choke. Ferox drew his sword. Chieftains shouted in anger and confusion. Crispinus crouched down in a ball. 'He made me!' he babbled. 'He made me!' Arviragus had his own sword out, was slashing at his sister, and Ferox spun in time, grabbing her by the shoulders and pushing her down. Men called for their attendants and their swords. Some were jostled and turned angrily on their neighbours. One stocky old warrior with no more than a fringe of grey hair around his bald head slammed his fist into the man beside him, knocking the other chief and a couple more onto the ground.

Vindex cradled his father, who gasped for breath, froth bubbling from his lips. Longinus stood over Ferox and Enica, sword in hand, and Arviragus cursed him and ran, pushing his way to the door.

'We need to go!' the veteran said.

Audagus died, his face a ghastly pallor, yellow drool down his chin. Vindex was glassy-eyed, and Ferox took his shoulder. 'I'm sorry, so sorry. Will you stay or come with us?'

The attendant was beside him, a younger version of Vindex, and the scout nodded and passed the corpse over onto the other man's lap. 'I'll come.'

The hut was clearing, men running because they feared treachery and death. A servant girl shrieked hysterically, while another sobbed. Longinus led them out to the horses, Ferox supporting Enica, who was a little dazed after being flung onto the ground. 'Poison?' she gasped at last.

'Yes.' Ferox wished he had thought to bring Crispinus with him or just kill the man, but decided he could not risk going back. They saw their horses. Shapes came out of the darkness. Longinus grunted as a spear struck him in the side. Ferox let go of his wife, stamped forward and drove the tip of his gladius into a guardsman's face. Vindex slashed at another man, hacking through the shaft of the spear that tried to block the blow, and then he cut again into the man's neck and once more before the corpse fell. Blood spattered all over his face and he kept stabbing at the dead man. Ferox grabbed him.

'We need to go.'

They mounted, Enica's long skirts hitched up so that she could sit in the saddle, and urged the horses into a run. Men shouted at them as they galloped away, but it was hard to tell in the chaos whether they were enemies, friends or simply confused.

Ferox saw them first, when he glanced back to check that Vindex was with them. Five or six riders, it was hard to be sure in the darkness, but they were following fast and he had little doubt that they were the prince's men.

He urged his horse to catch up with Longinus who was leading.

'Trouble?' the veteran said, his speech a little slurred. Ferox told him about their pursuers. 'It's the bridge then.' On the way down this morning, they had crossed a narrow stone bridge, dismounting and leading the horses in single file. It was about a mile from where the rest of the men were camped.

'Are you all right?' Ferox remembered the spear hitting the veteran.

'Just fine,' Longinus hissed back, and kicked his horse to drive the animal faster. Ferox let the other two pass before he followed. The pursuers were getting closer. By the time they reached the bridge they were no more than three hundred paces behind. Longinus jumped down, grunting as he landed, and led his horse across, cooing to the beast when it tried to pull away. Enica did the same, the hem of her dress snagging on one of the pommels until she tugged it free, and crossed. Vindex rode, his knees barely squeezing between the walls on either side of the little bridge. Ferox looked back. The prince's men had gained another fifty paces, and he wished that Sepenestus was with them, because even at night his bow would have killed anyone trying to cross.

Ferox leaped down, still holding the reins, and went over. Enica and Vindex were already riding on, and then he saw Longinus slap the rump of his horse to drive the beast away.

'I'll be Cocles,' he said. He had taken his shield from its strap before he sent the horse away.

Ferox came alongside. 'It's my job. You take my horse, and I'll catch yours when it's done.'

'No.' Longinus reached out and brushed the palm of his hand across Ferox's cheek. It was wet and he smelled the fresh blood. 'I'm not going any further tonight – not quickly anyway. And you need to make sure your wife is safe. As long as she is, a lot of the Brigantes will back her or at least wait and see who wins.'

'I'm not sure she's really my wife.'

'Please yourself. But she matters, and I don't any more. We'll see. They'll have to come one by one and my strength will last a while yet. Farewell, Silure.'

'Farewell, Batavian.' Ferox hauled himself into the saddle. The pursuers had stopped, perhaps a hundred or so paces away. They must have seen the bridge and been wondering what to do next.

'Go! Vindex is half-mad and she's confused. They need you to get them away. If you see Lepidina again then tell her this was what I had to do.'

'You love her, don't you?' The horsemen were walking forward.

'Like the daughters I once had and lost.'

'Did you kill Narcissus?' he asked, because he had to know before it was too late. 'And Fuscus?'

'You planning on arresting me?'

'Nothing serious.' Ferox realised he was grinning. 'But it could mean stoppage of pay and furlough cancelled.' The horsemen were almost within javelin throw. They halted again and all but one dismounted. Ferox could see that there were six in all.

'Yes. They were after her because of that idiot brother and you, you halfwit. They came after me too, although who would care after all these years? Both were better off dead, so I killed them. She told me about luring you to the amphitheatre, how she hated doing it, but had to. I said she was right to do it, and that you could look after yourself. And you did, didn't you?'

The Brigantes began to walk forward, clashing spear shafts against the edge of their shields.

'What about the slave girl at Vindolanda? The one who hanged herself.'

'Nothing to do with me. Now go!' Longinus hissed. 'This is my time – or it isn't and I'll see you again. Go! I was a prefect and a prince and lord of the Empire of the Gauls and you are just a little shit of a centurion, so go or I'll kill you as well.'

Ferox clicked to his horse and she answered readily. Vindex and Enica were dim shapes far ahead, but the path was an easy one. If they got to the camp of their men they might return in time.

'I am Julius Civilis, prince of the Batavi!' The voice boomed out across the little valley and Ferox's horse slowed, either by instinct or because it sensed its rider reacting. He drove the animal on. 'I am an eques of Rome, decorated for valour many times,' the old man thundered his challenge. 'I was lord of an empire, the man who broke legions and burned cities, and I beg you to come to my sword and be killed!'

The Brigantes stopped chanting. As Ferox rode into the darkness, he heard the first clash of weapons and a long scream.

'Come, my sword thirsts!' The veteran's challenge echoed faintly.

XXVI

THE NEXT MORNING they buried the veteran at the top of a pass. There was little time, for more pursuers were bound to be on their trail, and Ferox hoped the old man's spirit would forgive him, as he dropped back a half mile to stand guard. When they had got back to the bridge with the rest of the men, three of the Brigantes were dead, another moaning softly as he lay with blood pumping out of his thigh, and the other two fled. Longinus was propped against the wall, and as they arrived, he opened his mouth to say something, but only blood came out. He slid down and did not move again. His horse had not gone far and they put his corpse on it. An hour after dawn they halted, and the Batavians dug a shallow hole, using their swords to cut the turf and their cloaks to carry the spoil. Gannascus and the others gathered stones to pile into a cairn. The dead man was wrapped in his own cloak, fully armed and his shield at his feet. Claudia Enica took a ring from her finger and placed it on his chest, and if it was not really an equestrian ring, the troopers understood the gesture and were grateful.

All this Ferox learned later, as they rode north, driving the animals as hard as they dared.

'Where are we going?' Enica asked, breaking the solemn silence that seemed to envelop them all.

'My people have a saying,' he said. 'Tomorrow for mourning, today for revenge.'

'Charming, although I suppose it is apt.'

'Let's get back to the army and be with them when they take that revenge.'

'Aye,' Vindex growled. 'Blood calls for blood. Where will the army be?'

'Let's head home and find out.'

Enica frowned. 'Home?'

'Close enough anyway,' Ferox said, meaning Syracuse and he guessed Vindolanda, and soon they lapsed back into silence. The death of Longinus bothered him less than he expected, and not simply because the man had confessed to helping Sulpicia Lepidina betray him. As the veteran had said, he had survived, and it was done. There was no going back for any of them.

Ferox spent most of his time riding ahead of the rest, searching for the best route and trying to pick up any rumours from the few folk he saw. The murder of Audagus, the attempt on Enica's life and the bloodshed at the tribal council was spoken of in whispers, and some went on to speak of Acco and the end of times. 'Brother set against sister, friend against friend and kin against kin. It is not good.' Everyone he met was armed, even if it was simply with a wooden club or stave sharpened into a crude spear, and many openly carried swords, shields and spears. Without the conspicuous helmet, the rest of his clothes covered by his cloak, Ferox could have been any traveller, at least when he was on foot. His horse with its brand and harness was too obviously an army mount. Several times he walked down to farms to speak to the occupants. They eyed him nervously, for a hard-faced man wearing a sword at his belt could mean danger at the best of times, let alone now. The call to war had gone out, and he was sure some would soon walk or ride away to muster under their chief, who in turn would lead them to a greater lord. Few seemed sure whether they would then serve brother or sister or someone else. That was not their place to decide.

Ferox saw no Romans, let alone soldiers, but since they kept away from the roads and the better paths that was not so surprising. On the third morning they woke to find snow covering all the fields, stiffening their blankets for they no longer had any tents. There was food for them for another day, perhaps with a little left, but the last of the grain was given to the horses that morning. The ride was hard, for they climbed to yet another high pass and the snow grew deeper and deeper until it reached the horses' bellies. Most of them got down and led the beasts, half dragging them through some of the drifts. Gannascus walked ahead of Enica, stamping a path through so that she could ride. The German gave every appearance of enjoying the whole thing.

Around noon they saw a dark shape moving behind them. It was steadily catching up, until Ferox could make out the little figures of horsemen, with bronze helmets, heavy cloaks and blue shields. As they climbed into the snow, the riders slowed down, and for the rest of the day no longer gained.

Ferox pushed ahead once again, although the snow forced him to keep to the main track. The path led down, and gradually the going grew easier, taking him through patches of fir trees, still green amid the white. Rounding a corner, he saw two troopers walking their horses towards him. They both were on bays, had drab cloaks and shields covered in calfskin to protect the painted design.

'Halt!' one called. Both riders levelled spears.

Ferox stopped, and his hand slid underneath his cloak and checked that his gladius was ready to draw. It should not have been cold enough for it to freeze in place, but it was better not to take a chance.

One of men trotted towards him. The other came more slowly, riding around between the trees to come at him from the side.

'Who are you, and what is your business?' The man's breath steamed as he spoke. A thick black beard peeked between the cheek pieces of his helmet and he did not look much like one of the Brigantes. 'Centurio regionarius at Vindolanda.'

'It is too.' The other trooper had come out of the trees and was staring at Ferox. 'Served alongside him two years ago. And saw him when he called on the prefect.'

Ferox sighed with relief. 'You're with Petriana?' He guessed, for the man did seem vaguely familiar and so did the size of the horses. Ala Petriana was one of the finest alae in the province, the proud command of Aelius Brocchus. They were based at Coria, a good few days' ride to the north. 'What are you doing here?'

The one with the black beard glanced at his comrade who nodded. 'We're marching south, sir. With the legate. Going to sort out the rebels.'

'Which legate?'

'The governor, sir. They say he came by sea and just popped up. Someone's certainly been lighting fires under everyone's arse ever since.' His comrade coughed. 'Sorry, sir, forgetting myself. We'd better take you in, sir. The turma is back a short way, and the main force a couple of miles on from that.'

Ferox finally brought his hand away from the handle of his sword. He smiled. 'First I have to fetch some friends.'

Brocchus pumped his hand so hard that Ferox wondered whether the arm would come out of its socket. He beamed even brighter when Claudia Enica was introduced.

'An honour, a true honour. My wife has told me so much about you, my dear.'

'Indeed it is,' Neratius Marcellus agreed. 'Especially as we had heard that you were dead. In fact, that you were all dead, even if we were more concerned about some than others!' He arched his eyebrow as he nodded to Ferox. 'Though I confess I might almost not have recognised you. A princess of the Brigantes in truth as well as a fine Roman lady.' Enica was in breeches, heavy tunic and her Thracian boots, with her long hair loose around her shoulders.

The provincial legate had a bandage just above his right knee, and scars on his left hand, but neither seemed to slow him down. As the trooper had said, the governor had come north by sea eleven days ago, landing at the tiny fishing port of Arbeia with an escort of twenty of his singulares and half as many officers and staff. They had ridden hard for Coria, and on arrival the legate sent gallopers off with orders for all the posts to the west and south. They were to muster every man able to march, issue hard tack, wine and smoked bacon for fourteen days and bring them to Coria by the third day after the Nones of December.

Some four and a half thousand fighting men had marched south from Coria at dawn on the next day.

'If the Selgovae or Novantae decide to be lively, we could be in trouble,' the legate said cheerfully as a tribune summarised the situation for the benefit of the newcomers. Around the folding table in the legate's grand tent were Brocchus, Cerialis, Rufinus, commander of cohors I Vardulli, who had shaved off his beard since their last meeting, and three more prefects he did not know. The tribune was from Legio XX, while the vexillation of II Augusta was commanded by its newly promoted *princeps posterior*, who nodded affably.

'With the legate's permission, I'll happily take Ferox here back to Augusta. I've only one other centurion, since Pudens went down with fever.' Julius Tertullianus was a burly man with an incongruously high-pitched voice. 'I could do with another lad who knows the score.'

Neratius Marcellus raised his a hand and smiled. 'Peace, my dear fellow, peace. We shall see in due course. Give the poor fellow a chance to rest – and shave – before we set him to new labours.

'Gentlemen, I shall bid you all good night. Rest, for soon we will have need of all our strength.' The legate was not the sort of man to give unnecessary reminders to attend to their duties. 'Orders for tomorrow's march to be issued at the start of the sixth hour of the night. Good night to you.' He glanced at Ferox, who understood that he was to stay.

Cerialis and Brocchus stopped on their way out. 'You have seen our wives?'

'Yes, my lords, although it is many weeks since I was in Londinium. When I last saw them they and the children were all well.'

'Thank you. It is a great comfort. No letters have come for some time.' Cerialis smiled warmly as he spoke. Brocchus said nothing, but there was moistness in his eyes when he patted Ferox on the shoulder.

Claudia Enica hesitated, looking questioningly at the legate. 'Dear lady, please refresh yourself.' A slave appeared without any obvious sign of being summoned. 'Give the lady everything in our power,' the governor commanded. 'There is a tent set aside for you with hot water, food and wine.' Seeing the challenge in her expression, he smiled. 'We shall speak later. First I must get a full report from the centurion.'

That took a long while, and Ferox sat by the table while the governor of the province circled him, pacing relentlessly. He asked few questions, and mainly listened, apart from a roar of laughter when he spoke of Acco marrying them on Mona.

'Truly! How extraordinary. The old rogue married you and then planned to kill you straight away! I suppose some would count that as a mercy. Sorry, my dear fellow, one should not be flippant. And do not worry, although it is an offence for a centurion to marry without his commander's permission, we can let this one by! Please go on.'

Ferox spoke of Acco's strange hesitation, his suspicion that the druid wanted to be killed, and their rescue, escape and how he had killed the old man.

'He is dead then,' the legate grunted, pausing in mid-stride. 'After all the trouble he has caused it will be a relief, although I suspect a part of me will grieve.' He saw the puzzled look. 'With him passes another world. Such things are always sad, whether or not the vanished world was a good one.' The legate stood still while Ferox told him about who the druid really was. How he had once been a narrow-stripe tribune, was captured by the druids and somehow became one of them. He guessed that he was the red boy Longinus had seen on the beach at Mona.

'Strange, the twists of fate. Ovidius would no doubt say something about the gods having a sense of humour. A more serious mind might wonder who each of us really is, deep down. No matter. Oh, the old fool is recovering well by all accounts. I dare say he will outlast us all.' He sighed. 'Especially if I make a mistake in the days to come. For the moment, let me hear the rest of your tale. You met up with Crassus, did you not?'

'Yes, my lord.' Ferox kept his account of the battle plain, trusting the legate to understand. Neratius Marcellus was on the move again, and punctuated the narrative with snorts.

'Well, it could have been worse,' he concluded. 'And perhaps will all turn out better in the long run. Perhaps. Please continue.'

On their arrival, they had said only a little about the tribal council, but now Ferox told all that he could remember, adding in things Enica had explained in the days that followed. He held nothing back, telling of the governor's nephew being led in chains into the assembly and Crispinus' attempt to poison Enica.

'Bad business,' Neratius said once he had finished. 'Very bad, although again it could have been worse. If she had died leaving him as sole choice for high king...' He trailed off, and paced in silence for long while. Ferox knew the legate's ways well enough to wait.

'Very well,' Neratius Marcellus said at long last. 'Yes, very well. We might wish things were different, but they are not so let us not waste breath lamenting them. So be it.' The legate stopped pacing and sat on a chair opposite Ferox. In him, it was a gesture of serious intent.

'I am glad that you were surprised to find me here,' he said, fingers drumming a rhythm on the table top. 'Arviragus will have known for days, of course, for one cannot hide an army of this size. Still, it is to be hoped that we gave him a scare when he first got the news. Yet more chiefs are bound to have joined up with him after his victory. The tribe must be divided even more after the treachery at the council. We must spread the word that the princess – no, of course high queen – is alive and well and on our side. That may deter some from joining him, and perhaps even win us allies willing to fight.

'Some chieftains still send me word, wherever their sympathies truly lie. None say that the prince has fewer than ten thousand men in his army, and some claim there are many more. Reports from the garrisons are fewer. Perhaps because the commanders are scared and perhaps because the messengers have been intercepted. As yet I do not know definitely of any defections to the prince and his '"true emperor", and it is to be hoped that none occur. The little that has come through says much the same as the chieftains.

'So I can assume that he has twice my numbers at the very least, although most of them will be warriors, who are brave enough but lack discipline.'

Ferox thought back to Crassus' contempt for his opponents until they routed his force. The legate's column was bigger and all he had seen suggested that the troops were in better shape for a campaign.

'Yes,' the legate said, as if reading his thoughts. 'Those are tall odds. The royal guard are real soldiers, and the Brigantes as a people are formidable. Not like the rabble who followed the Stallion and that was a hard enough fight. We cannot afford to make a mistake. Still, neither can Arviragus. He is near Cataractonium. I have not heard from the prefect in command there for nine days, so at best the fort is under siege and perhaps it has fallen. Crassus is marching north from Eboracum with nine thousand men, including most of the Ninth. Yes, I know the man is a fool, but he is a vengeful fool and this time he has a far bigger force, but knows he must be cautious. He has orders to move slowly. I want Arviragus to see his chance. If he strikes quickly he can face just me, with numbers on his side. If he faces Crassus he will be about even. If he waits then the two of us meet and we will have the bigger force. I sense you have a concern?'

Ferox was a little disappointed to think his expression had betrayed his thought.

'Food, my lord. It's December and it will be hard to stay in the field for long, even if the snows hold off.'

'For the prince as well as us. In that sense his numbers count against him. We have enough for another eight days and after that will rely in reaching a fort with its brimming granaries. I do not think the prince is a patient man. And he believes in his destiny. My spies have watched the conspirators for months. The prince has always urged swift action. He acts as if he is sure of victory and great things.'

'He believes that Julius Caesar is his ancestor.'

'Hah!' Neratius Marcellus slammed his hands down on the table. 'Truly? I had not heard that before. Explains a lot. Yes, it will make him more likely to strike hard and fast and trust to his luck. Venus bringer of victory, or the Morrigan?' The legate pronounced the word haltingly, but was pleased when Ferox nodded. 'He will be all the more eager when word gets out that his sister is with us. We will march straight down the road and let him pick his spot, and, however strong it is, I must attack and smash him. Everything comes down to that. It is really simple, and once again I must "fish with a golden hook", as you used to be fond of saying. You and the divine Augustus!'

Ferox said nothing. The decision was made and there was a logic to it all. Like Caesar at the Rubicon, going ahead put them all in great peril, but there was nothing to be gained by holding back.

'You have not asked about my nephew.' The legate stared intently at Ferox. 'And whether or not I think him a traitor or a captive whose spirit is broken? The law would probably say he is a slave now, assuming we count Arviragus as a foreign enemy.' Neratius Marcellus sighed softly. 'The boy often says your obstinate silences are more frustrating than your open impertinence.'

'In Londinium I saw him at a secret meeting with Fuscus and other conspirators, including Domitius, who was really Acco.'

'Would it surprise you to learn that the tribune has been acting on my orders all the time?'

'No, my lord.'

'Then I am obviously less inscrutable than I had hoped.'

'My people are not inclined to trust others,' Ferox said.

'Your people are the Romans, Flavius Ferox. And I dare say our history should teach everyone to be suspicious all the time. Well, let me tell you that for almost a year reports have come in of discontent and wild talk among the chieftains of many tribes and especially the Brigantes. Over the summer it became more definite, and there were signs that the procurator was involved. Crispinus discovered some of this, and came to me with the idea that he seek the conspirators out and become one of them. As the weeks passed – broken only by your adventures over the summer – it grew obvious that there would be trouble at some stage, and it seemed best to bring it to a head. My nephew came up with the idea of urging them to spread rumours that Trajan was dead and that I sought the purple for myself, but was doomed to fail. That would give them the confidence to act and reveal themselves. Better now than in a year's time, for orders have arrived to send more troops away from the province. In the spring Trajan will attack Dacia and he is assembling a bigger army than we have seen for almost a century to undertake the task. He must have a clear, unambiguous and grand victory to prove his fitness to rule and a defeat here, even a small one, would be embarrassing. Our emperor remains vulnerable, but we had to gamble and provoke rebellion before we became even less able to cope with it.' The legate bounded to his feet, the suddenness making Ferox flinch, and then the governor was pacing about again.

'The first great gamble! Then Acco helped by preaching a great change, but I began to worry that the revolt would turn into something too big altogether. What would victory mean if the province lay in ruins? Yet the pebbles were already rolling down the cliff and more and more boulders joined them. Someone killed Fuscus, but he had already done his mischief, driving chieftains into debt before offering them a way out if they joined the plot. My nephew thought we could weaken Acco by beating him to the treasures on Mona. It rather sounds as if that old rogue was reading our purpose and waiting. Still, since he was also Domitius and part of the conspiracy, perhaps we should not be so surprised. Arviragus made it all more complicated, and I do not know whether my nephew colluded with him from the start. What do you think of my nephew?'

'An able man, my lord, clever and ambitious. I should not say that he is ever troubled by conscience.'

The legate spun around, grinning. 'Yes, that is about right. I would like to believe that he still feels he is doing his best for me and our princeps, if only because he must realise that we remain most likely to win. Yet who knows?'

Ferox wondered whether Crispinus was acting under the prince's orders when he tried to poison Enica. Did he think the murder would strengthen Arviragus or make the chiefs hate and distrust him? He did not like to think of her choking her life out, and Audagus had been a good man, who had not deserved that death. He sat there, making no answer, for it was clear the legate expected none.

'I have orders for you, Ferox.'

He stood obediently. 'My lord.'

'When we win, Arviragus must die. A prisoner might be inconvenient, so I need his head and nothing else. Your task will be to bring it to me. Find him on the battlefield or hunt him down afterwards. You may have as many men as you wish, but find him and kill him. My nephew I would prefer alive. His presence with the enemy would be embarrassing if it become common knowledge. His death would be disturbing. He needs to be found in one piece and then perhaps we can learn what he has been doing, and make sure no one else ever learns of it. If he has to die, it will be in the weeks to come. Perhaps a fall while riding or a sudden fever.'

'My lord,' Ferox said, his voice flat.

The legate rubbed his chin. 'Go and rest. Soon I shall have a word with your wife, if that is what she is. Do you know that Crispinus suggested months ago that you become her consort to strengthen her claim to rule the tribe?'

'He hinted, my lord. It sounded improbably bizarre.'

'Yes, that is what I thought, so I was inclined to dismiss it. And I felt sorry for the poor girl – well, wouldn't anybody? Still, now that I learn she is so fluent with a sword, perhaps it is too dangerous a task for anyone else.' The governor smiled.

'I am not sure we are married, my lord.' Each time he repeated it, the words seemed a little more hollow, but he was too tired to explore the idea.

A legionary led him to a tent on the far side of the row of horses and mules brought by the legate and his staff. It was one of the larger ones, the type given to a centurion on campaign, and to his surprise it was empty of other occupants. A wide straw mattress lay on the floor, with blankets and furs. There was a platter with fruit, bread and wine, and a bowl of water. The fatigue was overwhelming him, but when Philo appeared, it somehow did not seem strange.

'The legate brought me from the south,' the boy explained. 'Gannascus' girl as well, although she is safe at Coria.'

Ferox let himself be shaved and cleaned, for he no longer had the will and strength to resist. Philo took his clothes, nose wrinkling even more than usual in his disgust at their state. He had brought his master a long tunic for the night and everything he needed for the next day. Eventually the boy left and Ferox sat cross-legged on the ground and poured a cup of wine. It was expensive, a present, he guessed, from the governor, and he shuddered a little as he sniffed it. In the old days when he had drunk to cover his emptiness, he knew that he would not have shuddered and that encouraged him.

He was just about to go to sleep when the flap of the tent was lifted and she came in, closing it behind her. She was wrapped in a heavy fur cloak, but her hair was coiled and curled like a Roman lady and when she let the cloak fall she wore a sleeveless dress. There was something bunched in her hands.

'Are we married, do you think?' Claudia Enica asked in a soft voice.

'I do not know. What do you think?'

'I do not know either, but I think it is meant to be.' Her seriousness surprised him, but then she managed a smile. 'You are mine, as I have said.' She opened her hands to show a piece of material. 'It is more red than orange, but the best I could find.'

Claudia Enica lifted the veil and covered her head. A Roman bride wore the flamma, an orange veil. She was more nervous that Ferox had ever seen, even when Acco had stood by them with the sacrificial blade. He sensed that she was afraid, and a wave of tenderness swept over him.

'*Ego Gaius, tibi Gaia,*' he whispered. Where I am Gaius, you are Gaia – and it sounded so natural that it surprised him. They were the old words of two become one, male and female halves of the same whole. He wondered whether Acco laughed from the Otherworld.

'*Ego Gaia, tibi Gaius,*' she replied.

Ferox lifted the veil and they kissed. Enica was enthusiastic, if clumsy like a child, and he felt her body stiffen nervously. He pulled away a little.

'It will be all right,' he whispered.

Claudia Enica hung her head, knowing that he was surprised. 'I talk a lot,' she said.

'I'd noticed that. Do not worry.' He ran his fingers lightly over her arm. She must have been cold with her short sleeves, but she did not shy away from his touch. He leaned forward and kissed her again, and their bodies merged, Gaius and Gaia become one.

Ferox woke before dawn, to the sound of the camp stirring. Enica was gone, but the veil lay beside him. He reached out and held it tightly.

XXVII

THE ARMY MARCHED south under a grey sky, and most of the time Ferox rode with the legate, for in spite of Tertullianus' pleas for an additional centurion with his first cohort of II Augusta, Neratius Marcellus wanted an extra officer for his own small staff.

Enica had gone, not just from his tent but from the camp, and Vindex had gone with her, as had Sepenestus and Gannascus. The legate obviously knew where they had gone, but said nothing other than to assure him that they would be as safe as they could be with the column. 'Some loyal Brigantes went with them.' Ferox wondered why the legate had changed his mind about the advantage of trumpeting the presence of the high queen with the column. Even more he hoped that the legate had judged the loyalty of the tribesmen well.

Last night was a like a dream, save that it had not faded in memory. Ferox felt a contentment he had not known for a long time, deeper even than the thrill after the first time he had lain with Sulpicia Lepidina. Oddly what little anger he had felt at Lepidina's betrayal had gone as well, leaving the fondness of happy memory. Their son was a wonderful gift, even if Ferox could never declare his love openly, and he still trusted the lady to care for him.

Early in the day Ferox was sent back with orders for Cerialis, who was in command of the infantry forming the rearguard, mostly composed of his own Batavians, with their moss-topped helmets looking like fur until you came very close. The prefect was affable, and Ferox felt an odd relief that the affair with the man's wife was now over forever. He had always liked Cerialis too much to enjoy cuckolding the man, even though he knew the marriage was one of advantage rather than affection, let alone love.

'There are worse deaths,' Cerialis said, after receiving the warning that they would be crossing a bridge soon, so that the rearguard was to halt and wait while this brought its inevitable delays. The legate suggested that he let his men light fires and cook. The Batavians had returned to their cohort and spread the word of the death of Longinus. His true identity was a jealously guarded secret, and Ferox was one of the few outside the unit to be admitted to it. 'In a way, I am relieved,' the prefect said. 'He went out bravely, and performing a good act. All his family are long gone, and he had already stayed with the cohort long after he should have retired. Where could he go?' He reached out his hand. 'The lads know you were not to blame. They know too that he liked you.'

Ferox shook the proffered hand. Amused tolerance was more his sense of Longinus' feelings towards him, but perhaps he was wrong. As well as prefect, Cerialis was of the royal line of his tribe, and he spoke as both on a matter all the Batavians felt deeply.

'No hard feelings,' the prefect told him. 'You did your best for him, and you brought most of the lads home.'

As Ferox rode back to the legate he found himself wishing that the prefect's generosity extended to his affair. As far as he knew, Cerialis had not the slightest idea of any of it, and it was surely best that he never did. How could any husband forgive a man who slept with his wife and fathered a child with her?

Ferox brooded as he rode, and then as he waited for the baggage train to file slowly across the bridge, poorly greased axles screamed on the wheels of the carts. The drivers always claimed the noise warded off evil spirits and he did not know whether this was true. The galearii were slaves owned by the army, given a basic uniform and menial tasks like driving the transport. They were a strange, insubordinate bunch who kept themselves to themselves, jealous of the rare freedom they received. On one of the nearest carts a woman sat suckling a baby, and he guessed she was probably the 'wife' of a galearius rather than a soldier. She had a sullen expression and deeply lined face, whether from the harshness of her life in general or the more recent rigours of giving birth.

An image formed in his mind of Claudia Enica holding a newborn babe as he stared down, brimming over with love for them both. It was strange to realise that he had come to love her, even if he had not the slightest idea of when this had happened. Desire had been there from the start, but that was no more than the natural instinct of any man seeing an attractive woman. Respect had grown over time as they had travelled together, but the love he now knew was altogether different.

The woman on the cart lifted the baby and placed it on her shoulder, patting gently until it belched with surprising loudness. She glared at Ferox, perhaps thinking he was leering at her uncovered breast.

It was all a dream, for how could they have a future? He could not imagine the elegant Claudia living as the wife of a mere centurion, let alone one who had long since ruined his career and found himself on the edge of the world. Neither could he see himself as her consort, the pair of them puppet rulers of an allied tribe. The Brigantes would surely not accept him and he could not spend all his life scowling to order. That way lay only boredom, despair and drink. Enica deserved better, as the legate had said; certainly better than a man who had seduced another's wife. She was beautiful and young, a queen now, at least assuming the legate won his battle and she survived it all. What was he? He felt the blackness grow inside him, the despair and self-pity and hate that made the oblivion of drink call out to him.

The wind picked up and as it made the covering on the cart flap noisily, he half thought he heard Acco's laughter and his grandfather's scorn. 'Live with what you have done, whatever it is,' the Lord of the Hills had said. 'No magic in this world can change the past and wishing things were otherwise is the part of a fool and a coward.'

The cart was across, and before the oxen on the next one were goaded into lurching forward, Ferox cantered across, ignoring the protests of the weary optio guiding the traffic. Once across he left the road and gave the animal its head, pounding past the transport as the draft animals plodded along in an unearthly chorus of squeaking metal. At least the sight helped convince him that the legate was as well prepared as possible for such a hastily planned campaign. There were more than ninety carts and wagons, some of them big four-wheeled affairs pulled by a team of eight. Almost all were drawn by oxen, so that they were lucky to make ten miles in a day, but along with the hundreds of mules and ponies they carried bread, flour and salted meat. He was pleased to see that some also had bundles of firewood, for they could not be sure to find enough wood for fires along the way.

Everything about the little army was reassuring in a way so different from Crassus' force. It was hard to believe that was only a few weeks ago. Neratius Marcellus marched with more of everything, soldiers as well as supplies, and that was part of the difference, but only part. As it went south the column torched no farms, great or small. The legate had given strict orders that no one was to be treated as an enemy unless they attacked the Romans. Even the sight of men carrying arms was not to be seen as a mark of rebellion unless they made use of them. These were the lands of allies of the Roman people, old friends to be treated with respect and courtesy, for the soldiers were here to protect them, not fight them. Anything taken from the land, from livestock, hay or food, was to be paid for in coin. Ferox wondered how many people would risk coming forward to speak to the soldiers, and was surprised when during the day several farmers appeared. The column had followed the legate's orders since the march began and word was spreading.

He rode past the contingent of II Augusta, Julius Tertullianus waving to him as he passed. The princeps posterior commanded his own cohort, the double-strength First, its numbers topped up to almost its regulation strength of eight hundred by volunteers from the rest of the legion. They carried the eagle, but since today it was their turn to take second place to the vexillation from Legio XX Valeria Victrix, the gilded bird was concealed behind a protective leather cover.

The Victrix supplied almost as many men in two cohorts, and both contingents had spent the last year in the north, drilling and training. The governor had gathered a major force to hold manoeuvres over the summer, ready for a campaign if necessary and for grand exercises if it was not. Now they had their campaign, and Ferox had to wonder whether the legate had had this possibility in mind all those months ago. Tertullianus and some of his men had fought against the pirates during the attack on the island in the far north so had a recent victory to feed their confidence. Some of the auxiliaries were even more experienced, having fought in several campaigns. Cerialis' Batavians and Rufinus' Vardulli each mustered six hundred infantrymen as well as turmae of cavalry. There were two hundred and fifty more from cohors IV Gallorum, and three hundred and fifty archers, lean Syrians from cohors I Hamiorum. Supporting these were just over a thousand cavalry, drawn mainly from ala Petriana and ala I Hispanorum Asturum and the cavalry of the cohorts. It was not simply that Neratius Marcellus had more men, they all marched with an assurance and ease that had been utterly lacking in most of Crassus' force.

On the next day the outlying cavalry patrols saw bands of horsemen watching them. There were more of them the day after, and once or twice javelins were thrown on each side, with no more result than a horse taking a graze. Neratius Marcellus had his army march in *agmen quadratus*, the main force moving in a long rectangle, the baggage in the centre on the road and the fighting units ready to turn outwards and face an attack from any direction. Bands of tribesmen were visible from time to time, especially on the hills to the west, watching and waiting. The legate ordered his own cavalry never to push too far away from the main force, and not to be too aggressive unless they were pressed. The warriors did not press close, so that the two sides watched each other as the Romans trudged south.

Halfway through the morning of the fourth day since Ferox had joined the column, Brocchus with the advance guard sent a rider back to say that there was an army waiting to meet them. The prefect estimated that the enemy numbered at least twelve thousand men, and when Ferox was sent to join him he judged the number about right. This time Arviragus had not blocked the road, and instead his army stood on hills to the west. It was a decent position, the left flank strengthened by the grassy walls of a long-abandoned fort and the right with good, gently rolling ground ideal for cavalry and beyond that thick woodland. Any attempt to outflank would be seen long before it posed a threat, and in any case would mean attacking up even steeper and more difficult slopes. Ferox saw men at work in front of the main line, finishing off a turf rampart that would cover much of the slope.

'Bit of a cheek,' Brocchus said, for the wall was being raised using the army's routine technique. Ferox could see that most of the men doing the work were the royal guard.

Neratius Marcellus did not hurry. He let the column arrive at its own pace and when the leading auxiliary infantry arrived he formed them into a line facing west, and a good half-mile from the enemy. One of the cohorts of XX Valeria Victrix soon joined them, and then after that he set the remaining legionaries to digging the camp, which had already been marked out on the ground with flags showing where everything was to go.

The legate sat on his horse alongside Ferox, Brocchus and other officers and scanned the enemy line.

'Will they attack, sir?' the tribune in charge of the vexillation from Legio XX asked. The enemy had made no move so far, and most of the warriors sat or wandered around, while the guardsmen toiled away to make their rampart. Arviragus was riding a grey, and was clearly visible supervising the work and watching the Romans just as they watched him.

'Oh, I should not think so. After all the trouble they have gone to, making their little wall, they must be desperate to make use of it.' The prince's plan was obvious. He wanted the Romans to attack him. The rampart would not only make that attack harder, but it would help restrain the enthusiasm of his own warriors. Let the Romans come up the hill and be killed. In the meantime his cavalry, whose numbers looked far larger than the Romans', would hold the right of their line, until the attack was spent or beaten back and then they and any warriors he had held back could sweep round and through the Roman left, rolling up the whole line.

Ferox wondered whether to speak, and was prevented when Neratius Marcellus proceeded to give an almost identical summary to the narrow-stripe tribune. 'Let him sleep thinking he has us beaten,' the legate concluded, 'and worrying that we will try a night attack. We will attack an hour after dawn.'

'Is it worth considering the night assault, my lord?' The tribune must have commanded an auxiliary cohort before he was given his post, but may well have seen little service.

He was a pale man, with narrow lips, and darting eyes, with the air of someone trying not to be noticed.

Neratius Marcellus smiled. 'I could be Alexander and tell you that I will not steal a victory in that way! Or just say that I am getting old and need a good night's sleep. The truth is that a December night is too long and too cold. The men need rest and food, and I do not want everyone blundering about in the dark. Let us do things in what passes for sunlight here in the north, and make sure that we do everything to perfection.'

The legate expanded on the theme in his *consilium* that night, as he issued orders to all the senior officers and commanders of cohorts and alae in the army. There were only seventeen men all told, including Ferox and the two cornicularii who struggled to keep pace with the governor's rapid dictation. Each officer would then take written orders and pass them on to his subordinates. The whole army would be armed and in formation in the road behind the ramparts an hour before dawn. That was normal practice, but they were to form so that they could march out and easily take up their allotted place in the battle lines.

The night was clear and cold, the grass crunching underfoot as it froze. Men were glad whenever they could stand or sit near a fire, and listening to the low conversations Ferox felt their confidence. They wanted the campaign over so that they could get back to warm barracks and a quiet winter. No one seemed to doubt that they would win, or if they did, like good soldiers they kept it to themselves. They moaned about the food, and the cold, and bastards from the other units who did not know how to use a latrine, and all the usual things legionaries and auxiliaries liked to complain about. At the third hour of the night Ferox went to visit the picket outside the main gate. The duty fell to the Batavians that night, and he found Cerialis there. They had lit fires thirty paces beyond the picket, which meant that they would get a bit of warning of any attack. A lot of units did this, although Ferox thought it was wrong because it made it impossible to see anything beyond the fires.

'Tomorrow we kill you!' a voice yelled from the darkness.

'He's back,' muttered one of the soldiers.

'We're going to cut off your pricks!' This came in a deeper voice than the first.

'He must have found a friend,' one of the older soldiers said. 'In this cold he'll be lucky to find anything.'

'Speak for yourself,' another of the Batavians replied, and then raised his voice. 'Piss off, you daft buggers!'

'You are all traitors!' Ferox thought he saw a pale shape moving in the dark and knew the voice of Arviragus. 'Trajan is dead, and your legate a traitor who will die along with all his supporters.'

'That's nice!' a soldier shouted back.

'Tell your officers to give up,' the prince continued.

Cerialis took a couple of paces forward and cupped his hands to shout louder. 'Lord prince, you are the traitor and rebel. Trajan lives and we all serve him, true to the oath you have broken. You must all lay down your arms and trust to his mercy!'

Arviragus' laughter was loud. 'Will you give a message to Flavius Ferox?'

Cerialis glanced back, wondering whether the centurion wanted to declare himself, and then nodded in understanding. 'I will give it.'

'Tell him that bitch, my sister, is dead. Tell him that. As high king I ordered her death and that of all those with her. They are all dead. Tell him that.'

A grey horse shone as it bounded forward, the prince whirling something bulky around in his hand before he flung it forward. It bounced on the grass and rolled a little before it stopped. One of the Batavians flung a javelin, but it fell several paces short and the prince had wheeled his horse and galloped away.

Ferox ran forward, trying to fight down his fears. He could see that the prince had thrown a head, but when he came close he saw it was large and must be a man's. For a moment he worried that it was Gannascus, until he picked it up and saw that the hair was short and the chin clean shaven.

'I do not know him,' he said.

'I do.' Cerialis was alongside. 'It is the prefect in command at Cataractonium.'

XXVIII

'I T IS RARELY wise to be too clever.' Neratius Marcellus repeated what he had said in the consilium the night before. 'He expects us to attack him and so we shall. But in our own time and way.'

An hour after dawn and everyone was in place. On the left, both alae formed up, each in two lines of turmae. Ala Petriana was furthest forward, with the other ala behind and to its left. They would let the enemy horsemen come to them, rather than driving too deeply forward. The Gauls stood between the cavalry and the main force of infantry. A cohort of Legio XX was on the left, formed in two lines, each six deep. Two hundred paces to their right was the first cohort of Legio II Augusta, in a matching formation, with the eagle shining in the middle of the reserve line surrounded by five signa from the centuries of the first cohort and the vexillum flag of the detachment. The gap between the legionaries was filled by ten scorpions, light artillery, firing heavy bolts with tremendous force and uncanny accuracy and some of the archers in open order. The rest of the archers formed an extra rank at the back of the leading lines of legionaries. Behind them all, the other cohort of Legio XX acted as an immediate reserve.

'Silly fellows,' the legate said to his staff. 'Ought to have thought more about what he was doing.' The rampart built by the enemy covered most of their front line and was continuous, without the weak spot offered by a gate. Yet that also meant that there was no easy way through for their own warriors. A shrewder commander would have had openings every few hundred paces. What this meant was that the Romans could choose where to attack and not be too worried about their flanks, at least until they had got past the rampart. Neratius Marcellus planned to attack in two places with his legionaries. At the same time Cerialis' Batavians, supported by the Vardulli, would storm the old hill fort. The cohort cavalry would provide the legate with his ultimate reserve.

Ferox was with the governor as he rode along the line of scorpions. He had asked for permission to lead some of II Augusta or anyone else in the first assault. Neratius Marcellus had refused, no doubt informed by Cerialis of what the prince had said. 'No, I need you. I have few enough officers as it is, and none who know the tribes as well as you.'

As Ferox watched the crew of one of the engines load a bolt and start cranking the slide back to something like full tension, he tried to fight off a black mood. He did not believe that Enica was dead. Her brother had surely lied, for otherwise he would have shown them some trophy as proof; not her head, since taking the head of any woman would have disgraced a chieftain, let alone the self-proclaimed high king, but something else.

Enica lived, he was sure of that, just as he was sure that her life hung by a thread, and perhaps the same was true of Vindex and the others. What Ferox did today would decide her fate and theirs, and no doubt the gods would demand a heavy price. He might die today, and if that was what would happen then there was no point trying to hide, so he had asked to be at the forefront. There was no point trying to explain this to the legate or any Roman, for he could not say how he knew. Understanding had come slowly, as he'd lain awake through the last hours of the night, and in the red dawn he was certain. A man could not kill a druid and walk away. Acco was at work, or the magic the druid had unleashed, and the gods would play their games, and perhaps the chaos the old man had foretold would erupt here. If both brother and sister died then the Brigantes had no clear leader and the chiefs would fight each other. If the legate was defeated or died in the battle, the other restless and desperate leaders in other tribes might well decide to challenge Rome and the druid would prove right and flame and sword sweep through the province.

Ferox did not fear death, and if it saved his wife then he could almost welcome it. He found it hard to worry much about all those who would perish if the rebellion begun by the prince spread throughout the lands. Instead he thought of the girl in his arms, her softness and his surprise because at first she had been so timid and nervous. Was it just another act? He did not think so, but who could say for he had been wrong before.

It did not matter. Ferox knew that they must win and that he must accept any challenge or danger without hesitation. If death came then it came. He feared the half-death, to suffer wounds leaving him blind and crippled, eking out the long, slow years of life, dependent on the kindness of others, always knowing that his soul would carry the scars into the

Otherworld. Yet if that was what the gods demanded, he would suffer it for her. Saving his wife gave Ferox's own life purpose and meaning, and perhaps his craving for these was deeper that his newfound love.

'Ready, my lord.' A *tesserarius* from XX Valeria Victrix was in charge of the artillery, and now saluted the legate.

Archers stood in pairs between and behind the scorpions, with another group formed as a reserve, and a centurion commanded them, but they were out of bowshot of the rampart. Ferox looked at the row of faces peering over the parapet. Few wore helmets, and as far as he could see all were tribesmen fighting with their own weapons. Some probably had slings, although the Brigantes were not known for their skill with slings. Perhaps one or two were bowmen. Otherwise, they would be able to do nothing to the enemy until the Romans came close enough to hit with a javelin or stone hurled by hand. At least the rampart meant that the warriors could not surge forward before Arviragus was ready, as they had done in the last battle. A standard shaped like a cockerel bobbed up and down in front of them, and beside him stood a big man with a tall helmet and armour of bronze scales.

'You may begin,' the legate told the artillerymen. 'An *aureus* apiece for the crew who nail that shiny fellow and the one with the bird.'

The tesserarius grinned, showing teeth that were yellow and broken. 'Pick your targets!' he shouted. 'Shoot when you are ready.'

The first scorpion cracked like a whip, as the metal slide slammed forward. Ferox watched as the bolt flashed through the air and whipped several feet above the men on the rampart. The crews of the neighbouring artillery pieces jeered.

'Silence there! Get on with your job!' the tesserarius bawled at them. 'Next peep out of any of you and I'll have the bugger flogged.'

'Oh the raven! Oh the wolf!' The tribesmen began their chant. A lone man with a tall carnyx horn blasted out a challenge.

More of the scorpions cracked and slammed. The next two bolts drove deep into the turf of the wall.

'Come to me and I will give you flesh!'

The trumpeter blew another rousing blast, which stopped with an abrupt clang as a bolt struck the boar's head of the carnyx, flinging it back beyond the wall and leaving the player dazed, his mouth bloody.

'Stop playing games, Marcus. Kill the mongrels!'

'Oh the raven!' Ferox thought of Enica hearing her people's old song and hating the fact that she was on the other side.

The tall armoured chieftain took a bolt through the eye and vanished behind the parapet. His standard-bearer was leaning over him when another missile hit his neck and burst out the other side. The singing faltered. By now, the scorpions had the range, and their crews worked mechanically, cranking and loading, lining up on a target, loosing the bolt, and then doing it all over again. A few of the victims screamed, and there were jeers from the defenders whenever a man ducked in time or the bolt struck the parapet or whisked past overhead. Soon most of the shots struck a man in the shoulders or face, and more and more men bobbed down behind the parapet. No one was yelling back any more, let along chanting.

The last men hid out of sight or were killed, but Neratius Marcellus let the scorpions shoot for a little longer, before raising his hand. 'Archers to advance. Scorpions to follow and set up fifty paces from the rampart. You can shoot over the bowmen if any of those fools feel brave again.' He turned to Ferox. 'Ride to the Augusta and tell them to advance when I signal. And then come back. I need you here.' As he rode away he heard similar orders being issued to go to XX Valeria Victrix and the auxiliaries under Cerialis.

A warrior cautiously raised his eyes above the parapet, now that the bolts had stopped. He must have shouted something, although Ferox did not hear, for others joined him. Then the arrows started, and although no one was hit they were close enough to make everyone duck back down.

Ferox passed on the orders and trotted back to the legate, taking his horse parallel to the rampart and within range of a well-thrown javelin. None came his way, for the defenders remained in hiding, so there was no real test of whether the gods planned to claim his life. Neratius Marcellus raised one eyebrow when he saw the centurion wheeling round to join his staff, but made no comment. The legate gestured to the tubicen who trailed behind him and the man sounded the signal for orders. Then the vexillarius dipped his square red flag, embroidered with its golden figure of Victory, three times. Cornicines in all of the leading units blew the three notes of the advance.

They were closest to Legio XX, on its unshielded side, so Ferox saw the legionaries step out as neatly as if they were on parade, with the clinks and soft thump of soldiers on the march. A centurion ahead and to the right of the front half of the cohort was walking backwards, so that he could keep a close eye on his men. It was a gesture of contempt for the enemy, if a weak one, since the enemy remained invisible, save for the horsemen on their right and the distant figures of the men in the old fort.

The legionaries were silent apart from the calm voices of centurions, and the sharp rebukes from the optiones following each line whenever a man spoke or wandered out of place. In the distance, Ferox just caught a low murmur as the Batavians began the barritus, the old war cry of Germanic warriors. Men in the fort answered with cheers and blasts of horns, for there were no archers over there to keep them down. On the opposite side the cavalry of each army watched each other, neither making any move, until Ferox caught a flicker of something out of the corner of his eye and saw a chariot shoot out between two of the bands of Brigantian horsemen. The car was painted a pale blue, the team one black and one grey, and the warrior in the back wore silvered helmet and mail and carried a deep blue shield. More chariots followed, some red, some green and some white, with warriors capering as they brandished weapons and shields high. It was bad luck to drive with ponies of the same colour, or so most of the tribes believed, so Ferox was surprised to see one car painted black and pulled by black animals. Its warrior was stark naked, his body painted, and he was standing on the shaft between the ponies as the wheels thundered across the grass.

'Well, there's a sight,' the legate said, as if commenting on a statue or painting. 'A glimpse of Homer, perhaps! What a shame Ovidius is not here to see it.' Ferox would have been glad to see the old fellow, and simply to know that he was well, and did not bother to remind the legate that the philosopher had seen plenty of chariots in Hibernia that summer.

The infantry pushed on steadily.

'Good boys! Keep it steady there.' The centurion going backwards did not shout, and simply spoke very loudly, his voice carrying easily along the first line formed by the cohort.

The chariots did not advance too far from their own cavalry, and then turned sharply, riding back and forth as the warriors showed off. Ferox saw ripples in the front rank of ala Petriana. He doubted the horses had ever seen or heard something like this, and more than a few were spooked by the flashes of metal and the spinning wheels as they crunched across the frosty grass. One beast turned and tried to push past the horses behind, its rider tugging desperately at the reins to stop it. At last he managed to drag his mount back around. Fortunately the Britons had not charged, for even a little bit of confusion could easily turn into panic. Ferox suspected that no one had seen the opportunity.

'Pity we did not put some archers over there with the cavalry,' the legate said wistfully. He glanced at the scorpions, but all were between the two leading formations of legionaries, and it would take time to bring a couple back so that they could see the chariots.

One of the warriors leaped down from his chariot and strode towards the Roman horsemen. Ferox could imagine him calling out his name and lineage and asking for a fitting opponent to face him in single combat. He wondered whether a few months ago the same man had been dressing in a toga and taking pride in speaking Latin, or whether this was one of those noblemen who had clung tightly to the old ways.

Aelius Brocchus galloped out from his station at the head of ala Petriana straight at the warrior, yellow-brown cloak billowing behind.

'Damned fool,' the legate muttered, half admiringly.

The Briton threw a javelin and the prefect deflected it with his shield. Brocchus had his own spear low down, and he urged his horse to go even faster, as the warrior drew his sword. The prefect leaned low and to the right, shield held up to protect his horse's head, the reins hanging free as he steered the animal with his knees. The Brigantian raised his long sword, but before he could sweep down, the spear point drove into his stomach and through his body, lifting him off his feet. Brocchus struggled with the weight, for he was not a big man, and after a moment gave up and dropped both spear and the writhing warrior impaled on it.

'Ferox,' the legate said quietly. 'Go and tell the prefect well done, but if he tries that again I'll have him on a charge and dismissed from his post.' He shook his head. 'Really, a man of his years. And, Ferox?'

'Yes, my lord.'

'Come straight back.'

Brocchus grinned as his men cheered him. Other warriors were on foot now, issuing their own challenges.

'Stay in ranks!' Brocchus shouted. 'Keep order.'

Decurions echoed the command. 'Stay in line, you bastards!'

The prefect nodded as he received the order. 'Please don't ever tell my wife,' he added with a smile. 'Oh well, so much for heroism, let us do this like proper soldiers.' He ordered a turma to ride out and skirmish with the chariots.

By the time Ferox rejoined the legate, the legionaries were at the wall. Now and then a defender bobbed up, throwing a javelin or rock down. Few risked the time needed to aim properly, because the archers and scorpions were waiting. One legionary was behind the line, as a medicus tied a bandage around his bloodied head, while another lay still, a spear in his throat, but those were the only casualties. Men were working with dolabrae, using the wider head of the pickaxe to prise apart the turves in the wall. Others used crowbars or simply their hands, eating away at the hastily built rampart. Each legion was working on two breaches in the wall.

Something was wrong. Ferox's instincts were calling to him that it was all too easy. Even with the risk from the arrows and bolts, the Brigantes seemed too cowed, as they let their defences be destroyed with no real effort to hinder the work. Ferox heard a distant roar as the barritus reached a crescendo and the Batavians charged. The defenders shouted back, hurling javelins at the auxiliaries as they scrambled up the grassy slope. Cerialis had orders not to press the attack too hard until the legionaries had crossed the wall, but such caution was all too easily forgotten in the heat of the moment.

Brocchus' men worked in pairs, one covering the other so that they always had at least one javelin ready to throw. Two of the chariots lay as shattered ruins of men and ponies, brought down by killing one of the animals or the driver when they were going at full pelt. Three more warriors were wounded, and only one managed to get back on board and escape, and the cost was one trooper hit in the thigh and two horses wounded. Ferox did not think that Arviragus was with the chariots, although at this distance it was hard to be sure. As he watched, the naked warrior with the black chariot and team burst forward. A javelin twitched the mane of one of the ponies without doing harm, and another struck the warrior's shield and stuck fast so that he dropped it. His own javelin hit the top of a trooper's raised shield, but the auxiliary was slow and all he did was deflect the missile up into his face. The chariot raced past, and the warrior had his sword ready. He dodged the javelin of the trooper's companion, and the auxiliary was still fumbling with his spatha when the chariot skimmed along past him and the long sword swept. Blood fountained high as the trooper's head and helmet sailed through the air, and the black team was turning, galloping away to safety. Ferox could not help admiring the skill.

With a soft, almost gentle rumble, part of the rampart collapsed forward, the legionaries bounding back out of the way. The soldiers cheered, and a moment later more of the wall gave way to form a second breach.

'Beware the Boars,' the centurion who had started the advance going backwards bellowed out in triumph. Legio XX used a boar as its symbol on some of its standards, although its shield bore the device of Jupiter's lightning bolts and the wings of thunder.

Valeria Victrix had broken the rampart before the other legion, and no doubt they would remind Augusta of this at every opportunity. Ferox imagined Tertullianus cursing in his high-pitched voice, until the wall started to crumble and their two breaches formed.

'Capricorns!' II Augusta had the capricorn symbol of the divine Augustus on its red shields.

As the dust cleared javelins came whipping through the breaches. Julius Tertullianus died in the moment of triumph as a spearhead struck him in the mouth and drove so deep into his head that the rear of his helmet was dented. Most of the men using the tools had laid aside their shields to work and now they paid for this, with half a dozen falling to wounds in the legs, and one whose mail failed to stop a powerful throw.

There was no check. A few men hurled pila through the gap, but most did not bother and raised the slim javelins to use as spears. Some stayed with their tools as they climbed up the slope made by the debris of the wall and charged inside. There was a dull roar of rage and an answering shout of anger from behind the wall.

'Someone go and see what is happening!' the legate gasped, and before he could say anything else Ferox put his horse into a run. Four mobs of legionaries attacked through the breaches. Formation was impossible and the lack of order could not be helped, but by now Ferox's instincts were screaming even louder and he was sure that this was a trap.

He rode past the scorpions and archers, heading for the wall near one of the breaches made by II Augusta. From beyond the ramparts there were shouts, the clash of weapons, and screams of agony. More and more legionaries were pushing their way through the gaps, and behind them the reserve lines were close, ready to reinforce. The rampart was not high, so that when Ferox reined in beside it, the crest of his helmet was barely lower than the top of the parapet. There was no sign of any defenders. For a moment he wondered about trying Enica's trick of standing on the saddle, before deciding not to risk it. This was a borrowed horse and rather skittish. Instead he jumped down and called to a couple of the archers.

'Give me a hand.'

Putting a foot in one man's cupped hands, he pushed up, and with a hefty shove from the over grabbed the top of the parapet and managed to get one boot on the narrow ledge in front of it.

'Thanks, lads.'

Ferox pulled himself up, and to his relief no warrior was kneeling behind the barrier, waiting for this moment. A corpse with a bolt in its chest sprawled on the walkway, one arm hanging down, and apart from a few more dead and badly wounded warriors the wall was empty. Below there was fighting and he could see that the Romans were winning and steadily pushing forward. Dragging himself over, Ferox squatted next to the dead warrior and looked down. Most of the men from the first attacking line were already inside, in four groups in front of each of the breaches. As they cut their way forward, they spread a little with each pace gained. The reserves were starting to follow them, and he saw the eagle waving amid the other standards as the lionskin-headdressed standard-bearers advanced with their comrades.

'What's happening?' Neratius Marcellus shouted from behind. The legate had come after him, too impatient to wait.

Ferox did not answer. He tried to count the warriors fighting the legionaries. They were little more than a mob, clustering around the Romans, so that the best he could get was an impression, but it was obvious that there were too few of them. Perhaps there were a few score more Brigantes than Romans, although that would soon change as the reserves caught up.

'Damn it, Ferox, what is happening?'

He glanced to the right. The Batavians had not yet broken into the old fort and for the moment the two sides had separated and were lobbing javelins back and forth. On the left, the cavalry still waited, although from here he could see that the Britons had well over two thousand horsemen and more might be concealed by the woods. The royal cohort stood just a little back from the line of the rampart, each man with his shield resting against his legs and his spear in his hand as he waited in silence.

'It's a trap, my lord,' Ferox called back. Everything pointed to that, for if this was all that was left of the prince's army and the rest had deserted then why would he have fought at all? Ferox stared behind the clusters of Britons fighting the legionaries. There was just grassland for a couple of hundred paces before the ground rose to a low ridge, but it was hard to believe that the rest of the army could be so far away as behind the heights. He looked closer, saw the grass ripple in the wind, passed on, and then brought his gaze back. There was no wind.

Someone grunted as they landed on the parapet beside him. The legate stood up, brushing himself down. 'Go on, lads!' he shouted, as the legionaries made another surge forward. He turned. 'Send up the other cohort.' The tubicen called out and the vexillum waved as a signal.

'Wait, my lord!' Ferox watched the grass no more than seventy paces behind the retreating Britons, before he saw a head, then another peering out. 'Look there!' Once he had seen it, the shadow on the land was obvious. There was a gully, running all the way across the field, invisible until you knew where to look, but big enough to hide men – lots of men.

The warriors fighting the legionaries were going back faster now, leaving a lot of dead and wounded behind them. As they pushed on behind the front ranks, Romans jabbed down with pilum or sword to kill those who still moved, for it was never wise to take a chance and spare an enemy before the battle was won. A carnyx blew, the harsh quivering call loud even above the fighting, and the Britons turned and fled. Some died because they did not turn fast enough, and then more as the legionaries streamed after them, the wounded and slow being killed first. A great cheer of victory went up from the legionaries as the enemy broke. No one shouted any orders and the two cohorts just rushed ahead, eager to finish the job.

Then the prince sprang his trap.

XXIX

THOUSANDS OF WARRIORS sprang up out of the ground, pouring over the lip of the gully and charging, and their great shout was like the crashing of waves against the shore. Many of them wore armour and helmets of army pattern, spoils from the defeat of Crassus.

'Hercules' balls!' the legate gasped as he saw them.

They were not in neat ranks, but there were so many of them and they came on eagerly, Arviragus leading them with a dozen of the royal guard around him and his standard of the horse overhead. The fleeing Britons either joined them or were pushed to the ground and trampled by the oncoming horde. Legionaries halted, and those who had gone the furthest were first to die.

Trumpets sounded and the royal cohort picked up its shields and marched forward. Facing them was cohors IV Gallorum, outnumbered more than two to one. Beyond them the Brigantian cavalry started to walk their horses towards the Roman left wing

'Form up!' Neratius Marcellus screamed at the legionaries in front of the rampart. 'Form ranks!'

Ferox grabbed his arm, and the legate started in surprise, eyes angry. 'He means to sweep round through our flank while our army is split by the wall,' he explained.

Neratius Marcellus was breathing hard, but nodded in understanding, and Ferox could see him calculating. 'Archers, up on the wall!' he yelled, and then grabbed the parapet to shout down orders to his staff. 'All the archers, up here, quick as you can! Send the cohort cavalry to support Brocchus. He must stop their horse until we can win here. The Gauls to hold their place and die where they stand if need be. Tell them I am counting on them and know that they will not let me down.' Cerialis' men still faced the old fort and there was no need to give them fresh instructions. 'Tell the reserve cohort of Victrix to wheel to the left, but wait for my orders!'

As the legate shouted his instructions, the legionaries were coming back, still in no sort of order, but drawn towards the wall. More warriors kept swarming up out of the gully. Ferox guessed there were five thousand or more and still men boiled over the lip. Somehow a rough line was forming, the legionaries clustered in some places and thin in others. Some eleven hundred men had broken through and were still on their feet, stretched in a ragged line across the half-mile strip of grass in front of the rampart. The Britons were close enough to stab with spears or swords and it had all happened too fast for anyone to throw javelins or pila. Behind the front ranks of warriors, all of them in mail, was a vast crowd and some of these men managed to fling a spear forward, but most were too tightly packed. Legionaries who found themselves in the front rank dropped pila if they still had them because there was so little room, and instead slid out their swords.

'Come on!' the legate said, and ran down the bank of the rampart, heading for the eagle. 'Rally, boys! Rally,' he shouted as he went. Ferox went after him, slipping on the grass so that he skidded on his backside down the ramp.

'Don't play the fool, man!' the legate snarled.

The Roman line was only twenty paces or so from the wall. There were no optiones behind it, or trace of proper formation, and in places it was two deep and sometimes five or six deep. Men shouted as the Brigantes attacked, blade clashed against blade, or struck helmet, armour or shield and after a flurry of fighting the Roman line shuffled back a few more paces.

'Steady there!' the legate called, his trained voice booming out over the legionaries' heads. Steady, the Boars! Steady, the Capricorns!' Just behind the line, the aquilifer of II Augusta stood with the other standard-bearers, including two from Victrix who had found themselves here.

'Come on!' Ferox heard the prince yelling to his own men. 'Let them hear you! Oh the wolf! Oh the raven!' The singing was ragged, until more and more of the Brigantes joined in. 'Come to me and I will give you flesh!'

'Ferox, you take charge of Augusta. I will sort out Valeria Victrix or find someone who can.' The legate saw the questioning look. 'Do it, man, there's no time for debate.'

'Sir!' Ferox drew his gladius. 'Good luck, my lord.'

'And to you, centurion.' The legate ran off to the left. 'Steady, lads! Hold them! Hold them!'

'Any centurions left?' Ferox asked the aquilifer.

'Don't know, sir.' The eagle-bearer tried to smile. A javelin lobbed high above the legionaries whistled, and Ferox was lunging forward with his free hand, trying to push the man out of the way, but was too slow and the leaf-shaped point drove into his neck through the scarf he wore to stop his mail from chafing. Blood jetted out, the man's eyes rolling up as he slumped forward. Ferox managed to catch the eagle before it fell.

A young soldier was at the back of the line and turned, staring in horror at the dying standard-bearer. He was tall, for II Augusta liked to have a first cohort of tall men, and must have had a good record otherwise he would not have been with the cohort at all.

'You, boy, what's your name?'

'Caecilius, sir.'

'Oh the raven!'

'Let's have your shield, Caecilius.' Ferox thrust the precious standard towards him. 'You are to carry this,' he said. The boy's eyes widened. 'It is a sacred trust for this is the honour of our legion and we are II Augusta, the best legion in the army, and we have work to do. You follow me. All of you.' He hefted the shield as the boy passed it over, and looked at the standard-bearers. 'We will make this a day the legion will still be marking in two hundred years' time.'

'Oh the wolf!' The singing was getting louder as the Brigantes readied themselves for a fresh charge.

Ferox had deliberately chosen a place where the line was only a few men deep. He snarled and shouted at men to let him through, and reached the front, the warriors only two spear lengths away. Facing him was a chieftain he remembered from the council, although he could not think of his name. The man was clean shaven and short-haired, with a sly face and eyes that never looked at someone when he spoke to them.

'You!' he said, breaking off from the war chant, although he still did not look Ferox in the face.

'Give in. Lay down your arms and the legate will be merciful!' Ferox had spoken in Latin out of habit, but now switched to the language of the tribes. 'All of you, surrender now and accept the governor's mercy!'

'Come to me and I will give you flesh!' The words were almost screamed at the Roman line and turned into a roar as the Brigantes surged forward. The chieftain with the sly face had a spear, a bronze helmet with an elaborate plume, mail and an oval shield. He came for Ferox, finally looking straight at him, spear over his shoulder, ready to jab down. The centurion raised his borrowed shield, felt it shudder as the iron head struck it, and swept very low with his gladius. The blade bit into something, the slim face broke into a yelp and the man staggered. Ferox flicked the sword to thrust up and the chieftain squealed as the long triangular point came under his mail and into his groin.

As the chieftain fell back, shrieking, Ferox stabbed the man standing beside him, the blade sliding past his shield and punching through the iron rings of his mail shirt. The warrior gasped, dropped his sword, and the legionary beside Ferox stamped forward and finished him with a jab through the eye. On his left, the legionary attacked with too much force, and his opponent pushed the blade aside with his shield and then slashed down, severing the Roman's right arm. Blood pumping out, the soldier dropped his scutum and clutched at the wounded limb. The long sword slashed down again, clanging as it struck his helmet with such force that the iron broke open as the man went down. Behind him a legionary still carried his pilum and aimed carefully as he jabbed forward, the little point driving into the warrior's eye.

The Brigantes gave way and stepped back a few paces. It was the first time that the Romans had not been the ones to retreat and that was something, even if all along the line Ferox could see many dead on the grass and the wounded being dragged back.

'Still with me, Caecilius?' he asked.

'Yes, sir.'

'Good lad. Keep that eagle high.'

'We're holding them, boys,' he shouted. 'They won't break the Capricorns.' His back was slick with sweat and he had only fought for a short time.

Arrows whipped overhead to fall deep among the mass of warriors in front of them. He heard cries of pain, and saw men in the rear ranks raising their blue shields to meet this new attack. The Hamian archers were up on the rampart, and that would help, but the front lines were too close together for them to shoot at the enemy leaders and their boldest men. Ferox saw Arviragus some way over to his left and wished that he could get at the prince, but the legionaries were only just holding on and he did not want to try to work his way around behind the line in case they thought he was running. If the Romans broke, then most would die, because they would be trapped against the wall, and if they died then he doubted Neratius Marcellus would win his battle, even if he did not die along with them.

The arrows stung the Brigantes into another attack, which brought more of them closer to the legionaries again. A very tall man, a good six inches higher than him, though lean as a reed, yelled as he came at the centurion. He had an axe in his hand, the sort most men would save for chopping wood, and he tried to hook it over the top of Ferox's shield and pull it down. Behind him a spearman as tall and rangy as the first man thrust a spear over his shoulder. They looked alike, perhaps twins, so strange with their hollow cheeks and spiked hair that they might have come from a legend.

Ferox had his sword up, elbow bent, and stabbed forward, but the tall man was too far away from him to reach. Again the axe swung, and rather than let it catch on his scutum he jerked the shield up, so that the blade sliced through the brass edging and gouged a hole in the wood. The spear thumped against it, not hard enough to penetrate, and Ferox brough his right arm low behind his shield, lunging at waist height, only to strike against the warrior's shield.

These strange twins were dangerous, working together well. Beside him, the soldier on his right had lost his helmet and was bleeding heavily from his scalp, but managed to drive his opponent back a pace. Another legionary on his left fell, this time with his left leg almost cut through beneath the knee, and he was dragged into the enemy ranks and stabbed a dozen times before he lay still. A comrade stepped forward into the gap.

Suddenly the tall warrior sprouted an arrow from his eye, his head snapping back with the impact, and Ferox blessed the archer who had taken such a risky shot. He stamped forward, pushing the corpse with his shield, and lunged up into his twin's neck. The legionary on Ferox's right was struggling to see as the blood streamed down over his eyes, and he slashed wildly and so quickly that he beat his opponent's shield down, twice struck sparks off his mail shirt without breaking the rings, and finally nicked his face. Then a spearmen behind the warrior thrust hard, bursting through where two plates of the man's segmented cuirass met. The Roman grunted, slumping forward. A legionary standing in the next rank still had a pilum and threw it with all his strength into the warrior. The head punched through the man's shield, the shank sliding hungrily through the hole, splitting two rings on his mail as it forced its way into his belly. He too dropped back, and it was as if that was a signal for the whole line to pull away.

'Well done, boys, we're holding them.' Ferox gasped for breath. His arms and legs felt like lead, and his muscles throbbed. No one who had not fought in a battle line ever understood how quickly a man became exhausted. He knew that holding the enemy was not enough. The Romans were outnumbered and so many Britons were packed behind the leading ranks that it would be hard for any of them to turn and flee. If it came to a long slog, then the legionaries were more likely to become exhausted before the enemy.

Arrows snipped above his head, thunking into the shields the Brigantes were holding high. Ferox had no idea what was happening in the rest of the battle. Even the governor, who was probably no more than a few hundred paces away, might as easily be alive or dead, or on a journey to the moon, for all he could tell. He wished that he was up on the wall again, able to see what was going on, but he could not leave.

'Right, boys,' he shouted as loudly as he could, trying to sound as if victory was inevitable, but his throat was thick and all that came out was a croak. He spat to clear it.

It was not enough to hold their ground. They had to win, because if any part of the Roman army collapsed then the rest could easily follow. 'Those bastards have killed some of our commilitones. No one does that and gets away with it.

Come on, Capricorns. Follow the eagle! It's going through those sods in front of us, so unless we want to lose it, we will have to go with it!'

He took a deep breath. 'Caecilius.'

'Sir.'

'Stay behind me, boy. Every step of the way.'

He thumped the flat of his gladius against the side of his shield. 'Let 'em hear you!' He struck again and again. 'Come on, Capricorns, let 'em hear us coming!' Men copied, pounding swords or shafts of pila against the rectangular shields.

'Charge!' Ferox yelled, and did his best to run at the enemy, in spite of the heaviness in his legs. They were only a few paces away, but he saw the warrior opposite him, teeth bared as he grimaced over the top of his shield. The man had a legionary helmet, the top dented, and he wondered whether its previous owner was dead or had thrown it away to run faster. Ferox punched with all his weight behind the heavy scutum, the dome-like boss high to smash into the warrior's face, breaking his nose, and if the man had been waiting he could have killed Ferox then and there, thrusting low with his sword. No blow came back, and the warrior staggered from the impact, so Ferox punched again, without the force of going forward, but savagely enough. Then his gladius was up and jerked forward, brushing the bottom cheek piece before it found the warrior's neck. Blood spattered over Ferox's face and shield as the Brigantian dropped.

Ferox stamped forward, boot on the man he had just killed, and the warrior behind tried to go back, but could not because of the press behind him. He beat aside a sword attempting to parry, twisting his wrist to angle the thrust down. The tip grated on a collar bone, then slid down. Gasping for breath, the warrior was finally able to step back as the men behind him reacted. He was hurt, but not fatally. Ferox had a moment of freedom and swept again back and to his right. His gladius was starting to blunt by now, so the steel cut only part way into the warrior's neck, and his head flapped down but did not fall. Then Ferox turned back, facing ahead, and the Brigantes gave ground again, stepping back a couple of paces.

'Still there, Caecilius?'

'Course I am, sir.'

Ferox was panting, his mail armour like great weights pressing down onto his shoulders. On either side of him the Roman line had advanced and taken a tiny patch of ground, so that it bulged forward. Elsewhere the two sides were where they had started. He blinked because there was sweat in his eyes. Glancing up to the right, he could see Batavians and Roman standards on the grassy mound of the old wall, and the defenders still facing them. There were not many arrows overhead this time, and he guessed the Hamians must have nearly emptied their quivers. The winter sun had climbed as high as it would go, which meant that it was noon, and he tried to work out where the hours had gone.

'Another few paces, boys!' Ferox croaked. 'That's all we have to do, just drive these mongrels back a a few more paces!' He had a vague memory of a general telling his men to give him one more step for victory. Was it a Greek?

'Come on, boys!' Caecilius yelled so suddenly that Ferox would have jumped if he still had the energy. The boy was waving the gilded eagle. 'Follow the eagle! Follow the eagle.'

'The eagle!' one of the signifers repeated. 'The eagle.'

Maybe it was just the men still in the rear ranks and not quite so drained, but the legionaries started to chant.

Ferox searched for Arviragus among the enemy and could no longer see him. It did not seem to matter any more.

'The eagle!' he screamed, and lurched forward, his legs heavier than when he strapped weights to them to make exercises harder.

The Brigantes came to meet them, and the shouts faded as the two lines of men drew on the last dregs of their strength to fight. Ferox's shield banged hard against an opponent's. Neither man gave way, and the warrior was in mail, with a Roman sword and a bandaged head, and he watched the centurion warily. They tested each other, each of their worlds down to just the man trying to kill him.

Ferox feinted a high thrust, failing to draw his opponent's guard the wrong way, so he put his shoulder behind his shield and rammed it forward again, his foot slipping on the blood-soaked grass so that there was even more force than he had intended. The warrior was barged back, but by the time Ferox recovered balance the man's guard was up again. On his right the warrior fell with a gladius driven through his head, and the legionary let the weapon go and went over the corpse, pounding the enemy with his shield, until he was among them and a sword swung and took him behind the knee. He went down on the other leg, and they swarmed around, but he kept blocking them with his shield and the blows that got past pounded armour and helmet and did not break through. Barely conscious, somehow the legionary squatted there and defied them until he sagged.

The warrior slashed down hard, his blade striking Ferox's shield where the edge was already broken and biting deep into the three layers of wood. It stuck fast and as the man tried to wrench it free, the centurion cut upwards, through the man's chin and mouth. Letting go of his own sword, the man staggered. Ferox twisted the gladius free and sliced through the warrior's neck. Blood sprayed over his face and eyes and he struggled to see. He shook his shield, but the dead man's sword was stuck fast and weighed it down.

Caecilius was beside him, eagle in his left hand, and the lad stabbed a warrior in the stomach. A spear came from the second rank, denting one of the plates of the legionary's armour. It had a huge head, the edge serrated like the ones heroes used in the old songs.

'Get back, you fool!' Ferox gasped. He cut at the spear shaft, throwing off splinters, but another man came at him from the front, and with his cumbersome shield there was only just time to block the sword as it swung down. The impact shuddered the shield and the great split in it widened. Another hard blow and the sword dropped down, but the scutum was in ruin. Ferox flung it at his opponent, and then had to slash desperately at a man coming from his right. The gladius rang as it struck the torc the warrior was wearing with such force that it snapped his neck and he dropped.

Caecilius screamed as the spear broke through the lowest plate on his cuirass and went into his stomach. The warrior twisted the weapon, not to free it but to widen the wound, and then let the spear go. Caecilius dropped his sword, and somehow drove the spike of the aquila into the ground before he collapsed. The ground was hard, and his strength ebbing away, so that the eagle-standard leaned forward at a sharp angle.

Ferox spun around, lunging to take the warrior who had killed Caecilius in the side, the point of his gladius driving deep through muscle and flesh. A Brigantian was reaching for the eagle, so the centurion ripped the blade free and slashed at him, slicing down through the man's skull. Something hit him hard on the side of the helmet, snapping the chin strap and spinning the helmet round until it fell off. His head throbbed and there was wet blood in his hair. The gladius was stuck fast in the man he had killed, the corpse's weight dragging him down. Ferox let go, nearly tripped on a corpse, and reached the eagle, grabbing it with both hands. There was a blow against his shoulder, where the mail doubled over to fasten, and the rings held, although he was bruised.

Horns blew, dozens and dozens of horns, but they were far away. They did not sound like army signals and Ferox wondered whether thousands more warriors were rushing out to swamp the last Romans, or did he hear the armies of the dead still fighting forgotten wars in the Otherworld?

Ferox wrenched the aquila from the ground and swung it in a great arc at the Brigantes. The gilded bird on top of the pole scarred the air, and took a man in the jaw, breaking teeth and spraying blood from a split lip. One wing bent back with the impact. He swept it round savagely and the warriors made room.

'Come on, you mongrels!' he screamed at them in their own language. 'Let me feed you to the wolves and ravens!'

The horns blasted out again, closer now, and Ferox knew the end would be soon. He no longer cared or thought about anything. There was just the faces of the warriors watching him, waiting for their chance, and all that was left was hate.

Let the bastards come and he would pound as many as he could into slush before they got him.

A warrior stepped forward, sword up ready for the swing, and Ferox twisted the heavy standard so that the blade hit the pole, leaving a gouge, but he twisted again and drove the long butt spike into the man's face.

Ferox laughed like a madman, revelling in the warrior's death.

'Come on, you mongrels!' If he was about to journey to the Otherworld then he would not go alone.

Again the horns called, and this time Roman trumpets answered, blaring out their own challenge.

Ferox let the body fall and swept the aquila at his enemies. They stepped back, so he turned the standard around again and went for them. He no longer felt tired and the pain did not seem to matter. With all his strength he carved the air, the bird pounding against the warriors' shields, and still they gave way.

'Bastards! Fight me!' he begged, but the men took another step back.

Someone was shouting, their voice clear and high. Ferox ignored them. He swung the eagle again, sweeping it higher than before, and was rewarded because one of the warriors had turned to look behind him, so the bird slammed into his head and knocked him to the ground.

'Stop!' The voice was still shouting, and it was an odd sound for a battlefield, but he did not care. His enemies were running now, fleeing from him, and he hated them for their cowardice. He went to the one he had knocked down, turned the standard again and drove the spike through the warrior's belly and into the ground. The man was pinned, badly hurt, but not dead and Ferox watched the terror and agony in his face and rejoiced in it.

'It is over!' The enemy had gone, at least from this part of the field. One of the signifers came up to him, and the man's face was pale with fear.

'Stop! It is over!' Ahead of him, beyond the gully, was a chariot, the car painted white and the team a grey and a dark bay, both in bright red harness. A man squatted at the reins, and behind him stood a woman in gleaming white, save for the scale armour of alternate gilded and silvered plates. She carried a spear and a blue shield and had long red hair down her back.

Was this how it ended? Gannascus had once told him that goddesses came to lead the soul of a great warrior into the Otherworld.

'Husband, it is over!'

Thought came slowly and with effort. Strength had left his limbs and he felt weary and battered. Even breathing was hard work.

'Ferox, you fool, it is over! We have won!' The words were in Latin.

That was Enica, and she was alive. Ferox sank to his knees beside the man pinned to the ground. Someone touched his shoulder lightly, and he saw it was the signifer, who looked as if he was afraid the centurion might attack him.

'I'd better take this, sir.' The standard-bearer reached for the eagle and yanked it free. The warrior clutched at his intestines as they spilled from the gaping wound in his belly.

Ferox put his hands over his face. He was alive. He did not know whether this was good or bad.

XXX

'TODAY FOR VENGEANCE, tomorrow for mourning,' Vindex said firmly, and drew his sword. His spear was buried in the royal guard and the shaft had broken when he tried to pull it free. The scout smiled. 'As long as you think this is a good idea!'

Sepenestus had killed the other two, and his arrows came out much more easily. He wiped the heads on the hem of his tunic and put the arrows back in his bag.

'There are nine left and the prisoner,' Ferox said. 'You've already done enough and don't have to come.'

The archer sniffed at that and patted his sword, an army-pattern spatha. Gannascus nodded approvingly. 'We cannot wait for more of them to arrive, so it will just have to be unfair,' the big man rumbled, saying almost as much as he had done in the three days of pursuit.

As Enica had shouted out, the battle had been won, and a lot of the credit went to her. Cerialis had taken the old fort after a bitter struggle. The stocky little Vardulli were saying that they had rescued the Batavians and the big men from the Rhineland were denying that they needed any help. Both prefects had been wounded, but managed to stay on their feet until it was done. On the left Brocchus and the cavalry had fought a long, whirling fight, charging, driving the enemy back, before being chased in turn. Numbers were with the Brigantes, and they were on the higher ground, so that they did not break easily. Gradually, the auxiliaries made headway, until their main lines were on top of the hill. Next to them the royal cohort had met the Gauls, who had fought for a long time before weight of numbers drove them back. Somehow, Neratius Marcellus had got an order to the reserve cohort of Legio XX and the Victrix had plugged the hole in the line. Beyond the rampart, men had fought and died where they stood, and it was only Ferox and the men around him who had begun forcing that vast crowd of enemies back. Soon, someone's will would have broken. It only took a few to turn and run and others would follow. It might have been the Romans, especially at the rampart, for there it was hard for the Britons to give way with so many men pressing behind them.

Then the horns sounded. Enica brought no more than five hundred warriors to the fight. Quite a few were Carvetii, led by Vindex's half-brother, who was on his way to seek vengeance even before the high queen sent out her call. A lot of men were sympathetic or simply hated her brother for what he had done, but some were afraid, and there was simply not time to gather the rest. Enica needed men with horses, and gratefully took the chariot and team from a chieftain too old to walk, let alone fight. She also wanted horns or trumpets, and took any she could find. Vindex had told her the story of when they had caught Rufus and the others, and she had liked the idea. Nearly seventy of her riders carried something to blow, so that when she reached the battlefield, horses foamy with sweat and too weary to do more than trot, it had sounded like a vast host ready to fight.

The deception worked. The Brigantes were fighting hard, but had not yet won and were growing tired. When a host of their kin appeared behind them, lining the crest of the next row of hills, they doubted. When Enica rode among them, calling out for all of her people to follow her and she would ensure they were free to go, all but a few grasped at the chance of life. Arviragus escaped. None of his people would hinder him, and probably some of Enica's men felt the same, not wanting royal blood on their hands. No more than twenty or so men went with him. Many of the guards fought until Enica implored them to lay down their arms if they wished to carry them in her service. Here and there across the field little groups fought to the last, but the result was no longer in doubt.

Philo was delighted when Ferox told him about the ploy. The young slave was almost as delighted, and a good deal more scared, when his master told him that he would have his freedom as soon as the documents could be prepared. There had not been time in the two hours Ferox was given to get ready for the pursuit. To his surprise, Enica did not want to come.

'A sister should not shed a brother's blood, even after he has tried to kill me. It is better this way.' She stood tall and proud, every inch a queen, and he found it hard to believe that they had any future. Still, perhaps the gods still meant him to pay for her life with his own, and it was with that gloomy thought he rode off, taking the others with him as well as five Carvetii scouts.

Arviragus headed north, and as they followed Ferox began to recognise more and more of the country. He wondered whether the prince hoped to reach the tribes beyond the province, trusting them to give him shelter. Gannascus was dismissive when he suggested this.

'Tincommius will not want to provoke the Romans.'

The fugitives did their best to confuse the pursuit they must have known was following, and snow might have saved them, but the brooding skies gave only drizzle hour after hour, so that their horses left prints that were easy for Ferox to track. Most of the men rode cavalry mounts, but there were several ponies and two very big horses, one of which surely carried the prince.

Late on the second day the trail split, eight men heading west into the high hills. Two of them rode the big horses.

'I can't see anything,' Vindex said after he had stared at the prints for a long while.

'Different rider,' Ferox insisted with more confidence than he felt. There was something odd about the prints he had found in a long patch of mud. Only a few from one of the big horses were good enough to see apart from the muddle of all the rest. He wondered whether he really saw something or just sensed that this was a ploy because it was the sort of thing he would do if he was trying to escape. It could be a bluff, although he doubted Arviragus had the subtlety to think that way.

In the end he compromised, sending the Carvetii after the smaller trail, and taking the others after the main party. They had only gone a mile or so after the decoys, so not much time was lost. During the next day, Ferox knew that they were gaining, and close to dusk they caught up with them. Thirteen horses were in the pens around five round houses, crammed in with the livestock spared the winter slaughter. It was a farmstead like any other, although not yet quite close enough to his region for him to know the people who lived there.

Three of the royal troopers acted as sentries, and Sepenestus shot two while Vindex stalked and killed the third. They were tired, not keeping a good watch, and Ferox could only hope the same exhausted despair had fallen over the rest of the party.

'You know the prince?' Ferox asked the bowman.

Sepenestus nodded.

'You must not kill him.' Just as Enica must not be a part of her brother's death, so the prince, even though he was a rebel, must have the chance of an honourable death, toe to toe with his pursuers. Perhaps then the rifts torn among the Brigantes would heal more quickly. Ferox was not sure, but his wife and the legate might be right and those were his orders. The bowman went to their left, hanging back a little as the other three strode towards the farm. Vindex had one of the horns they had used in the battle and managed a rasping blast.

'Come out, lord prince!' Ferox yelled as loud as he could. 'Come out and face us!' Vindex stood on his left, and the towering German on his right. 'You must kill us if you ever wish to leave this place.'

There was silence, so Ferox nodded and the scout blew the ox horn trumpet again and he repeated the challenge. 'This is Ferox,' he added. 'The noble Neratius Marcellus and your sister have sent me to find you.'

Arviragus wore the torc and the helmet and armour of Venutius, even though he must now know that the last two were not genuine. He bent down to come through the door and then stood.

'Just four of you,' he said, his voice as weary as it was disappointed. 'It would be you, wouldn't it, Ferox – leading the wolves on my trail.' He drew his sword. 'I will not go back.'

'I know, lord prince. But if you are to go on, you must face us first.'

Arviragus smiled and seemed to grow taller as if some of his spirit returned. He walked towards them as his men appeared. Four troopers of the royal guard came from another house and stood on his right. Another, along with Brigantus, a chieftain and another warrior joined him on the left. The warrior was naked in spite of the cold, his body a whirling network of blue woad, and Ferox remembered this man in his black chariot. He dragged Crispinus by a chain, and the tribune crawled like a dog. The warrior kicked him, until he lay down next to the wall of a pen, moaning.

There was no ditch around the farm, or even a wall or fence, and the courtyard between the pens and houses simply opened up into the meadow where the three men stood.

Gannascus gave a deep-throated chuckle.

'Oh well,' Vindex muttered, and they started to walk forward as the Brigantes came for them.

Sepenestus loosed an arrow. The trooper on the far right raised his oval shield to block it, but did not realise the appalling power of the archer's bow at this range. The arrowhead was slim and pointed, similar to the head of a pilum, and it drove straight through the shieldboard and into the man's eye. A second arrow was in the air, and the next trooper held his shield up firmer and further from his body, so that when the head came through it did not reach him. He shook from the impact.

Ferox had borrowed a cavalryman's oval shield from a Batavian trooper, and it was much lighter than a scutum. There was a notch on the blade of his gladius, courtesy of the man with the torc, and he had not had time to work on it. The memory the battle had faded, as it always did, and there was little left of the wild joy he had felt when he had brandished the aquila as a club. His own helmet had been trampled and bent, so he had also borrowed a fur-topped one from the same soldier.

Another arrow banged against the trooper's shield, making him stagger again. Then the next went under the rim and struck just above the knee. That was wonderful shooting in the gloom, and the man gasped, dropping his shield and spear to clutch at his leg. He was hit again, hard in the chest, and fell.

Arviragus yelled and ran at Ferox, the others taking up his cry. One of the troopers threw a spear at Vindex, who deflected it with his shield. The other cavalryman had a sword and the scout parried the blow with his own blade. Gannascus bounded forward, lunged with his own spear to spit the chieftain, who fell, gasping for breath. The German barged Brigantus out of the way with his shield as he reached for his sword. The bodyguard was showing none of the speed he had been famed for in his days as a gladiator.

The naked man was on Ferox's right, the prince on his left, and both watched him. He feinted at the warrior, who stepped back and then slashed at him as he tried to turn and attack the prince. Their swords met, throwing off sparks in the darkness, and the prince cut faster than he expected, giving him a glancing blow on the helmet. Ferox's head rang.

Each of them faced two men as Sepenestus watched for a clear shot. Vindex managed to give one of the troopers a cut on the chin, but before he could regain his balance, the other one slid his blade past his shield and punctured his mail shirt. Gannascus was forcing his two opponents back, moving with a speed truly uncanny in so big a man. His shield was scarred by their blows, but he kept coming, pounding them with it.

'Never trust that bitch!' Arviragus spat the words at Ferox. 'She'd kill any man without a thought.'

Ferox did not reply. He had realised that the warrior was faster than the prince, so now he loosened his grip on his shield, wanting to use the prince's taunts.

'Don't trust Crispinus either. He's done more than you know. Hanged a girl at Vindolanda. Humped her first, though. Only a slave, but still... Bet he's rutted with my sister as well!'

Ferox bellowed, trying to sound enraged, and, letting go, he hurled the shield at the prince, something only a madman would do. Arviragus flung up his own shield to block it and went back. As he did so Ferox dived and rolled, swordpoint under the warrior's guard as he pushed it deep into his groin. The shriek was piercing, and he yanked at his sword, taking a moment to tear it free.

Gannascus killed the trooper as the man was distracted by the scream of agony. One of the men facing Vindex tried to work around him and took an arrow in the back. The scout hooked his shield around the edge of the other man, ripped it away and rammed his sword into the man's chest, snapping the scales of his armour.

Ferox was pushing himself up, and then was beaten face down onto the ground by a sword slamming against him. He rolled away, but felt a bitter stab of pain as the point went into his side.

'Poisoning bastard!' Ferox had never heard Vindex so full of rage. 'That was my father.'

'I did not do it,' Arviragus maintained, but his voice trembled.

Vindex came at him, arm whirling as he slashed down again and again. The prince took the blows on his shield, which started to split as the relentless scout came after him. Ferox pushed himself up. Gannascus had beheaded Brigantus, but stayed back, understanding that this was something Vindex had to do on his own.

'It was him!' Arviragus gasped. 'Not me!' He sounded like a child caught stealing apples. His shield collapsed into fragments. He lunged desperately, and Vindex was so wild that he had left a gap and the sword broke mail rings and came back red. Arviragus smiled, and then the scout stabbed him through the mouth. Vindex held the corpse upright for what seemed like a long time. Then he spat in his face and let him fall.

Ferox was sitting up, his back and side burning with pain. Vindex sat beside him, hand clamped to his side, which was clearly the nastier of the two wounds he had taken. A pale face peered out at them from one of the huts.

'Trouble?' Ferox asked.

'They may help. Unless they are bound by oaths to the prince. Then they probably won't be so friendly.'

Gannascus went over to the corpse of the prince and prised off the torc.

'My king sent me for this,' he said.

'Take it.' Ferox said. He had always suspected Tincommius wanted more than to simply help his Roman allies. He did not care. 'Tell him to keep it.'

'We go now.'

'I'm not going to stop you!'

'No, you won't, but some Romans might try, so we will not give them the chance.' Gannascus came over to stare down at them. 'You will live,' he announced. 'Probably.' He gave them a big grin. 'I hope we will not be enemies one day.'

'I'll try to send you the girl,' Ferox said.

'Keep her. I don't think she would like the north very much. And she's fond of that boy of yours.'

'Philo?' Ferox had not had the slightest idea, and it felt odd that the massive German had realised what he had not seen.

'Farewell. You are my friends always.' The grin was back. 'Unless the king says otherwise. Farewell.' He and the archer strode off, going back to the horses

Ferox and Vindex sat in silence side by side. The scout began cutting up his cloak to bandage their wounds. There were faces in the doorways, and hopefully soon the people would come and help them. He doubted that they owed any particular loyalty to the prince, and the Brigantes were hospitable folk as a rule. Crispinus still crouched by the pen, muttering to himself, and he wondered what they had done to him and whether his wits would ever return. The prince's words were in his head, but he did not have the energy to think about them.

'Still think this was a good idea?' Vindex said.

Ferox laughed, and his side hurt, which only made him laugh the more.

HISTORICAL NOTE

LIKE ITS PREDECESSORS, *Brigantia* is a novel set at a
time when very little indeed is known about events
in the Roman province of Britannia. While I have
tried to depict the Roman army and government, and also
Roman and tribal societies, as plausibly as possible, the key
events of the story had inevitably to be invented.

Some of the people were real. Lucius Neratius Marcellus
was the provincial legate at this time and was probably
accompanied to Britain by his friend Quintus Ovidius,
but we do not know much about either of them. Similarly,
Cerialis, Lepidina, Brocchus and Severa appear solely in
the Vindolanda writing tablets, which give no more than
glimpses of their lives. Thus their characters in the story are
invented, although I have done my best not to contradict
anything we do know about them.

Much of the rest of the cast, from Ferox and Vindex
through to Acco and the Brigantian royal siblings, are pure
fiction. The name Arviragus occurs in Juvenal's *Satires*, where
he seems to have been a British king who fought against the
Romans during Domitian's reign. He is otherwise unknown
and I have simply taken the name. There is no evidence for a
succession dispute among the Brigantes at this time or indeed

for any rebellion in Britannia. In fact, there is no certain evidence for any revolt in lowland Britain after Boudicca in AD 61. Recently, one scholar has re-interpreted the hundreds of skulls found in the Thames at Walbrook as signs of Roman reprisals after a rebellion in the area during Hadrian's reign. It is an intriguing possibility, and I was sorely tempted to twist his chronology and use this material for our story, but did not feel justified in doing this. Perhaps one day Ferox will get caught up in that business, whatever it proves to be.

The Brigantes were the largest tribal group in Britain described by the Romans, who sometimes used the name as synonymous with Britons. The true relationship between the Brigantes and neighbours like the Carvetii and Textoverdi is unclear, as is the extent to which any of these groups were politically united. In some cases the Romans imposed clearer structures on indigenous peoples, most probably for administrative convenience. We know, for instance, that the boundaries of the three Galatian tribes, Gauls who had migrated to Asia Minor in the third century BC and settled there, were altered by the Romans. Written evidence for Britain comes solely from Roman sources and post-dates conquest, often by a very long time, so apart from the strong chance of cultural misunderstanding it is always possible that tribal structures had changed by the time they were described.

In AD 43 some or all of the Brigantes were ruled by Queen Cartimandua, who allied with Rome from the start and remained steadfastly loyal to this alliance. We know nothing about her age or ancestry. Mandubracius was a king of the Trinovantes and was supported by Julius Caesar, and the similarity in name has led to the speculation that he was an ancestor of the queen. We know of at least one Gallo-Roman aristocrat who claimed descent from Caesar on the basis of an alleged affair with one of his ancestors, so there seemed no reason not to have Arviragus believe the same thing.

At some point Cartimandua fell out with her husband Venutius, taking his armour bearer as her new consort. This led to war between them and Roman intervention to rescue her on one or possibly two occasions. The passages describing this are confused and no one is sure whether the historian Tacitus describes two separate incidents or gives slightly different versions of the same event. The huge walled enclosure at Stanwick may well have been the main centre of Cartimandua's power, although as usual nothing is certain. We do not know when and where she died, just as we do not know the age of Caratacus in AD 43 or how long he lived on as an exile. An early phase of the villa at Holme House, near to Stanwick and also not far from the Roman fort at Piercebridge, had both a rectangular stone structure with a veranda on each side and a very substantial round house beside it. The date would just about fit for our story, and I liked the idea of an elderly Cartimandua returning 'home' in her last years and living in a way that allowed her to be both Roman and Brigantian.

The goddess Brigantia appears on inscriptions from the second century AD onwards. Her origins are unclear. She may have been promoted or even created under Roman rule as a unifying central cult for the tribe. For this reason she barely appears in the story, but the name has a good ring to it hence its use for the title of the book. Ruling dynasties survived in many communities for generations after the imposition of Roman rule. In most cases the families had become Roman, were often equestrians and might have careers in imperial service. We do not know what happened with the Brigantes, but it is quite possible that pre-existing tribal structures of kings and other aristocrats adapted to the new circumstances and continued within the empire. The Roman inclination was to let provincial peoples run their own affairs as far as possible, not least because the empire lacked the resources and enthusiasm for direct rule. The monument to her is an invention, while the presentation of her as a mystical figure owes a lot to the early Medieval Irish literature, especially Medb of Connaught in the Ulster Cycle.

The latter sources, combined with snippets from Greek and Roman authors describing the Gauls as well as the Britons, and material from other societies in other eras has fleshed out the depiction of the tribes in the story. It is reasonable to suppose that there were many differences between the tribal communities, in language, dress, customs and social and political structure. Therefore I created the tribal gathering of the Brigantes, and their 'proverbial' loyalty to friends. The duty of a host to shelter and protect guests under his roof appears in sources for the Celts and in many societies throughout history, so is reasonable to assume the some for the tribes of Britannia.

The druids are poorly recorded in our sources. Caesar tells us that they refused to commit anything to the written word, while they were one of very few cults actively suppressed by the Romans. In AD 60 Suetonius Paulinus crossed the Menai Straits to destroy the cult centres on Mona (modern-day Anglesey). He did not stay long, for news soon arrived of Boudicca's rebellion, and the island is relatively large, which makes it unlikely that every shrine was destroyed. However, it does appear to have ended the religion as a formally organised cult, which in the past may well have arbitrated in disputes between the tribes. The Romans cannot have wanted a supra-tribal structure independent of their authority and this, combined with distaste at such rituals as human sacrifice, provoked Rome's hostility. Druids who appear in later years seem little more than wandering medicine men – or occasionally women – making it clear that what survived of the cult bore little relation to its pre-Roman importance. Yet the beliefs did not die out instantly. We hear of a Gallic aristocrat who was a Roman and an equestrian being executed for possessing a druid's egg, presumably some form of magic talisman. Acco and Prasto are inventions, as are their stories, and Longinus' description of the landing on Mona substantially embellishes the account in Tacitus.

Scholars continue to debate the impact of Roman conquest on the communities in Britain – and indeed throughout the empire – and the reality was no doubt complicated and subject to constant change. It is easy to fall into the trap of sympathising more readily with one group rather than the other. In the story I have tried to present a mixed picture, with virtue and vice on display in every community and group, and with the towns and cities significantly more 'Roman' than some parts of the countryside. No one could have ignored the presence of Rome, since this meant taxation and regulation different from anything that had happened before. Even if someone in the countryside rarely saw a representative of the empire, the shadow of Roman rule was always there. Leaders inevitably came into far more contact with Roman authority and the culture of the empire. Tacitus tells us that his father-in-law, Agricola, encouraged the tribal aristocracy to have their children educated in the Roman fashion and to build monuments and houses in Roman style. No doubt other governors were just as enthusiastic.

Similar trends placed aristocrats in other provinces under great strain, as they spent lavishly to compete with each other in demonstrating how Roman they had become. Such competition replaced the political and military competition between and within the tribes prior to conquest. Inevitably some lost out, and many more ran up huge debts in the process and had little or no hope of paying their creditors. The desperation of indebted tribal aristocrats, most of them citizens and *equites*, underlay the rebellions in Gaul under Tiberius and contributed to Boudicca's revolt and the disturbances in the Rhineland in AD 70. I drew upon all of these as inspiration for the rebellion in our story. The Batavian revolt in the Rhineland in AD 70 was led by Julius Civilis. We do not know his age at the time or what happened to him and his family, so this permitted the creation of Longinus, the old rebel leader living anonymously as an ordinary soldier.

Even by AD 100, Londinium was growing into the largest city in Roman Britain. Our knowledge of the city is patchy, since most lies under the heart of modern London, but it is steadily growing as rescue archaeology occurs before new building projects. A collection of writing tablets similar to the ones from Vindolanda was recently published and it is to be hoped that more will be found in due course. One of the surprises in these documents was the impression of just how quickly the city recovered after being sacked by Boudicca's warriors. Many mysteries remain about the city at the time of our story. The abandoned earlier fort described in the story has been found, and within a generation a permanent fort was built, but so far we have no idea where any soldiers lived while in Londinium c. AD 100.

If you ever have the chance, then a visit to the Museum of London is highly recommended, not least for their reconstructions of a series of rooms dating pretty much to the time of our story – https://www.museumoflondon.org.uk/museum-london/permanent-galleries/roman-london. They also produce the very handy *Londinium. A new map and guide to Roman London*, which shows the traces of the Roman city overlaid on a modern map. It is also possible to see remains of a Roman amphitheatre under the Guildhall – https://www.cityoflondon.gov.uk/things-to-do/visit-the-city/attractions/guildhall-galleries/Pages/londons-roman-amphitheatre.aspx. Like the stone fort, this was built a little later than our story, and in the book the action takes place in its wooden predecessor.

A few years ago a TV documentary suggested that a grave of a woman from the Roman period in London was that of a gladiator. While possible, the evidence was poor, relying mainly on the inclusion of an oil lamp with a picture of a gladiator among several forming part of the grave goods. However, there is evidence for women gladiators from other parts of the empire, not least the stone monument from Asia Minor in honour of two fighters called Amazon and Achillia now in the British Museum. Domitian included a display of women fighting midgets at one of his games. More usually, female gladiators were matched against each other, and it is likely that they represented a small minority of the professional fighters.

More historical background will appear on my website – adriangoldsworthy.com, where you can also find supporting material for the other stories about Ferox.

GLOSSARY

accensus: senior clerk and doorman on the staff of a Roman governor.

ad stercus: literally 'to the shit', the expression was used in military duty rosters for men assigned to clean the latrines.

agmen quadratus: literally a square battle-line, this was a formation shaped like a large box and used by a Roman army threatened by attack from any side. Units were deployed to form a rectangle, sheltering baggage and other vulnerable personnel and equipment inside.

ala: a regiment of auxiliary cavalry, roughly the same size as a cohort of infantry. There were two types: *ala quingenaria* consisting of 512 men divided into sixteen *turmae*; and *ala milliaria* consisting of 768 men divided into twenty-four *turmae*.

aquilifer: the man who carried the eagle standard (or *aquila*) of a legion.

aureus (pl. aurei): a gold coin equal to 25 silver denarii.

auxilia/auxiliaries: over half of the Roman army was recruited from non-citizens from all over (and even outside) the empire. These served as both infantry and cavalry and gained citizenship at the end of their twenty-five years of service.

barritus: Germanic battle cry that began as a low rumble of voices and rose to a crescendo.

Batavians: an offshoot of the Germanic Chatti, who fled after a period of civil war, the Batavians settled on what the Romans called the Rhine island in modern Holland. Famous as warriors, their only obligation to the empire was to provide soldiers to serve in Batavian units of the *auxilia*. Writing around the time of our story, the historian Tacitus described them as 'like armour and weapons – only used in war'.

beneficiarii: experienced soldiers selected for special duties by the provincial governor. Each carried a staff with an ornate spearhead.

Brigantes: a large tribe or group of tribes occupying much of what would become northern England. Several sub-groups are known, including the Textoverdi and Carvetii (whose name may mean 'stag people').

caligae: the hobnailed military boots worn by soldiers.

centurio regionarius: a post attested in the Vindolanda tablets, as well as elsewhere in Britain and other provinces. They appear to have been officers on detached service placed in control of an area. A large body of evidence from Egypt shows them dealing with criminal investigations as well as military and administrative tasks.

centurion: a grade of officer rather than a specific rank, each legion had some sixty centurions, while each auxiliary cohort had between six and ten. They were highly educated men and were often given posts of great responsibility. While a minority were commissioned after service in the ranks, most were directly commissioned or served only as junior officers before reaching the centurionate.

clarissima femina: 'most distinguished woman' was a title given to women of a senatorial family.

classicum: the late afternoon/evening meal taken by soldiers.

cohort: the principal tactical unit of the legions. The first cohort consisted of 800 men in five double-strength centuries, while cohorts two to ten were composed of 480 men in six centuries of eighty. Auxiliaries were either formed in milliary cohorts of 800 or more often quingeniary cohorts of 480. *Cohortes equitatae* or mixed cohorts added 240 and 120 horsemen respectively. These troopers were paid less and given less expensive mounts than the cavalry of the *alae*.

colonia: a city with the status of colony of Roman citizens, which had a distinct constitution and followed Roman law. Many were initially founded with a population of discharged soldiers.

commilitones: 'comrades' or 'fellow soldiers'.

consilium: the council of officers and other senior advisors routinely employed by a Roman governor or senator to guide him in making decisions.

contubernalis (**pl.** *contubernales*): originally meaning tent-companion and referring to the eight soldiers who shared a tent on campaign. It became more generally used as 'comrade'.

cornicen (**pl.** *cornicines*): trumpeters who played the curved bronze horn or cornu.

cornicularius: military clerk.

cuneus: the triangular or wedge-shaped seating in an amphitheatre. It was also used for a military formation that may have had a similar shape or simply been a narrow column.

decurion: the cavalry equivalent to a centurion, but considered to be junior to them. He commanded a *turma*.

dolabra (pl. *dolabrae*): The military pick-axe, very similar in shape to the entrenching tool used by the army today.

duplicarius: a senior auxiliary soldier/NCO who earned double pay.

equestrian: *(eques, pl. equites)* the social class just below the Senate. There were many thousand equestrians in the Roman Empire, compared to six hundred senators, and a good proportion of equestrians were descendants of aristocracies within the provinces. Those serving in the army followed a different career path to senators.

exactus (pl. *exacti*): military clerks attached to a governor's staff and in charge of the archives.

frumentarii: soldiers detached from their units with responsibility for supervising the purchase and supply of grain and other foodstuffs to the army.

galearius (pl. *galearii*): slaves owned by the army, who wore a helmet and basic uniform and performed service functions, such as caring for transport animals and vehicles.

gladius: Latin word for sword, which by modern convention specifically refers to the short sword used by all legionaries and most auxiliary infantry. By the end of the first century most blades were less than 2 feet long.

hastile: a spear topped by a disc or knob that served as a badge of rank for the optio, the second in command in a century of soldiers.

lancea: a type of spear or javelin.

lanista: the owner of a gladiatorial school.

legate (legionary): the commander of a legion was a *legatus legionis* and was a senator at an earlier stage in his career than the provincial governor (see below). He would usually be in his early thirties.

legate (provincial): the governor of a military province like Britain was a *legatus Augusti*, the representative of the emperor. He was a distinguished senator and usually at least in his forties.

legion: originally the levy of the entire Roman people summoned to war, legion or *legio* became the name for the most important unit in the army. In the last decades of the first century BC, legions became permanent with their own numbers and usually names and titles. In AD 98 there were twenty-eight legions, but the total was soon raised to thirty.

lemures: ghosts or unquiet spirits of the dead.

lillia: lilies were circular pits with a sharpened stake in the centre. Often concealed, they were a comman part of the obstacles outside Roman fortifications.

lixae: a generic term for the camp followers of a Roman army.

ludus (pl. *ludi*): a school of gladiators.

medicus: an army medical orderly or junior physician.

murmillones: heavily armoured gladiators wearing a masked helmet.

omnes ad stercus: a duty roster of the first century AD from a century of a legion stationed in Egypt has some soldiers assigned *ad stercus*, literally to the dung or shit. This probably meant a fatigue party cleaning the latrines – or just possibly mucking out the stables. From this I have invented *omnes ad stercus* as 'everyone to the latrines' or 'we're all in the shit'.

optio: the second in command of a century of eighty men and deputy to a centurion.

phalerae: disc-shaped medals worn on a harness over a man's body armour.

pilum: the heavy javelin carried by Roman legionaries. It was about 6 to 7 feet long. The shaft was wooden, topped by a slim iron shank ending in a pyramid-shaped point (much like the bodkin arrow used by longbowmen). The shank was not meant to bend. Instead the aim was to concentrate all of the weapon's considerable weight behind the head so that it would punch through armour or shield. If it hit a shield, the head would go through, and the long iron shank gave it the reach to continue and strike the man behind. Its effective range was probably some 15 to 16 yards.

posca: cheap wine popular with soldiers and slaves.

praetorium: the house of the commanding officer in a Roman fort.

prefect: the commander of most auxiliary units was called a prefect (although a few unit COs held the title tribune). These were equestrians, who first commanded a cohort of auxiliary infantry, then served as equestrian tribune in a legion, before going on to command a cavalry *ala*.

princeps posterior: a grade of centurion in a legion, the second most senior officer in a cohort.

princeps: a Roman emperor was called the princeps or first citizen/first servant of the state.

principia: headquarters building in a Roman fort.

procurator: an imperial official who oversaw the tax and financial administration of a province. Although junior to a legate, a procurator reported directly to the emperor.

pugio: Latin name for the army-issue dagger.

raeda: a four-wheeled carriage drawn by mules or horses.

regionarius: a centurio regionarius was placed in charge of a set territory or region, where he performed military, diplomatic and policing functions.

res publica: literally 'public thing' or state/commonwealth, it was the way the Roman referred to their state and is the origin of our word republic.

sacramentum: the military oath sworn to the emperor and the res publica.

salutatio: traditional ceremony where people came to greet a Roman senator – and especially a governor – at the start of a working day.

scorpion (*scorpio*): a light torsion catapult or *ballista* with a superficial resemblance to a large crossbow. They shot a heavy bolt with considerable accuracy and tremendous force to a range beyond bowshot. Julius Caesar describes a bolt from one of these engines going through the leg of an enemy cavalryman and pinning him to the saddle.

scutum: Latin word for shield, but most often associated with the large semi-cylindrical body shield carried by legionaries.

sica: curved sword particularly associated with Thracian gladiators.

signa: the standards carried by Roman army units and often used as shorthand for 'battle-line' or in the sense of 'with the colours'.

signifer: a standard-bearer, specifically one carrying a century's standard or *signum* (pl. *signa*).

Silures: a tribe or people occupying what is now South Wales. They fought a long campaign before being overrun by the Romans. Tacitus described them as having curly hair and darker hair or complexions than other Britons, and suggested that they looked more like Spaniards (although since he misunderstood the geography of Britain he also believed that their homeland was closer to Spain than Gaul).

singulares: the legate of a province had a picked bodyguard formed of auxiliary soldiers seconded from their units.

spatha: another Latin term for sword, which it is now conventional to employ for the longer blades used mainly by horsemen in this period.

speculator: a soldier tasked with scouting.

tesserarius: the third in command of a century after the *optio* and *signifer*. The title originally came from their responsibility for overseeing sentries. The watchword for each night was written on a *tessera* or tablet.

thetatus: the Greek letter theta was used in some military documents to mark the name of a man who had died. This developed into army slang as thetatus meaning dead/killed.

tiro (**pl.** *tirones*): a new recruit to the army.

tribune: each legion had six tribunes. The most senior was the broad-stripe tribune (*tribunus laticlavius*), who was a young aristocrat at an early stage of a senatorial career. Such men were usually in their late teens or very early twenties. There were also five narrow-stripe or junior tribunes (*tribuni angusticlavii*).

triclinia: the three-sided couches employed at Roman meals.

tubicen: a straight trumpet.

Tungrians: a tribe from the Rhineland. Many Tungrians were recruited into the army. By AD 98 a unit with the title of Tungrians was likely to include many men from other ethnic backgrounds, including Britons. In most cases, the Roman army drew recruits from the closest and most convenient source. The Batavians at this period may have been an exception to this.

turma: a troop of Roman cavalry, usually with a theoretical strength of 30 or 32.

valetudinarium: a military hospital.

venator (pl. *venatores*): a type of gladiator who specialised in fighting animals in the arena.

vexillum: a square flag suspended from a cross pole. Detachments were known as vexillations because in theory each was given its own flag as a standard.

via praetoria: one of the two main roads in a Roman fort. It ran from the main gate to join the other road at a right angle. On the far side of the other road, the via principalis, lay the main buildings of the fort, including the praetorium and principia.

vicus: the civilian settlement outside a Roman army base.

vitis: the vine cane carried as a mark of rank by a centurion.

ABOUT THE AUTHOR

ADRIAN GOLDSWORTHY STUDIED at Oxford, where his doctoral thesis examined the Roman army, and became an acclaimed historian of Ancient Rome. He is the author of numerous books, including *Caesar, The Fall of the West, Pax Romana*, and most recently *Hadrian's Wall*. *Brigantia* completes the trilogy of novels about Flavius Ferox including *Vindolanda* and *The Encircling Sea*. He is currently working on a new trilogy of Roman stories.

Visit adriangoldsworthy.com